He lowered his face over hers, kissing her deeply. When he pulled away, she felt almost dizzy. "I love you very much, *chérie*. You believe that, don't you?"

She blushed. "I hope you do."

"You mustn't *hope*. You must *know*." His voice had deepened, and his eyes flashed. As exciting as Nicole found Paul's intensity, sometimes it disconcerted her. She'd had several boyfriends over the years, but Paul Dominic wasn't a boy. And he wasn't just any man. He was brilliant, a musical genius, famous, wealthy. He was also the most dazzlingly handsome man she'd ever seen. Occasionally the force of his very being overwhelmed her young and relatively inexperienced psyche. Although she knew she was pretty and she'd always been popular, nothing in her life had prepared her for the larger-than-life whirlwind that was Paul Dominic, and sometimes this relationship seemed more like the dream of a teenager instead of reality. But it wasn't. Her certainty of Paul's love, as incredible as it seemed, had allowed him to become her first lover, and she knew she could never love anyone else as she loved this man.

TONIGHT YOU'RE MINE

CARLENE THOMPSON

St. Martin's Paperbacks

Thanks to Pamela Ahearn,
Kevin Thompson,
and Keith Biggs

This is a work of fiction. All of the characters, organizations, and events portrayed in this novel are either products of the author's imagination or are used fictitiously.

TONIGHT YOU'RE MINE

Copyright © 1998 by Carlene Thompson.
Excerpt from *You Can Run...* copyright © 2009 by Carlene Thompson.

All rights reserved.

For information address St. Martin's Press, 175 Fifth Avenue, New York, NY 10010.

Library of Congress Catalog Card Number: 92-97108

ISBN: 0-312-35713-3
EAN: 978-0-312-35713-9

Printed in the United States of America

St. Martin's Paperbacks edition / December 1998

St. Martin's Paperbacks are published by St. Martin's Press, 175 Fifth Avenue, New York, NY 10010.

15 14 13 12 11 10 9 8 7

IN LOVING MEMORY OF MY
FATHER

ONE

Candles flickered in the big room, their flames casting dancing shadows on the wall, their clean scent of vanilla filling the air. Nicole lay on the cool shining hardwood floor, her blond hair spread across a fringed tapestry pillow. Beside her a man rested in perfect stillness, holding her right hand. His eyes were open, but she knew he saw nothing in the room. His vision was fixed on a world created by the music.

She closed her own blue eyes, letting the music flow over her. *Rhapsody in Blue*. Huge stereo speakers sent the sensual jazz classic throbbing through the room. On the recording, Paul Dominic, the man next to her, played the piano with all the expertise and passion of the world-famous virtuoso he was.

Nicole felt Paul tense as he listened to the four-bar passage that bridges the long piano cadenza into the famous *Andantino moderato* melody. Then the music soared and Nicole's own heart beat faster as the song moved into the development of the slow theme, trading off with the orchestra until the rhapsody was brought to its spectacular conclusion.

Paul rolled toward her, propping himself up on one elbow. "So you liked it, *chérie*?"

Nicole took a deep breath. "I *loved* it." She thought she sounded like a breathless teenager and wished she had a critic's sophisticated vocabulary to express her feelings. Instead, she reached up and touched the man's black hair. "I can't believe I'm with you, Paul," she whispered. "I can't believe I'm with a man who's capable of playing such glorious music. To have that kind of talent . . ." She shook her head. "You're a genius."

"I'm no genius," he said with a self-deprecating laugh. "The music is one-fourth gift, three-fourths very hard work. Besides, I'm not as good as I should be."

"That's not what the critics say. They say you're the ideal Gershwin pianist."

He smiled. "You've been reading my reviews."

"Of course. I also know your concerts all over the world are always sold out." She frowned. "What on earth does someone like you see in me?"

His penetrating hazel eyes gazed into hers. "Do you believe in destiny, Nicole?"

"I'm not sure I've really thought that much about it."

"I believe in it," he said intensely. "I believe I was destined to come back to Texas and meet you again." He touched a strand of her hair. "You were only seven when I first saw you in your father's store, and I thought you were the most beautiful little girl I'd ever seen. You were sitting at your father's finest baby grand piano playing 'Down in the Valley.' "

Nicole rolled her eyes. "One of my most requested numbers, very hot at family parties." She laughed. "I'm surprised Dad let me actually bang out a song on that expensive piano. I have no musical talent, you know that."

"But you have feeling, Nicole. Your little face was so concentrated, almost rapt. It was one of the most touching things I've ever seen. I think I fell in love with you that day. Or rather, the woman I knew you'd grow up to be." He grinned, the lean, aristocratic lines of his own face softening. "As for your father letting you play that piano, he could deny you nothing."

"Except you."

Paul's expression sobered. "You're only nineteen, a sophomore in college. I'm ten years older and I've seen a lot of the world. He's just trying to protect you. He thinks you're a temporary diversion for me while I'm here looking after Mother during this siege of pneumonia."

Nicole's eyes darkened. "It doesn't bother you that we have to sneak around to see each other? That we can't go out in public to dinner or a movie, that he would be furious if he even knew I was *here* with you instead of studying at the library?" She held up the white rosebud he'd handed her as soon as she walked in the door this evening. "I can't even take this home."

"It bothers me that we can't be open about our relationship," Paul said calmly, "but I understand it. Aside from my being older, your father always thought I was strange, even back in the days when I was a kid who used to haunt his music store.''

"How could he have thought you were strange?" Nicole asked indignantly.

Paul smiled. "I *am* strange. Ask anyone I went to school with.''

"They didn't understand a musical prodigy," Nicole protested. "Not even Dad, although he had his own aspirations at one time. Maybe that's his problem. Maybe he's jealous of you."

Paul shrugged. "Whatever. Local opinions hurt at one time, but they don't matter now." He raised his arm and looked at his watch. "What does matter now is that it's almost ten o'clock. Your parents will be wondering where you are."

"I wish I had an apartment," Nicole fretted. "It's ridiculous to be nineteen and still living at home. I hate it there."

"Soon you'll be married to me and living in New York City," Paul said. He rose with the fluid grace of a dancer, his strong, slender body outlined in the candlelight. He was dressed in black jeans and a black T-shirt, the slender silver and turquoise cross she'd given him for his birthday hanging on a chain around his neck, glinting in the light from the candles. He reached down and clutched her hand, pulling her lightly to her feet. "You should go home now before your father gets suspicious."

"I guess it is fairly late. I also have to stop by the library and get at least one book. If I come home empty-handed, he'll know I lied about where I was this evening."

"You should have told me earlier." Paul looked at his watch. "I'll walk you out to the car."

A woman appeared at the door. Her dull black hair was pulled into a long braid and she wore a high-necked maroon dress. "Señor Paul, your mother asks for you," she said in her Spanish accent.

"I thought she'd be asleep by now."

"She was." Nicole didn't like the Dominics' housekeeper, Rosa. The woman looked at Paul with flat black eyes and an expression of deep disapproval although her tone was civil. "Your music woke her."

Paul briefly shut his eyes. "I keep forgetting I'm not living alone anymore. Sorry, Rosa. Tell her I'll be there in a minute."

"Very well, but you should hurry. The loudness of the music disturbed her. She rambles in French. I cannot understand her.

I'm thinking she should return to the hospital." Her words simmered with rebuke, but Paul either didn't notice or chose to ignore her. His tone remained cordial.

"Go back to her, Rosa. Tell her I'll come after I've walked Miss Sloan to her car."

"That really isn't necessary, Paul," Nicole said hastily, annoyed with herself for being intimidated by Rosa's unflinching stare. She'd caught fleeting glimpses of the woman's teenage son around the house a couple of times, and she wondered if he were as cowed by his mother as she would have been. Probably. Only someone with Paul's self-confidence would be oblivious to her perpetually reproachful manner. "Your mother needs you and my car is right outside."

"But not in the driveway." Paul looked troubled. "I don't like you walking around late at night by yourself."

"Now you sound like Dad." She stood on tiptoe and kissed his taut cheek as Rosa slowly turned away, her face heavy with disdain. "I can make it safely across your front lawn and half a block away to my car."

They walked down the curved staircase. The Spanish-tiled entrance hall was empty, lit only by an antique Tiffany lamp throwing rich, luminous colors into the shadows. Paul said the house had been built in the 1920's, bought in the fifties when Texas oil had brought the Dominics from New Orleans, and Nicole thought it resembled the Spanish mansion of a grand silent-movie star— maybe Rudolph Valentino's Falcon Lair. She could picture him and his mysterious wife, Natacha Rambova, doing the tango across the tiled floor. A movie director couldn't have chosen a more perfect home for a man like Paul Dominic to have grown up in. It suited his drama and elegance.

Paul pulled her close to him. "Will I see you tomorrow?"

"I'm not sure. I only have two classes in the morning, but I have to go to the Mission San Juan to finish my research. My paper is due Monday morning."

"Then I'll meet you at the mission."

Nicole grinned. "Paul, the last time you met me there we spent all day wandering around taking pictures of each other and talking."

"It was one of the happiest days of my life."

"Mine, too, but I didn't get a thing done. I only have two

paragraphs of notes and no pictures without one or the other of us posing like tourists.''

Paul smiled. ''All right, my scholar. This time we'll be very professional, I promise.'' He held out his hand. ''Deal?''

She put her hand in his. ''Deal. I'll be there around one o'clock.''

He lowered his face over hers, kissing her deeply. When he pulled away, she felt almost dizzy. ''I love you very much, *chérie*. You believe that, don't you?''

She blushed. ''I hope you do.''

''You mustn't *hope*. You must *know*.'' His voice had deepened, and his eyes flashed. As exciting as Nicole found Paul's intensity, sometimes it disconcerted her. She'd had several boyfriends over the years, but Paul Dominic wasn't a boy. And he wasn't just any man. He was brilliant, a musical genius, famous, wealthy. He was also the most dazzlingly handsome man she'd ever seen. Occasionally the force of his very being overwhelmed her young and relatively inexperienced psyche. Although she knew she was pretty and she'd always been popular, nothing in her life had prepared her for the larger-than-life whirlwind that was Paul Dominic, and sometimes this relationship seemed more like the dream of a teenager instead of reality. But it wasn't. Her certainty of Paul's love, as incredible as it seemed, had allowed him to become her first lover, and she knew she could never love anyone else as she loved this man.

He released her from his embrace and kissed her lightly on the forehead. She handed him the white rosebud. ''Put this by your bed tonight and think of me.''

''I will,'' he said, taking the rose and holding it to his lips. ''Good night, my love.''

She stepped out into the February night. Not until she'd reached the end of the front walk did he close the front door.

The temperature had been in the low seventies during the day but now hovered around sixty. A breeze blew from the north, swirling her hair around her face as she walked south to her car. She pulled her jacket tighter, listening to the heels of her boots click on the road and the sound of the wind rustling the limbs of the live juniper.

She hadn't been worried about time when she was with Paul, but now she suddenly wondered if she could make it back to

Trinity University, retrieve a couple of books from the library, and get home at a convincing hour. She had to be more careful, she told herself. If her father found out about her relationship with Paul, he would be furious.

Still, he couldn't keep her away from him. No matter what rules he set down, she would find a way to circumvent them. She loved her father deeply and didn't like the idea of deceiving or defying him, but for Paul she would do anything. "You're just not brave enough to be open about it," she muttered. "Some fearless romantic heroine you are."

She reached her white Mustang. She never bothered locking the doors in this quiet upscale neighborhood and she hurriedly climbed inside. Fishing around in her purse, she found her keys and was inserting one in the ignition when a large hand closed over her mouth, jerking her head back and smothering her scream.

"Visiting your boyfriend?" a razor-edged male voice asked in her ear.

Panic raced through her, stopping her breath in a freeze response. While trapped air stretched her lungs, her legs spasmodically shot out, thrusting against the pedals of the car, smashing them to the floor. The car wasn't running and nothing happened. Her hands clenched, nails digging into her palms, and her arms locked, bent at the elbows. Finally breath poured from her nose, easing the pain in her chest. Without thinking, she moved her hand toward the horn. Then she felt a cold blade against the side of her throat beneath her right ear, halting her hand in midair. "Do you know how easy it is to slice through the skin here?" the voice grated from the backseat. "Important vessel in the throat. What you call it? Juggler?"

"Jugular." Another voice. Oh God, Nicole thought in horror. There were two men in the back. "And don't forget the carotid. It's an artery." The first man had a Spanish accent. This one didn't and his voice was smoother. "Blood shoots like it's coming from a fountain when the carotid's cut."

"Ah, the Brain. Should've been a doctor."

Both men laughed hysterically. Nicole smelled wine. Wine and perspiration and cigarette smoke. Her heart was beating in slow, heavy thuds and she was now growing almost calm despite her terror. Slowly she reached for the door handle, but the knife pressed harder against her neck. "Are you stupid?" the one with the accent asked harshly. His voice was older than the other's. The rough, sandpaper quality made it sound as if the vocal cords had been injured. "I will slash your throat if you try to get away," he ground out. "Do you understand me?" Nicole's hand dropped away from the door handle. "I asked you a question, little bird. Do you understand me?"

Nicole moved her head slowly up and down while the other man broke into another spate of convulsive giggling. "Little bird? Where'd you get that? Some book of poetry?"

The other laughed. "Sure. I read poetry all the time. You read poetry, little bird?" His face came closer to hers. She felt the stubble of his beard on his cheek and the cold metal of a hoop earring. He breathed rapidly, his breath reeking of sour wine and filthy teeth. "Sure you read poetry. The pretty college girl with the nice car. Daddy loves you, huh? Daddy gives his little bird whatever she wants. She goes to the right schools. She wears expensive clothes. She reads poetry." He snickered. "And still she sneaks off in the night to meet men. Fancy clothes on the outside, but a *puta* inside."

"But she goes to a *rich* man," the other said, then hiccuped. "A rich man in a mansion. What else for her? No slumming with guys like us. No sir, not for her. When she wants a little action, she goes to her own kind."

How did they know she'd been to see a man? Nicole wondered inanely.

"I want you to start your nice car," the older one said. "I want you to pull away from the curb slow, understand?" Nicole managed another tiny nod. "You better understand 'cause you try *anything* and this knife goes in your throat. One slice, little bird, and you're dead."

The blade of the knife was not so cold now. It had pressed against Nicole's skin for over a minute, long enough for her to realize it was serrated and diamond-sharp. It was also held in a jittery hand tight with tension. One small tremor would split her skin. A stronger one would pierce blood vessels.

Her fingers had turned icy. She realized she still clutched the keys, and she raised her right hand, fumbling as she tried to insert the proper key into the ignition.

"Hurry up!"

"Trying," she mouthed against the callused hand covering her mouth.

The big hand moved down to her chin, still holding her head backward in a viselike grip. "What?"

"Trying."

"Try harder."

Blindly she fumbled with the keys on the ring. They jangled and slithered as if alive in her trembling hand. She tried one, then another. Finally the third slipped in the ignition. She turned it and the car started smoothly. She hadn't shut off the radio and Queen's "Radio Ga-Ga" boomed through the interior. The knife pushed dangerously against her throat and she gasped. "Turn that thing off!" the older one shouted.

Nicole didn't need to see to find the radio she listened to constantly. Her hand immediately shot sideways, but her stiff fingers slipped off the knob before she'd completely clicked off the instrument. The music played on, softly. "That's okay," the younger one said pleasantly. "Good song. Great concert group. The windows are closed. No one can hear. Leave it on."

The other one sighed. "Such a spoiled baby. Always got to have music. Okay. You want music, we'll have music. Little bird, turn on the headlights."

Nicole fumbled along the dash until she found the headlight knob. She pulled and the lights came on low beam.

"Good. Now go."

"Can't see," Nicole croaked, the angle of her head constricting her windpipe.

"What you mean you can't see? You got lights."

"Can't see."

"You got her head jerked back too far," the younger one said casually. "Ease up some, man."

"Don't give me orders!" The knife trembled against Nicole's neck. She could feel his rage rising like a sharp wind.

"Okay. Don't freak out. It was just a suggestion."

A grunt before the knife-wielder abruptly complied, lessening the pressure of his hand on her jaw. "Okay, now *go*!" Fighting to control her shaking, Nicole lowered her head, shifted into drive, and crept away from the curb.

"Good, little bird," the man said gently. "Drive nice and slow. No tricks."

Nicole eased the car down the residential street. No tricks? She could always try jerking the steering wheel to the right and slamming into a parked car, but she knew the serrated knife would be in her throat at the moment of impact. No, there would be no tricks. At least not for now.

The younger man had begun to sing along with the music in a surprisingly strong, melodic voice. I *know* that voice, Nicole thought with a jolt. She hadn't recognized it when he was speaking, but now it was familiar. She'd heard this guy *sing* before. But where? When? Her memory blurred when the older man began to sing off-key in his own rough voice before they both stumbled over the lyrics and fell into raucous laughter.

Hollow with fear, Nicole kept the car at a steady fifteen miles an hour, desperately scanning the road for potholes. If she hit even a small one, the sudden movement could send the knife into her throat.

Vaguely she was aware of lights on in the houses she passed— big, luxurious houses where people sat in safety. They had no idea what was happening just a few hundred feet from them. How ironic, she thought. Help was so close, yet so far from her reach.

They came to the end of the street. "Turn here," the man said. "Nice and slow." Nicole obeyed. "Good. Now turn again."

They were on Dick Frederick Street, heading out of residential Olmos Park into the empty grounds of Basin Park. Lights glowed dimly from the dashboard. She knew that if she glanced in the rearview mirror, she could see the face of the man holding the knife. But that would be a mistake. He might panic if he thought she could identify him later. If, please God, there *was* a later.

They passed no other cars on the narrow road. Suddenly it seemed more like three in the morning than ten o'clock at night, Nicole thought in frustration. Where *was* everyone?

One of the men made a soft snorting sound, gasped softly, then let out a sigh of delight. "Want some?" the younger one asked.

"In a minute. I'm busy with the knife right now."

Drugs, Nicole thought. Not just liquor but drugs. Cocaine? No, more likely crystal meth. It was cheaper. That explained the excitability, rapid breathing, tremors. They were hyped up, acting on false courage. And if Nicole remembered correctly, one of the symptoms of amphetamine abuse could be assaultiveness.

"All right, now pull your car off the road."

"What?" Nicole whispered with a sinking heart.

"Can't you hear?" the man shouted in her ear as she cringed. "Pull your car to the left, off the road. Way off the road, into the brush."

As Nicole slowed the car, she was relieved the man moved the knife away from her throat a fraction when they jolted into the undergrowth. The headlights picked out spiny shrubs, empty aluminum cans, and crushed Styrofoam cups. This was the kind of place people passed by quickly, never stopping. A deserted place abandoned to weeds and trash. Suddenly it seemed to Nicole as if until this moment the whole experience had been a terrifying dream. Now it was becoming real and she felt as if she were sinking in quicksand. The more she cooperated, the deeper she sank. There was no way out. She was doomed to endure whatever these two had in store for her. Her mind shuddered away from the possibilities.

They nearly bumped into a small mesquite tree and Nicole stopped. "Now turn off the car and the lights."

Do something! her mind screamed as she switched off the headlights and the ignition. But do what? Even honking the horn wouldn't help at this point. No one could hear. She had no weapons, not even Mace in her purse.

"Take the knife."

The sharp edge of the knife lifted from her throat for a moment as the knife changed hands. Then the dangerous points pricked at her skin again. Someone took hold of her hair, yanking it so hard she yelped. "You gonna get out of the car very, *very* slow," the razor-voiced one said. "You can't run because I'm holding you. Besides, Ritch—" He broke off sharply. "There's a knife at your throat, little bird. You can't outrun us. You won't even try, will you?"

"No," she whimpered. "But you don't have to do this. My father has money. He's not rich, but my boyfriend is. If you just let me go, they'll both pay you."

Foolish, adolescent-sounding snickering emerged from the backseat. The younger one. "Okay," the razor-voiced one said. "We'll let you go. Then tomorrow we'll go to your daddy's house and your boyfriend's house and they'll both hand us envelopes full of money. So simple." He wrenched her hair so hard she couldn't believe it didn't come out in his hand. "You think we're fools?"

Nicole's insides twisted as they both fell into that awful, maniacal laughter again. Idiot, she thought. This wasn't a television show. How could she have thought she could talk her way out of this with offers of money?

"Not even a very smart try," the older one said with a mixture of amusement and disgust. "Maybe you're dumber than you look. Just a *puta* they let in college because she's got a pretty face and a daddy with money. Get out of the car."

"Please," Nicole begged in a thin, ragged voice. "Please, I haven't done anything to you—"

"But I'm gonna do things to you. Things you'll never forget." He twisted her hair another painful notch tighter and she cried out, tears beginning to run down her cheeks. "Quit squealing like a pig and get *out*!"

In numb resignation, Nicole opened the car door. The interior lights came on. If only a car would drive by, she thought desperately. Please, *please* let a car pass.

But the road was empty and dark.

She stepped from the car, staggering with the weakness of fear. For a moment he released her hair. Even if the moment had been longer, though, she was too helpless to run. Her legs shook and she knew she couldn't get away from these two lunatics whose reflexes were sharpened by amphetamines. By the time her feet were firmly on the ground, a muscular arm in a sweatshirt gripped her around the waist and the knife again pressed into her throat. She heard car doors closing and the interior lights blinked off.

"Into the brush," he ordered.

She stumbled forward, the long dry grass crunching under her boots. A few trees grew in the area, their branches bare against the night sky. In the distance she heard cars, saw the flash of lights. She looked up and stumbled over an abandoned tire, almost falling. The arm around her tightened, and the knife finally slightly pierced her skin. The man cursed violently. A thin trail of warm blood oozed down her neck, tickling slightly as it slithered over her collarbone.

Suddenly he threw her to the ground so hard he knocked the breath from her. She landed on her back, a rock jabbing excruciatingly into her hipbone. Silent with the shock of the pain, she looked up and saw an overpass. Interstate 281, she thought distantly. That's where all the cars and lights were. Hundreds of cars sped over 281, none of their passengers knowing what was going on below them in the dry Texas grass. I'm only half a mile from home, she realized. Half a mile from love and safety.

Nicole felt the weight of a body descend over hers. She closed her eyes and turned her head to the right, letting out a tiny sob. "Relax," the sandpapery voice crooned in her ear. "You gonna enjoy this, baby. You never had anything like this." He paused. "Hold her."

Hands pinned her shoulders to the ground. Suddenly she felt her jeans being jerked from her body. Every time he jerked, trying to pull off the tight jeans, her hipbone hit the sharp stone again. "Damn," he spat. "Why couldn't you wear a skirt?"

Later, Nicole couldn't remember what made her begin to fight at this moment. Seconds earlier she'd been limp with fear and resignation, but now adrenaline flooded her body. With an animal cry she didn't recognize as her own voice, she kicked out, eliciting a pained shout from her attacker. He hit her face with his fist so hard she thought she was going to pass out, especially when she heard a bone crack, but she didn't stop fighting, thrashing wildly against the weight of two male bodies.

But the men were too strong for her. The next few minutes were a nightmare of pain, terror, and humiliation. Her face grew wet with their saliva, her ears rang with their wild laughter and their shouts of triumph as they reduced her to something less than human.

Through it all she'd kept her eyes squeezed tight, trying to shut out at least part of what was happening to her. Even when she realized the sexual assault was over, she wouldn't look although she no longer thought an ability to identify them might jeopardize her life. She had abandoned the hope of saving her life. She just didn't want her last earthly memory to be of their savage, hated faces.

For a few seconds, while she lay quietly wishing she could pass out and escape the pain, she heard only their panting, a few grunts, a high-pitched snicker. Then the older one said, "Now we gotta do her."

"I thought that's what we just did," the younger one giggled.

"No. I mean really *do* her."

Slowly the giggling stopped. "You mean kill her?"

"Sure, man."

Nicole heard movement in the grass, as if one of them were attempting to stand up. "Look, Magaro, rape's one thing. I didn't count on murder."

"What did you think? We're gonna beat and rape a girl like this, then just leave her alone? You don't think she's goin' to the police?"

"She doesn't know who we are. She never looked at us. I made sure. She doesn't know who we are."

"She didn't *look* at us?" the older one spat out. "How do you know she didn't sneak a peek? Besides, you couldn't help showing off your voice in the car. Maybe she's heard the band. Maybe she recognized the voice. And, *genius,* you just said my name."

"I did?"

"Yeah. Now we *got* to kill her."

Nicole, cold, in physical and emotional agony, lay motionless, her eyes still closed, but she heard the younger one's voice begin to betray anxiety. "Look how still she is. Maybe she's already dead."

"She's not. Are you, little bird?" He hit her face again, splitting her lip, dislocating her jaw, and a moan escaped her.

"I . . . I still don't think she knows who we are. We can get away with it. I mean, God, *murder.* I don't . . ." Nicole was aware of a sharp intake of breath. "Listen, man, I don't think I can do it."

"Oh, you *can't?* A little short on courage? Well, I'm not gonna do it alone."

"Magaro—"

"Shut *up!* You hold her down again."

"Look, man, I told you—"

"I said hold her! Do it now, or I swear to God I'll kill you, too."

"Me?" the younger one squeaked.

"If something goes wrong, I'm not gonna be the only one guilty of murder. You're gonna be—what they call it? An accessory. That way you won't talk."

"*Talk?* You think I'm gonna tell anybody about this?"

"Who knows? You get all crazy on your wine and meth and you could say anything. I don't trust you. Now do what I say.

Hold her down." Nothing happened. "Hold her *down*. I mean it, Zand. Hold her or I'll kill you, too. You know I will."

"Okay, okay," the younger one said shakily. "Just cool it. I'll hold her, man. I'm with you all the way."

During this exchange a tiny flame of encouragement had flickered in Nicole's ravaged body and mind. But when she heard the fear in the young one's voice, the flame died. Hadn't she known all along that the experience would end this way? The best thing to do would be to send her mind somewhere else, somewhere beautiful and far away where she wouldn't feel the pain, wouldn't feel the frightening darkness of death descend.

But when hands pressed on her shoulders again, unexpected desperation flowed into her. She began to flail with the strength of a madwoman, her right hand connecting with an eye socket. The man's scream was followed by a spate of cursing as her knee sank into a groin. Writhing with all her strength, she fought grappling hands and efforts of strong bodies to pin her to the rough ground. A fist connected with her temple, and another punched into her abdomen, forcing the air from her.

During it all Nicole had been aware of noise—the men's voices, one high-pitched, the other growing even more guttural than before in its fury. Then, as the excruciating pain of the blows overwhelmed her and her surge of strength dissipated, she heard another sound. She slowed her weak attempt at fighting, straining to listen. Could it be? Could it *possibly* be? *Yes!* A car.

Both men stiffened as the car drew nearer. "Stay low," the rough-voiced one she knew as Magaro ordered. "They'll go by and never see us."

But the car didn't whiz by as Nicole expected. It slowed. She heard gravel crunch as it pulled off the road. Then headlights swept over them. In the shock of the brightness, Nicole's eyes snapped open. In five seconds she saw two faces clearly—one in its early twenties with blue eyes, clear skin, a slightly broad nose, and shoulder-length light brown hair. The other was at least ten years older, acne-scarred, the dark eyes narrow and mean, the lips so thin they were almost nonexistent.

A car door opened. "Hey, what's going on here?" a man demanded.

"Run," the younger one quaked.

"It's not the cops. Gotta kill her!"

Nicole flung herself to the left, missing the slash of the knife aimed at her throat. She screamed with all the strength she could muster.

"I've got a gun!" the man in the car shouted.

"He's lyin'," Magaro hissed.

Suddenly the sound of a shot tore through the night.

Hands released Nicole's shoulders. "I'm gettin' outta here!"

The knife swept past Nicole's throat again, this time nicking the skin. She shrieked frantically and another shot rang out.

Then she fainted.

TWO

FIFTEEN YEARS LATER

"Though nothing can bring back the hour
Of splendor in the grass, of glory in the
flower..."

Nicole Chandler stood motionless, staring at the coffin holding her father. Bright sunshine played over the stiff funeral flower arrangements she knew he would have hated. She'd told her mother he would have preferred a donation made to charity in lieu of flowers, but Phyllis Sloan had flatly refused. "It's bad enough that he gave up his faith and made us all promise he wouldn't have a religious funeral service," she'd snapped. "I'm honoring that promise, but he didn't say anything about not having flowers, so we're having them."

Countless arrangements rested around the coffin. Clifton Sloan had a lot of friends in San Antonio. Most of them were at the funeral. But there were many others, people Nicole had never seen before, and she wondered how many had come out of curiosity just to view the funeral of a man who for no apparent reason had put a .38-caliber revolver in his mouth and pulled the trigger.

A wave of queasiness swept over her, and she shut her eyes, still hearing the funeral director's voice:

"We will grieve not, rather find
Strength in what remains behind..."

Oh, Dad, how could you do such a thing? she cried mentally. *Why?* The simple word had echoed through her head a thousand times since the Wednesday morning just three days ago when her mother had called her, her voice a stunned, thin monotone, saying that Clifton was hurt, he needed an ambulance, but she was feeling a bit faint from all the blood, would Nicole make the call?

Shrill with horror, Nicole had asked over and over *how* her father was hurt. Phyllis finally managed ''shot'' and ''store'' before she uttered a ragged moan and hung up. Nicole touched the reset button on the phone, then punched out 911 for help, certain that her father had been shot by someone trying to rob his music store downtown. Only later did she learn that sometime in the night he'd left his home, gone to his office in the back of the store, and killed himself. She couldn't have been more surprised if someone had said the world was going to end in a week.

Pressure on her hand forced her to open her eyes again. She looked down at her nine-year-old daughter Shelley, whose clear forehead was furrowed in concern. ''Okay?'' she mouthed, her periwinkle blue eyes, so like Nicole's, looking troubled and watery from unshed tears.

Nicole squeezed Shelley's hand and gave her a slight smile. The girl had been so close to her grandfather. It was Clifton who'd always made her eyes light up with joy, who could make her laugh in spite of almost anything, who could bring perspective back to her young world when things went wrong, just as he had with Nicole. Phyllis, autocratic and critical, elicited the same response from Shelley she always had from Nicole—dutiful attempts at affection and an inevitable stiffening with repressed resentment when the complaints began in spite of all attempts to please.

> *''In the faith that looks through death,*
> *In years that bring the philosophic mind.''*

Am I supposed to find strength in years that bring the philosophic mind? Nicole wondered as the funeral director's surprisingly eloquent voice concluded the stanza of Clifton's favorite poem. Will I ever feel philosophic about my father killing himself without leaving so much as a brief good-bye note to me, especially now when I need him so much?

Immediately she felt ashamed. Obviously her father had been deeply troubled to do something so drastic, so seemingly irrational, and all she could think about was that he'd deserted her when her life was such a mess. Well, according to Elisabeth Kübler-Ross, wasn't anger one of the stages of grief? Which one? The second or third? She was sure her husband, Roger, could tell her. Or rather, her soon-to-be ex-husband.

She glanced across her father's coffin at Roger Chandler, standing tall and distinguished and properly solemn. He didn't look much older than he had when they'd met at a graduate student party twelve years ago. She'd just begun work on a Master's degree in English while he was finishing his doctoral dissertation in psychology. They'd married a year later. He'd always been so strong, so sure of himself, so certain of what she needed, and if his dominance had sometimes gotten on her nerves, she'd still been grateful she could always depend on him and his unwavering love.

Then, a few months ago, she'd noticed that he seemed to be away from home more than usual, spending time in his office at the university at night working on his book, or so he claimed. After three months of this diligent writing, one evening he'd lit a few candles around the living room, put on a Debussy CD, fixed her a snifter of very good brandy, and after some pointless small talk abruptly announced he'd fallen in love with another woman and wanted a divorce. Nicole had stared at him for approximately thirty seconds, then begun to giggle. The whole scene was so dramatically staged, Roger's expression so lugubrious, his voice so tender and tragic, that the only thing penetrating her brain was how ludicrous they would appear to a sophisticated theater audience. She'd laughed until tears ran down her face, and Roger's stiffening posture and his expression of bruised dignity mixed with fear that she was going into hysterics made her laugh even harder. It wasn't until the next day that her tears no longer streamed from laughter.

At least he'd had the decency not to bring the little twit to the funeral, she thought. The girl, one of his students, was twenty years old, exactly half Roger's age. Naturally all her friends assured her this was just a midlife crisis, that he'd never go through with the divorce but simply expend his passion in a rather embarrassing show, then slink home, repentant.

Nicole knew better. Roger's need to be needed was overwhelming. He felt that she'd outgrown him, that the days were gone when she hung on his every word, that in a room full of people he was no longer the only person who existed for her. In a way, she felt rather sorry for him. For all Roger's intelligence, he'd never realized that while for several years her dependence on him had been abnormally strong, and that she'd always cared deeply for him, he'd never been the center of her life as he thought.

He looked up. She saw the flash of guilt in his eyes before he managed a tight, awkward smile she knew was meant to be bracing. Nicole merely stared at him, and a moment later his gray gaze dropped. She supposed she could have been more gracious, but she was too shaken and heartsick to worry about Roger's feelings right now.

Suddenly Nicole became aware of her mother moving forward to place a rose on Clifton's coffin. Phyllis sniffled into a lace-edged handkerchief, but Nicole's eyes were painfully dry as she laid a red rose atop the casket. She knew the grief would hit her swiftly and violently, but so far she'd been outwardly calm, her hurt throbbing inside her like a heartbeat, steady and invisible. She held Shelley's hand while the girl reached forward with her own rose, murmuring, "Bye, Grandpa."

The three of them stepped back, and others began moving as if a silent bell called them forth. Nicole couldn't look at the many hands dropping already wilting flowers onto the coffin. Her father had always said funerals were ghoulish affairs. "They're lovely ceremonies where people can say good-bye," Phyllis had argued heatedly. "Say good-bye to what?" Clifton had shot back. "A corpse full of formaldehyde?"

Nicole knew the retort was calculated to get a reaction out of the high-strung, traditional Phyllis, and it always worked. Although she'd told her mother a hundred times that if she wouldn't respond so fervently to Clifton's teasing, he'd stop it, she nevertheless usually found herself smothering smiles as her mother let out a loud hiss of disgust and stomped out of the room, appalled by her husband's apparent irreverence for all she considered sacred.

A slight breeze blew up, catching a lock of Nicole's long hair and sweeping it across her face. She pushed it aside, looking beyond her father's coffin to the grounds of the cemetery rolling beyond. It was February, an unusually warm seventy-five degrees, and the breeze that blew her hair skimmed over the short green and brown grass and blew the small, many-limbed junipers abounding in the cemetery along with the masses of bright artificial flowers decorating the graves. When she and Roger had lived in Ohio, she'd noticed that only on Memorial Day did the Northerners decorate as abundantly as they did in San Antonio year-round.

Suddenly her gaze stopped at the figure of a man standing nearly a hundred feet beyond beside a sprawling Pinchot juniper. He was tall and slender, wearing jeans and a jacket, and beside him sat a dog—a Doberman, its black coat gleaming in contrast to its red collar, its ears clipped to alert points. Even from such a distance, the dog's dark eyes seemed to meet and hold hers. The moment was almost hypnotic, as if the dog were trying desperately to convey a message. Abruptly the world narrowed for Nicole, becoming nothing but the sleek, shining canine. Then, slowly, the dog turned its narrow head, looking up at its master. Nicole's own keen eyes followed. The tall man stood as still as the dog and gazed at her just as unflinchingly. For a few seconds she boldly stared at him in return. Then the outlines of his face sharpened in her vision. She could clearly see the line from his high cheekbones to his strong jaw, the hair as black as the dog's, and the intense eyes that never left hers. . . .

Nicole's heart slammed against her ribs. She swayed, her vision darkening, cold beads of perspiration breaking out all over her face.

"Mommy? Mommy?" Shelley's voice floated toward her from far away. "Mommy, are you okay?"

"Wha . . ." Nicole had the desire to speak, could even hear herself trying to mouth a word, but her voice seemed to be coming from underwater.

"Grandma, something's wrong with Mommy!"

"What? What *now*?" Phyllis hissed, grabbing Nicole's hand. "What's wrong with you? Everyone's looking."

Slowly Nicole's vision cleared as Phyllis's voice hit her like a dash of icy water. The brightness of the day hurt her eyes. She blinked, frowning into the sun, her gaze seeking the tree. The man and the dog were gone.

Phyllis's gaze searched her face. "You're pale as a ghost. Are you going to faint?"

"No." Nicole's voice was thin and breathy.

"Well, get hold of yourself," Phyllis ordered *sotto voce*. "All we need is for you to pass out and fall head first into the grave."

Nicole looked at her mother in shock, then almost burst into one of her nervous laughing fits at her mother's sadly preposterous response. At a time when Phyllis should be stricken that she'd lost her husband of thirty-six years, all she could think of were possibly embarrassing scenes. Suddenly, Nicole realized her mother was furious with Clifton, and she didn't believe Phyllis was going through Kübler-Ross's stage of grief labeled "Anger." She was livid that Clifton had killed himself, had made people wonder about his sanity, had drawn unseemly speculation down on her family.

Again. First it had been she, Nicole, fifteen years ago, who'd been the talk of the town, the victim of a gang rape followed only weeks later by the suspicion that she'd instigated or at least inspired the double homicide of the rapists. Now the attention was focused on Clifton, the man who'd blown off his head in his own store. Sorry we keep embarrassing you, Mom, Nicole thought bitterly. Sorry Dad and I have compromised the pride of the daughter of General Ernest Hazelton.

"Are you all right?"

Beside Nicole stood Carmen Vega, her best friend since grade school. Carmen's depthless dark eyes showed worry. "I'm fine."

"What did you see?" Carmen asked quietly.

Nicole looked at her sharply. "I didn't see anything. It's just the occasion."

Carmen's eyes turned from worried to knowing. "No it isn't. I was watching you. You saw something."

When had she ever been able to hide anything from Carmen? She muttered, "Tell you later," as Phyllis turned curious, reproving eyes on her.

"What are you two whispering about?"

"Nothing, Mom," Nicole said tiredly. "I think we should be going back to the limousine."

Shelley clutched her mother's hand as they walked toward the long black car, her small face pale, her eyes sad. Safely inside the cool confines of the limousine, Nicole gave her a firm, encouraging hug.

"Well, that was a dreadful service," Phyllis declared.

"I thought it was nice," Nicole said.

"It wasn't. And Shelley's dress is inappropriate. Too short. Too gay. She looks like she's going to a party, not like she's in mourning."

"Mom, this isn't the nineteenth century when children went to funerals swathed in black."

"She could have worn *navy* blue, not light blue."

"Who cares what color it is?"

"*I* do."

"You're being absurd, Mother."

Phyllis's face assumed a devastated look. She sniffled into her handkerchief. "I know we don't get along, Nicole, but do you have to attack me even on such a tragic day?"

Oh, God, Nicole thought, sighing as she leaned against the back of the seat, her head beginning to pound. Please let this awful afternoon be over soon. I need time to rest. I need time to think about Dad.

And I want to think about who I saw in the cemetery today, she added mentally with a shudder and a rush of chills down her arms as she pictured the lean, handsome face. Or who I *thought* I saw because it *couldn't* have been . . .

"We're home," Phyllis announced. Nicole had been so distracted, she hadn't even noticed the limousine turning onto their street. "Now comes the *really* hard part," Phyllis went on. "Nicole, I hope you won't desert me. I simply *cannot* handle all these people by myself."

Nicole couldn't keep the exasperation from her voice. "What on earth makes you think I'm going to desert you? I've done all I could to help—" She stopped short, seeing Shelley tense and Phyllis's mouth begin to twitch again. Just be quiet and get through it, she told herself sternly.

When they stopped at the Sloan residence, Nicole emerged from the limousine, trying vainly to smooth the wrinkled skirt of the ill-fitting black linen dress she'd bought yesterday. Phyllis, however, looked trim and stylish in an expensive black silk shantung suit, her prematurely white hair tucked into its usual perfect French twist. Nicole remembered that even when she, Nicole, was a child, her mother had worn that gleaming, flawless hairstyle.

A few of Phyllis's friends had skipped the funeral service so they could set out the food. The large house, decorated to perfection in cool, neutral tones with an occasional touch of aqua, looked pristine, not a knickknack out of place. Phyllis glanced around approvingly, then took her place at the door. "Nicole, you and Shelley stand beside me," she ordered. "We must greet the mourners."

What did you think we were going to do, Mom? Nicole thought sourly. Stampede to the table and begin gobbling food as fast as we can? But Phyllis wasn't happy unless she was giving all the commands, even if they were unnecessary.

As they took their places inside the door, Nicole suddenly felt the desire to bolt and run down the street, never looking back. Her mind skittered, trying to recall how relatives of the deceased had acted at other funerals she'd attended. Sad, of course. Subdued. But what had they said? Her mind went blank.

And as soon as people began filing in the door, she realized why she, who was usually good with words, was nearly speechless. This wasn't like any funeral she'd attended because it was for a man who had killed himself. There was something strikingly different about the funeral of a victim of suicide. Everyone seemed embarrassed because they too were at a loss for words. No one could say, "At least he's out of his misery now," because if he'd been in misery, no one seemed to know it. Two weeks ago when Nicole had last seen him, Clifton had been the essence of cheerfulness although he seemed a bit tired. No one could say, "It was God's will," because Clifton Sloan's death was entirely of his own will. Most couldn't even say, "He's in a better place," because they believed no one who committed suicide went to a better place.

And of course they were speculative. Had Phyllis or Nicole done something to drive him to this? Had Clifton suffered a financial disaster? What was the real story? What was the family hiding?

As a result, almost everyone merely muttered a strained, "I'm so terribly sorry," to which the family said over and over, "Thank you." As the line of mourners filing through the door was nearing its end, all Nicole could hear was Phyllis, then herself, then Shelley, each saying "Thank you," in increasingly mechanical, scratchy voices.

Phyllis finally gave Nicole a gentle nudge in the ribs and said, "That's everyone. Now circulate. And do *not* discuss the nature of your father's death.'' She then glided forward, handkerchief clutched in her right hand, face wan and a bit vacant. No one would dare ask *her* any details, Nicole thought. She looks as if she'd keel over if they did. But in reality, Phyllis Sloan was the strongest woman Nicole had ever known. Even at this moment, she could probably stand up to a prolonged police interrogation if she chose.

Shelley clutched her mother's hand again, and they wandered into the living room. This was the room Phyllis insisted be kept perfect for company, but Nicole suddenly remembered childhood Christmases when the tree had stood in front of the window, and on Christmas morning brilliant paper and ribbons had lain all over the pale carpeting.

"Clifton, look what a mess she's making," Phyllis would fret. "Nicole, open the packages carefully. Don't tear at the paper or squash the bows. We might be able to use some of the trimming next year."

"Oh, for heaven's sake, Phyl," Nicole's father would laugh loudly, knowing how much Phyllis hated the shortening of her name. "We're not headed for the poorhouse. I think we can afford new paper and bows next year. Nikki, rip and tear and throw the wrapping all you want." So while Phyllis's lips pressed tighter and tighter together, the child Nicole had done exactly as her father ordered while he recorded her every movement on film in the days before video cameras.

Although her father dominated her memories of those happy times, her mother was always there in the background, a nagging but stable force. Mom may have been difficult, Nicole mused, but at least she hadn't deserted her family like Roger did. Such a thought would never have crossed her mind. In her annoying, idiosyncratic way, she tried to be the best wife and mother she could.

As if sensing her thoughts, Roger walked up. "How are you two doing?" he asked gently.

"We're okay," Nicole said, noting that he was wearing his glasses with the thin silver rims. He couldn't wear contacts and when he really cared about his appearance, he wouldn't wear the glasses, fearing they made him look older.

Roger glanced down at Shelley, a frown forming between his light brown eyebrows. "I didn't think you'd be here, sweetheart."

"It's Grandpa's funeral."

Roger raised an eyebrow, then looked at Nicole. "I don't approve of children attending funerals."

Shelley, who'd grown hostile toward her father although Nicole had been careful never to criticize him, said hotly, "I *wanted* to come. I'm not a baby!" She looked up at Nicole. "Can I go get some cake now?"

Nicole nodded and as Shelley scampered away, Roger fixed Nicole with cool gray eyes. "You're turning her against me."

Nicole took a deep breath, trying to hold her temper. "I have bent over backward not to turn Shelley against you, but she's not two years old. She's aware it was your decision to move out of our home, and you've made no attempt to keep your relationship with that teenager a secret from her."

"She is *not* a teenager," Roger said stiffly. "She's twenty."

"Had a birthday, did she? Gee, pretty soon people will stop thinking she's your daughter."

"Please don't get nasty at a time like this."

Chastened, Nicole said quietly, "You're right. I'm sorry."

Roger glanced over at her mother. "Phyllis seems to be holding her own."

"She always does."

"I think she's mad as hell," Roger stated. Nicole remained silent although for once she agreed with him. "Do you have any idea—"

"*Why?*" Nicole interrupted. "Why my father killed himself? No."

Roger turned his searching gaze back to her. "We aren't exactly close these days. How do I know you're being honest with me?"

"Roger, I have never lied to you," Nicole said tautly. "But even if I knew why Dad killed himself, why would I be obligated to tell you? It's none of your business."

"Yes, it *is* my business. Clifton was my daughter's grandfather."

"What are you hinting at?" Nicole flared. "Some kind of genetic weakness?"

He gave her a patient look. "Of course not. You know I believe we're products of our environment. I'm worried because if there was some kind of serious trouble in the family that caused Clifton to do this, I should know. After all, Shelley adored him. She was around him too much these last few months. This whole mess has really rocked her young world.''

''I know of no serious trouble in the family except for you leaving me, which I hardly think would drive my father to suicide,'' Nicole answered coldly. ''And I am well aware of the effect this has had on Shelley. I'm doing everything I can to restore some normalcy and happiness in her life.''

''That's what I wanted to talk about,'' Roger said earnestly. ''I think Shelley should spend the next few weeks with me.''

Nicole stared at him in disbelief. ''Forget it.''

''Don't give me one of your knee-jerk reactions. Think about how much sense it makes. You're desolated by your father's death. Your mood can't be doing Shelley any good, and you're not up to giving her the attention she needs.''

''I see. And living with you and your girlfriend will return her good spirits in no time?''

Roger's jaw tightened. ''Her name is Lisa Mervin. And we don't live together.''

''She only spends all her nights at your apartment.'' He opened his mouth to protest, but Nicole cut him off. ''You haven't been discreet, Roger. We're professors at the same university. Do you think I'm not aware of your lifestyle? Lisa is your student, for God's sake. Sleeping with a student on the sly is one thing. You're openly living with her. Have you ever heard of dismissal due to moral turpitude? It can happen, especially when you don't have tenure to protect you. At this rate you might not have a job next year.''

Roger's face had paled, his gray eyes hardening. ''All you've heard are rumors. Why don't you let *me* worry about my job?''

''You misunderstand. I don't *care* whether you lose your job over this girl or not. Shelley is another matter.''

''Nicole, you are *not* going to use my having a woman in my life to keep me away from my daughter.''

''I'm not trying to keep you away from her, but she isn't going to stay with you and your little live-in nymphet. Besides, there's no point in going into this now. We'll work out visitation at the custody hearing.''

''Visitation? I think you mean joint custody.''

''Over my dead body!''

Carmen Vega appeared beside them. "Your voices are rising," she said pleasantly. "Phyllis is going to glare a hole through each of you if you don't quiet down."

Roger's nostrils flared slightly. He was ready for battle now, but Nicole's energy immediately flagged when she realized the potential scene they were creating. "Carmen is right. A funeral isn't the time for this discussion."

Roger gave her a searing look. "I agree, but don't think I intend to crawl away and let you have Shelley all to yourself. She's my daughter, too, and I am *not* going to give her up. Don't forget your past emotional problems, Nicole, *or* the police investigation you underwent. I've got a ton of ammunition on my side, too, and don't think I won't use it."

He strode away, heading for the front door. Nicole sucked in her breath, feeling as if he'd just kicked her in the abdomen.

"Creep," Carmen muttered.

"Sometimes I don't know why I ever thought I loved him, and I could just slap myself for getting in a fight with him." Nicole ran a hand across her forehead. "If the pressure inside my skull gets much worse, my eyeballs are going to pop out."

Carmen gently took her arm. "Come in the kitchen with me."

Nicole glanced around the room. Phyllis was talking with a good-looking, dark-haired man Nicole didn't know. Shelley sat in a corner, nibbling on a piece of cake.

In the kitchen, Carmen poured ice water in a glass. "Where does you mother keep the aspirin?"

"Cabinet to the right of the sink."

In a moment Carmen handed her the glass and a bottle of white pills. "Sit down at the table. Take two of these and about five deep breaths."

Nicole obeyed, sinking down at the table and swallowing the aspirin. Then she leaned her head forward onto her folded arms. "I didn't need a confrontation with Roger on top of everything else."

"He probably started it," Carmen said, sitting down beside her. "He's the most self-centered person I've ever met, Nicole."

"He wasn't always that way, Carmen. You never got a chance to know him well, but a few years ago he was very protective and considerate."

"Well, he isn't anymore. In a few months you'll see that the end of this marriage is one of the best things that's ever happened to you."

"I already see it," Nicole said wearily. "I'm not saying the whole thing isn't upsetting and disruptive, but I know eventually I'll be a much happier person because of the divorce. It's Shelley I worry about."

"Shelley is a strong little girl, just like her mother. She'll be fine."

Nicole smiled wanly. "Do you really think I'm strong?"

"I've known you since you were six." Carmen grinned. "I'll never forget the day we were on the playground and that terrible big bully José was pulling my braids. I was flailing around, helpless and squealing. The other kids were laughing. Then you marched up, at least two inches shorter and fifteen pounds lighter than José, and kicked him with all your might in the knee. He howled like a baby all the way back into the school building."

"And I got detention for a week."

"And the undying respect of everyone else in the first grade he'd bullied. Nearly twenty-eight years ago," Carmen said, shaking her head slowly in amazement. "Sometimes I still feel like that little girl on the playground."

"I don't feel like that fiery-eyed little kid who rescued you. I feel like a rag doll who lost all her stuffing. Carmen, it's so strange. I'm numb. I haven't even cried over Dad. Not once."

"You're in shock. I was the same after my baby boy died. Be grateful. In a couple of days, you'll feel awful." Carmen's long curly black hair had been brushed into an unnaturally smooth style. She ran her hands through it, shaking loose some of the curl. "What caused your face to turn chalk-white at the cemetery?"

Nicole wiped at a drop of water running down the side of her glass. "I saw a man and a dog standing on a slope watching the funeral."

"I saw them, too."

"You did?"

"Yes. It was that student of yours, Miguel something."

"Miguel Perez? No, Carmen, it wasn't."

"Well, I only met him once at your Christmas party. Maybe not. Who did you think it was?"

"Carmen, did you *really* look at the man? Didn't he remind you of someone?"

Carmen's lovely tanned face grew bewildered. "I told you—Miguel."

"No, Carmen, it looked like Paul."

"Paul who?" Carmen's eyes widened. "Paul *Dominic*?" Nicole nodded. "That's impossible! He died in a car wreck fourteen years ago."

"Did he? After the explosion there wasn't enough of the body left to make a positive identification. They didn't do DNA testing back then."

Carmen couldn't hide the astonishment in her eyes before her gaze dropped and she bit her full lower lip the way she did when she was troubled. Finally she said, "Nicole, the last few months have been so hard on you. First the move back to San Antonio with all its bad memories. I know you would never have come except to please Roger. Then he left you. And now your father . . . Well, you can't be thinking too clearly right now."

"You think I'm hallucinating?" Nicole asked, stung.

"No. I saw the man, too. I don't remember Paul as vividly as you do, but the height, the slimness, the black hair . . . Under the circumstances, being so tired and overwhelmed, I might have thought the same thing for a moment if I were you."

"But the way he was looking at me . . ."

"The way he was looking at you?" Carmen reached out and put her strong, long-fingered hand on Nicole's. "He was so far away. How can you be sure of exactly *how* this man was looking at you?"

"But I *am* sure. His gaze was so intense . . ."

"Nicole, you're a beautiful woman. Lots of men look at you intensely."

"But I thought . . . I was almost sure . . ." Nicole trailed off, embarrassed, knowing how unbelievable her story sounded. And thinking back on the incident, she wasn't certain why she'd believed the man in the cemetery was Paul Dominic just because he resembled him. Was it because she'd never been able to accept the death of a man she'd once worshiped just as she couldn't accept her father's?

"Are you all right?"

"I guess. Nerves, grief, shock. This hasn't been one of my

better weeks." Anxious to change the subject, she asked, "Where are Bobby and Jill?"

"Bobby's minding the store and waiting for Jill to come home from a friend's birthday party."

"I'm glad you didn't make her come. I agree with Roger that funerals are no place for children, but Shelley couldn't very well be absent from her grandfather's, although I would have saved her the ordeal if I could." Nicole glanced at her watch. "We've been in here fifteen minutes. Mother will be annoyed."

"Your mother is always annoyed about something, so what difference does it make?" Carmen giggled. Nicole joined her, knowing no one but Carmen could have made her laugh even briefly today.

When they entered the living room, Phyllis turned her head away from Kay Holland, Clifton's longtime assistant at the store, and shot a burning look at Nicole to let her know her prolonged absence had been noted. At the moment, Nicole didn't care. Her eyes scanned the room. It was only half as full as when she'd gone to the kitchen. People obviously had no desire to linger and visit at this particular house.

"Are you feeling better, Mrs. Chandler?"

Nicole turned to see the dark-haired man her mother had been talking to earlier when Carmen led her off to the kitchen for aspirin.

"I'm feeling much better. Just a headache."

He smiled easily. "A day like this could certainly give you one, although I have to congratulate you on the stamina you've shown. Both you and your mother, today at the funeral and Wednesday morning."

Wednesday morning when Clifton Sloan had been found dead in his office. Nicole looked at him inquiringly. "You'll have to forgive me. You look so familiar, but I can't place where we've met."

"I'm Raymond DeSoto. I was one of the detectives called to the scene of your father's death."

Nicole's mind flashed pictures. A black-haired man wearing clear plastic gloves bending over her father's body. His quick, nodding acknowledgment of her and her mother. His quiet instructions to uniformed officers and what she supposed were forensics people, and later the scalding look he'd thrown his older, black partner who questioned Phyllis and Nicole stridently.

"Detective—"

"Actually, it's Sergeant."

"Sergeant DeSoto, I'm sorry I didn't recognize you. You were very kind to my mother and me that day. I appreciate it. Unfortunately, I was so shaken that the whole scene seems like a kaleidoscope in my memory."

"That's understandable."

Nicole noticed the strong lines of his square face, the large, warm dark eyes, the thickness of his black hair. She guessed him to be in his very early thirties and noticed he didn't wear a wedding ring. Despite her quick appraisal, she was not looking at him as a potential romantic interest. She had always been observant. At one time the police had congratulated her for being such a good witness. Her mind veered from the dangerous memory.

"I thought the service was very dignified," DeSoto was saying. "I did notice, though, that it wasn't religious."

"My father was reared a Catholic, but he stopped going to church many years ago. He claimed to be an agnostic."

"Claimed?"

Nicole knew the question wasn't as nonchalant as it sounded. DeSoto was interested in learning more about Clifton Sloan, but she answered anyway. "Every once in a while Dad said something that made me think he firmly believed in a supreme being, but maybe he was only echoing phrases he'd heard all his life, not expressing his true feelings."

"I see," DeSoto said offhandedly. "Well, I suppose in adulthood we all reexamine childhood beliefs and feelings, but I don't know how often we really change, not deep down anyway. I've heard cold-blooded killers suddenly start begging for God or their mothers when they know there's no way out for them."

A tremor passed through Nicole, and he must have seen it. "Sorry again, Mrs. Chandler. Sometimes I think I'm only fit to talk to other cops."

"It's all right, really. I was just thinking about how easy it is for some people to kill." She paused, then asked a trifle nervously, "Sergeant DeSoto, I don't mean to make you feel unwelcome, but is there a reason you're attending this funeral? I mean, you *are* convinced my father's death was a suicide, aren't you? Because I know . . . I mean I've read . . . that sometimes policemen come to the funerals of murder victims because they think the killer might be there. I believe the theory is that the killer likes to see all the grief he's caused.''

DeSoto smiled reassuringly, showing even white teeth. ''Yes, sometimes that's true. But not in this case. I'm here because I used to have an interest in music. I visited your father's store quite a few times. He was always very kind and patient with me, although it was obvious I had no talent and no money to buy any of the expensive instruments he handled.''

Nicole relaxed and smiled. ''Dad cared more about a person's passion for music than their actual talent,'' she said, then abruptly pictured a dark-haired man with mesmerizing hazel eyes talking earnestly about her feeling for music, about how rapt her seven-year-old face had grown when she was trying to play ''Down in the Valley'' on a grand piano. ''Would you like something to eat?'' she said in a brisk, loud voice unlike her own. ''More coffee? I see that you've finished yours.''

Sergeant DeSoto glanced at his empty cup, frowning slightly, obviously sensitive to her sudden change in mood. ''I've had plenty of coffee, thank you. I think I should be on my way. I stayed longer than I meant to.''

From across the room Nicole caught Phyllis's hard stare. She swiftly made her way to them. ''I hope you two aren't discussing details of dear Clifton's death.'' Her tone was sad but with a trace of steel underneath. ''It's all so morbid, you know, Sergeant DeSoto. I don't like for Nicole to get more upset than she already is.''

Nicole resisted rolling her eyes. The idea that her mother's prime concern at the moment was Nicole's emotional state was nonsense. Phyllis was only worried that they were discussing the suicide. She seemed to believe that if they didn't talk about the specifics of Clifton's death, the cause would turn into a dignified heart attack.

''Your daughter was just offering me some more coffee,'' Sergeant DeSoto said smoothly, ''but I'm afraid I must get back to work.''

Phyllis smiled graciously. ''We certainly understand. We also appreciate your attending the service. That was really above and beyond the call of duty. But then you knew my husband slightly, didn't you?''

"Yes, ma'am, although I hadn't seen him for years—"

"Oh, everyone is *so* busy these days," Phyllis rattled on, steering him unobtrusively though expertly toward the front door. "Life used to be so much slower, more relaxed . . ."

Nicole hung back, listening to her mother. No doubt Phyllis had been deeply distressed to see the man at the funeral. She was afraid other people would know DeSoto was a policeman and his presence might stir up even more curiosity and discussion.

After everyone else had left, Carmen and Kay Holland stayed to help clear away the food. Nicole had always liked her father's thin, birdlike assistant, Kay. She remembered her as a young, energetic woman with surprisingly dreamy violet eyes behind thick glasses. The woman had never married, seemingly content with her job, the piano lessons she gave part-time, and her cats. But when Nicole returned to San Antonio in August, she'd been amazed at how much Kay had aged since she'd seen her a year before. Kay couldn't be more than in her late forties but she looked closer to sixty, her slenderness turned to boniness, her skin pale and waxy.

Kay insisted that Phyllis and Nicole relax on the couch while she and Carmen did most of the work. Within an hour all the food had been put away and Kay placed a slender book from the funeral home on the sideboard listing the dish, contents, and giver so Phyllis could write thank-you notes.

"Kay, you're a gem," Phyllis said with a genuine smile. "Clifton always depended on you so much. No wonder. You're the most efficient person I know."

Kay looked pleased in spite of the deep lines of sadness etched on her face. "Anything I can do to help, Mrs. Sloan. All you have to do is let me know."

Phyllis stood. "Kay, dear, you've worked so hard you look absolutely exhausted. I want you go home and rest."

"All right, Mrs. Sloan," Kay said, flashing an entreating look at Nicole.

"After all, we can't have you breaking down over this thing."

Another meaningful look at Nicole from Kay. Suddenly Nicole realized Kay wanted a private word with her, although Phyllis was leading her relentlessly toward the door. Luckily, at that moment Shelley called for her grandmother from the kitchen.

"Mom, you go see what Shelley wants," Nicole said quickly. "I'll walk Kay to the door."

Phyllis hesitated, clearly as surprised by her granddaughter's calls as Nicole was, then she smiled ruefully. "I hope she hasn't spilled something. Kay, I'll speak with you soon, and thank you again."

As soon as she'd left the room, Kay took Nicole's arm in her thin, cold hands. "I wanted a moment alone with you."

"What is it, Kay?"

"I've never had a chance to talk with you since your father's . . . death." She looked down, blinking back the tears welling in her eyes. "You know how *very* sorry I am."

"Of course, Kay. It's not what you wanted to talk to me about, though."

"No. I don't mean to be mysterious, but I don't feel . . . well . . . free to talk here. I wouldn't want your mother to overhear. The store will be closed tomorrow, but I'll be there cleaning out Mr. Sloan's desk. Do you think you could stop by?"

Startled, Nicole realized Kay knew something about Clifton Sloan's death. "Kay, why don't you call me tonight—" She broke off, hearing Phyllis talking to Shelley as they passed through the dining room, headed for the living room. "All right," Nicole murmured. "Shelley is supposed to spend tomorrow with her father, so I'll come by as soon as he's picked her up."

Kay nodded vigorously as Phyllis entered the room. "Shelley wanted me to show her one of her great-grandmother's crystal birds, now of all times. Nicole, you're not detaining Kay, are you? She looks tired enough to drop."

"I was only giving my regrets to Nikki," Kay said, using Clifton's nickname for his daughter. "I *am* tired. I'll be on my way now, but remember what I said. I'm on twenty-four-hour call if you need me."

"I'll remember," Phyllis said. "Good-bye, Kay."

Nicole and Kay walked to the front door in silence. Before Kay stepped out the door, she patted Nicole's arm and muttered, "To-morrow. Please."

Nicole nodded and watched as the stick-thin figure meandered down the front walk. She used to stride, Nicole thought. She used to seem as if she had the energy of ten people contained in that small body.

As Kay climbed into her five-year-old Chevrolet, Nicole looked beyond her. At first she merely glanced at the dog sitting on the other side of the street. Then her eyes narrowed. The dog was a large, gleaming black Doberman with a red collar. This close she could even see a small gold medallion hanging from the collar. The dog sat perfectly still, its dark eyes meeting hers with that strange look of knowledge she'd seen before. But this time it was alone. At least it appeared to be alone. Nicole had the odd feeling that its master was not far away. Her gaze remained locked with the dog's while Kay pulled away from the curb. Nicole stepped out on the porch. "Come here, dog," she said softly, then more loudly, "Come to me!"

The dog moved slightly, leaning forward. She had the distinct impression that it wanted to come to her. Slowly she sauntered down the front walk, smiling and holding out her hand in a gesture of friendship. She'd always had a way with dogs, a trait that drove Phyllis wild when she constantly brought home strays. Shelley had the same gift.

"Come here, please," she repeated to the beautiful dog. "I won't hurt you."

The dog stood. It was even bigger than she'd realized and its stance demonstrated excellent breeding. It took a step toward her. Suddenly high heels clicked on the porch behind her and Phyllis demanded, "What in the world are you doing? Trying to drag another dog home? Honestly, don't you think you're getting a little old for this, Nicole?"

Instantly the dog's head snapped to the right. As if responding to a command, it bolted, disappearing behind the house across the street. Furious, Nicole turned on her mother. "Did you have to come barging out right at that moment?"

Phyllis glared at her in outrage as Carmen appeared by her side. "What was it?" she asked anxiously.

Nicole looked at her solemnly. "Carmen, the dog we saw at the cemetery was here."

"The dog from the cemetery?" Carmen repeated doubtfully.

"Yes. And I think its master was here, too."

THREE

1

Nicole brushed off her mother's questions about the dog as deftly as possible and whisked Shelley back to the peace of their own home in a neighborhood close to the branch of the University of Texas where she taught. The small white brick house with its neat front yard had never looked so good to her.

"I'm tired," Shelley said as Nicole pulled her Buick Regal into the driveway and shut off the car.

"In your nine years of life I don't believe I've ever heard you say that. You're getting old, kid."

Shelley sighed. "I know. Ten is just around the corner."

Nicole burst into laughter and was rewarded by Shelley's giggle. "Let's go in and see Jesse. I'll bet he's missed you like crazy today."

But their entrance was delayed. Nicole kept her car keys and house keys on separate rings, and she now searched frantically for the house keys. "Oh, this is just great," she moaned, feeling as if she were going to burst into tears.

Shelley looked at her patiently. "You lost the keys."

"Yes."

"No windows open?"

"No. We'll have to go over to Mr. Wingate's house and call a locksmith."

The elderly man who lived across the street was happy to see them, and insisted on serving fresh lemonade and cookies while they waited for the locksmith.

"What a thing to happen on a day like this," he said, his face wrinkled in concern.

Nicole grimaced. "It's typical for me. I don't seem to be doing anything right lately."

Mr. Wingate gave her his endearing smile. "We all have peaks and valleys, dear. You're just in a valley. You'll come out of it."

"You think so?"

"Yes. I predict sunny days not far in the future." He turned toward Shelley, who seemed to be a particularly favorite friend of his. "And how is young Mr. Jesse today?"

"Probably hungry. It's past his dinnertime, and he gets cranky when his meals are late."

Mr. Wingate closed wrinkled eyebrows, pretending to concentrate. "No. I sense that Jesse isn't cranky at all. He's just anxious to see his lovely young mistress."

Mr. Wingate was correct. Half an hour later, they were inside their house thanks to the help of the locksmith. At the sight of Shelley, the little black dog jumped around ecstatically and emitted the series of high-pitched barks that used to drive Roger crazy.

Nicole remembered the day Shelley had found Jesse on their front porch in Ohio. She'd seen him around the neighborhood a few times and had always taken time to pet him, worrying over the fact that she didn't think his "parents" were taking good care of him. Finally he'd vanished for over a month. Nicole feared he'd been killed, but one winter morning Shelley screamed when she discovered him curled up in a corner of the front porch, trembling, malnourished, his back bare from mange, a front leg badly broken and bleeding, apparently the result of being struck by a car.

Roger had been disgusted by the sight of the mange and loudly commanded Shelley and Nicole not to touch him. "I don't take orders from you," Nicole had snapped as she covered the dog with a warm blanket and brought him food and water while Shelley stood crying quietly, her father holding her firmly by the shoulder so she couldn't go near the dog. Looking back, Nicole remembered the shocked look on Roger's face when she flared up at him, refusing to do as he said. She'd always been diplomatic about her few rebellions before. Now it seemed to her that things had never been quite the same between them again.

After Roger left that day, taking Shelley with him to school, Nicole took Jesse to the veterinarian. Enduring weeks of Roger's protests, she and Shelley nursed the dog back to health although the veterinarian said his leg was too badly damaged to ever be normal again. Once Jesse was well, Roger admitted defeat, giving Shelley permission to keep the little dog although he hated him. The feeling was mutual. Nicole always thought Jesse would like nothing more than to take a sizable chunk out of Roger's ankle, but he wisely contained his dislike to an occasional baring of teeth when Roger's back was turned, or one of his well-timed messy sneezes on Roger's shoes just as he was leaving the house.

Shelley was another matter. The dog, whom the veterinarian had pronounced "probably part terrier, part cocker spaniel, and who knows what else," was wild about his young mistress. Small and crippled though he was, Nicole hadn't a doubt he would give his life to protect Shelley from harm if the occasion arose.

"Were you lonesome without me?" Shelley asked. Jesse yipped, giving her a lick on the cheek. "You wouldn't have had any fun if you'd come. It was Grandpa's funeral. You don't know what a funeral is, but it's sad, especially when it's for someone you loved. You loved Grandpa, didn't you? He loved you, too, and I know he's looking down at you from Heaven. Someday you'll go there, too, and Grandpa will play ball with you again."

Nicole's insides wrenched. She wished she knew the proper thing to say to a child at a time like this, but she didn't. Maybe there wasn't anything, although she was sure Roger would disagree. But Roger wasn't here anymore. Neither was her father.

Shelley always insisted on feeding Jesse herself. "I'm gonna give him some biscuits," she told Nicole. "He didn't even pull the pillows off the couch like he usually does when we're late. I think his manners are getting a lot better."

"They are." Now if the same could only be said for your father, Nicole thought as she remembered the scene at her mother's house earlier today. But she had to be fair. There wouldn't have been an unseemly argument if she hadn't let Roger bait her into it. She had to learn to ignore him. That was just a difficult task when she was still so angry with him. Wanting a divorce was one thing. Flinging his girlfriend in Shelley's face was another. The child could spend tomorrow afternoon with him as planned, but his intention to use Clifton's suicide as leverage to make her agree to Shelley spending the next few weeks with him and his young lover was another matter.

She kicked off her high heels, wiggling her pinched toes, and looked around the living room. She loved the thick pale blue carpeting and eggshell-colored walls, the large thirty-gallon aquarium with its rainbow of tropical fish floating in perpetual tranquility, the painting of a beautiful Indian girl wading in a shallow, light-reflecting stream. The only off notes in the room were the overstuffed dark brown couch and chair that Roger had selected. She'd always disliked the pieces, but they hadn't looked so bad in their older, rather dark house in Ohio. In the pale sleekness of the San Antonio home, they reminded her of big brown bears lolling around the living room. As soon as she could afford it, she would buy new pieces. At least the kitchen was perfect if small, all white and bright yellow with a skylight and well-placed shelves for plants which grew in abundance. She walked in to see Jesse devouring canned food as if he hadn't eaten for a week.

"Now that Jesse's taken care of, how about a bath and early bedtime for you?"

"It's *too* early for a Saturday night, but okay," Shelley said reluctantly. "Can I use some of your bubble bath, the fancy stuff that smells like that drink piña colada?"

Nicole swooped over her, clasping her in a tight hug. "Ah, you want to be the little señorita tonight?" she asked with a heavy Spanish accent. "Do you want the dangling earrings? A rose for your teeth? How about I play the guitar and serenade you during your bath?"

Shelley giggled hysterically. "Mommy, you can't even play the guitar. You're so silly!"

"I know. It's part of my inexhaustible charm. Use all the bubble bath you want, sweetheart. Just don't overflow the tub."

Shelley scampered off to her bedroom, Jesse in hot pursuit. Nicole went to the refrigerator and poured a glass of iced tea, sweet and heavy with mint, the way she loved it. She took a deep drink, then wandered over to the sink, looking out the window above. The street was quiet and the driveway looked empty without Roger's Ford Explorer.

"He's been gone almost two months," she said to herself, "and I'm still not used to it." The days when he took Shelley were always the worst. Then she was really alone. But tomorrow would be different because she would be going to see Kay Holland, perhaps to learn why her father had killed himself.

2

Two hours later, after Shelley had fallen into an unusually deep and early sleep, Jesse curled on the bed beside her, Nicole sat on the ugly couch, glass of chardonnay in her hand, wearing jeans and an oversized sweater, listening to a Pretenders CD on the state-of-the-art stereo system she'd selected a couple of years ago. Although her taste for only the best equipment had been honed by her time with Paul Dominic, she rarely listened to classical music and never Gershwin.

She tried to think about her father. To her despair, his healthy, smiling face stubbornly eluded her memory. When she closed her eyes, all she could see was his horribly blood-splattered office. Was that all that was left of him in her mind—the imagined memory of a man with a revolver stuck in his mouth, the awful blast that sent bone and blood and brain tissue all over the wall?

She jumped when someone tapped on the front door knocker. Who would be coming by unannounced at this hour? Roger, no doubt. He probably wanted another go-around about taking Shelley. Already stiffening for a confrontation, Nicole set down her wine and went to the door. Peering through the peephole, she saw a tall man with long dark hair pulled back in a ponytail. Her heart skipped a beat before she realized she was not looking at the man with the dog from the cemetery, but her student, Miguel Perez.

Surprised but unafraid, she opened the door. "Miguel! This is unexpected."

He smiled. "Sorry to bother you, Dr. Chandler, but you dropped your keys at the cemetery." He held up her gold chain with the three house keys.

"Oh, thank goodness you found them!" Nicole exclaimed. "It took a locksmith to get Shelley and me in this afternoon."

A moth fluttered around Miguel's face, drawn by the porch light, and Nicole stepped back. "I'm forgetting my manners. Come in."

"I don't want to bother you."

"You're not bothering me. I'm glad for the company." She smiled regretfully. "It's been a rough day."

"I won't stay long."

He stepped in and slipped out of his light tan jacket. He was a good-looking young man, somewhere in his late twenties, tall, slender, with long black hair pulled back with a small silver ornament. The first semester Nicole taught at the university he was in her Creative Writing Fiction class. This semester he was taking Major American Writers. He was a bright student with an above-average imagination and a polished prose style. Roger had always claimed the guy had a crush on her, but she'd never noticed any signs of romantic interest.

"Miguel, I didn't see you at the funeral."

"I stayed in the background."

Nicole looked at him sharply. "You weren't standing beside a tree with a dog, were you?"

He looked at her blankly. "A dog? No. What made you think that?"

"Never mind." She frowned, taking the keys from Miguel. "I usually carry big, utilitarian bags. Today I carried a small purse. I stuck the house keys in the side pocket. They must have fallen out. Why didn't you give them to me at the cemetery?"

"I found them when you were leaving, just getting into the limo. I couldn't catch up to you without yelling, and that didn't seem appropriate. I'm sorry I didn't catch you, though. I could have saved you a locksmith's fee."

"Don't worry about it. I deserved the punishment for being so careless. I appreciate your coming to the funeral and for retrieving my keys. They're my only set."

"If I'd known, I would have come by your mother's house and dropped them off. You should have a spare set."

"Oh, well, no harm done. I have them now. How about some iced tea or a Coke?" He hesitated, and she looked at his mature face. Because he was her student, she often forgot that Miguel wasn't a teenager but a man who'd simply gotten a late start in college. "Better yet, how about a glass of wine? I have chardonnay or some very good Beaujolais Roger left behind."

Miguel smiled. "I'll take a little of the Beaujolais if you don't mind."

Miguel sat down in an overstuffed brown chair, sinking back so far his booted feet lifted off the floor and he almost spilled his wine. "*Damn!*"

Nicole smiled. "Isn't that an awful chair? One of these days it's going to swallow someone and they're never going to be seen again.''

Recovering awkwardly, Miguel grinned. "You should see some of the monstrosities in my mother's house. She calls them antiques, but I've got my doubts.''

"Do you live at home, Miguel?'' she asked as she poured the wine.

"Yeah. It seems silly to pay apartment rent when I live so close to the university, but I miss my freedom.''

"I know what you mean. I lived at home when I went to Trinity.''

"I thought you went to the University of Virginia for your undergraduate work.'' Nicole handed him a glass, looking at him inquiringly. "You mentioned it in class last semester.''

"Oh. Yes, I did go to Virginia later, but I was here in San Antonio for my freshman year and part of my sophomore.'' She felt color creeping into her face, wondering if Miguel knew what had driven her from San Antonio. The story had been in all the newspapers. But that was fifteen years ago. Besides, her last name was different now.

Jesse, hearing voices, had crept from Shelley's bedroom and ran into the living room. Miguel had been to the house a couple of times, once when Nicole invited a few of her most interested creative writing students over for an informal evening session, and later when some of her students had come for a pre-Christmas barbecue.

"Jess, *amigo*!'' Miguel exclaimed, setting aside his wine glass. "You get better looking every time I see you.''

"He's a beauty, all right,'' Nicole said wryly.

The dog had formed one of his immediate attachments to Miguel. "He knows how much I love dogs,'' Miguel had said. Jesse rolled happily at his feet, then ran twice at top speed around the living room, showing off. "I'll never figure out how he can run so fast on that leg.''

"Sheer willpower.'' Seeing Jesse reminded Nicole of the scene at the cemetery. "Miguel, during my father's service did you see a man with a Doberman standing some distance away, looking on?''

"A man with a Doberman? Someone you thought was me?'' She nodded. "I don't recall seeing anyone like that. Did you know him?''

Nicole's eyes shied away from his. "He looked very much like someone I used to know, but it's been such a long time since I've seen him, I could have been mistaken."

Miguel looked concerned. "Did he seem threatening or weird?"

"No," Nicole said quickly, perceiving Miguel's protectiveness. "Not at all. It probably wasn't who I thought." She didn't mention seeing the man's dog outside her mother's house. She had a feeling she'd said too much already. "It was a strange day. I'm probably imagining all kinds of things."

"You do look tired."

"I'm exhausted."

Miguel stood immediately. "Then I'll leave so you can go to bed. You won't be back to school this week, will you?"

"I've been off since last Wednesday, so I'll be back this Wednesday."

Miguel retrieved his jacket. "Thanks for the wine."

"Thank *you* for returning my keys. You saved me hours of frantic searching, not to mention the trouble it would have caused if someone less honest had found them."

"Glad I could be of some help." He bent and patted Jesse on the head. "So long, little *hombre*. You're the man of the house now, so take good care of the ladies." He smiled up at Nicole. "See you later this week, Dr. Chandler. Try to get some rest. You deserve it."

Yes, I guess I do, Nicole thought half an hour later after she'd checked on Shelley, turned off the music, and carried the wine glasses to the kitchen. As she placed them beside the sink, she couldn't help looking out the window, her eyes scanning the street.

But there was no sign of the large, watchful Doberman that had haunted her day.

3

"Daddy loves you, huh? Daddy gives his little bird whatever she wants."

The razor-edged voice grated in Nicole's ear. She was back in that white Mustang fifteen years ago and Luis Magaro held a knife to her throat. She moaned and turned over, fighting to wake up, but she couldn't.

Abruptly the scene changed. She was no longer in the car. Now she was barefoot in the brush of Basin Park. Magaro and Ritchie Zand sat close together on the ground. They were laughing, that same high-pitched, wrought-up laughter she remembered so well.

"She thought she had us," Magaro said.

"She almost did."

"No she didn't. It would have been better if we could have killed her like I wanted, but she still couldn't hurt us. I got too many friends, man. I *told* you I'd come up with an alibi. I said I'd keep you out of prison, didn't I?"

"Yeah, you did."

Magaro laughed again. "And you promised me something in return."

"Yeah."

"I'll tell you what I want. No more of this roadie stuff. I got talent, man. I shouldn't be hauling around equipment. I should be on the drums."

Their words blurred as in the dream Nicole moved closer, drawn closer although she was so frightened of them. Then she heard a crunching in the grass, a crunching not made by her own feet—

A shrill scream dragged Nicole from her dream. She kicked wildly at the covers for a moment, then realized she wasn't hearing some dream figure. It was Shelley.

She jumped out of bed, ran across the hall, and flipped on the overhead bedroom light, blinking in the sudden glare. Shelley huddled beneath her window, whimpering. Jesse, front paws propped on the windowsill, barked at the top of his high-pitched voice.

"What *is* it?" Nicole cried, rushing to Shelley, enfolding the trembling girl in her arms. "What did you see?"

Shelley raised a white tear-stained face to her mother. "A monster!"

"A *monster*?" Nicole rocked her as she buried her face in Nicole's chest. "Honey, you were dreaming."

"No I wasn't! I heard a noise at the window and I got up and looked. I was wide awake. Besides, if I was just dreaming, why is Jesse barking?"

"You scared him when you screamed."

"Then why is he *still* barking?" Ever since she was young, Shelley had possessed a strong sense of logic. "Jesse saw the monster, too!"

Jesse looked at Nicole and emitted two sharp yips, as if in agreement.

Nicole sat down on the floor, legs folded, and pulled Shelley onto her lap. "All right, tell me what this monster looked like."

"Well, not like Dracula or Frankenstein or any of your *famous* monsters," Shelley explained solemnly. "Also not like an alien with a great big head and huge black eyes."

"Maybe it was a dog."

"A dog! I wouldn't be scared of a *dog*!" Shelley said disdainfully. "But it did have pointy ears and lots of hair on its face like a wolf, but not a nice wolf like White Fang in the movie. But . . ." She frowned ferociously, thinking. "I saw something like it on television once with Daddy. It was an old movie and he laughed and laughed. He said the name was *I Was a Teenager Wolf*."

"*I Was a Teenage Werewolf*?"

"Yeah, that's it. Whenever there was a full moon, this real cute boy turned into a really awful-looking wolf and tore people apart."

"So you think you saw a werewolf."

"Yes. Should we call the police?"

"I don't think the police would come. They might not believe us. Besides, the monster seems to be gone. Maybe I could go outside and look around—"

"*No!*" Shelley exclaimed, clutching at Nicole. "It could be hiding out there."

Nicole thought, The child is showing more common sense than I am.

"We'll pull down the shade." She lowered the patterned window blind beneath the sheer organdy curtains. "That way no one, neither man nor beast, can look in. Tomorrow, when the sun's out, I'll check around. Okay?"

"Okay, but I still think you should call Detective DeSoto."

"Detective DeSoto?" Nicole said in surprise. "How do you know who he is?"

"I heard you talking to him at Grandma's."

"Were you eavesdropping?"

"No, *honest*!" Shelley protested, having been warned against the impoliteness of eavesdropping. "I was just walking by and I heard him say something about *other* cops, like he was one, too. Besides, he looks like a policeman."

"How do you know what a policeman looks like?"

"I watch TV," Shelley said indignantly. "I think he looks kind of like Bobby Simone on *NYPD Blue*."

"You mean the actor Jimmy Smits?" Nicole's mouth dropped. "Have you been watching *NYPD Blue*?"

"Well . . . uh . . . yeah."

"Where? At your father's?"

"No, here."

"Here! *When*?"

"Oh, sometimes when I can't sleep," Shelley said airily.

"I never heard you watching television after nine o'clock."

"Earphones, Mom. You bought them for me."

"Obviously a mistake." Nicole paused. "Do you really think Raymond DeSoto looks like Jimmy Smits?"

"Absolutely."

"I don't see it. He's not as handsome as Smits."

"But he *is* cute, Mom."

"Well, yes. Also, he's a sergeant, not just a detective."

Nicole jerked her mind back to the issue of television. "But that's not the point. *NYPD Blue* is too grown-up for you."

"I understand it. I'm not a little girl, Mommy. I'm almost ten. Anyway," continued Shelley, master of changing the subject, "Sergeant DeSoto looked nice."

"Yes, he did."

"I bet he'd believe us about the werewolf and come."

"Maybe, but he's probably not on duty. Besides, I don't think we need a policeman tonight. Right now we both need sleep. Remember, you're spending tomorrow with Daddy."

Shelley sighed. "Do I have to?"

"Come on, Shel. You promised not to be mad at Daddy because he and I are having trouble. You'll have fun."

"Oh, okay. But I'm not gonna tell him about the werewolf. He'll probably try to make me come live with him if he knows, and I *don't* want to live with him."

"I know you don't, honey."

"But I'm still a little worried about the werewolf. Can I sleep with my lamp and radio on?"

"Yes, if you *can* sleep through all the noise and light."

"I can."

Ten minutes later, a thin scarf thrown over Shelley's bedside lamp to dim the light, her radio turned low, Jesse settled firmly by the child's side, Nicole returned to her room. She looked out the window, wishing they had a stronger dusk-to-dawn light out there.

What had come with the house looked like an old-fashioned gaslight and put out only a dim glow.

No doubt their prowler was merely a teenager wearing a mask, but she didn't like the fact that he'd appeared outside Shelley's window, which faced a backyard encircled by a six-foot-high wooden fence—a fence whose gate Nicole had padlocked shut after some neighborhood kids opened it and let Jesse loose, nearly resulting in his being hit a second time by a car. Whoever had peered in Shelley's window must have taken the trouble to climb the fence. There were many other houses in the neighborhood without fences, and it wouldn't have been easy to scale six feet of smooth boards, indicating a determination that made her uncomfortable.

Quietly Nicole dragged her dressing-table chair to her closet, stood on top, and began rummaging through shoe boxes. Finally she found the one where she'd hidden the gun. It was a Smith & Wesson .38, not an expensive model, but one that could do some damage if necessary. After her attack, she'd asked her father to buy her a gun and let her take lessons. He'd refused, abhorring firearms, but when she left San Antonio, she did as she pleased, buying a handgun and going regularly to a firing range until she developed a respectable skill. When she married Roger, he insisted she get rid of the gun, saying she had no need of it when he was there to protect her. She'd acquiesced, as always, even though she didn't know how Roger intended to protect her. He'd never even been in a fistfight in his life.

Once again on her own, she'd bought the gun after Roger left, knowing he'd be outraged if he knew she was keeping a gun in the house. "But you walked out and left me alone with a child," she muttered to an invisible Roger. Besides, the locks on the doors had been changed since he moved out, so there was no danger of his walking in unexpectedly and accidentally being shot by a panicky wife. That's why she had only one set of keys—so *no* one else could come in. She was also careful to keep the windows locked.

Nicole started to put the gun back in the closet, then decided it would do her no good if it took her ten minutes to find and load it. Instead she loaded it and put it in the drawer beside her bedside table. Then she locked the drawer and tucked the key under her mattress.

Taking another quick look around the backyard, Nicole climbed into bed. She was so tired, she expected to fall immediately asleep. Instead, she tossed restlessly, haunted by the dream Shelley had interrupted.

She'd always had vivid dreams and relived the attack many times over the years in nightmares, but this one had been different. Never had she seen Luis Magaro and Ritchie Zand sitting beneath the overpass talking about the rape.

Talking about the rape. Talking about the rape as if it had already happened.

Nicole sat up in bed. Why on earth would she dream that they were talking about the attack as if it were in the past? How could she have overheard a conversation like that?

"You didn't," she said aloud. "It's impossible. You have no idea what they said to each other later. It was a *dream*, Nicole, just a dream."

But it didn't feel like a dream. It felt like a memory.

FOUR

1

The next morning Nicole awakened early, and before even letting Jesse into the backyard, she went out by herself for an inspection. The gate was still padlocked shut. She walked the perimeter of the yard. There were no scuff marks on the tan painted fence, and they hadn't had rain in weeks so the ground was bone-dry, leaving no hope of finding a footprint.

The intruder had left behind one trace of his night visit, however. For some reason, Jesse had chosen two spots for hiding places. One was beneath a live oak at the back of the yard. The other was against the foundation of the house directly beneath Shelley's window. Here, where the intruder had looked in Shelley's window, Nicole found the back half of a running-shoe print. It was much larger than hers.

Looking at it, she wondered if she should call the police. But what could they do? Tell her she'd had a prowler? She already knew that. No, the police could do nothing with the little bit of evidence the prowler had left behind. He hadn't even done any damage except to scare a little girl. If she called, they'd simply tell her it was probably a teenage prankster. Worse, they could label her a woman unused to living alone and given to hysterics. In that case, if anything more serious happened, they might even believe she was literally crying "wolf" and not give the matter the attention it deserved.

When she came back inside, Shelley was up. "Did the werewolf leave clues to show the police?"

"No clues, I'm afraid, and it's awfully hard to convince the police of a werewolf sighting. Besides, I think it was just someone wearing a mask."

"Well, of course," Shelley replied, all calm sophistication in the light of day. "But you can't be too careful."

"Yes, Mom," Nicole droned in a beleaguered, teenage voice. Shelley giggled. "You get cleaned up, kiddo. We have church this morning."

Nicole and Shelley were just returning from mass when Roger's Ford Explorer pulled in behind them. Nicole glanced at her watch. Ten forty-five. He wasn't supposed to arrive until noon.

Annoyed but trying not to show it, she forced a smile as she emerged from her car. "A little early, aren't you?"

Roger, wearing beige khakis, a denim shirt with long sleeves rolled up to the elbows, new Gucci loafers and designer sunglasses she'd never seen before, grinned cheerfully. "Couldn't wait to see my sweetheart."

"Roger, you'll make me blush."

His smile vanished. "I meant my daughter."

"I *know* that, Roger. What's happened to your sense of humor?"

"I thought you were being sarcastic."

"No, just teasing. I'm not in the mood for a fight." Roger seemed to relax. "Well, as you can see, Shelley is dressed up. She needs to change clothes. And she hasn't eaten."

"She can change clothes in a flash, and I'll take her out for a nice lunch."

Nicole looked at the child hovering near the car. "Shel?"

"I'll change real fast," she said obligingly. "And Daddy, can we have lunch at Planet Hollywood?"

Roger detested the raucous atmosphere of Planet Hollywood on the River Walk, which Shelley knew quite well. Nicole pretended to cough to keep from laughing when Roger forced a broad, artificial smile and said heartily, "Of course, honey! Sounds terrific!"

They walked to the front door together and Nicole withdrew her keys from her purse. "My key doesn't work anymore," Roger said.

"There's a reason for that."

He raised an eyebrow, understanding that she'd changed the locks. "Was that really necessary or just an act of anger?"

She opened the door and Shelley ran ahead of her toward her

bedroom. "You don't live here anymore. There's no reason for you to have unlimited access to the house."

"What if I need to get in?"

"For what reason?" Roger stared at her, momentarily stumped. "Tell you what," Nicole said. "I'll give you a new key to this house if you'll give me a key to your apartment."

That should successfully end the subject, Nicole thought. She was right. Roger ignored her, walked to the awful brown chair, sat down, and let out a groan of comfort. She thought of Miguel floundering in the monstrosity. "Don't you want your couch and chair?" she asked. "I know how you love them."

"Not now. My apartment is furnished. I'll probably want them later, though."

"How much later?"

He looked irritated. "What difference does it make?"

"They look awful in here."

"They look fine," Roger said firmly, as if that settled the matter. "May I have something to drink, or is the refrigerator under lock and key, too?"

"Not on Sundays. What do you want? Iced tea? Coke? Milk?"

"Water. Lots of ice."

He gulped down the glass and asked for another. Nicole knew this meant he'd drunk heavily the night before and was dehydrated. That's why he wouldn't remove the sunglasses—he didn't want her to see his bloodshot eyes. He used to drink in moderation, but his alcohol consumption had increased dramatically since he started spending so much time away from home, even before he left for Lisa Mervin.

Nicole sat down on the couch. "What do you have planned for Shelley today?"

"I thought I'd take her to Sea World."

"She'll love that!" Nicole exclaimed. "She hasn't been there since we first moved here."

"I know. Then I'll take her out to dinner."

"That sounds fine. I do hope you'll have her home by seven, though. She needs a bath and time to settle down before bed. She has school in the morning."

"Seven it is."

Nicole hesitated. "It will be just the two of you today, won't it?"

Roger feigned confusion. "What do you mean?"

"You know what I mean. Lisa isn't going along, is she?"

Roger's lips tightened in annoyance. "Why is that an issue? Just because you don't like her—"

"Hold it!" Nicole said sharply. "I've never even met the girl. Maybe under different circumstances I'd like her very much. But this doesn't have anything to do with *my* feelings. Shelley resents her—"

"I wonder why?" Roger interrupted acidly.

"Don't blame me for her feelings. I don't talk against her to Shelley. You, however, have tried to cram Lisa down her throat ever since you left, and she hates it. It's not fair to Shelley. To Lisa, either, if you plan to marry her."

"How considerate of you to worry about Lisa."

"Promise me, Roger. Just you and Shelley."

Roger set his glass on the end table. "All *right*. Any further orders, General?"

"I think that will do for now," Nicole said coolly. "And I assume by calling me 'General' you're referring to my grandfather."

"You do seem to be developing a few traits in common with the famous General Ernest Hazelton."

"Whom you never knew."

"No, but your mother has told me *all* about him." He gazed up at the ceiling. "A virtual paragon among men was the general. Bigger than life." He looked back at Nicole. "Phyllis is a case of the classic Electra complex if I've ever seen one."

Her jaw tightening, Nicole stood up and called, "Shelley, are you about ready? Daddy can't wait to get to Planet Hollywood."

"Very funny," Roger muttered.

Jesse appeared, made a beeline for Roger, and promptly emitted a loud sloppy sneeze all over his Gucci loafers. "Goddammit!" Roger exploded, jumping up. Jesse artfully dodged a kick, tearing back to the bedroom. "Nicole, get me some paper towels. I don't know why you keep that mangy, flea-ridden little—"

Trying to stifle her laughter, Nicole went to the kitchen for paper towels. When she gave them to Roger, he began working on the shoes, still muttering furiously. "I'm sorry, Roger," Nicole managed. "Those *do* look like very expensive shoes. They're new, aren't they?"

"They weren't expensive," Roger lied, "but they are new. Now look at them. He did that on purpose."

"Oh, I'm sure he didn't," Nicole said blandly.

Roger glared at her before Shelley dashed out of her bedroom wearing jeans, a blue T-shirt, and new Keds, her long blond hair pulled back in a ponytail and secured with a blue scrunchie. "I'm ready!"

"Have a *really* good time today," Nicole said, holding Shelley tightly and giving her a smacking kiss on the cheek.

"You, too, Mom. What're you gonna do?"

"Oh, I've got all kinds of exciting things planned."

Like going to visit Kay Holland and perhaps finding out why my father killed himself, she thought with a chill, forcing herself to wave merrily as Roger and Shelley drove away.

2

After they left, Nicole dressed, thinking about her father's store. The place where she'd spent so many happy hours as a child "helping" her father and Kay with the business was now a site of horror where her father had retreated to violently take his life.

Now Kay had something to tell her about her father's death. She wondered if it were really significant. Maybe the woman was only imagining she had important information. Imagination and a sense of drama didn't seem to be Kay's strong points, though.

Sunday traffic was light and she drove down into the older section of town near the Plaza de Las Islas. As always she admired the beautiful San Fernando Cathedral built by settlers from the Canary Islands in the 1730's. Near it was the Bexar County Courthouse. "What year was the courthouse built?" Nicole could hear her father ask. "In 1895," the young child Nicole would answer dutifully. "And what's it made of?" "Red Texas granite and sandstone." "Brilliant!" her father would crow. "This little girl deserves an ice-cream cone." So long ago.

Parking was not a problem today. She pulled into a spot directly in front of the large store that had stood here for eighty years. It had always been a music store, owned by one family until Clifton Sloan bought it in 1959. He'd told her once that although it became fairly successful in the late sixties, only a generous inheritance from a maiden great-aunt who shared his love of music allowed him to keep the store going in the early years. Later he used part of the inheritance to make lucky investments in the stock market, enabling the family to live on a much higher scale than the income from the store ever would have allowed.

The front door was locked. She pecked on the glass, and in a few seconds Kay hurried to unlock it. "Hi, Nikki," Kay said nervously, locking the door behind Nicole. She looked alarmingly thin in a dark green skirt and print blouse hanging out of her waistband on the right side. Her short brown hair lay in its usual perfect helmet of curls, but she wore only a streak of heather-colored lipstick over dry lips. Without her usual subtle application of eye shadow and mascara, her eyes had a wide, surprised look.

"How's the work going?"

"The work?" Kay repeated blankly. "Oh, you mean emptying your father's desk. Well, there wasn't much of a personal nature. Mostly just business papers."

As they walked through the store, Nicole glanced around, realizing she hadn't been here for months. Drums, horns, organs, pianos—uprights and baby grands—guitars, violins, a thousand pieces of sheet music. "Here I was surrounded by a world of musical opportunity, and I didn't have a lick of talent," Nicole lamented.

"I always thought you had a very sweet little singing voice," Kay said diplomatically.

Nicole grinned to herself. She, the closet rock star, had never wanted to be described as having "a sweet little singing voice," but poor Kay was giving the most honest compliment she could.

"I put some tea on earlier," Kay said as they headed for the office. "Would you like some? Chamomile. Very calming."

Nicole, who hated tea, especially herbal, smiled politely. "I drank about three cups of coffee before I left home. I think I'm waterlogged."

"Too much caffeine isn't good for you, dear, especially at a time like this. You don't need anything else rattling your nerves."

As they neared the office, Nicole's steps slowed. "Actually, my nerves *are* a little rattled by whatever you have to tell me."

"I probably said it all wrong yesterday, scared you when I

shouldn't have." Kay walked into the office, then turned around and stared at Nicole, who'd stopped dead on shaky legs. "What's wrong, dear?"

"The office." Nicole's mouth was dry, her voice unsteady. "I don't think I can . . ."

"Oh, my goodness!" Kay exclaimed. "How thoughtless of me. It's been completely cleaned and I've worked for hours in there, so I just didn't think about the effect it would have on you, not having been in there since . . . Oh, Nikki, I'm sorry!"

"It's all right, really. But I'd prefer to stay out here if you don't mind. You go ahead and get your tea."

"I don't need tea. I've drunk gallons the last few days. Just habit." Kay looked stricken. "You sit down on that piano bench and catch your breath. Want a glass of water?"

"A pint of Scotch would be better."

Kay's eyes fluttered around the room. "I don't believe we have any."

"I was just teasing. I don't even like Scotch."

"Oh." Kay looked confused.

"I'll be fine. Sit down here on the bench beside me and tell me about Daddy."

Kay sat down and began smoothing her skirt with pale, faintly bluish hands. "Your father wasn't himself the last few months."

Nicole was puzzled. "Mom didn't say anything about it."

"I'm sure he tried to hide any unhappiness from her. He always did, you know. But there were things she had to notice. First he started looking tired. He got circles under his eyes and became sallow. I asked him about it and he said he wasn't sleeping well. Claimed he'd tried some of those over-the-counter remedies, but they weren't working."

"Did he seem concerned enough to see a doctor?"

"If he saw one, he never told me. Then one day I went in his office and found him asleep in his chair. I was so glad he was getting a little rest. I was being quiet as a mouse, looking for an invoice, when suddenly he started mumbling. I couldn't make out any words except 'shouldn't' and 'Nikki' in a frightened voice. Then he jerked awake. He came to himself quickly and acted embarrassed. Brushed it off as a little catnap. I didn't say a word about him talking in his sleep."

"About a month later, it happened again," Kay continued. "It could have been happening every day, but once again I just happened to be there. Well, this time he wasn't muttering. He *shouted*, 'Nikki! Could've been killed, the bastards!' "

"It was the rape," Nicole said softly. "He was dreaming about my rape."

Phyllis had always insisted that if Nicole's experience must be mentioned at all, it was to be referred to as "the attack." She noticed Kay's face pinkening at the word "rape," but Nicole had rarely been one to use euphemisms.

"Yes, I do believe that's what he was dreaming about."

"Do you have any idea what could have triggered all this?" Nicole asked.

"I've wondered if he were ill. Maybe there was something seriously wrong with him and he wasn't thinking so clearly anymore. He did seem to dwell on the past more than he ever had. Even before he became so depressed lately he left the church. He said your mother was very unhappy about it."

"Yes."

"After that he gradually lost interest in the business. Not completely, you understand, but he just wasn't on *top* of things anymore. That's another thing that made me think he was seriously ill."

Nicole stood and began walking around the store. "Now that you mention all this, I realize I was vaguely aware of it. But only vaguely. I was so wrapped up in myself—the move back to San Antonio, my new job, Roger leaving." She hit her fist on the top of a piano. "Why didn't I pay more attention?"

"Don't blame yourself, Nikki. The changes were subtle, and I'm sure he always put on a good show for you. Your mother, too."

"But not you?"

Kay flushed. "I was around him all day, every day. It would have been hard to hide something from me. Besides, he wasn't as worried about my feelings as yours and your mother's."

But you were worried about his, Nicole thought. You've been in love with him for years. I always sensed it. I wonder if Mother did? I wonder if *he* did?

Knowing that Kay had loved her father made her both happy and sad—happy because Phyllis was so difficult, so critical; sad because Kay had devoted herself to a man who, even if he returned her love, would never have left his wife and daughter, would never even have had an affair. At least she didn't think he would have had an affair. She wasn't sure she had known her father at all.

"Kay, was there anything else?" she asked, trying to steer her mind away from what might have been between Kay and Clifton.

Kay clasped her hands. "Yes. And this is what's most disturbing. I sorted the mail and I should have noticed *long* before I did, but there's so *much* mail. Anyway, now that I think back on it, about the time your father started having the nightmares, letters came for him marked 'Personal.' "

"Just regular-looking letters?"

"No. They were large clasp envelopes, always heavily taped as if it were very important they stay sealed."

"Was there a return address?"

"No. And the postmark was local. Then, on Tuesday . . ." Her voice thickened and tears welled in her eyes. "Last Tuesday another envelope came. It was padded—the kind you send photographs in—but it was marked 'Personal.' I took the mail in to your father as usual and he spotted it right away." She pulled a tissue from her pocket and dabbed at her eyes. "The color drained from his face. He said, 'Thank you, Kay,' in a strained voice. I hovered around a moment. He said sharply, 'Did you need anything else?' I said 'No' and left. Then he did something he'd never done before—locked his office door in midday."

She took a deep shuddery breath. "About ten minutes later, I thought I heard a noise back in the office. Something like a groan. I had a bad feeling, but I didn't do anything. Nikki, I didn't *do* anything!"

"Calm down, Kay," Nicole said, although her own heart was pounding. "What could you have done besides beat on the door and demand to know what was going on? Dad would have hated that. He was a very private man."

"Yes, but I feel so guilty. Anyway, minutes later I smelled smoke coming from the office. This time I *did* knock on the door. Your father didn't answer. I tried the door and it was still locked. I pounded on it, ready to phone the fire department, when he finally opened the door. He looked ten years older, Nikki. Ten years older and devastated, but he tried to act normal. He said the fire was in the wastebasket. He said he'd tossed an ashtray in and a cigarette stub was still burning and it set some papers on fire.'' She turned pain-filled eyes on Nicole. "But your father *never* emptied an ashtray into a wastebasket during the day. Ashtrays were only emptied in the mornings, when he came in, so a fire couldn't start during the night."

"It was the same at home." Nicole bit her lip. "Could he have been distracted and done it by accident?"

"I'd say that was a possibility except that the fire was still burning. He ignored it. When I tried to push past him to reach the pitcher of water on his desk, he blocked me. And Nikki, his *eyes*! If someone had just called and said you were dead, they couldn't have looked more awful. He set that fire himself!"

"And what did I do?" Kay cried. "Nothing. I should have stood right up to him and said, 'Clifton Sloan, I've been your friend for thirty years. You tell me what's wrong or I'm calling a doctor!' But did I? No. I just stood there, blithering like my mother always said, not enough nerve or presence of mind to be any help at all."

Nicole empathized with Kay's frustration with herself. There had been a thousand times when she wished she'd handled situations differently. But now she was more interested in what her father had said and done, not what Kay hadn't. Trying to hide her impatience with the woman's detours into self-flagellation, she prodded determinedly.

"Kay, what did Dad say after giving you that excuse about the wastebasket?"

"Nothing! He shut the door in my face. He'd *never* been so rude. I was astonished. No, that's not the right word. *Appalled,* that's it. Over the whole scene, you understand, not just his shutting the door on me. Afterward, all was quiet in the office for about half an hour, then your father came out, told me he wasn't feeling well, and left. He said he was going home." Her mouth trembled. "I never saw him alive again. That very night he came back to the office and . . ." Kay choked back a sob.

Nicole put her hand on Kay's bony shoulder. "Don't think about that part now."

Kay wiped her nose, wadded her tissue, and stuffed it in her pocket. "Your father left the office about half an hour later and locked his office, but I was worried that maybe the fire in the wastebasket wasn't out completely." She looked down at the floor. "That's not completely true. I was curious," she said meekly.

"Anyone would have been."

"I used my own key and opened the office. The fire was out and almost everything in the wastebasket was ashes. *Almost* everything."

Nicole's interest quickened. "What was left?"

"It's in the office file cabinet. I understand that you don't want to go in there, so I'll get it—"

"I'll go with you."

"Are you sure?"

"Yes. I can't stay out of there forever, especially if Mother keeps the store. I was just feeling a little queasy earlier."

Nicole followed Kay into the spacious office carpeted in pale gray. Her father's large mahogany desk was unnaturally neat, an expensive gold pen-and-pencil set sitting close to an oversized turquoise ashtray on one side, photos of her, Shelley, and Phyllis forming an arc in gold frames on the other. The blotter was missing. Of course, Nicole thought, her stomach clenching. The blotter had been covered with blood.

Nicole quickly switched her attention to Kay, who was unlocking one of the file drawers. She withdrew a white legal-sized envelope. Gingerly she lifted a small piece of paper and held it toward Nicole. "I found this still smoldering under the padded envelope." Her face colored and she looked miserably self-conscious. "I didn't show it to the police. I didn't want to stir things up again."

"Stir up what things again?" Nicole asked, accepting a piece of charred paper.

"Well . . . just things best left in the past."

Baffled, Nicole stepped closer to the window behind the desk, tripping over an oriental rug. It flipped back, exposing a rusty stain. Nicole gasped. Kay clutched her throat. "Oh, Nikki, I'm sorry. The walls cleaned up beautifully, but the carpet is so pale they just couldn't get out all the—"

"Blood," Nicole said briskly. "It's all right." She flipped back the rug with her foot, her stomach tightening as she fought nausea. Focus on what's in your hand, she thought sternly.

Light streamed in the window. She held up the piece of paper. It was a photograph, but at first she couldn't make out what she was seeing. It was upside down. She turned the fragment around until it took recognizable form.

She felt as if everything inside her wrenched into a painful knot. Shining black hair, a hazel eye, an arched eyebrow, a high cheekbone, a fragment of a straight, chiseled nose, the corner of a full, sensual mouth.

She was looking at the burned remains of a photo of Paul Dominic.

FIVE

1

Nicole felt as if she were in a trance as she drove from the store to her mother's. Kay had asked if Nicole thought she should give the fragment of the photo of Paul Dominic to the police and tell them about the letters.

"No," Nicole had answered sharply, realizing she sounded like her mother, wanting to keep everything quiet, desiring as little interference from outsiders as possible. But something told her now was not the time to reveal the letters to anyone. "Let's keep this between us for now, Kay." Kay had agreed, looking relieved.

When Nicole pulled up in front of her parents' French Provincial house, she saw another car in the driveway, a blue Cadillac. One of her mother's friends. Maybe today's visit hadn't been necessary at all, but she hadn't even spoken to her mother on the phone since yesterday.

She opened the front door without knocking and heard the chatter of voices from the living room. Before she got the door closed, Phyllis had come to greet her. She wore slim black slacks and a white silk blouse, every hair of her white French twist in place, a slender necklace of real pearls—the last Christmas gift from her husband—around her neck. The only signs of her grief were faint mauve shadows beneath her eyes.

"Nicole, how nice to see you," she said, aiming a kiss at Nicole's cheek and just missing. This was the way her mother had always kissed her. "The No-Smear Kiss," Nicole had come to call it, referring to Phyllis's concern that her lipstick always look perfect. "I called earlier, but no one was home."

"Roger took Shelley to Sea World, and I took a drive." That

wasn't really a lie, she told herself. She *had* driven. "I see you have company."

"Mildred Loomis is here." She steered Nicole into the living room where a plump middle-aged woman with daffodil-yellow bleached hair, bright blue frosted eye shadow, and a vivid pink suit with red poppy appliqués on the jacket sat on the couch. "You remember Mrs. Loomis, don't you?"

"Yes, of course." Now that *was* a lie, Nicole scolded herself, but the woman was beaming at her, obviously remembering *her*. "It's been a long time, Mrs. Loomis."

"I'll say it has," the woman agreed. "And please call me Mildred. Why, honey, I haven't seen you since you recited that poem you wrote to your mother's reading circle."

No wonder Nicole hadn't remembered her. She hadn't seen her for nineteen years. Now she recalled that even all those years ago, she'd wondered why the woman looked so blowzy despite her husband's wealth. Certainly all that money could have improved her hair and makeup, if not her weight. "Oh, that dreadful poem," Nicole groaned.

Mildred beamed again. "Why, I thought it was precious." At the time, Nicole had thought it terribly profound. "It rhymed so nice," Mildred continued. "I just hate poems that don't rhyme. I don't think they should even be called poems if they don't rhyme, do you?"

"Well—"

Obviously Phyllis saw that Nicole was about to argue and cut her off. "Mildred and her husband just got back from New York last night. That's why they didn't come to your father's funeral."

Mildred's beaming face immediately fell into a mask of woe. "Oh, Nicole, I am *so* sorry. What an *awful* thing. I was just tellin' my husband, Willard, this morning, 'What an *awful* thing! What would make a man who has everything want to stick a gun in his mouth—' "

"I suppose we'll never know," Phyllis interrupted sharply. "Nicole and I have decided not to speculate. It's too upsetting."

Sufficiently quelled, Mildred lapsed into a nodding, doleful silence. Phyllis looked at Nicole. "Would you care for some tea?"

Why did everyone keep offering her tea? she wondered. Especially her mother, who knew she couldn't stand tea. "I think I'll pass, Mom."

"I could make coffee. We have a delicious pound cake that Mildred brought."

"No, thank you." She smiled at Mildred, who was slicing off a piece of the cake. Nicole was certain it wasn't her first. "I'm really not hungry now, Mom, and since you have someone to keep you company for a while, I wonder if you'd mind if I went upstairs and looked for something in my old room."

Phyllis allowed herself a small frown. "Look for what?"

"My school yearbooks." Lie number three, she thought. A lot of good mass did this morning. "Shelley was interested in seeing what her mother looked like in high school."

"Pretty as a picture," Mildred managed around a mouth half-full of pound cake. "I always told Willard you were the prettiest girl I ever saw. You've only improved with age."

"Thank you," Nicole said.

"Your mama tells me you're gettin' a divorce. Our boy W. J.'s divorced, too." She pronounced *W* as *dub ya*. "He's only a couple of years older than you and a fine figure of a man, if I do say so myself. Maybe you two could go out to dinner or to the movies or somethin'."

"That sounds very nice," Nicole said woodenly, suddenly remembering W. J. Loomis as an oxlike creature whose claim to fame in high school was dropping water balloons out of second-floor windows on the heads of passing girls.

"I could give him your phone number," Mildred continued hopefully.

"Well . . ."

"You run on upstairs," Phyllis said quickly, rescuing her. "Mildred and I are having a very nice conversation. We won't even miss you, will we, Mildred?"

Mildred, stuffing another piece of cake in her mouth, waved a puffy hand in dismissal. Phyllis gave Nicole an unexpected wink, and Nicole felt like hugging her. Her mother rarely came to her rescue.

Nicole hurried up the stairs before Mildred could ask for her phone number. Nicole knew the woman couldn't pry the number out of her mother, but that didn't mean W. J. couldn't get it from Directory Assistance. Maybe I should get an answering machine so I can screen calls, Nicole thought.

Her bedroom looked almost as it had when she moved away

fifteen years ago. The thick pale green carpet seemed like new. The ultramodern white lacquer furniture was spotless, just like the snowy white bedspread adorned with decorative pillows in mint, forest, and ivy-green. The heavy pale green draperies hung over snowy sheers. A large framed print of "Idle Hours" by J. Alden Weir graced one wall. The only ornaments on the dresser and chest of drawers were framed photos of a four-year-old grinning Nicole wearing a bunny outfit at a dance recital, and her formal high school graduation picture.

She shut the door to her bedroom and went to the walk-in closet. One side was for clothes, the other lined with built-in shelves for books. Garment bags hung on a rod. Nicole knew they held Easter dresses and prom gowns from her youth.

But she wasn't interested in clothes. She turned to the shelves. Books stood rigidly in place, so many she'd read over and over as a teenager such as *Wuthering Heights* and *Jane Eyre*. A few schoolbooks stood among the crowd. At the end of one shelf were her school yearbooks and two photo albums.

Nicole gathered up the yearbooks and albums and placed them on the floor by her bed. Then she went back to the closet.

When they had moved into the house, she'd been delighted to find a small cabinet built into the base of the shelves. She called it her hiding place, but it wasn't safe enough for her *really* private things like her diary and valentines she received from boys, so when she was twelve, she bought a padlock. Phyllis had been outraged, and even Clifton had complained. "What kind of secrets could my baby girl have that even her daddy can't know?"

Nicole had ignored both of them, though, tucking away what she considered top secret property and keeping the key to the padlock with her at all times. Until she moved away seven months after the rape, that is. Then she'd left the contents of her hiding place *and* the padlock key behind. Now she picked up her graduation picture and slid the photo from behind the glass. On the cardboard backing was taped the short, thin key. She'd never liked the picture, but it had been good for something.

Nicole untaped the key and rushed back to the closet. The lock was stiff and at first she thought she'd have to sneak back with lubricating oil, but at last the lock clicked open. The hinges creaked as she swung open the storage-cabinet door.

Sitting on the floor, she withdrew five diaries. "All full of torrid secrets, no doubt," she mumbled, noticing they only covered her years between twelve and seventeen.

At the bottom of the cabinet was a photo album. This was what she'd been looking for, although it wasn't a traditional album. Her hands trembled slightly as she pulled it from the cabinet. Her hands had also trembled when she'd put it together.

She dusted it off and sat down on the bed. Are you sure you want to dredge all of this up? she wondered. No, but after what Kay told her, she must.

She opened the cover. On the first page beneath a plastic protector was a yellowed newspaper clipping. The headline blared, "Daughter of Local Businessman Assaulted in Basin Park." The story went on to describe how Nicole Marie Sloan, nineteen, a sophomore at Trinity University, had been raped and brutally beaten by two men. A male passerby had scared off the men with a handgun. Sloan's rescuer had not seen the men's faces, but Sloan had identified her attackers. Their names were being withheld until arrests were made. Nicole Sloan was in serious but stable condition.

Nicole took a deep breath and moved on to the next page. Here was the story of the arrest of Ritchie Zand, lead singer of the local rock band The Zanti Misfits, and one of the band's roadies, Luis Magaro. Magaro, thirty-two, had a previous record of assault. Zand, twenty-three, had been arrested three years ago for statutory rape, but the charges were dropped. Magaro and Zand had been positively identified by Nicole Sloan.

A light tap sounded at the door. Nicole jumped and almost dropped the album, knowing that if her mother saw it, she would jerk it from her hands and immediately destroy it. Instead, the door opened and Carmen stepped in. "What's going on? Hiding from Mrs. Loomis?"

Nicole let out her breath. "Partly."

Carmen's curly dark hair framed her face. She wore jeans and a long-sleeved peach-colored shirt. Except for the weight she'd gained lately, she looked almost exactly the same as when they were teenagers. "When I couldn't reach you at home, I figured you were here. I thought you might need a friend today."

"Thanks. I do."

"What are you looking at?"

"Memories. Close the door and come on in."

Carmen joined her on the bed. Her smile disappeared when she saw the clippings in the scrapbook. "You kept all this stuff?"

"Yes. The album's been hidden in this room since I moved away. I've never taken it home because I didn't want Shelley to find it."

"My God, Nicole. I had no idea. Why are you looking at it now?"

"I'm not sure. I heard something today . . ." Carmen's dark eyebrows rose and reluctantly Nicole began telling her Kay's story, knowing Carmen would never repeat it.

When she finished, Carmen looked at her quizzically. "Why would someone send your father a picture of Paul Dominic?"

"I have no idea. But I know that he started acting strange when those damned letters began coming. And because of what he mumbled in his nightmares, I'm sure the letters had something to do with what happened to me."

Carmen tapped a long peach-polished nail against her perfect teeth. "That sounds logical, although I still can't imagine what in those letters could have upset your father so much. The picture of Paul hints that it was something about your assault and the murders, but it's not as if your dad didn't know exactly what had happened to you and everything that took place afterward."

"I know. I'm not even sure why I'm looking at this. Maybe it's because of Dad. Maybe it's because I want to see if I've really put it behind me. I thought I had—until lately."

"Until you thought you saw Paul at the cemetery." Nicole nodded. "You were exhausted and emotionally drained. I agree that the guy looked like Paul. But it wasn't."

"Probably not, but I still want to go over this stuff. Will you stay with me?"

Carmen smiled. "Sure. But we'd better keep a sharp ear for your mother. If she sees this—"

"We're dead meat," Nicole said melodramatically.

Carmen smothered a laugh. "You're still a big goof, do you know that?"

"Thank you. Only you and my daughter seem to appreciate my sense of humor."

"Okay, if you're determined to do this, turn the page. I don't know how much more cake Mrs. Loomis can hold, and as soon as she leaves, your mother will be right up the stairs to see what we're doing.''

Nicole obeyed. The next page displayed an article dated two days after Zand's and Magaro's arrests. A picture showed a triumphant Zand waving to a crowd. And why wouldn't he be looking triumphant? Nicole thought. Suddenly Magaro and Zand had alibis. According to two sons of a prominent San Antonio family, at the time of Nicole Sloan's assault, Magaro and Zand had been with them. The brothers had gone to Mexico the day after the attack and had only just returned to San Antonio. Otherwise, they could have cleared Zand and Magaro immediately. ''Yeah, sure,'' Nicole said aloud. ''In other words, it just took a while to find a couple of suitable guys willing to lie for them. Probably die-hard fans of Ritchie's band. Either that, or Magaro was their drug supplier.''

''Are you sure you should go on with this?'' Carmen said tentatively. ''It only gets worse.''

''Yes.'' Nicole noticed the steely edge in her voice. ''I'm sure.''

She turned the page and the headline seemed to scream: ''Two Men Found Murdered in Basin Park.'' Nicole scanned the article, although she knew the details by heart. Ritchie Zand and Luis Magaro, who only four weeks earlier were arrested then released for sexual assault and battery, had each been found shot in the head. The bodies were hanging from trees near the Interstate 281 overpass. The weapon was a .44 magnum. Both men had died instantly from the gunshot wounds. In a bizarre touch, black hoods had been placed over their heads. Some speculation existed that the men had been the victims of a ritual execution.

The article went on to talk about the promising career of Ritchie Zand, lead singer of the rock group The Zanti Misfits, named for an episode of the science fiction television show *The Outer Limits*. Only a week before the killings, the band had been given a recording contract with Revel Music. Without Zand, however, the future of the group was unknown.

''The Zanti Misfits,'' Carmen said softly. ''Ritchie Zand was slime, but he had that fabulous voice. Remember it?''

Nicole shuddered. Oh, yes, she remembered him singing ''Radio Ga-Ga'' in the backseat while Magaro held a knife at her throat.

"Without him, the band fell apart," Carmen continued, "but Bobby still talks about it constantly."

"He does?" Nicole answered absently. Then her memory flashed. "Carmen, I completely forgot! Bobby was the drummer for The Zanti Misfits."

"That's right. He's certain that if Ritchie hadn't been killed, they would have gone on to stardom. He would have been a millionaire, lusted after by hundreds of groupies, a household name. Instead he's plain old Bobby Vega, co-owner of a trinket shop on the River Walk."

"I'd hardly call Vega's a trinket shop," Nicole said. "But I cannot believe I forgot about Bobby being in The Zanti Misfits. I thought I remembered *everything* about the events, the people . . ."

"Apparently you don't. I'm not surprised that you forgot about Bobby, though. He wasn't mixed up in any of this."

"No, of course he wasn't, but you were dating Bobby at the time. Didn't he talk to you about it?"

"Yes."

"And he believed Zand was guilty, like I said?"

Carmen looked at her in surprise. "Yes, Nicole. He knew Zand was no angel. Why would you ask such a question?"

"Because I've always gotten the feeling Bobby doesn't like me."

Carmen shrugged. "He *is* different around you. I've noticed it. Maybe it's because he's afraid you associate him with that awful time, that maybe you don't like *him* because he was friends with Ritchie Zand."

"Good heavens, and I didn't even remember he was in the band. So much for crossed wires. Sometime Bobby and I will have to have a talk." Nicole drew a deep breath, her mouth getting drier. "Now for the worst part."

"Nicole, you're looking very pale. I think you should stop—"

But Nicole had already turned the page. She was right. This *was* the worst part. Here was the article about the arrest of Paul Dominic for the murders of Magaro and Zand. According to the article, the day after the discovery of the bodies, an anonymous tip had sent police to the home of Dominic. There they found a Smith & Wesson .44 magnum, registration numbers filed off, wrapped in a shirt belonging to Dominic. The shirt was smeared with AB Positive blood, the rarest kind, and that belonging to Ritchie Zand. Both the shirt and the gun were stuffed in a trash can. Ballistics verified the magnum as the murder weapon. In addition, Dominic had no alibi for the time of the murders. Finally, several people claimed that Dominic had threatened to get even with the men who allegedly had attacked Nicole Sloan, with whom he was romantically involved. Miss Sloan herself told police that Dominic said to her he would kill Magaro and Zand.

"I don't remember saying that," Nicole said faintly. "But everyone says I did."

"You were heavily medicated after hearing about the murders, Nicole."

"That's right. You would have thought I'd have been glad Zand and Magaro were dead. Instead I got hysterical. The police insisted on questioning me. Dad was in Dallas on a trip. Mom was uncharacteristically flustered and called a doctor who sent me spinning with a bunch of tranquilizers."

"I remember. You were probably babbling to the police things you would never have said if you'd had your wits about you. And after all, Paul did tell you he'd kill them."

"What I said in such a medicated state should never have been quoted. I shouldn't have been questioned at that time. I can't believe what I said in that condition would have been admissible in court. Besides, Paul was just talking, just raging. He wasn't a killer, Carmen."

Carmen looked compassionate but dubious. "You'd only known him a couple of months when all of this happened. How well do you really get to know someone in eight weeks?"

"I knew Paul," Nicole maintained firmly.

"And I'll bet you thought you knew Roger, too. Yet after all those years of being married to him, you found out you didn't." Carmen reached over and touched her hand. "I wonder if we really ever know *anybody*."

She's right, Nicole thought. I believed I knew Roger. I believed I knew my father. But Paul . . . It was different with Paul.

Numbly she went to the next article, which described how Paul had been released on one million dollars bond. And finally she reached the last clipping, which announced that Paul Dominic had fled. A nationwide search was being conducted for him, but so far police had no leads.

"And he was never found," Nicole murmured. "That handsome, wealthy, miraculously talented man just vanished off the face of the earth."

Carmen shook her head. "No. Less than a year later he died in that car wreck. They found some of his possessions that had been thrown clear of the wreck, Nicole. And the body—"

"Was never positively identified," Nicole interrupted.

Carmen sighed. "All right, let's say he *is* alive. What would you have to fear from him? He loved you. He *killed* for you."

Nicole looked at her with anguished eyes. "I don't believe he killed them. I've never believed it. But he was arrested for their murders because of me. My rape gave him a motive. And what was one of the most damning pieces of evidence against him? My telling the police that he'd sworn to kill them."

"Nicole, other people swore he'd said the same thing."

"No. They said he threatened to 'get even' with Magaro and Zand. It's not the same." Tears filled her eyes. "Carmen, don't you see? I was the girl he loved, the girl people thought he killed for, and I was the one who supposedly told the police he planned to do it. I betrayed him. He had a fabulous life, and it was ruined because of *me*, because of what had happened to me, because of what I said to the police. If he's alive, he must hate me. Now, just seven months after I moved back to San Antonio, I think he's returned." She looked at Carmen, tears streaming down her face. "What if he's come back because he wants revenge?"

2

Nine thirty-five. Nicole sat at the kitchen table staring at the clock as if she could turn back time to seven o'clock when Roger was supposed to have brought Shelley home.

Nicole had called his apartment three times, each time getting the answering machine and each time leaving an increasingly angry message. The child should be bathed and in bed by now. Instead, Nicole had no idea where she was, and she didn't know where else to call.

"What does Roger think he's doing?" she asked Jesse, who lay curled at her feet the way he always did when she was upset. "Is he purposely trying to make me worry? Is that more important to him than Shelley's welfare?"

Jesse looked up and tilted his head. "You're right, Jess," she continued. "Roger may be a jerk, but he loves Shelley. He wouldn't abuse her just to hurt me."

Talking with Kay and reading the old newspaper clippings had set her nerves on edge earlier in the day. Mrs. Loomis had stayed until she nearly finished the cake and Nicole was too nervous to wait out her visit, so she had never gotten a chance to talk to her mother about her father's nightmares or his behavior at home, which frustrated her even more. Now Roger was over two hours late with Shelley.

She drummed her fingers on the table, angry and increasingly concerned. Where could they be? Certainly Roger would be wearing down by now after spending a whole day with his energetic daughter. After all, he hadn't looked in top condition when he'd picked her up before noon.

A thought suddenly pierced her mind like a dagger. "What if they've been in an accident?" she asked aloud. "My God, it never occurred to me to call the hospitals!"

She jumped up and ran to the phone directory. She was looking up the number of the South Texas Medical Center when Jesse began barking and ran to the front window. Headlights flashed in the driveway.

Nicole didn't remember running out of the house. She even forgot to put on Jesse's leash. They both dashed across the front lawn and through the brilliant glare of the headlights, which Roger had on high beam, to see Shelley emerging from the back of the Explorer. "Shelley, where have you *been*?" Nicole yelled, not from anger but from fear and relief. "Didn't I tell you to be home at seven?"

The child's tired face crumpled. "I'm sorry," she quavered, shying away from a blazing-eyed Nicole and bending to clutch Jesse who was jumping ecstatically at her legs. Roger clambered from the car. For a moment Nicole thought he was going to fall down before he regained his footing.

"Where the *hell* have you been?" Nicole raged.

"Lower your voice," Roger said stiffly. "You're making a scene."

"Answer my question!"

Roger hung on the door of the car for balance. "One of my friends from the department was having a dinner. We went."

"So you decided to take Shelley along to a dinner party without telling me?"

"I told you I'd give her dinner."

"Buying her dinner at a restaurant and taking her to a dinner party are two different things."

"Oh, settle down, Nicole. Listen, the guy's wife is from Vietnam. Fabulous cook. I thought it would be a good experience for Shelley to taste some genuine Vietnamese food and talk with Mai—that's the wife—about her life in . . . well, whatever the hell the name of her village was."

"I guess you also thought having Shelley watch you get drunk and then drive her home in that condition would be a good experience, too. You're not even wearing your glasses."

"I am *not* drunk." Roger overenunciated the way all drunks do when trying to prove they're sober. "I had a couple of drinks. So what?"

"You've had far more than a couple. But whatever, you could have *called*, Roger. It's nine forty-five, almost *three* hours after you were supposed to bring her home."

"Sorry. I guess time slipped up on me."

"Sorry isn't good enough, not after what you've put me through this evening." Nicole's eyes flashed to the other side of the car. A young auburn-haired woman sat nervously in her seat. She didn't meet Nicole's eyes. "Lisa Mervin, I presume."

"Yes. What about it?"

"Roger, you promised me today was for you and Shelley only."

"I made no such promise."

"Yes you *did*!" Nicole shouted.

"I did not. I am not going to keep Shelley away from the woman I intend to marry!"

"I didn't ask you to keep her away forever. Just for today. You sat right there in our former house and promised me when you knew you had every intention of meeting Lisa."

Roger glared at her. "What's happened to you, Nicole? You've turned into a loudmouthed, carping, selfish bitch and I feel like slapping that sanctimonious face of yours!''

"Daddy!" Shelley exclaimed, fear edging her young voice.

Nicole stared at the man she'd once thought so stable, so caring. Her Rock of Gibraltar. The father of her beautiful child. Now here he stood, drunk, threatening to hit her, while his young girlfriend sat in the car watching. If she hadn't been so furious, she could have cried for him. "Roger, I don't know what has happened to *you* this past year, but it's a damned shame," she said quietly. "You used to be a very likable person."

"Likable," he spat. "*Likable*, not *lovable* like Paul Dominic. You would never have married me if he hadn't been killed, no matter what he'd done."

Nicole's spine went rigid at the mention of Paul's name, but she kept her voice steady. "Roger, please get back in your car and shut up. You're making a fool of yourself in front of your girlfriend."

"Lisa *loves* me!"

"She must to tolerate this kind of behavior. But remember, she's young, she's beautiful, and there are plenty of fish in the sea. Good night, Roger."

She wished Lisa would take over the wheel. She appeared more sober than Roger, and Nicole didn't want there to be a car accident. But she knew Roger. If he insisted he wasn't drunk and he would do the driving, he would brook no argument. Nicole felt almost sorry for Lisa. Almost.

Shelley ran past her into the house. Nicole watched Roger climb unsteadily back into the car and the headlights weave to the end of the street before he drove over a curb. Then Jesse drew her attention. He stood at the end of the driveway, his little legs stiff, growling low in his throat. Nicole followed his gaze.

On the opposite side of the street sat a big Doberman wearing a red collar. For a moment the significance of the dog's presence was overshadowed in her mind by her fear for Jesse. In spite of his small, battered body, Jesse had the heart of a lion. He didn't like other dogs on his turf, and no matter what their size, he would attack. The Doberman wasn't on Jesse's territory, but if it made a move . . . In a flash Nicole saw Jesse's throat ripped out by the powerful Doberman. Feeling slightly dizzy with the vision, Nicole called softly, "Jesse." The dog did not respond. "Jess, *please*," she said again. He wouldn't move.

Slowly she walked forward. She could feel the Doberman's eyes shifting between her and Jesse. She was probably being very foolish. Her mother would tell her she was being ridiculous to risk her own safety to try to save "that pitiful excuse for a dog." But she'd never acted with what her mother considered good judgment.

As she neared Jesse, she expected him to bolt. If only she had a leash, she thought in frustration. But she didn't. "Jess, I'm going to pick you up," she said cajolingly. "I'm going to take you to Shelley, where you belong. Now be a good boy and don't you dare jump out of my arms."

Normally Jesse rebelled at being lifted, but miraculously he held perfectly still. She stooped, wrapped her arms around his small body, and clutched him to her chest. With one look back, she saw the Doberman sitting calm and watchful on the sidewalk, its muscular body gleaming beneath a streetlight.

When she got inside, she placed Jesse on the floor, closed and locked the front door, and went to the window. The Doberman was gone.

She found Shelley sitting on the side of her bed, crying. "Mommy, I'm sorry to be late."

Nicole sat down beside her. "I know, honey. I shouldn't have yelled. It was stupid, but sometimes grown-ups act stupid when they're scared. I've been so worried, honey. So has Jesse. He's been biting his nails all evening."

This elicited a teary smile from Shelley. "No he hasn't."

"You're right. He's too vain to ruin the manicure he got at the vet's last week." The dog jumped up on the bed, climbed on Shelley's lap, and licked her on the chin. "Did you have a good time today?"

"Lunch at Planet Hollywood was fun although Daddy didn't like it too much. I knew he wouldn't, but I love it there." Shelley cocked her head. "I think I want to be a movie star, Mom."

"You're certainly pretty enough."

"But I won't do nude scenes."

"I'm glad to hear it. Grandma would have a heart attack."

Shelley giggled. "Anyway, Daddy was grouchy at Planet Hollywood, but he got real happy when Lisa met us at Sea World."

Shelley stroked one of Jesse's long ears. "Mom, I don't like her."

"You barely know her."

"But I still don't like her. She talks to me like I'm *six*."

"Maybe she hasn't been around children very much."

"She was a kid once."

"Yes, but as you get older, childhood dims. You forget what you knew at six and what you knew at nine, almost ten."

"I still don't like her," Shelley maintained. "She's always hanging on Daddy's arm and talking to him and I never get to say anything. And you know what else? In front of people she kisses him all the time *right on the mouth*!"

"Well, young lady, you know about mouth-kissing from *NYPD Blue*."

"Yeah, but that's just pretend kissing. Besides, there aren't a million people laughing like at Daddy and Lisa."

"I'm sure there weren't a *million* people *laughing* at Daddy and Lisa."

"Well, maybe not a million, but lots. They were smiling, and they weren't *nice* smiles. They were making fun." Shelley let out a huge, gusty sigh and rolled her eyes. "I was *so* em*bar*rassed!"

Nicole couldn't help smiling although she agreed this was inappropriate behavior between Roger and Lisa in a public place and in front of a child. Now she had one more grievance against Roger for today's performance.

"How about the party?"

"That was even worse! The food was yucky and that woman from Vietnam told stories about people starving and babies dying. It made me cry."

"I'm sorry, sweetie."

"But Daddy didn't want to leave. Lisa did. Nobody would talk to her. They acted like they didn't want her there, but Daddy still wouldn't go. Then the man whose house we were at said Daddy'd had enough to drink. Daddy got mad and we left. I don't think his friends like him anymore, Mom."

Nicole hugged Shelley. "Today didn't turn out just like you wanted, but at least you went to Planet Hollywood and Sea World."

"Yeah," Shelley said disconsolately. "But I sure wish Daddy was the way he used to be."

So do I, Nicole thought sadly.

Long after Shelley had finally fallen asleep, Nicole sat curled on the couch, thinking about the day. Who had been sending her father letters marked ''Personal'' for months and why had they apparently thrown him into a tailspin? As hard as it was to believe, she might have entertained the notion that perhaps he'd had an affair and was being harassed by the former mistress. But that little scenario was ruined by the final letter, the letter he'd set on fire, the letter containing a photo of Paul Dominic.

Paul. Her father had disliked him. He believed the suave man of the world had seduced his daughter, who in his mind was still around thirteen years old. He thought Paul was merely dallying with her while he was spending time in San Antonio. Most of all he blamed Paul for leaving Nicole unprotected, for not walking her to the car where Magaro and Zand waited. But he'd blamed himself too for not keeping a closer eye on his daughter.

Fifteen years ago. Such a *long* time. Who would be tormenting her father with reminders of Paul after all those years? And *why*? What had Clifton done? He was the gentlest man she'd ever known.

Finally, she wondered what Paul Dominic had to do with all this. He'd vanished fifteen years ago. He was presumed dead.

But she would swear she'd seen him at the cemetery. Could he have been sending her father the letters? For what reason? Clifton Sloan might have disliked him, but he had nothing to do with Paul's fate. Although he was briefly considered a suspect himself, the police proved he wasn't even in the city when Magaro and Zand were killed. Still, he'd never accused Paul publicly or privately of the murders. In fact, he'd told her he believed the original theory that Zand and Magaro had been killed by a cult, therefore the strange hoods on their heads.

Finally, she wondered what on earth was going on with that beautiful, strange Doberman? Who did it belong to and why did it keep turning up, almost as if it were watching her?

The phone rang. Nicole glanced at the clock. Eleven-thirty. Who would be calling at this hour? Roger with another tirade? No. He'd be passed out by now. Maybe her mother with an attack of late-night blues.

She picked up the receiver of the cordless phone beside the couch on the second ring before it awakened Shelley. ''Hello?''

"That man who calls himself your husband won't dare talk to you so cruelly again," a slightly familiar, smoky-voiced male said softly. "Tonight I'll give him a warning. But if he continues, *chérie*, I will kill him."

SIX

1

Shelley was eating toast, her good spirits renewed after last night's scene, when the phone rang. Nicole picked up the receiver and before she could even finish her "Hello," Roger shouted, "Just what the hell do you think you're doing?"

"I believe I'm having breakfast with my daughter," she said coolly, although she could feel the hot blood of anger rush to her cheeks. Shelley had heard her father's loud, angry voice and sat wide-eyed, her toast suspended in midair. "What's the problem?"

"What's the problem?" Roger repeated in a saccharine voice. "You know damned well what the problem is."

"Sorry, but I haven't been gazing into my crystal ball this morning. Why don't you just tell me?"

"Okay, I'll play along. Four slashed tires and a smashed windshield, that's the problem!"

"What?"

"You heard me, dammit!"

"Yes, I heard you, but I don't understand. Please stop cursing at me and explain."

"What's to understand? I went out to the car this morning and found your handiwork."

"*My* handiwork!"

"Yeah. Did you think I wouldn't guess? You wanted to get back at me for taking Shelley out with Lisa and then getting her home late, but I think you went a bit far, don't you?"

"You think *I* damaged your car?"

"Certainly. Who else could have done it?"

"Since I'm the only criminal in San Antonio, I understand your logic." She sighed gustily. "Roger, you really are losing it."

"No, *you're* losing it. I know you're furious because I don't want to be married to you anymore and that I've found love with a gorgeous woman *fourteen years younger* than you." Nicole mentally began counting to ten. "However, those are the facts. You have to accept them."

"Roger—"

"Look, Nicole," he said in a softer voice, "I understand your hurt and resentment, but if you don't get your emotions under control and you keep up this kind of behavior, then I'll be forced to get a restraining order."

Nicole's breath came shallow and fast. "Roger, I have no desire to be anywhere near you. Now you listen to *me* for a change. Don't you dare ever call here again with a lot of wild accusations or *I'll* be the one getting a restraining order." She slammed down the phone.

"Mommy, what's going on?" Shelley asked timidly.

Nicole had completely forgotten that the child was sitting there listening to the furious exchange. She and Roger *had* to stop these destructive scenes in front of Shelley.

"Somebody banged up Daddy's car and he blames me."

"*You?* Is he really mad?"

"Yes, but he's probably just—" Hungover, she started to say, but caught herself. "Grumpy. He doesn't really think I'd do something so mean. In a few hours, when he's feeling better, he'll be sorry he said all those things."

"Maybe. Mom, what's a 'straining order'?"

"Nothing you have to worry about." She walked over and kissed Shelley. "You don't have to worry about *any* of this. Daddy's car is insured. The insurance company will pay for the damage, he'll get the car fixed, and then he'll be happy again."

"But will he ever come home? Will things ever be like they used to be?"

Nicole hesitated. There was no point in lying, in building false hopes. "I don't think so, honey. But that doesn't mean you and Jesse and I can't be happy."

"I guess not," Shelley mumbled disconsolately.

Later, as Nicole drove Shelley to school, she tried to say something cheerful, but all she could think of was Roger's battered car and the voice on the phone saying, "That man who calls himself your husband won't dare talk to you so cruelly again. Tonight I'll give him a warning. But if he continues, *chérie*, I will kill him.''

The only person who had ever called her *chérie* was Paul Dominic.

2

Bobby Vega placed a valuable clay pot carefully on a shelf and looked out the front window. "Plenty of people on the River Walk today."

"All the better for us," Carmen said. "I feel lucky today. I'll bet we do over a thousand in sales."

"You're dreaming. What I see are a lot of lookers and few buyers."

"Do you have mind-reading powers I'm not aware of?"

Bobby turned. "No. They just have a look about them. They're the tourists who buy T-shirts, not our kind of merchandise."

Bobby was only a couple of inches taller than Carmen, with a square build that made him seem stocky. His face was pleasant, although it bore little resemblance to the poster-boy cuteness he'd been known for in his teens and early twenties. He had not aged well, his dimples turning into furrows, too many lines cutting horizontal paths across his forehead, his eyes narrowed by eyelids whose once sexy droop at the corners had turned into definite sags. He was thirty-seven, but he looked ten years older.

Carmen's youthful face grew serious. "Bobby, you're worrying about the business, but we're doing all right."

" 'All right' isn't what I had in mind for us. We're too cramped in the house since my father had to move in and we can't afford anything bigger."

"We're at the store all day and Jill is at school. Things are only crowded at night. Besides, much as I hate to say it, your father will probably be in a nursing home by this time next year."

"Crammed into a ward because I won't be able to afford a private room for him. Then there's Jill."

Carmen frowned. "Jill! What's wrong with her?"

"College. How are we going to afford it?"

"The same way a lot of kids do—college loans. Besides, with her grades, it's likely she'll get a scholarship." She went to her husband and placed her hands on his shoulders. "What's wrong today?"

"It always bothers me when I have to bring Dad to work because his 'baby-sitter' didn't show up and he can't be left in the house alone."

Raoul Vega's Alzheimer's was a constant source of sadness mixed with irritation to Bobby. The man who had started this shop, who had once been a maker of exquisite jewelry, now often had trouble remembering his granddaughter's name or how to make coffee.

"Well, cheer up. Things could be worse. At least we're happy together and your papa is doing fine for the time being. He's going over the inventory right now and doing a good job. How would you like to trade places with Nicole?"

Bobby turned and walked back to the shelves, rearranging the pieces he'd just arranged. "How's she doing?"

"Not too well."

"Lots of tears and dramatics and leaning on friends who have their own problems, no doubt."

Carmen looked at him so sharply her dangling silver earrings swung. "Where did *that* come from?" Bobby shrugged. "For your information, Nicole is doing none of that. However, I did have an interesting conversation with her yesterday." Bobby didn't answer and Carmen continued. "She was looking at some newspaper clippings she kept about the time of her attack."

"You were looking at them with her?"

"Yes. Do you know Nicole had completely forgotten that you were with The Zanti Misfits?"

"Really made my mark, didn't I?"

"Bobby, that's not my point. Nicole said she's always felt you don't like her. I told her *I'd* noticed you usually seem uncomfortable around her, reserved." She waited for Bobby to answer, but he'd begun straightening paintings. "Anyway, we wondered if maybe you thought she *did* remember that you were with The Zanti Misfits and believed she held it against you that you'd been friends with Zand and Magaro."

Bobby finally looked at her, his dark eyes defiant. "I was never friends with Magaro. Ritchie was another matter." One corner of his mouth lifted in a sardonic smile. "So Nicole thinks I'm cool around her because I'm afraid she holds the rape against me?"

"Actually, I thought it. Is it true?"

Bobby sighed. "Carmen, what's the big deal about Nicole this morning?"

"It's not a big deal. It's just that she *is* my best friend. I'd like for my best friend and my husband to get along."

"Have Nicole and I ever had an argument? Have I ever been rude to her?"

"Come on, Bobby, you know what I mean."

Bobby finally abandoned the paintings and walked toward her. His hair was mostly gray, but he dyed it black. He brushed a lock off his forehead. "Frankly, I don't think about Nicole that much, just like she doesn't think about me. Hell, she didn't even remember that I was the drummer in what would have been one of the top bands in the world."

"*Might* have been," Carmen corrected. "You know how unpredictable show business is. The band might not have caught on."

"I don't believe that," Bobby said fiercely. "We would have been great, still going strong."

Carmen lifted her hands in defeat. "Bobby, you can't possibly know what would have happened. But you do know *one* thing. The failure of the band was the fault of Ritchie Zand."

"Because he was murdered?" Bobby demanded, growing angry.

"Because by raping Nicole he set in motion a chain of events that *got* him murdered."

"He had an alibi for that rape."

Carmen looked at him in disbelief. "Oh, Bobby, not even *you* can believe he and Magaro didn't rape her."

"Okay," Bobby said reluctantly. "He was getting loaded a lot in those days. Maybe he *did* have sex with her."

"Have *sex* with her? He *raped* her. He and Magaro would have killed her if they'd gotten a chance, and I'm glad Paul Dominic killed them."

Bobby stared at her. "You always hated Ritchie because you thought he and the band were taking me away from you."

Carmen blinked at the venom of his words. Then she answered quietly, "I didn't hate the band. I hated Zand and Magaro. They were changing you, getting you into alcohol and drugs and—"

"And groupies. Let's bring it up *one* more time, Carmen. I

screwed around a little. I was young and those were wild days. But I *loved* you. I *married* you.''

"You married me because I was pregnant.''

"I don't want to talk about our dead son," Bobby said crisply.

"Neither do I. But would you have married me if The Zanti Misfits hadn't fallen apart?''

"Sure.''

"I wonder," Carmen murmured doubtfully as Bobby turned to greet the first customer coming in the door. "I really wonder.''

3

Nicole sat up in bed, pillows piled behind her. Day after tomorrow she had to return to the university and she was reviewing notes for her Major American Writers class. Wednesday they would begin on Herman Melville. Now she had to compose an introductory lecture that wouldn't put everyone to sleep. She began, as always, writing in a spiral notebook on her lap. Tomorrow she'd switch to her computer.

She was only on the third paragraph when a huge yawn threatened to unhinge her jaw. She looked at the clock. Midnight. Maybe she should just give up for tonight and hope sleep would infuse her with inspiration.

She gathered up her notes and notebook and carried them to the dresser. Then she turned off her bedside lamp, flipped on the dim night-light she'd never slept without for fifteen years, and crawled into bed.

Almost immediately she felt as if she were drifting, hovering in a huge candlelit room where ''Rhapsody in Blue'' throbbed from huge stereo speakers. "So you liked it, *chérie*?" a deep, gentle voice asked as intense hazel eyes gazed into hers.

Strident barking pulled her from the dream world. "No," she mumbled as the music, the deep voice, the intense hazel eyes drifted away. "No, please . . .''

Suddenly Jesse was on her bed, yipping shrilly, turning in circles. Nicole shot into a sitting position as the dog leaped off the bed, ran to her window, and stood on his hind legs, barking, spraying the glass with saliva. Nicole looked at the window and drew in her breath. The wolf's head stared directly at her.

With a calmness that later surprised her, she reached under her mattress and retrieved the key. The soft glow of the night-light allowed her to unlock the drawer of her bedside table without fumbling. She took out her loaded gun and aimed straight at the window.

In a flash the figure disappeared. She jumped out of bed and joined Jesse at the window, kneeling beside the dog. The weak bulb in the outside light illuminated enough of the yard for her to see someone tall heading for the back fence.

"Mommy, what *is* it?"

Simultaneously, Nicole turned to look at Shelley and slid the gun beneath the bedside table. "Apparently our werewolf is back."

"What?" Shelley quaked.

Nicole held out her arms and Shelley rushed to her. "It's just a person wearing a mask, remember? Your window blind was down, but mine wasn't, so he came here."

Jesse still barked frantically, jumping at the window, fully prepared to tear apart the intruder. "Settle down, Jess," Nicole said as she and Shelley watched. When the person reached the back fence, he grabbed a rope and began climbing up the fence. He topped it and reached for a branch of the live oak. "So that's how he did it the first time," Nicole said. He climbed into the tree and began his descent, disappearing from their view behind the fence. "Well, there he goes."

But in a moment a shout pierced the night. It was so loud, they could hear it from behind the closed window. Then came the sound of a dog barking. A *big* dog who'd obviously cornered the intruder. In a moment Nicole saw a form climb back up the tree and huddle in the branches.

"What's going on?" Shelley asked.

"Good luck for us, honey!" Nicole reached for the phone. *"Now* we can call the police because there's a great big dog out there that's got the creep cornered."

Ten minutes later Nicole heard a siren. By this time she had on jeans and a sweatshirt, but as she slipped her feet into loafers, her heart sank as the barking of the big dog abruptly stopped. The police pounded on her front door. Why in heaven's name were they making so much noise? she wondered angrily. First the siren, now the pounding. You'd think this was a bank robbery.

While Shelley held Jesse on a leash, Nicole explained to two young patrolmen where the man was. She and one policeman went through the backyard to the fence. The other patrolman went around the block to the yard of the vacant house that abutted Nicole's property. "No dog, no man," he called.

"Damn," Nicole muttered. "If only the dog hadn't run off."

"Maybe it was the sound of the siren," the young patrolman suggested.

No kidding, Nicole thought. She watched the beam of a flashlight dancing on the other side of the fence. Then the other policeman yelled, "The dog got hold of him. There's some blood on the tree trunk and some on the grass. Not a lot. Couldn't have been a bad injury. Wait a minute. I think I see something else. A piece of gold jewelry." Nicole could only see slivers of light between the boards of the fence as the policeman bent to inspect his find. "It's fancy," he shouted. "Some kind of religious symbol." He paused. "It's a brass Saint Francis medal."

"Saint Francis, the patron saint of animals," Nicole murmured.

Finally, the policeman laughed. "Well, can you believe this? It's a pet ID tag. It says, 'Jordan,' and there's an address. At least a partial. The number's scratched, can't make it out, but the rest is Hermosa Street. That's in Olmos Park. The dog's a long way from home."

Nicole stood frozen as the world of her familiar backyard and her little brick house disappeared and she saw a long Spanish-style mansion with a fountain on Hermosa Street in Olmos Park. The home of Paul Dominic.

SEVEN

1

Nicole awakened with a dull headache. She took two aspirin with a glass of orange juice before fixing Shelley's breakfast.

Unlike her, the child was in high gear, excited by last night's commotion. "Can I tell everyone at school about the werewolf and the policemen?" she asked, spooning Cheerios and strawberries in her mouth.

"No."

"Why?"

"It might scare the other kids. They might get ideas about playing the same kind of trick."

Shelley frowned over this for a moment and Nicole thought she was going to raise objections. Instead, she nodded. "I think you're right. I bet Tommy Myers would buy a wolf mask and go scare somebody tonight. Mom, he's so *mean*. And you know what else? He likes *me*! He wants to go steady. Yuck!"

Nicole took a sip of orange juice, thinking. One level of her mind was working on how ridiculous it was for nine-year-olds to be talking about going steady. Another part gnawed at a different question. "Is Tommy Myers very big?"

Shelley nodded. "He's taller than most of the guys in class. Why?"

"No reason."

Shelley stared at her for a moment, then assumed an owlish look. "You're wondering if that was him last night. No way, Mom. That was a grown-up guy."

"I just wondered." Or rather, I hoped, Nicole thought. "You have a milk mustache."

Shelley quickly wiped it away. "Our teacher said women used to take baths in milk."

"They thought it was good for the skin."

"Who'd want to sit in a tub full of cold milk? Besides, you've got real pretty skin anyway. Prettier than Lisa's. She's got freckles."

"There's nothing wrong with freckles."

"Well, I don't like them," Shelley announced emphatically. "Or orange hair or green eyes. And she's too tall. She's also got *real* big boobs and she rubs them against Daddy all the time!"

"Shelley!" Nicole exclaimed, torn between shock and laughter. "Those aren't nice things to say."

"I don't care. I like blond hair and blue eyes and little boobs like yours."

"Thank you, dear," Nicole said dryly. "And would you please stop saying 'boobs'?"

"What should I say instead?"

"I don't know. I'll think of something. And for the record, her hair is dark auburn, not orange, and she's about the same height as Aunt Carmen."

"She looks taller. *Huge.*"

"Well, she's not. Are you finished with breakfast?"

"Yeah. I wasn't too hungry."

This morning Nicole let Shelley take the bus to school. A couple of hours later, she climbed into her car, intending to head straight for her mother's house. The impulse she'd had all morning was too strong, though, and in twenty minutes she found herself in Olmos Park.

Although the Dominic home was less than three miles from her parents' house, she had not been here since her last night with Paul. How romantic that tryst had begun. How horrifyingly it had ended.

As she drew near the Dominic home, she slowed down and parked on the opposite side of the street. The once perfect lawn now looked shabby, the hedges untrimmed, the white fountain, topped by its beautiful figure of Diana the Huntress, dry and stained from rusty water. She remembered once taking a picture of the sun shining through the sparkling spray.

Like the lawn, the house itself also showed signs of neglect. Its pristine whiteness had dimmed to a dirty eggshell color, and several of the dark red Spanish roof tiles were cracked or missing.

Paul's father had been much older than his mother, Alicia, and died when Paul was in his early twenties. Nicole wondered if Alicia Dominic still lived here. She'd looked for the name in the telephone directory and found nothing, but that could mean the woman had an unlisted number. There were no signs of life around the house, though. Of course if Mrs. Dominic still lived here, her only companion might be the housekeeper, Rosa. How strange, Nicole mused. She hadn't thought of Rosa for ages. Neither she nor her son. What was his name? Juan. She'd only seen him a few times and never said more than ten words to him. Besides, he would be a man by now.

But she wasn't looking for people. She was looking for a Doberman. If not the dog, some sign that a dog lived here. She pulled farther up the street and stopped again, looking backward so she could get a view of the rear lawn. No fence. No doghouse. No dog.

Well, what did you expect? she wondered as she started the car and pulled away from the curb. Paul Dominic sitting on the lawn playing with his dog?

No. If Paul were alive and in San Antonio, he didn't intend to make himself easy to find.

2

Her mother opened the door immediately. "Nicole! I didn't expect to see you again today."

"I wanted to talk to you yesterday, but I didn't get a chance."

Her mother gave her a small smile. "Mildred's sympathy call exhausted *me* and added five pounds to *her*."

"I guess she means well."

"Yes, she has a good heart. It's just that her social skills need work." She motioned toward the living room. "Come in, dear. Do you want something to drink?"

"No, thanks." She gazed at her mother closely. "You look tired."

"I haven't been sleeping too well. I suppose that's natural."

"That's exactly what I came to talk to you about." Nicole took her mother's arm and led her into the living room. "Sleep."

"You're not sleeping well, either?" Phyllis sat down on the couch, crossing her long, sleek legs. "You should have been a Rockette with those fabulous legs," Clifton used to tell her. "Or maybe in the *Folies-Bergère*. You would have made hearts melt in those scanty little outfits."

"Clifton, you are full of more nonsense than any man alive!" Phyllis would huff, but she couldn't hide her pleasure at the compliment. Nicole had always been aware that her mother made a special effort to look nice for Clifton, careful to change clothes and freshen her perfume and makeup before he came home. And once, when she was fourteen and alone in the house, she'd sneaked into her parents' room to look in the dresser drawers. When she opened one drawer, her mouth literally dropped open at the sight of her mother's nightwear. She'd been both astonished and embarrassed by the sexy negligees with labels from Christian Dior. For the next two weeks she kept picturing her mother in the scanty nightwear and, to Phyllis's bafflement, Nicole couldn't look at her without either blushing or bursting into torrents of adolescent giggles.

"I'm sleeping all right," Nicole said, deciding not to mention her strange dreams or the intruder. The latter would elicit an unending campaign to make Nicole and Shelley move in with her. "It's Dad's sleep that I've been wondering about. Mom, was he having trouble sleeping in the weeks before . . ."

She stopped when she saw Phyllis's face pale. "Nicole, do we have to talk about this? It's so upsetting."

"Yes, Mom, we do," Nicole said firmly. "Every time I ask questions about Dad, you put me off. Now I insist on getting some answers."

"I really don't think it's your place to insist."

"I was his *daughter*, for God's sake. It *is* my place and I'm not leaving until I get some answers."

"Aren't you the charming one this morning!"

"You're not going to put me off with sarcastic remarks. I want to know. Was Dad sleeping badly?"

"All right, yes."

"How about nightmares?"

Phyllis gave her a penetrating look. "Why are you asking me these things?"

"Kay. She told me Dad said he wasn't sleeping well. He kept falling asleep in his office, and a couple of times he woke up in the middle of a nightmare. He was saying my name and something about how I could have been killed."

"Kay shouldn't have told you that."

"I think she should have, and don't you dare get angry with her because she did."

"Nicole, I'm not quite the ogre you think. I'm not going to get angry with Kay. And yes, the same thing was happening here. Nightmares, calling out your name, waking up drenched in perspiration."

"Why didn't you tell me?"

"I didn't think it was any of your business."

"My father was in torment and you didn't think it was any of my business?"

"Oh, Nicole, sometimes you simply wear me out. I get tired of arguing with you."

"I get tired of it, too, Mom," Nicole said softly. "Why can't we, just for *once*, have a normal mother–daughter conversation?"

Phyllis stared at her. Nicole was aware of a mental battle going on behind her bright blue eyes. Then she sighed. "All right. If you want the truth, I'll give it to you. Your father was still deeply troubled about your attack."

"But *why* was it still troubling him? It happened so long ago."

A tiny crease formed between Phyllis's perfectly penciled brows. "Nicole, a parent never gets over their child being brutalized. I know I'm not open with my emotions like your father was, but do you think I haven't suffered for you, too? Good lord, I can still barely stand to talk about it."

Nicole looked at her in amazement. "I thought that's because I'd embarrassed you."

"*Embarrassed!* You thought my main concern was embarrassment?" Her mother closed her eyes and shook her head. "You and I have never been close, but I didn't realize just how little you thought of me."

"It's not that I don't love you, Mom, but I've never understood you," Nicole said meekly.

"I suppose that's partly my fault for always being distant with you. As I said, I've never been good at expressing emotion. But it's partly your father's fault, too. From the time you were born, you were *his* child. I know I shouldn't speak ill of the dead, but he did everything he could to cut me out of your life. Maybe it was because he knew I couldn't have more children, so he wanted the one we *did* have to be his alone.''

''That's a terrible thing to say!''

''I'm not saying it's true. I'm only speculating. But you must remember, Nicole, that your father wasn't a saint. He dominated your time and constantly countermanded my rules.''

Nicole shifted uncomfortably. What her mother was saying was true. ''Well, I certainly was Daddy's girl,'' she admitted reluctantly. ''I wish I'd gotten a chance to know you better, Mom, but you didn't make it easy.''

Phyllis seemed tense during the exchange, intimacy with her daughter still difficult. Perhaps forever impossible after so long, Nicole thought. She decided a quick change of subject was necessary before her mother retreated into her usual unapproachable shell. ''Back to Dad's nightmares, Mom. Why did he suddenly start having them? Was he sick?''

Phyllis abruptly stood and paced around the room, fingering the diamond stud earrings she wore. ''I can't believe that if your father were seriously ill, he wouldn't have told me. Even if he wouldn't, Harvey Weber, his doctor, would have. Considering how your father died, Harvey wouldn't have clung to the ethic of privileged information between patient and physician.''

''You're sure?''

''Absolutely. I talked to Harvey the day after Clifton killed himself. He assured me that there was nothing organically wrong with your father, although at his last checkup, just two weeks before he died, Clifton was showing signs of anxiety and depression. He said he suggested your dad see a therapist. Obviously the problem was even more serious than Harvey realized.''

''You didn't tell me.''

Phyllis raised her hands in resignation. ''I couldn't talk about it. I didn't *want* to talk about it.''

Nicole sat in silence for a few moments, absorbing what her mother had told her. Then she made a decision. ''Mom, Kay says Dad was getting some strange mail.'' She told her about the envelopes marked ''Personal'' and the final one which he had set on fire, but she couldn't bring herself to divulge that a partial photograph of Paul Dominic had been left.

"I can't imagine what could have been in those envelopes," Phyllis said, coming to sit beside Nicole. "Could someone have been blackmailing Clifton?"

"*Blackmail!* Who? Why?"

"I don't know. It was just a thought." She sighed. "I wonder if all this letter business is as important as Kay is making it seem. Perhaps there's no connection except in Kay's mind."

"I've never known Kay to imagine things, Mom. She's fairly literal."

"Usually, but you can't have missed the fact that she's not well."

"Hardly. She looks awful."

Phyllis hesitated. "She didn't want anyone to know this, but your father found out. She has cancer, Nicole."

"Cancer!"

"Yes. She has a brain tumor and she let things go on too long. It's inoperable. She took chemotherapy treatments for a while. You've probably noticed her hair is always such a perfect little cap of curls—it's a wig. She only has about four months to live."

Nicole felt as if she had been kicked in the abdomen. "Oh, no," she moaned.

"That's why I've decided to sell the store. If she were in good health, I'd keep it and take it over myself. After all, Kay is only forty-nine and the store is her life. That and her cats. But with Clifton dead and Kay so soon to go—well, I just couldn't bear to walk into the place with both of them gone."

"I understand," Nicole said sadly. "She doesn't know that you know?"

Phyllis shook her head. "I try to act as if everything is perfectly normal. I even sat here and let *her* help Carmen put away the food after your father's funeral because it's what she would expect of me."

A tear trickled down Nicole's face. "It just isn't fair, Mom. She had such an empty life—just the store and a few kids she gave piano lessons to, and some cats."

"She had your father."

Nicole looked at her mother warily. "You don't suspect an affair between Dad and Kay?"

"No, but Kay was in love with him. She always has been." Nicole's eyes widened. "Oh, don't look so surprised, dear. Even you knew it long ago. When you were a little girl, I happened to be passing your room and heard you telling Carmen you thought Kay had a crush on Daddy."

"Secrets certainly weren't safe with me."

"I wouldn't say that. You certainly kept your involvement with Paul Dominic a mystery." Nicole flushed. "You also kept quiet about the problems in your marriage."

"There weren't really any until—"

"I know what you're going to say," her mother interrupted, "but you'll never convince me there was nothing wrong until Roger suddenly met this young slut at the university."

Nicole smiled ironically. "Okay, Mom, you're right. Things had been going downhill for about three years. Nothing major. As far as I know Lisa is his first affair and there was never any violence, but lots of arguments, then lots of silence." She hesitated. "Mom, as long as we're being so honest, Roger said he thought you were more angry than grief-stricken about Dad's death."

"Well, score one for Roger. He's brighter than I thought."

"Then it's true? You're angry about Dad's death?"

Phyllis looked away. "His death. You mean his *suicide*!" she said vehemently. "And yes, I *am* angry. I'm furious!" She twisted her hands, looking out the window. "I know what everyone thought. 'How does genial, gentle Clifton put up with that tartar of a wife?' "

Nicole took a breath, wanting to deny what her mother said, but she couldn't because it was true. "Well, today you want honesty so you'll get it," Phyllis went on. "It was your father who was the strongest one of us. When we were dating, most people believed my father would disapprove of him. General Ernest Hazelton, the man of iron, wanting his daughter to marry a man whose dream was to own a music store?" She laughed harshly. "The other officers at Fort Sam Houston thought it was either a joke or that Father was losing his mind.

"But Nicole, your grandfather saw something in Clifton that the other officers didn't—his strength. He also saw Clifton's intelligence and his devotion to me. He'd raised me to be strong because my own mother was so fragile, but he knew I was too strong for most men, that they would not tolerate me and the marriage would be destroyed. Father was a devout Catholic, so when I married, he wanted me to marry for life. He wanted for me someone who appreciated my strength but could control it. He also never wanted me to be a military wife, moving from base to base. And most important, he wanted someone who would put me, not his career, first. That's what Father did, moving us all over the world, always putting his career above everything, and it broke my mother. She was the saddest woman I've ever known. I think she was relieved to die when I was only fifteen. My father didn't want the same fate for me.''

"You never told me all this," Nicole said in wonder.

"We've never really talked. But maybe now you understand why I'm so angry. Clifton was ideal for me. He put up with all my idiosyncrasies and bossiness and critical nature and old-fashioned ideas and loved me anyway. It may not have looked like it to outsiders, but our marriage was just about as perfect as a marriage can be. And then, the man I'd depended on, leaned on, *adored* for thirty-seven years, crept out of our house one night while I slept and shot himself in the head. He didn't even leave a note, Nicole.'' For the first time in her life, Nicole saw her mother's blue eyes fill with tears although her voice turned fierce. "Clifton Sloan, loving husband and father, didn't even have the decency to leave his family a goddamned *note*!''

EIGHT

1

"And thus ends our section on Hawthorne." Avis Simon-Smith, fiftyish, reed thin with large dark, baggy eyes, gave the students a narrow-lipped, insincere smile. "Dr. Chandler will be back tomorrow. I do hope you'll all be especially nice to her after the tragic suicide of her father. As if she hasn't had enough trouble this year."

Miguel Perez closed his notebook and threw the woman a baleful look. Did she have to emphasize that Dr. Chandler's father had committed suicide? Couldn't she just have said "death"? And by mentioning Nicole's "other" troubles, she was purposely reminding everyone of Roger Chandler's affair. Miguel had taken Dr. Simon-Smith for one other class and not cared for her. Now he positively disliked her.

"I hope you've gained something from our sessions," Avis went on in a falsely pleasant voice. Students had begun to rise from their seats but now collapsed back into them when they realized she wasn't ready to shut up. "I'm sure you all know I walked into this class cold, no time for preparation, and I *am* teaching four other sections, which is a full load. It has been *quite* a strain, let me tell you, but I was glad to help out Dr. Chandler."

Yeah, sure you were, Miguel thought.

The students started to rise again. Class was supposed to have ended two minutes ago, but Avis continued. "Now that I've imparted to you an appreciation of Hawthorne, I hope all of you will read *The Scarlet Letter*."

"I think I'll rent the movie," one student wisecracked, leaving although they hadn't formally been dismissed. "I'd rather see Demi Moore rolling around naked in the hay than read about some chick in a gown with a giant *A* sewed on her chest.''

Other students twittered, but Avis Simon-Smith was not amused. She was rarely amused by anything *she* hadn't said, and she shot the student a withering look, which went unnoticed by almost everyone piling out of the room.

Later in the day, as Miguel prowled an upper hall of the Humanities and Business Building searching for Nicole's office so he could slip a "Welcome Back" card under her door, he passed Dr. Simon-Smith standing in the hall talking to another professor whose name he thought was Silver. The woman looked slightly younger than Avis and carried a load of papers under her arm. Just as Miguel located Nicole's door, Avis began speaking loudly.

"I simply get sick of all the breaks she gets around here, Nancy." Fretful lines made her thin, plain face look almost ugly. "When *I* started here, I was allowed to teach *only* Basic English and Composition for *two* years. *Two* full years. But she prances in with her pretty face and blond hair and good figure and in the second semester she's teaching Major American Writers.''

The other woman, balancing her own papers and a mug of coffee, gave her a placating smile. "Avis, you must remember that we had a different department director when you came. He had a few pets and they got all the good classes. The rest of us were treated like dirt. Thank God he didn't last long.''

Miguel hovered at Nicole's door, pretending to study the office hours posted. Then he stole a look as Avis shifted to her other foot, planting a hand on a razor-sharp hipbone. "Oh, Nancy, you know she's getting preferential treatment. A whole week off because of a death in the family! And is it fair for a totally inexperienced teacher to be given Major American Writers?''

Another stolen look told Miguel that Nancy Silver looked uncomfortable. "Avis, *you* got a week off when your mother died. And Nicole isn't inexperienced.''

"Oh, that's right," Avis sneered. "She taught *one whole year* in Ohio.''

"And she had an article published on Fitzgerald in a prestigious journal.''

"I read it. Trash. She doesn't know what she's talking about.'' Avis paused. "I'm beginning to wonder if she's as free with her sexual favors as her husband. If so, unlike Roger she has the sense to give herself to administrators, not students. Maybe *that's* why she's doing so well in the department.''

Miguel's fists clenched. Jealous bitch. Suddenly he realized she was staring at him. ''Did you need something, young man?''

He met her eyes, his own cold. ''No. I was just leaving something for Dr. Chandler.'' He bent to slip the card under the door.

''Stop! That should be taken to the office.''

''I'd rather leave it here.''

''I said it shouldn't be left there.'' She jerked a thumb over her shoulder. ''Down the hall in the office.''

Miguel shoved the envelope under the door, stood, and walked past her without a word.

''Honestly!'' Avis huffed. ''Some of these Mexican kids are *so* arrogant!''

''Avis!'' the other woman gasped. ''What an awful thing to say. He *heard* you!''

''I don't care. It's true and he knows it.''

''Avis, you've been a friend for a long time, but you're getting out of control. The department director has already spoken to you about your unseemly comments.''

''As if I care what *he* thinks! I should have his job and he knows it.''

Nancy Silver shook her head. ''A word of advice, Avis. If you don't tone yourself down, one of these days that bitter tongue of yours is going to land you in *big* trouble.''

2

Shelley was in her bedroom, supposedly asleep, but probably watching something totally unsuitable on television. Nicole knew she should check, but it was nine-fifteen and she sat at the kitchen table, frantically composing her introductory lesson on Melville. She'd planned to have it done an hour ago so she could go over material for her other classes, then get to bed early, but the talk with her mother had destroyed her concentration for the rest of the afternoon. She felt as if she'd had a conversation with a woman she'd lived with over half her life yet never knew.

Now, no matter how hard she tried, she couldn't add electricity to her lecture. This was the first section of Major American Writers she'd taught and she wanted to do a good job, not send everyone out of class vowing never to read Emerson or Melville or James again. "Maybe you're just trying too hard," she muttered. "This *is* a lecture on serious subject matter, not a tabloid article."

The knocker tapped lightly against the front door. "Oh, great," Nicole groaned. She looked down at the gray sweatsuit she'd slipped into earlier when she thought a brief session of exercise might charge up her mind as well as her body. She stood, looking down at her heavy gray socks. Reeboks lay discarded somewhere in the living room along with her ten-pound weights, and she knew her hair was stringing down from its ponytail. Oh, well, it was probably only Roger here to pick a fight. Just what she needed.

She looked out the peephole in the door to see a surprising face. Opening the door, she was aware of alarm in her eyes. "Sergeant DeSoto! Is anything wrong?"

He smiled. "I wish my visits didn't immediately strike terror."

She returned his smile. "I'm sorry. That wasn't a very polite greeting."

"I'm used to it. Actually, nothing is wrong. I just wanted to give you some information."

She opened the door. "Come in. I'm afraid both the house and I are a mess."

"I should have called before I came. Besides, you look fine."

"Have a seat," Nicole said, motioning toward the awful brown furniture. "Would you care for something to drink?"

"Only if you're having something."

"I've been drinking coffee all evening and I'm wired tight. I think I could use a glass of wine. How about you, or are you on duty?"

"I'm not on duty and wine sounds great. Whatever kind you're having."

As she passed a mirror on the way to the kitchen, she cringed. She looked even worse than she thought, no makeup, tired circles under her eyes, an ink smudge on her cheek. She turned off the laptop computer, dashed to the sink and scrubbed at the ink mark with a wet paper towel. She thought she heard a faint groan from the living room. DeSoto trying to settle onto the voluminous, consuming furniture.

She poured the wine and when she walked back to the living room, DeSoto was sitting on the couch, his legs stretched in front of him, flipping through a copy of *Vanity Fair*. He laid it aside and accepted the wine, smiling again. He really was good-looking, she thought, although she didn't agree with Shelley that he looked like Jimmy Smits.

"I apologize for dropping by like this. I have a feeling I'm interrupting something."

"I've been driving myself crazy all evening over a lecture. Tomorrow is my first day back at school. But don't apologize. I needed a break."

"All right. I'll try to be as brief as possible." He took a sip of his wine, then began casually. "Today I read the report about your intruder."

"I'm surprised such a trivial matter crossed your desk."

"Normally it wouldn't, but because of your father's death . . . well, anyway, I saw that it wasn't the first time you've had a visitor."

"Our werewolf, my daughter Shelley calls him. He wears a wolf mask."

"So I heard. I also learned that he's entering the yard by climbing a tree, then sliding down a rope. But that's not what interested me the most." Nicole tensed, certain that she was about to get a lecture about pointing her gun and the dangers of civilians owning handguns, although she couldn't remember mentioning it to the policemen who were here last night. "It's the dog."

This was worse than the gun. Nicole swallowed. "The big dog that bit the intruder?" she asked innocently.

"Yes. We did a check of local hospitals and no one came in last night with an animal bite, so apparently the dog didn't do any real damage." He paused. "There were no fingerprints on the ID tag, but it gave an address in Olmos Park. The numbers were scratched, but we finally made them out." Nicole stared at him, her mouth dry as sand. "Mrs. Chandler, I know all about what happened to you fifteen years ago and your relationship with Paul Dominic."

"Oh," she said weakly.

"The address on the tag is that of Alicia Dominic, Paul's mother." Nicole opened her mouth, but nothing came out. "But then you knew that, didn't you?"

Nicole swallowed again and finally found a thin version of her voice. "I didn't *know*. I just suspected."

"Why would you suspect that the dog belonged to Alicia Dominic?"

Nicole took a deep breath. "I don't think it belongs to Mrs. Dominic. I think it belongs to Paul."

For the first time DeSoto showed surprise. "Why do you think that?"

"I believe I saw him at my father's funeral." DeSoto raised his eyebrows. "He was at a distance with a dog. And then there was a call the other night." She described the contents of the call threatening to give Roger a warning and the man calling her *chérie*.

When she finished, DeSoto looked at her dubiously. "Mrs. Chandler, have you been in contact with Paul Dominic in the last fifteen years?"

"No."

"You do know that he's presumed dead."

" 'Presumed' being the key word as far as I'm concerned."

DeSoto sipped his wine, then gazed at her seriously. "Are you absolutely certain you saw Paul Dominic at the funeral and heard his voice on the phone?"

Under DeSoto's probing brown eyes, Nicole's confidence flagged. "Well, he was standing some distance away, and as I said, I haven't seen or spoken to him for a long time. But it *looked* like him and it *sounded* like him on the phone. No one else has ever called me *chérie*."

"I see." DeSoto looked away from her, focusing on the aquarium. "That's beautiful."

"I think so." Nicole stared at the neon tetras, red moons, black mollies, painted glassfish, and kissing fish. Plastic ferns waved gently against the blue gravel and various shades of coral on the bottom, and bubbles from the aerator rose beyond the castle, the skull, the diver, and the catfish hovering above the gravel. "The fish always look so calm."

DeSoto nodded but remained quiet. Finally Nicole said, "I feel like you have something else to tell me."

"It's not much. I went to the Dominic house today."

"Oh." Nicole was nonplussed. "I would have thought you'd just call."

"Sometimes you learn more from a personal visit than from a phone call."

Which is why you're here tonight, Nicole thought. "So what did you learn?"

"I only talked to the housekeeper."

"Rosa?"

"You know her?"

"Not really. I just remember her. She's been there forever. She never liked me."

DeSoto smiled. "She doesn't seem like the type who likes anyone."

"Except Mrs. Dominic."

He shrugged. "Maybe. She certainly acts like a pit bull protecting the woman."

"She wouldn't let you see Mrs. Dominic?"

"No. The housekeeper said she's an invalid—a weak heart. She suffered a stroke last year."

"How sad. She's not very old. Did it appear that anyone else lived in the house besides Rosa and Mrs. Dominic?"

"I didn't get past the entrance hall. The place looked fairly neglected, though, and it was quiet as a tomb."

When it used to vibrate with music, Nicole thought, remembering an evening when she'd held a white rose and listened to "Rhapsody in Blue" throb from huge stereo speakers. She wondered how long it had been since music had soared down the house's halls.

"What did you find out about the dog?" she asked.

"Nothing. The housekeeper claims they *never* had a dog, even when Paul was young."

"And the other boy?"

"What other boy?"

"Rosa had a son. Juan. He was quite a bit younger than Paul."

DeSoto shook his head. "I didn't know anything about another boy and she didn't mention him. I don't think it would have made any difference, though. The woman was adamant—no dog, *ever*. Looking around the grounds, I didn't see any signs of a dog."

"I didn't, either." DeSoto glanced at her questioningly. "Okay, I took a spin past the house earlier today," she admitted.

"Did you go to the door?"

"Heavens, no! I haven't even been in Olmos Park since . . .

well, let's just say I didn't have any desire to linger.'' She paused.
''Do you believe Rosa about the dog?''

''Yes.''

''Then why would the dog be wearing a tag listing the Dominic
address?''

''It could have been a mistake. One digit wrong could make a
big difference.''

''But what about my seeing a big dog with a man who looked
like Paul, then finding the Dominics' address on the ID tag?
Doesn't that seem like a bit of a coincidence to you, Sergeant
DeSoto?''

''It's Raymond. Ray.'' He glanced down at his wine glass, then
looked at her solemnly. ''No one has seen Paul Dominic for fifteen years. Do you know how unlikely it is that he would suddenly turn up in San Antonio after all this time and come to your
father's funeral?''

''You don't believe me,'' she said, her disappointment obvious.

Ray's eyes strayed from hers, back to the aquarium. ''I'm not
saying I don't believe you. I'm just saying what you're thinking
is unlikely. However,'' he added, suddenly smiling at her, ''unlikely isn't synonymous with impossible.''

Nicole let out a big sigh. ''Thank goodness you're not just
dismissing me.''

''I would never do that. So you think the intruder in the wolf
mask might be Dominic?''

Nicole frowned. ''It crossed my mind, but now I'm sure it isn't.
I believe that dog wearing the ID tag with the Dominic address
belongs to Paul. The intruder was attacked by that dog. Why
would Paul's own dog attack him?''

Ray twirled his glass in his hands. ''Did you get a look at the
dog that bit the intruder?''

''No. It was on the other side of the fence. But I'd seen the
Doberman *three* times prior to that night and I'd noticed a brass
tag hanging from its collar. I believe it was the tag the police
found.''

''All right, let's say it *is* the same dog, it belongs to the man
you saw in the cemetery, and it wouldn't attack him. Who do you
think is coming into your yard wearing a wolf mask?''

''A prankster, I guess.''

''Maybe one of your students?''

"Maybe, although I don't know who. Whoever it is, they don't seem to want to do anything except scare us."

Ray nodded. "You're keeping all your doors and windows locked?"

"Absolutely."

He nodded again, set down his wine glass, and gave her a penetrating stare. "If you're convinced Dominic is alive and here in San Antonio, why are you so afraid? I thought the two of you were in love."

"We were."

"He's a murderer."

"That was never proved," Nicole snapped, then softened. "I'm sorry. It's just so hard for me to believe that Paul could commit *two* premeditated murders. Besides, all they had was circumstantial evidence. That and hearsay." She sighed. "*My* statements being the most damaging. I'm afraid because he might think I ruined his life."

"You didn't," Ray said firmly. "He killed those men in cold blood and then he ran, too cowardly to stand trial."

"He did run," Nicole said reluctantly. "But he was arrested because of *me*."

"And because the murder weapon was found at his house."

"Nevertheless, I made damaging statements to the police."

"Statements that would have been considered hearsay."

"But they were from the woman he loved. How would you have felt in his place?" She leaned forward, speaking intensely. "Ray, don't you see that I *did* destroy his life? I'm afraid of him because what happened to him was because of me."

"Mrs. Chandler, calm down," Ray said gently.

Nicole became aware of how her voice had risen. She folded her hands in her lap and concentrated on slowing her breathing. "I'm sorry I lost control, but I'm certain Paul is back."

"He may be, but the evidence is thin. *Very* thin."

She looked at her folded hands and the gold wedding band it had never occurred to her to remove. "You're right," she said calmly.

"I'm glad you feel better."

She raised her eyes. "I don't feel better. I only meant you were right about the evidence of Paul's return being thin."

"So you still believe Paul Dominic is in San Antonio and he's trailing you?"

"Yes, I do."

"Well, I can't change your mind about that and I'm not going to try because there's a chance it's true. But it's only a small chance. I'd say a thousand to one." He smiled and rose. "I've taken up enough of your time for this evening. I'm sorry I upset you, Mrs. Chandler."

She walked him to the front door. "Please call me Nicole, and you didn't upset me. It was actually good to talk about this to someone besides my friend Carmen, even if neither one of you believes me."

"I don't disbelieve you. I'm just skeptical. It's my nature."

Nicole opened the door. She stared for a moment, then reached out and removed a long-stemmed white rosebud that had been tucked under the knocker.

Ray grinned. "You have an admirer who gives you white rosebuds?"

"Yes," Nicole whispered. "Paul Dominic always gave me white rosebuds."

NINE

1

Raymond DeSoto pulled away from the Chandler house, drove around a couple of blocks, then returned and parked four houses down from Nicole's.

So she was convinced Paul Dominic had returned. After her father's suicide, he'd heard all the stories about her assault, the double homicide of Zand and Magaro, and Dominic's arrest and subsequent flight into what seemed oblivion. He remembered that time, but it was long ago and whoever told him the story now gave a slightly different version after fifteen years, so Ray had looked up all the newspaper articles from the time to refresh his memory of how things were perceived back then.

What he'd come away with was the picture of a girl who had been badly traumatized over and over within a period of a few weeks. She was brutalized by Ritchie Zand and Luis Magaro. It was a miracle she'd escaped with her life. He was also aware of what the newspapers left out—the belief of a large portion of the police and the public that she'd asked for what happened to her, that by being beautiful, stylish, and out alone after dark, she'd gotten exactly what she deserved.

Then came the revelation that she was involved with Paul Dominic, a rich and famous concert pianist ten years older than she. The press attributed this bombshell to "an unnamed source close to Ms. Sloan." Ray was certain it wasn't her parents. He'd learned she'd been close to Carmen Vega at the time of the relationship with Dominic, although if she'd been the leak to the press, either Nicole hadn't known or hadn't let it affect their friendship. Of course, Carmen wasn't the only one who knew about Dominic. After all, Magaro and Zand had known exactly where to find Nicole that night—outside the Dominic home.

Now somebody was looking in Nicole's windows wearing a wolf mask. He smiled slightly at the crudity of the trick, but it frightened her. He wasn't as doubtful about Dominic being alive and returning to San Antonio as he pretended to be in front of her—she was right about there being a few too many coincidences. Still, he knew it wasn't Dominic trying to terrorize her in a wolf mask. As Nicole said, he wouldn't be attacked by his own dog.

But was Nicole right about everything else? Was last night a freak encounter between the dog and the prankster, or was Dominic following her? And if he were, what were his intentions? Nicole feared he wanted revenge for the trouble *she* had caused Dominic. Ray shook his head, letting out a sardonic grunt. Nicole hadn't done a damned thing to Dominic except tell the police about the death threat he'd made. Another cop who'd been on the case told him she'd been heavily medicated at the time of that statement. A lawyer would have made mincemeat of her words.

Other than that, Dominic had nothing to blame her for. Maybe he didn't want revenge at all. Maybe he thought he could rekindle their romance. Whatever his reason for following her, he was probably unstable, perhaps even insane. And he was stalking Nicole Chandler.

Ray had his evening planned even before he'd visited Nicole. He reached across the front seat, picked up a thermos, and poured a cup of strong black coffee. Then he sat back in his seat, his head barely visible to a passerby, and settled in for a long night.

2

For her first day back at school, Nicole donned an iris-blue suit with a white silk shell beneath the long jacket, faux pearl earrings and necklace, and a deep russet lipstick. She took special pains with the curling iron to turn her hair into a shining pageboy. No one was going to look at her and see a broken, weepy woman, she thought in satisfaction. "Always put your best foot forward," Clifton used to say. "Don't show your pain to the world." "I'm doing my best, Dad," she said aloud to her reflection in the mirror.

"Are you about ready, Shelley?" she called. "You have to take the bus this morning."

Shelley bounced into her bedroom, Jesse hot on her trail. "Mommy, how pretty you look!"

"Thank you, sweetie."

"Did Sergeant DeSoto ask you for a date last night?"

Nicole looked at her in surprise. "How did you know he was here?"

"We don't live in a mansion, Mommy. I heard voices and I peeked out the door."

"Sure you did. How about this scenario instead? You were watching *NYPD Blue* and you were making sure I was busy so I wouldn't catch you."

"Mommy, I really *did* hear voices!" Then Shelley grinned guiltily. "But it was during a commercial when I had the ear-phones out. It was a really good episode. You would've liked it."

Nicole shook her head, although she couldn't keep the right side of her mouth from lifting in amusement. "You are incorrigible."

"What's that?"

"Since you're so grown-up, you look it up in the dictionary."

"Well," Shelley persisted as Nicole slipped on her wristwatch. "Did he ask you for a date?"

"No."

"No!" Shelley wailed, thumping down on the bed as Jesse jumped up to join her. "Why not?"

"Did you feed the fish this morning?"

"Sure, but you didn't answer my question. Why didn't Sergeant DeSoto ask you out?"

"Shelley, even if he liked me that way, I'm married."

"That didn't stop Daddy."

Nicole paused. "No, it didn't, did it?" She looked down at her gold wedding band and abruptly slipped it off, dropping it in her jewelry box.

"Daddy doesn't wear his, either," Shelley said quietly. "Does this mean you hate each other?"

Nicole looked at her seriously. "Certainly not. Your father and I were very happy together for a long time and we'll always be close because of you. We're just not really married anymore, except in the eyes of the law, and even that will change soon."

She expected tears, a melancholy look, a plea for her and Roger to get back together again. Instead, Shelley said simply, "Okay. What about Sergeant DeSoto?"

Nicole rolled her eyes. "My matchmaking daughter. I told you he didn't ask me out."

"Then why was he here?"

"He came about our prowler."

"I told you he'd believe us about the werewolf!"

"He doesn't think it was a werewolf. He believes we have a prowler who dresses like a wolf."

"Are they going to do a stakeout to catch the guy?" Shelley asked excitedly. "Of course, even if they collar him, and he's smart, he'll lawyer-up and not say a word."

Nicole rubbed a hand across her forehead then burst into laughter. "Shelley, we *have* to cut down on your television time. You don't sound like a nine-year-old girl anymore. You sound like a homicide detective."

"I think that's what I want to be."

"I thought you wanted to be a movie star."

Shelley frowned for a moment. "Maybe I'll be a movie star who *plays* a homicide detective!"

"I'd rather you became a teacher."

"Oh, Mom," Shelley said in what Nicole feared would become a frequent teenage whine. Then she brightened, running toward the white rosebud in a bud vase on Nicole's dresser. "Mommy, how pretty!"

"Yes, it is."

"Is it from Sergeant DeSoto?"

"Honey, it's time for us to be going."

"You didn't answer—"

"No, it isn't from Ray."

"Ray?"

"Sergeant DeSoto."

"Then who's it from?"

Nicole adjusted her right earring and stuck a pack of tissues in her purse. "I don't know."

Shelley studied the rose, then her mother's face. "I think you *do* know but you don't want to tell me," she said impishly.

Nicole didn't answer because the child was exactly right.

3

Nicole's campus office seemed strange to her, a place she hadn't occupied for months instead of just a week. When she opened her door, she found a cheerful card from Miguel under her door. How thoughtful of him, she mused as she spooned grounds into the coffeemaker. Her first class wasn't for forty-five minutes, so as the coffee brewed, she sat down at her desk and began sorting through the mail that had collected during the week.

Five minutes later the phone rang. "Hey, teach, how's it going?" a cheerful voice rang in her ear.

"Carmen, how nice to hear from you. What's up?"

"I'd like to invite you out to dinner tonight."

"At your house?"

"No. I said 'out.' That's not 'out' to me. Let's go somewhere fun on the River Walk."

Nicole smiled. Considerate Carmen, knowing that her first day back at school would be hard on her and how much she loved the River Walk. "That sounds great. But were you thinking of including Shelley and Jill? If so, we can only have one drink each, watch our language, and act mature."

"But we want to have fun, so of *course* we're not taking the girls. I thought Shelley could spend the night with Jill. She'd like that, wouldn't she?"

"She'd love it! Jill's just two months away from being a bona fide teenager."

"Then why don't you drop her by the house around six? Bobby will baby-sit. He even volunteered to drive each of them to school in the morning."

"But Shelley's school is so far out of his way."

"He says he doesn't mind. You can meet me at the store."

"It's a date."

"My, *you* seem to be recovering from tragedy easily."

Nicole put down the receiver as she watched Avis Simon-Smith lounge in the doorway. "Hello, Avis. As for my recovery, it may not be as easy as it looks, but I'm making progress."

"*And* dates," Avis said coyly.

"Only with my best friend of almost thirty years." Avis kept looking at her, smirking maddeningly. Nicole had never been around anyone who made her so edgy, but she always tried to be friendly to the woman who seemed to be a fixture in the department. "Thank you for taking over my class in my absence."

"That's me, the department workhorse."

"I'm sorry you were so overworked," Nicole said mildly. "Would you care for a cup of coffee?"

"Is that all I get for my week of hardship?"

Nicole stared at her long, homely face. "I had intended to send you flowers—"

"*Flowers!*" Avis nearly shrieked, sounding as if Nicole had said "snakes." "God, do you want people to think we're *lesbians*?"

Nicole gaped before Avis broke into loud, braying laughter. "Oh, put your eyes back in your head. It was a joke. Lord, no one around here would ever think *you* were a lesbian with all the attention you pay to the young male students."

"I beg your pardon?" Nicole managed.

"Oh, forget it. No sense of humor. That's what's wrong with most of the people in this department."

Two of these humorless people walked by and glanced at Avis, but no one stopped. I don't blame you, Nicole thought. I wouldn't want to get involved in this, either.

"Yes," Avis said abruptly.

"What?"

Avis sighed. "You asked if I wanted coffee. *Yes*."

"Fine. Do you take cream or sugar?"

"Both. I've never had to worry about keeping this girlish figure."

"You're lucky."

"Lucky? Do you think I enjoy going through life looking like an anorectic?"

"You don't look like an anorectic," Nicole said, stirring Coffee-mate into the cup and wishing desperately the woman would leave.

"Nice try. That must be why people in the department like you so much. You're always trying to be sweet. A regular ray of sunshine."

Nicole handed Avis a cup and sat down behind her desk. "My mother would certainly disagree with you."

"I guess you save your charm for your career." Avis took a sip of coffee and wrinkled her sharp nose. "Too weak."

Nicole automatically started to say "I'm sorry," then stopped. If the coffee hadn't been too weak, it would have been too strong or too sweet. Avis always found something wrong.

"As I was saying," Avis continued, ignoring Nicole's silence, "you are the department sweetheart. Our beautiful young princess."

"Avis, I hope you're teasing," Nicole said evenly. "Otherwise, I'm going to think you're off your rocker."

"Oh-ho!" Avis crowed. "A little venom bubbles to the surface."

"Did you find that remark venomous? I thought I was teasing, just like you were."

Avis set down her cup, sloshing coffee on Nicole's desk. "But I haven't been teasing."

"Then you've gotten some wrong ideas somewhere. I'm certainly not the department princess. It sounds ridiculous for you to even make such a statement."

Avis stood abruptly. "I have to go. I know you're starting Melville today. I did an *excellent* job with the Hawthorne section. I hope you don't make a mess of the one on Melville."

"I'll try to maintain your magnificent standards," Nicole muttered dryly.

A moment later, while Nicole wiped up the coffee Avis had spilled, Nancy Silver stepped in. "Glad to see you're back."

"Thanks."

"Nicole, I couldn't help overhearing Avis." She stepped into the office, her dark hair shining under the light. "She's not well, you know."

Nicole looked up, thinking of Kay. "You mean she's ill?"

"Not physically. But she's taken a lot of blows lately."

"Tell me about it," Nicole said bitterly. "I know how it feels."

"But it's different for you. You're still young and beautiful and you have a child. Avis is all alone. No husband. No children. She had dreams of becoming a great scholar, but after a twenty-five-year career, she's had only one book published over twenty years ago and just three articles since then. The book she's been working on for five years has been rejected time after time.''

"That's unfortunate but—"

"Just ignore her for a few more months, Nicole," Nancy interrupted. "Next year she's going on a much-needed sabbatical. We're all hoping she can pull herself together and be the kind, sensible person she once was."

"Yeah, let's hope," Nicole said without enthusiasm. Something told her that no amount of time off would soften Avis's acrimony toward her, and after what she'd been through lately, she couldn't work up sympathy for a woman who hated the world just because her books hadn't been published. "I'm sorry, Nancy. I know you mean well, and Avis is fortunate to have you on her side, but I don't feel like discussing her this morning. If I don't hurry, I'll be late for class."

4

"Where are you and Aunt Carmen going to eat?" Shelley asked, dragging her tote bag into Nicole's room.

"I'm not sure. I thought I'd let Carmen decide."

"I don't see why Jill and me can't go."

"Jill and *I*." Nicole struggled into a new pair of jeans. "You can't go because it's a girls' night out."

She buttoned a long-sleeved beige blouse and stepped into black leather boots.

"Jill and *I* are girls."

"Not grown-up girls." Nicole added large gold hoop earrings.

"Gee, Mommy, you look like a teenager!"

Nicole bent and kissed Shelley on the forehead. "You are a dear, sweet child, and no, you cannot have a raise in your allowance and you cannot go tonight."

"Shoot," Shelley pouted. "Well, you still look young. As young as Lisa. And lots prettier."

Nicole stopped primping and kneeled, taking Shelley in her arms. "Shel, can't you try to like Lisa a little bit?"

"Why should I?"

"Because your daddy might marry her."

Shelley groaned. "I can't stand it if he does."

"Yes you can. You have to give her a chance."

Shelley thought this over. "Okay. I'll be polite to her, but I won't promise to like her."

"I guess that's all I can ask," Nicole said, thinking it was probably more than *she* could manage.

Forty-five minutes later Nicole dropped Shelley and her tote bag off at the Vegas' small adobe house. Bobby met them at the door, giving Nicole as cool a greeting as Jill's was warm. He took the tote bag. "Hey, what's in here, Shelley? Concrete blocks?"

"Just necessary items," Shelley announced in her most adult voice. Nicole knew she was attempting to act as sophisticated as she found Jill, who was two years her elder and already wore pale pink lipstick.

Raoul Vega, Bobby's father, appeared at the door wearing an old gray sweater, his thin hair bearing wet comb tracks. "Nicole!" he said joyously.

Surprised that he remembered her, Nicole smiled broadly. "Mr. Vega, how nice to see you."

"And you, as always, are a vision. Isn't she a vision, Bobby?"

"Yeah," Bobby replied flatly.

"I hope the girls won't be too much trouble tonight," she said.

Raoul gave her a waggish look. "Girls? Trouble? Hah! I raised six of them."

"Three," Bobby corrected.

"Was it three? *Seemed* like six." Raoul and Nicole laughed. Then, abruptly, Raoul's wrinkled face seemed to blur, the eyes to shift focus slightly. "How's that boyfriend of yours?"

"You mean my husband?"

"Did you marry him? The handsome one I made the cross for?" He clasped his hands together and looked at Bobby. "A beautiful cross set with turquoise and wings engraved on the back. Nicole said the wings were symbolic of inspiration." He glanced back at Nicole. "Did he like the present?"

"He loved it," Nicole said, her voice thickening as she remembered presenting Paul with the cross on his twenty-ninth birthday.

"Such a talented man," Raoul continued. "A genius. He appreciated art."

"Yes, well, I really have to be going." Nicole turned quickly so they wouldn't see the tears in her eyes as she remembered Paul opening the gift. It was that night he had proposed to her.

She drove faster than usual, blasting a Heart CD and singing "Crazy on You" at the top of her voice, until the image of Paul accepting the cross and proposing began to fade. So long ago, she kept telling herself. It didn't matter anymore.

Except that it did. It always would.

"And you are a fool," she said aloud over the music. "One minute you're in tears over an old romantic memory of him, the next you think he's stalking you for revenge. Roger would have a field day analyzing *you*."

By the time she reached downtown San Antonio, she'd relaxed slightly. She parked in the Nation's Bank Parking Building, ignoring a momentary flash of fear as she remembered all the scary movies she'd seen where women were attacked in parking buildings. But she wasn't going to be careless. She parked on the first floor and had armed herself with Mace tucked in her blazer pocket so she could reach it easily.

Emerging from the building, she headed for the River Walk. *Paseo del Rio*, Clifton had taught her to say when she was little, the River Walk ran along the San Antonio River twenty feet below street level. The entire area was built between 1939 and 1941, preserving a horseshoe bend in the river that in the 1920's city businessmen had wanted to cover with concrete and turn into a sewer. Wiser heads prevailed, and instead it had been converted into a wonderland that wound nearly two and a half miles through the heart of downtown San Antonio and had become one of the city's main attractions.

Nicole hurried down the stone steps into what had always seemed to her a magical world. Immediately her spirits rose. How many hours had she spent here with Carmen when she was a teenager, prowling the shops, sitting in the sidewalk cafes, and meandering through art galleries? The whole area looked like a fairyland tonight with a thousand tiny lights strung through the trees, music pouring from the cafes and nightclubs, river boats ferrying people on forty-minute excursions, and dining boats serving dinner by candlelight.

I *feel* like a teenager again, Nicole thought, glad she'd dressed young. She felt a stab of guilt for her light heart so soon after her father's death. She wouldn't comfort herself by saying, "This is what he would have wanted," or trot out the popular cliché she hated, "You have to get on with your life." For one evening she simply wanted to shake off her shock and devastation over her father's death, her anger at Roger, and her sudden fear of Paul. Tonight she wanted to feel young and carefree.

Throngs of people passed by her as she walked to Vega's. The CLOSED sign was up although lights burned and she could see Carmen moving around inside. She rushed to the door and let in Nicole. "You are ten minutes late!" she scolded in her slightly husky voice.

"Sorry. Traffic was heavy."

Carmen's dark eyes traveled over her. "I'd kill to fit into jeans like that."

"I haven't had much appetite lately or I couldn't have done it, either." She grinned. "I'm not even sure I'll be able to get out of them without Shelley's help. I may end up sleeping in them."

"Well, I'm eating enough for both of us. Even Bobby is starting to complain," Carmen said, slapping a substantial hip beneath loose brown slacks. "Too much of a good thing, he says."

"I just saw him," Nicole returned tartly. "It seems to me you might return the compliment."

Carmen glanced at her almost in alarm. "I'd *never* criticize Bobby's looks. You know how sensitive he is about them."

"No, I didn't know, but it seems to me turnabout is fair play. Why is it okay for him to comment on your weight but you can't let him know he's putting on a few pounds himself?"

"Bobby still sees himself as twenty."

"And they say women are vain! Sometimes I think you're too nice to him, Carmen. Oh, well, I'm *starving*. Where do you want to eat?"

"How about Tequila Charlie's? I'd love one of their frozen margaritas, and I'd say at *least* one would improve your mood. First day back at school didn't go so well?"

"With the exception of a visit from Avis Simon-Smith, it went beautifully."

"Is she that nutty woman who gives you such a hard time?"

"Yes, and she was in rare form today. They say she's going on sabbatical next year, but I bet she doesn't make it. I think she's on the verge of a breakdown." Nicole smiled. "But don't worry. I'm neither blue nor grouchy. In fact, I'm ready for some fun."

Carmen beamed. "Great! Just let me check to make sure the back door is locked and grab my jacket. Be back in a jiffy."

When Carmen disappeared into the back of the store, Nicole wandered around. Display cases showed a collection of lovely silver and turquoise jewelry. She hadn't needed Raoul's reminder of that long-ago day when she'd come in and asked him to make a special piece, a silver and turquoise cross with wings engraved on the back to give it added meaning. How happy she'd been that day. She closed her eyes and moved on.

Shelves held clay pots and valuable coiled Chumash baskets carrying the Spanish royal coat of arms, as well as objects carved from obsidian, white jade, and turquoise. A few paintings hung on the walls. Beside them were woven rugs with Southwestern designs. It was all beautiful. And expensive. Vega's had always been one of the classiest stores on the River Walk. Carmen had said that Bobby would like to improve business by handling some cheaper merchandise, although both she and Bobby's father objected. Nicole, too, would hate to see the quality of Vega's inventory decline, but she also understood Bobby's money concerns.

"Just a minute," Carmen called. "Can't find my purse, as usual."

"I'm holding on, although my stomach is growling."

Nicole passed around the store again. Suddenly she stopped. On the wall hung three masks—one of an eagle, one of a bear, and one of a wolf. She stepped closer to the wolf mask, although a closer look wasn't really necessary. She would have recognized it anywhere.

"Ready to go at last," Carmen said breathlessly, emerging into the showroom. "What's wrong?"

"Those masks."

"Aren't they beautiful? They're modeled on genuine Indian clan masks. They hung the masks outside their lodges to show which clan they belonged to, and the children of a marriage automatically became a member of the *mother*'s clan, not the father's. Isn't that interesting?"

"Yes," Nicole said distractedly. "Do you sell a lot of them?"

"Unfortunately, no. They're pretty expensive. Don't tell me— you want to buy one for your mother!"

"Just her style. Are these the only three you have?"

"I don't think so, but I'd have to check the stock. A friend of Bobby's makes them."

"A friend of Bobby's," Nicole said slowly. "He must sell them to Bobby for a pretty low price."

"Cheaper than we sell them for, of course." Carmen grinned. "Are you trying to buy at wholesale prices?"

"You know I never do that, but I'm interested in who's bought one lately. The wolf, for instance."

Carmen frowned. "Want to tell me what this is all about?" Then her expression changed. "Your werewolf! The prowler you told me about!" She burst into laughter. "Oh, Nicole, you *can't* think someone wore one of *these* masks to scare you."

"Why not?"

"Because of what they cost! If someone were just going to scare you, they'd buy a plastic mask, not one of these things. They cost around two hundred dollars and weigh several pounds!"

"How long have you been carrying them?"

"Only about a year. But Nicole, really—"

"I know the idea is far-fetched, but just to please me, can't you look up who's bought a wolf mask?"

Carmen shook her head. "As silly as I think this is, I'd do it to please you, but unless someone is leaving jewelry to be sized or engraved, we don't write down who buys what. After all, we don't give warranties on oil paintings or clay pots. However, if it'll make you happy, I'll ask Bobby about the masks tomorrow. He's the one who has them made. He loves them and I guarantee he'll remember how many we've sold and probably to whom."

Nicole smiled. "Thanks, Carmen. I know I'm being silly, but the mask just looks so *similar* . . ."

"I understand, but I think you're letting your imagination run away with you. You've only seen this guy in the dark. You've never even gotten a good look at the mask he wears."

Oh, yes I have, Nicole thought with assurance, unable to take her eyes off the mask she'd seen clearly through her and Shelley's bedroom windows.

TEN

1

Tequila Charlie's was crowded and they sat outside at a small table on the patio. The temperature had dropped to the mid-sixties with a soft breeze. Miniature white lights laced the oaks, crepe myrtles, cypresses, and willows lining the riverbank, reflecting over and over in the water. Nicole realized she hadn't felt so relaxed for nearly two weeks.

She and Carmen each ordered the steak and shrimp dinner and frozen margaritas. "Want chips and salsa with your drinks?" the pretty waitress asked.

"Yes, please," Nicole said. "Otherwise I might pass out from hunger." When the drinks came, Nicole took a deep, biting sip and licked the salt off her lips. "This is delicious."

"And let me guess—the first you've had since you came back to San Antonio."

"You know how Roger hates River Walk restaurants. Only Shelley can drag him down here. I understand he was delighted by his lunch at Planet Hollywood the other day."

"He *is* crazy about Shelley." Carmen paused, took another sip of her drink, reached for her fourth chip, then asked abruptly, "Why did he tell you he wanted to come to San Antonio?"

"He said it would be nice for Shelley to be near her maternal grandparents since she hardly knew them, but when we got here, he seemed to resent the time she spent with her grandfather. Roger also said it would be great if we both taught at the same school—so convenient because we could locate a house close to the campus and use the same car—and there were openings for each of us, which is rare."

"Did you tell him you didn't *want* to come back here?"

"About a hundred times. But he said I should face my memories—that it would be healthy for me."

"And you agreed?"

"About facing my memories? No. But the other stuff made sense. Besides, he wanted it so much. He was so persistent."

Carmen smiled a little lopsidedly. "And you accuse me of trying too hard to please Bobby."

"The pot calling the kettle black, right?"

"I guess." Carmen took another drink of her margarita and looked at Nicole. "Liquor has probably loosened my tongue. Bobby told me to keep my mouth shut about this, but I can't any longer. Every time I'm with you, I feel guilty."

Nicole's smile faded and her stomach tightened. "This sounds ominous. What is it?"

"Bobby knows Lisa Mervin's family."

"They're from San Antonio?"

"Yes. Last year she went to school in Ohio because they were trying to get her away from some weird guy around here. Unfortunately, Ohio is where she met Roger. Her family got wind of the affair and demanded she come home."

Nicole's eyes widened. "Roger was involved with Lisa last year, *too*?"

"I'm afraid so."

"Well, that son of a—" Nicole broke off and gulped her drink. "So Roger came here because of *her*. That jerk dragged his whole family halfway across the country to follow Lisa Mervin!"

"Yes," Carmen said meekly.

Nicole's eyes blazed. "Carmen, why on earth didn't you tell me before we made the move?"

Carmen looked affronted. "You think I wouldn't have if I'd known? The Mervins are Bobby's friends, not mine. I didn't know a thing about Lisa or an affair until this year."

"No, of course you didn't," Nicole said, calming down. "You would never have let Roger pull off something like that if you could have stopped it." She tapped her fingers on the tabletop. "So what about Lisa's family? How are they handling the affair?"

"They've had so much trouble with her over the years that they've finally disowned her. She's Roger's problem now."

"You mean he's *supporting* her?"

"Completely."

"And I'm suddenly living on one income instead of two."

"You mean he hasn't given you much to help with expenses?"

"A few hundred dollars."

Carmen looked appalled. "That's *all*?"

"Yes. I intend to get all that straightened out at the divorce hearing next month."

"But what about your father's will?"

"It was written before Roger deserted us. He left everything to Mother and a trust fund for Shelley. She gets it when she's eighteen."

"Can't you ask your mother for a loan?"

"Sure. But there would be *so* many strings attached, Carmen. She'd want Shelley and me to move in with her and then she'd try to take over our lives. She means well, but you know how Mom is." Nicole shuddered. "Shelley and I would be two birds in a gilded cage."

"Can't you put your foot down with her?"

"I don't know. I might have to try. We took a loss on our house back in Ohio because the move was so sudden, and our savings, which Roger controls, were depleted." Nicole sighed. "Carmen, how long have you known that Roger came here in pursuit of Lisa?"

"Only since Christmas, when Roger announced he was leaving you. I didn't tell you then because, as I said, I told Bobby I wouldn't. I was also hoping that as soon as Roger moved out, he'd realize he made a mistake. I thought you'd be more likely to take him back if you didn't know he'd brought you all the way to Texas in pursuit of this little tramp."

"Well . . ." Nicole said, flabbergasted at the massive degree of Roger's deceit, the incredible trouble and planning that must have gone into his scheme. "Well . . ."

"I'm sorry." Carmen nervously pushed her shining hair behind her ears. "We were out for a night of fun and I laid this on you. Bobby always says I'm too intense."

"Bobby is certainly good at keeping score of what he perceives to be your faults," Nicole snapped.

"Nicole, don't take your anger at Roger out on Bobby."

"Why not? Maybe you didn't know what was going on with the Lisa Mervin situation, but Bobby did. He doesn't like me very much, but I've known him for almost twenty years and as your husband he could have had the decency to let me know what was going on before we made a very expensive move and I was placed in this position."

"He just thought it wasn't his place to interfere in someone else's marriage," Carmen said unhappily.

Nicole looked at her. She didn't believe that excuse. She'd felt Bobby's dislike for a long time, and to her his silence wasn't a matter of minding his own business, it was his way of allowing something to happen he knew would end up hurting her deeply. But Carmen believed in her husband and she looked so distressed, Nicole couldn't allow herself to vent any more of her anger. The woman worshiped Bobby, God knew why.

"Don't look so shattered, Carmen," she said mildly. "It's not your fault. And I understand Bobby's silence on the matter." Boy, *do* I, she thought. He probably thought the whole thing was a big joke on me. "I just don't understand why, if Roger were so in love with this woman that he intended to leave me for her, he made me come to San Antonio, too. It would have been so much easier, and cheaper, to just leave me in Ohio."

Carmen took a deep breath. "I think it was *Shelley* he wanted here, Nicole, not you," she said reluctantly. "He couldn't leave you and come chasing out here after Lisa because Shelley would stay with you. He couldn't stand being away from either Lisa *or* Shelley."

Nicole tapped her forehead with the heel of her hand. "Of *course!* How could I have been so stupid? These days he's irresponsible when she's in his care because of his drinking, but he still wants her with him as much as possible. He's been a regular tiger about it. I wouldn't be surprised if he asks for full custody, even knowing that's impossible."

"Nothing Roger Chandler does would surprise me. Just watch your back. I don't trust him."

Nicole frowned. "Is there something else you're not telling me?"

"No, but I see the way he's treated you. Bobby would never do that to me."

Carmen's face lit up when she just mentioned him, and Nicole felt a tug of sadness. She'd never known what Carmen saw in Bobby Vega, even when he was a member of The Zanti Misfits.

"You really love Bobby, don't you?"

"Oh, yes, Nicole," Carmen said fiercely. "And I almost lost him to that damned band. God, how I hated Magaro and Zand! They were trying to take him away from me with their drugs and their groupies." Her gaze met Nicole's. "Oh, forgive me! How could I have brought them up in front of you?"

"Why not?" Nicole asked calmly. "I hated them, too."

"But I wanted to cheer you up tonight and instead I'm bringing up every painful thing in your life." She looked down into her margarita. "What do you suppose is in here?"

"Sodium Pentothal," Nicole said seriously. "I can't wait to hear what other secrets you're going to spill. I plan to steer you toward your sex life next, and I want *details*."

Carmen covered her eyes and laughed. "Good heavens, I think I've lost my mind tonight."

"I think you're just having a good time." Nicole was determined not to let Carmen see that some of the things she'd said had upset her deeply. "That's what we're here for."

The waitress stopped by and they ordered fresh drinks. "More chips, too?" the waitress asked.

Nicole looked in amazement at the empty basket, realizing she hadn't eaten one chip. "Yes, please," she said.

"Coming right up." The waitress smiled, assuring them that their dinners would be served soon.

"Then we'll be too drunk to care," Carmen said. "And I'm sorry I ate all the chips. *You* were the one who was so hungry."

"To hell with the chips. Here's something much more interesting than chips and salsa to spice up the evening while we wait for the food," Nicole told her, leaning across the table conspiratorially. "Don't look now, but Lisa Mervin's sitting three tables over with a girl and *two* young guys." Carmen's head snapped to the right. "I *said* don't look!" Nicole hissed.

"Oh, sorry, but she doesn't know me."

"She knows *me*."

"But she's not paying the slightest bit of attention to you. God, that guy she's talking to is handsome."

Nicole turned her head casually, then her eyes widened. Miguel Perez had had his head down when she'd looked before, his hair, free of its ponytail, partially covering his face, but now she could see him clearly. He was laughing at something Lisa had said.

Miguel and *Lisa*? She was flummoxed. She was also disappointed in Miguel.

"I thought he had better taste," she muttered.

"Who?"

"Carmen, *that* is my student Miguel."

"Oh, it *is*." She looked at Nicole closely. "Are you interested in him?"

"Me?" Nicole was genuinely shocked. "Carmen, he's my *student*!"

"What does his being your student have to do with anything?"

"I'm not Roger," Nicole said stiffly.

"And Miguel isn't Lisa. You're thirty-four. He's what? Twenty-eight, twenty-nine?"

"I haven't the faintest idea."

"Yes you do. He's not much younger than you and he's sexy as hell. He likes you, too."

"Apparently not as much as he likes Lisa."

Carmen grinned as the fresh drinks were delivered. "You're jealous!"

"I'm *not*! But I like Miguel—he's smart and charming and talented. You can imagine my feelings for Lisa. That's why I hate seeing him with her. He could certainly do better." She paused, then smiled slyly. "But it would serve Roger right if Lisa dumped him for someone so young."

Carmen and Nicole fell into a fit of giggles. "Those margaritas getting to you?" the waitress asked as she delivered their food.

"Apparently," Nicole managed. "This looks absolutely delicious."

"If you need anything else, let me know," the waitress said pleasantly.

During the next fifteen minutes Nicole and Carmen enjoyed their food, discussing Shelley and Jill, Nicole recounting Avis's bizarre visit to her office this morning, which now seemed funny. Then, leaving out the strange phone call, she told her about Roger's car being damaged and his blaming her.

"You'll be so much better off without him," Carmen said.

"Yes, but Shelley won't." Nicole's eyes grew troubled. "He's her *father*, Carmen. She's only nine and she's already aware of how silly he's acting. If he doesn't change drastically, in three or four years she's going to lose all respect for him, be humiliated by him. I want her to be proud of her father, no matter what's gone on between him and me. Instead I'm afraid she's going to see a womanizing drunk. It wouldn't matter so terribly if I could keep her away from him as much as possible, but—''

"Oh, God!" Carmen interrupted, her eyes growing huge as they looked in Lisa's direction. "I don't believe it."

Nicole's gaze followed, and she gasped when she saw Roger stride up to the table of young people. "So *here* you are!" he blasted.

Color washed from Lisa's face. Because everyone else on the patio had fallen silent, Nicole was able to hear her thin voice. "You said you had work to do tonight, Roger."

"And you said you were going to visit Susan so I could have some peace and quiet."

"I am with Susan." Lisa's voice wavered. She motioned to the other girl. "How did you know where we were?"

"Susan's roommate. You didn't say anything about going out with her and these two young studs." He glared at the one sitting next to Susan. "And you would be?"

The tall blond young man looked back steadily. "Not that it's any of your business, but my name is Toby."

"Toby," Roger boomed. "Now there's one fine name for you. Sounds like something you'd name an elephant in the circus." He turned and glared at Miguel. "And you are . . . no, wait, I *know* you. You're that guy who's always hanging around my wife." Miguel stared back coldly. "Perez. Michael Perez."

"Miguel. And I think you should either sit down and lower your voice, or leave."

Roger dismissed him with a glance. "Lisa, come with me," Roger commanded.

Lisa's face had gone from white to crimson. "Roger, these are just friends. There's nothing going on here. Besides, I haven't finished my dinner."

"Your *dinner*. What about *my* dinner?"

"What about it?" Lisa asked blankly.

"She didn't fix it for him," Nicole mumbled.

"Don't you care whether or not I eat?" Roger said loudly. "I *am* doing important work, you know. I can't live on air."

"So order a pizza," Miguel said equably.

Roger leaned on the table, nearly tipping it over. "This is between Lisa and me."

The owner of the restaurant appeared. "Sir, you are disturbing my other guests. I must ask you to either sit down or leave."

Roger glared at him. "I wouldn't be disturbing your guests if they'd all mind their own damned business." His gray eyes behind their glasses traveled belligerently over the crowd. "Mind your own business!" he shouted, then his gaze landed on Nicole. "Well, well, of all people, my virtuous *wife*. The gang's all here." He raised his voice even louder. "What are you doing, Nicole? Following Lisa?"

"Ignore him," Carmen whispered.

"I intend to," Nicole said, lowering her head.

"Nicole, you didn't answer my question." Nicole stared at her plate, possibly more embarrassed than she'd ever been in her life. Her cheeks burned and she felt as if she were going to start hyperventilating. "Not talking, are we?"

The manager tried again. "Mister, if you don't leave right now, I'm calling security."

Roger looked at him with great dignity. "I will be most happy to leave your sleazy little establishment." He reached down and grabbed Lisa by the arm. "Come on."

"Roger, you're hurting me!" Lisa cried.

"I said come with me. *Now!*" He jerked Lisa to a half-standing position as she cried out in pain.

In an instant Miguel was on his feet and around the table, yanking Roger's hand from Lisa's arm. "Let her go and get the hell out of here!"

"*Don't* tell me what to do, you long-haired—"

Almost before she realized what was happening, Nicole watched as Miguel hit Roger in the jaw. He staggered backward, sending the table behind him crashing to the patio, food splattering everywhere. Although Roger caught himself before he fell, the next few moments were a mixture of people gasping, laughing, cheering, and clapping. Nicole half rose from her seat in shock.

Carmen sat, convulsed with laughter, as Roger regained his composure. Nicole, her face frozen in astonishment, expected Roger to take a swing at Miguel. Instead, he turned, apologized to the people whose dinner he'd left on the patio, then looked at Lisa. She rose, and without a word they quickly walked away together.

Nicole sat numbly as waiters came to clean up the mess that had been Lisa's table. "He's lost his mind," she said vacantly.

"He's *drunk*," Carmen answered, wiping at her eyes with a napkin. "My God, that was hilarious."

Nicole looked at her in anguish. "Would you have thought it was so hilarious if it had been Bobby?"

Immediately the humor faded from Carmen's face. She reached both hands across the table for Nicole's. "I'm sorry. How insensitive can I be? Lord!"

"I guess it *was* pretty funny to an outsider," Nicole tried.

"I'm not an outsider. Even if I don't know Roger very well and can't stand what I do know of him, you are my best friend, closer than a sister. Please forgive me."

Nicole mustered a smile. "Don't worry about it. And don't sound so abject. Tomorrow I'll probably be laughing at it myself."

"Dr. Chandler?" Nicole looked up to see Miguel. "I'm sorry for the scene."

"It wasn't your fault," Nicole said coolly. "Roger started it."

"But maybe I went too far—"

"You didn't. He probably would have pulled Lisa's arm out of its socket if you hadn't stopped him."

Obviously aware of her remoteness, he backed away slightly. "Once again, I'm sorry for any embarrassment I caused."

"Everything is fine, Miguel," Nicole said formally. "See you at school."

As he walked back to where the others were gathering purses and jackets, Carmen raised an eyebrow. "You were a tad chilly."

"Was I?" Nicole said, sipping what was left of her drink.

"You resent him for defending Lisa, don't you?"

"No," Nicole said honestly. "Someone needed to defend her."

"Then what is it? No, wait. I *know*. You like this guy and you don't like seeing him here with Lisa."

"That's hardly a revelation, Carmen. I already told you that."

"But there's something else, something I pointed out to you the day of your father's funeral." Nicole raised her eyes in curiosity. "He looks like Paul Dominic, Nicole. It didn't really hit me until tonight. I wasn't paying that much attention to him at your Christmas barbecue, but don't tell me you haven't noticed it. He's even about the same age as Paul was when you were involved with him.''

"I'd like another drink," Nicole said briskly, signaling the waitress.

"Nicole?"

"Oh, okay. I've noticed. There *is* a faint resemblance but he's not Paul."

"Just keep in mind what I've said," Carmen answered slowly. "You barely know this guy. Don't trust him too much."

"Who said I trusted him?"

"The expression on your face when you saw him with Lisa. You looked completely betrayed."

And so I did, Nicole thought. Betrayed by yet one more man in my life.

2

"I'm glad we decided to stay," Nicole said. "I've had a good time, in spite of Roger's performance."

"Me, too." Carmen smiled warmly and looked at her watch. "But good heavens, it's nearly ten. I promised Bobby I'd be home by nine."

"I'm sure he'll survive."

"I'm going inside to call and tell him I'm safe or he'll be worried."

When Carmen had gone, Nicole leaned back in her chair, letting the cool breeze blow through her hair. Two more margaritas had temporarily calmed her earlier distress over Roger, although she knew in the morning it would return, along with a pounding headache. Oh, well, this hadn't been quite the evening she'd planned, but at least it had been an experience.

Carmen reappeared soon, her eyes apprehensive. "What's wrong?" Nicole asked, immediately thinking something had happened to Shelley.

"Nothing, really, except that Bobby's mad at me."

"Why?"

"Staying out so late, leaving him with the two girls and his father."

"I thought he agreed to it."

"He did, but I guess Raoul has been more trouble than usual."

"Has something happened to Raoul?"

"No. He's just in one of his garrulous moods. He keeps mixing up Shelley with you and going on and on about the past. You know how all that incessant talking drives Bobby nuts." No, I didn't know, Nicole thought, or I wouldn't have let Shelley stay. "Where is that girl with the check?" Carmen demanded.

"Carmen, are the girls all right?"

"What? Oh, yes. They're asleep."

"I'll stop by and get Shelley."

Carmen looked affronted. "No. I told you, they're perfectly fine. It would only make Bobby madder if he knew I'd said anything to you to make you think Shelley wasn't safe." She looked around nervously. "Where is the damned *check*?"

"Never mind the check," Nicole said steadily. "You head for home. I'll take care of our bill."

"That's not fair."

"You can settle with me later." Nicole was more concerned with Carmen's agitation than she was with splitting the bill. "Go on home. And don't drive too fast."

Carmen sighed. "Okay. Thanks so much." She stood and leaned down to give Nicole a brief kiss on the cheek. "You're such a good friend."

With that she was off, nearly running down the River Walk in her haste to reach home and a husband who'd decided to get mad because his wife wasn't back on time. Carmen was being silly, getting so upset over such a little thing, Nicole thought. Then she remembered the early days of her marriage, when she'd acted exactly the same way about Roger. The difference is, I grew out of it, she mused. Apparently Carmen hadn't.

After Nicole paid the check, she took a deep breath, suddenly feeling so tired she didn't know if she had the energy to get back to the car. Too much tequila and too much excitement, she thought before asking the waitress for a strong black coffee to go.

As she left the restaurant and started back through the River Walk, she thought about Roger. If two or three years ago someone had shown her a video of tonight's scenario, she would have laughed it off as a fake. Roger, what's happened to you? she thought. I don't love you anymore, but it still hurts to see you disintegrating before my eyes. She wanted to blame Lisa, but that was too easy. Lisa was a symptom of Roger's decline, not the cause. Maybe *I'm* the cause, Nicole thought sadly. Maybe he simply couldn't live with all the trauma I brought with me as his wife.

As soon as she began walking, Nicole was glad she'd bought the coffee. The breeze had grown sharper and she was certain the temperature had dropped to sixty. She took a drink of the steaming coffee, then pulled her blazer closer around her and buttoned it. A brightly lit riverboat cruised by, the passengers happily singing "Guantanamera," a song Nicole hadn't heard for years. She waved at them and most waved back.

Shops and cafes did not line all of the River Walk areas. Large spaces were empty, quiet and parklike with cobblestone walkways. When Nicole reached one of these, away from the music and sound of people talking and laughing, she suddenly became aware of the sound of water lapping against the concrete sides of the canal. It was a lonely sound, and although the canals were drained and cleaned each January, the water looked murky and smelled slightly brackish tonight.

The breeze suddenly stiffened considerably, sweeping her hair across her face. When she pushed it away, she realized how much the crowd had thinned, as if in the blink of an eye almost everyone had disappeared. Picking up her pace, she passed under one of the stone bridges arching the canal, lit underneath only by soft amber and green lights.

That's when she first heard the footsteps behind her. Normally she would have paid no attention, but these steps were different. They walked in perfect sync with hers. When she picked up her pace, so did they. When she slowed to take another sip of coffee, they slowed, too.

The temptation to look behind her was almost unbearable, but something told her that would be a mistake. Whoever was back there would be on her in an instant. Instead she looked across the canal. An older man and woman, the man moving slowly with a walker, were complaining steadily about the cold, the time of night, the cost of dinner, and the cobblestones while a middle-aged woman herded them along with loud, encouraging words. No one even glanced at Nicole, not that any of them could have been any help.

And she needed help. She'd only heard footsteps, but something primal told her she was in danger. This was *really* stupid! she thought furiously. The River Walk was not a high-crime area and she'd never been afraid here before, but then she'd never thought someone was stalking her before, either. Of all times to come down here, when she was worried about Paul Dominic following her! Of course, coming here wouldn't have been such a mistake if she hadn't stayed so long and left around eight-thirty with Carmen as she'd planned, but the evening hadn't gone as scheduled. Instead she'd become distracted by Roger and then dulled her senses with tequila, lingering around until after ten o'clock when the crowd began thinning because of the hour and the dropping temperature. Now here she was all alone with someone definitely following her.

She passed a set of stairs leading up to street level and her heart leaped. She started up them, hearing the footsteps slow behind her. Then she saw that a wrought-iron gate shut them off from the sidewalk above.

She felt like screaming, but instead muttered an "Oh shoot," and casually walked down the stairs as if she were in no hurry and had not noticed that she was being followed. She veered to the right, threw her disposable coffee cup in a trash can, and reached in her pocket for the Mace, holding it tightly but out of sight in the pocket. Two blocks to the steps that lead up to the street where the car is parked in the building, she told herself. Just keep walking. Don't think, don't run, don't throw off the scent of fear.

Up ahead was another archway. More green and amber lights glowed, although these seemed dimmer than the last. She tightened her hand on the Mace, looking around for someone who could help her. But no cruise ships went by, and no one else walked in the vicinity. The world seemed full of nothing but dull lights, water lapping, her heart pounding, and the footsteps tapping relentlessly behind her.

Under the archway, the air grew colder. The last one, she thought, perspiring in spite of the chill. This was the last bridge, she thought. Then she would reach the steps to the street where people walked, where policemen rode bikes.

Abruptly the footsteps behind her picked up speed. She pulled the Mace from her pocket and began to run when a body crashed against hers, knocking the Mace from her hand, propelling her toward the wall of the archway, slamming her against the stone, knocking the air from her. Pain shot through her back and head. She flailed helplessly, kicking her booted feet until she was rewarded with a grunt of pain. For an instant she saw a thin face with beard stubble, one front tooth missing and one gold. The smell of mildew and stale sweat nearly smothered her before a strong, filthy hand slapped her face so hard her vision dimmed. The hand covered her mouth before she could manage even a weak scream.

He tore at her purse, oblivious to her small, pummeling fists, and she felt the strap give way. Then he slapped her again and ripped her blouse, then her bra. Memories of the long-ago rape overwhelmed her as he forced her body down. Panic seized her, a panic even stronger than she'd felt with Magaro and Zand because she'd been through this before and knew the agony that awaited. Strong hands closed around her throat.

Suddenly she heard the sound of an animal growl. Dear God, she thought wildly, did that come from *him*? Then she felt the weight of a third body on top of hers. The snarls continued. The man screamed and Nicole caught a glimpse of an animal face. A Doberman, huge white teeth bared before they sank into the man's arm. He shrieked again and let go of her throat.

Stunned, Nicole lay still while the struggle between man and dog raged, the man's knees and shoes digging into her as he fought to get to his feet, the dog holding fast to his arm, then grabbing his upper calf, growling steadily the whole time.

The man kicked out and the dog yelped. At last he clambered to his feet, cursing and still kicking. "Hold!" someone yelled. The Doberman, slavering, sat still for a moment while the man abandoned Nicole and ran down the River Walk. Another form moved toward the dog. Nicole was aware of movement, as if someone were stroking the dog, looking for injuries. "Go!" the voice commanded again, and the dog was off, the man shrieking up ahead as the barking black streak pursued him.

Nicole struggled to a sitting position, her body weak and shaking, her blouse and bra hanging open, her vision blurred. She tried to stand but collapsed. Strong arms closed on her shoulders, pressing her back into a sitting position. "No, no please," she moaned, fighting weakly. But the big hands trapped hers. "You're safe now," a deep male voice said.

She struggled to see, but her eyes wouldn't focus. "Who . . ."

She heard voices, people shouting, footsteps running her way. "You are all right, *chérie*." The man slipped something around her neck. Cold metal touched the delicate bare skin between her breasts. She blinked. Her vision cleared for an instant and she looked into a man's burning hazel eyes. He kissed her on the forehead, rose, and vanished before anyone else reached her.

ELEVEN

1

The next few hours were a blur for Nicole. People appeared from all directions, a man helped her to her feet, a woman buttoned her blazer over her bare breasts, someone drove her to the police station. Was there someone she wanted to call? they asked. Roger? she thought, and almost laughed in spite of her condition. Her mother? No, she'd been through too much lately. Carmen? Carmen had her own troubles with Bobby. No, she didn't want to call anyone.

Later all she remembered was bitter coffee, questions about who might want to hurt her, more questions about what the guy looked like, and finally a grilling about how much she'd had to drink and what she was doing down there. "You always dress that way to stroll the River Walk alone at night?" a beefy, particularly offensive officer named Erwin asked. Time spun backward for Nicole. It was fifteen years ago. "You always wear tight jeans and prowl the town at night?" this cop's clone had asked.

"I want DeSoto," she said flatly.

Erwin looked at her with interest. "DeSoto?"

"Sergeant Raymond DeSoto."

"You two special friends?"

Nicole gave him a glacial stare. "You said I could call someone. I want Sergeant DeSoto."

"Well, I'm afraid he's not on duty, little lady. Got any other cop friends? Why don't you just talk to me?"

Nicole, battered, on the verge of tears, shaken to the core of her being, leaned toward Erwin and spoke softly. "If you don't call DeSoto, I'm going to scream down the walls of this place and claim you made sexual advances toward me."

"Nobody would believe you," Erwin said, his face puffing with anger although he didn't sound too sure of himself.

Nicole smiled challengingly. "Let's try it and see." The man's eyes wavered. "Call DeSoto *now*."

Fifteen years ago, another cop like Erwin had reduced her to sobbing humiliation. Now she wasn't about to let this lout demean her. I guess you *have* changed, she thought. Maybe the change was more drastic than she'd realized.

Twenty minutes later, Ray DeSoto approached her wearing jeans, a University of Texas sweatshirt, and a tan jacket. Erwin watched them closely, as if expecting them to throw themselves into each other's arms. Instead, Nicole raised an eyebrow. "Another night in paradise."

"So I see," Ray said, taking in her torn clothing, red cheeks, and the swelling under the eye. "What happened?"

"She got mugged wanderin' around on the River Walk," Erwin intervened. "I got the notes here."

"Thanks." DeSoto took the notes but barely glanced at them. "Want to tell me what happened from the beginning?"

Nicole sketched in her dinner with Carmen, mentioning the scene between Roger and his girlfriend, knowing she was doing it to explain why she'd stayed so late and drunk so much more than usual. Then she told him about hearing the footsteps behind her and the attack.

"So he just pushed you down, ripped your clothes, roughed you up some, and ran off with your purse?"

"He didn't run off voluntarily—"

"She says he was attacked by a dog," Erwin interrupted. He sounded as if he found this highly unlikely, but DeSoto's eyes met Nicole's.

"A Doberman?"

She nodded silently. "Hey, how'd you know what kind of dog?" Erwin asked.

"First thing that came to my mind," Ray said easily. "Did the dog do much damage?"

"It grabbed his arm hard enough to pull the hand off my throat, then it got his right calf. He kicked the dog. There was . . . a pause while it recovered," she said, skipping for now the part about the owner stopping the attack until he saw that the dog was all right before he ordered it to pursue.

"What did the guy look like?"

Nicole closed her eyes. "Wiry but very strong. Narrow face. One front tooth missing. The right front and . . . the left was gold. Long, dark, greasy hair."

"Eyes?"

"I'm sorry, I'm blank. What really sticks out in my mind is how *filthy* he was. And his smell—it was like mildew."

DeSoto looked up from his notes. "Mildew?"

"Yes. I know it sounds odd, but have you ever been in a dank, dirty bathroom and smelled the plastic shower curtain?"

"Can't say that I have," Ray said, a smile tugging at his lips. "Smelled a shower curtain, that is."

"Well, I don't make a habit of it, either." Nicole felt her face coloring. She sounded foolish. "Anyway, he smelled like mildew," she said stubbornly, "and really old perspiration. I'm sure he hadn't had a shower for days."

"Approximately what age?"

"I don't know," Nicole said tiredly. "Anywhere from early to late thirties."

DeSoto frowned. "That type doesn't usually hang around the River Walk. Market Square, yes, but not River Walk."

"Believe me, he was there."

"What did he get from you?" Ray asked.

"My purse. In spite of the dog attack, he didn't drop it. People looked everywhere around the area for it, but no luck."

"Anything else?"

"No."

"So he's got money, credit cards, and keys."

"Great," Nicole groaned. "I can't drive my car or get in my house."

"You don't have *any* extra keys?"

"No extra house keys. Extra car keys at the house."

"Then it looks like I'll be driving you home. But first you're going to the hospital."

"I don't need the hospital. Just a couple of aspirin."

Ray looked at her sternly. "Have you taken a good look at yourself? He knocked your head against a concrete wall and then slapped the hell out of you. Your eye is swelling half-shut. You could have a concussion. You should have been taken to the hospital immediately."

Nicole was too tired to argue although it was past midnight. However, she started to shake when the hospital examination began, remembering the last time she'd been brought in after an attack. Then she had lain on a table for what seemed hours, shivering and filthy until the humiliation of the rape-kit procedure had begun. She remembered her mother standing beside her, her face deathly white, her glacial blue eyes refusing to meet Nicole's. And she remembered feeling ashamed.

But this time was different. The examination was brief, the young doctor and nurse both jovial, trying to lift her spirits. Finally, after being poked and prodded and X-rayed, she was pronounced bruised but otherwise healthy, without a concussion, without so much as a cut or scrape. "You don't even have to worry about HIV," the young doctor told her. "But I doubt if you're going to sleep very well tonight." He put a pill in a small envelope. "This is Seconal. Don't take it until *immediately* before bed, but *do* take it. You need the sleep."

"*Now* you can go home," Ray said as she was released and trudged into the waiting room.

"Thank goodness Shelley is at Carmen's and I don't have class until early afternoon," she told him when they reached the car. "But how will I get into the house? No keys, remember?"

Ray winked at her. "Don't spread it around, but I pick locks."

"Thank goodness," Nicole breathed. "I don't want to call a locksmith tonight."

As they drove toward northern San Antonio, Ray said, "What did you think of Erwin?"

"I found him delightful," Nicole returned hotly. "God, what a sexist! You know, I see guys running in mesh T-shirts and shorts that barely cover their behinds but no one thinks they're out to get raped."

"That's true," Ray said mildly.

"Look, I've been really depressed since Christmas. Last night I felt good. I felt young and I wanted to have fun so I *dressed* young. I had the audacity to wear tight jeans, so Erwin seems to think I got what I deserved. Hell, if I'd worn a dirndl skirt and combat boots, would he have had some sympathy for me?"

"Not if you'd bothered to brush your hair and put on lipstick."

They looked at each other and burst out laughing. "I'm sorry," Nicole said, recovering. "I know I'm ranting. It's just that I've been through this before and guys like Erwin make me furious.''

"You should have been talking to a woman, but Erwin loves to pounce on these cases. It just makes his evening to embarrass some poor woman and make her feel guilty.''

"I pity his wife.''

"Don't. He's scared to death of her.''

Nicole laughed. A moment later Ray asked casually, "You ready to tell me the whole story now?''

She looked at his profile. "How did you know I wasn't being completely open earlier?''

"You seemed to be picking your words carefully. Feel like you can trust me?''

"Yes,'' she said slowly. "I didn't just see the Doberman, Ray. Paul was there.''

Ray's hands tightened on the steering wheel. "*Dominic* attacked you?''

"*No*. The dog, Jordan, saved me. After it ran off the guy, Paul appeared. He said I was safe. He called me *chérie* and kissed me on the forehead.''

Ray frowned. "Nicole, you were scared to death, you'd received a hard blow to the head. Maybe you just saw someone who *looked* like Dominic—''

"He put this silver and turquoise cross around my neck,'' she interrupted. "It was Paul's.''

Ray glanced sideways as she held out the cross on its silver chain. "Do you know how many silver and turquoise crosses there are in this area?''

She turned it over. "Not like this one. Paul's had wings engraved on the back, wings symbolic of spirituality and inspiration because of his musical genius. It also has the tiny initials R. V.— Raoul Vega. I know because I had Mr. Vega make the cross for Paul's twenty-ninth birthday.''

2

After Ray had gotten her back into the house, he checked both the first floor and the basement to make sure no one was hiding inside. Then he made her promise to cancel her credit cards, put a stop on her checks, and apply for a new driver's license and Social Security card the next day. Finally, after her many assurances that she wasn't afraid to stay alone, he left.

Nicole immediately went to the back door to let in Jesse. The dog, who wasn't used to staying out past eight, didn't run to her when she opened the door. "Asleep in his doghouse," she muttered. She walked outside and looked in his little house. Empty. "Jesse?" she called. "Are you hiding?"

Then she saw it—the fence gate swinging open. Nicole rushed toward it and let out a cry when she saw the smashed padlock. "Oh, no," she moaned. "Damn, damn, *damn!*" She ran through the open gate and out to the street. "Jesse?" she yelled. "Jesse!"

No high-pitched bark answered her. Without a car, she couldn't drive around looking for him. Instead, she walked two blocks in one direction and two in the other. Finally, exhausted by the evening, her legs trembling, she gave up and went home.

Inside, she flopped facedown on the couch. Jesse had escaped once before and returned unharmed, but luck didn't seem to be with her tonight, especially since the padlock was smashed. She didn't think any of the local kids would do that. Had the creep in the wolf mask come back and taken out his sick fantasies on a defenseless little dog? "Oh, please, *no*," Nicole moaned. "Please not that." If anything happened to Jesse, Shelley would be devastated. First her father, then her grandfather, then her beloved dog. All gone. Nicole's eyes filled with tears. "*Why* did I go out tonight?" she asked the walls, pounding her fists on the ugly couch Roger had bought and left behind as a reminder of himself and his lies. "Why *tonight*?"

She fumbled in her pocket until she found the envelope containing a red Seconal, knowing that taking it was the only way she would get any sleep. And tomorrow was a full day. She had to get back her car, have the locks changed, teach two classes, and worst of all, tell Shelley her dog was missing if he hadn't returned by the time school was dismissed.

She took a long shower, then looked at herself in the mirror. Red marks circled her throat where hands had clutched, and her eye was swelling. She didn't feel comfortable about Shelley being at Carmen's with Bobby, whom she no longer trusted. At the same time, she was glad Shelley wasn't here to see her in this condition.

Nicole slipped on panties and a filmy nightgown that wouldn't rub harshly against her sore body, tossed her blouse and bra in a trash can in the garage, went back inside to the kitchen, wrapped an ice cube in a washcloth, and peeked out the window. A patrol car was parked down the street. She managed a smile. She knew when she'd told Ray she wasn't afraid to be alone, he'd given in too easily. He'd sent someone to watch the house, and she was glad. The bum on the River Walk had taken her keys. There was no way she could lock him out.

She poured a glass of milk and downed the Seconal. Back in her bedroom, she turned on the bedside lamp, made sure the blind was pulled down, piled pillows behind her head, and lay back, holding the cold washcloth against her swollen eye. Drowsy already, she picked up the cross that lay on the bedside table. It was slender, the carving delicate, the piece of turquoise small and beautifully mounted, hanging from a gleaming twenty-inch chain. She turned it over. There were the wings, exquisitely engraved by Raoul Vega, a master of his craft.

She'd been so proud of herself for thinking of the special touch, and Paul had been impressed with her creativity. "This is a bond between us," he'd said. "One or the other of us will wear it all the time." And yet, after the car wreck fourteen years ago that had supposedly claimed Paul's life, she'd never heard of a silver cross found on the body or with the effects belonging to Paul.

She turned off the bedside lamp and, for the first time in years, drifted off to sleep without turning on the night-light. Suddenly she saw the image of Raoul Vega the way he looked a few hours ago, his face wreathed with smiles. "Did you marry him?" he'd asked. "The handsome one I made the cross for?" And then, "Such a talented man. A genius . . . he appreciated art."

She jerked awake, her vision blurry. Back then I told Mr. Vega I was having the cross made for my cousin Ellen, she thought. I *never* told him it was for a man, especially a man he would describe as talented, a genius. But he knew who it was for. He *knew*.

So who had informed him? she asked herself as she dozed back to sleep, but she already had the answer. She had told only one person about her relationship with Paul, she had told only one person for whom she was having the necklace made.

Carmen.

3

Izzy Dooley cruised slowly down the street in his twelve-year-old Plymouth. He spotted the small white brick house with no lights burning inside. He also spotted the patrol car parked one house down. His heart did an uncomfortable little flip at the sight. He settled down, though, when he saw the profile of the cop inside. His head was bent forward—asleep on the job, Izzy thought with a smirk. To Protect and to Serve—right. To eat doughnuts and to sleep was more like it. Izzy glanced at his watch. It was 3:20 A.M. Some guys just weren't night people, not like him.

Izzy thought of himself as a vampire, a creature of the night, moving around dangerously only after the sun went down. In fact, he'd seen the movie *Interview With the Vampire* five times and even decided he looked like Louis, played by Brad Pitt. Of course, in the movie Brad had all his teeth and a few less wrinkles, but the resemblance was definitely there, especially when Izzy's hair was clean and swung freely around his shoulders. He was always surprised more people didn't comment on it.

Izzy drove around the block and parked on the street behind the white house. Then he moved through the yard of the brown house facing the street, reached the fence surrounding the white brick, and half crawled, half ran around to the gate. It swung open, not even latched, and on the handle hung a smashed padlock. Izzy stole a look back at the motionless profile of the cop in the patrol car, then entered the backyard.

He froze when he saw the doghouse. It was a small doghouse, certainly not one that could shelter a Doberman like the maniac that had attacked him earlier. He'd gotten away from it, but his arm and his calf still throbbed from the bites.

Shaken by his earlier canine experience, Izzy waited five full minutes near the gate before he was certain no dog was going to charge him. Then he assured himself that even if a dog were in that little house, it would be small enough for him to handle. He was being overly cautious, wasting time.

He pulled the gate shut and latched it. Then he looked at the windows of the house. The blinds were pulled, but absolutely no light spilled around the sides. Even the dusk-to-dawn light was weak—just a five-foot pole topped by a glass ornament with a hundred-watt lightbulb inside. With the gate closed, the yard encircled by a tall wooden fence, no light inside the house, and the outside light so feeble it couldn't reach the corners of the yard, he felt safe. Nothing to worry about here.

He removed a switchblade from his pocket along with a ring of keys. He slipped forward to the back door and gently tried a key. It didn't fit. There weren't many others. He picked a second key. It slipped into the lock. Grinning, he turned it. The door opened with only a slight squeak.

He stepped in and stood quietly for a moment. Absolute silence. He left the door open behind him, not wanting to take a chance on making another unnecessary squeak when he closed it. An open door also meant a hastier retreat.

Izzy took three more steps into the house, stopping when he reached two doorways. He peered into the one on his right. Unfortunately, a vampire trait he'd not yet acquired was the ability to see in the dark. He squinted, as if this would help. It didn't. He couldn't resist creeping in a few inches. His foot collided with something large and soft and to his shame he almost screamed, thinking of the Doberman. But it was a stuffed animal. Some kind of big stuffed animal. Probably a kid's room, but he didn't hear the sound of breathing. Sorry, no one home.

He backed out of the room and turned toward the other one. He heard something and stiffened. What was that sound? Not a light being switched on. Not a telephone receiver being lifted. But a whisper of movement . . .

Blinding pain shot through his lower back at the same time a hand covered his mouth. Something—a knife—had plunged into the base of his spine, severing vital nerves with one powerful, vicious puncture.

Izzy fell to his knees, then slammed forward onto his face. He tasted blood from his broken nose, felt it running down his throat. Before he realized what was happening, a figure flipped him on his back and stuffed a big terry washcloth into his mouth so far back it brushed his throat, making him gag. By now his eyes had adjusted a bit to the darkness and he could see faintly. The figure above him sat back, and Izzy's eyes widened in complete shock.

A couple of grunts escaped him before a fist drove the washcloth farther into his mouth, cutting off most of his air. He shut up.

He felt himself being dragged. The lower half of his body was paralyzed so there wasn't much he could do but flail his arms. He tried to shout, but the effort only made the dry washcloth rub against his soft palate, choking him.

When they reached the door to the outside, Izzy tried to grab the door frame. He was able to hold on for a few seconds, but a hard yank finally pulled him free. His head thudded sickeningly as it bounced off the step onto the concrete walkway, landing sideways. From this angle he saw the little doghouse. For the first time he wished it weren't empty. A dog, even a small one, would cause a racket that could save him, rescue him from this totally unexpected and undoubtedly fatal turn of events.

But there was no dog. There was no sound except his body being dragged over the stiff, cold grass. Finally the dragging stopped. He looked up at the stars and mysteriously dredged up the ancient memory of his mother singing "When You Wish Upon a Star" to him before he went to sleep. How little he had been, how young and sick she had been. And then she was gone and no one ever sang to him again.

He felt the upper half of his body being lifted, then propped against the wooden fence. A small circle of metal pressed against his temple. He didn't have to see to know what *that* was. He felt strangely calm, as if his vampire spirit had moved outside his body.

He paid no attention to the gun. Instead he looked up. There were thousands of stars—distant, beautiful, but unlike in the song, uncaring. He made no wishes. Instead, he merely gazed longingly at the sparkling orbs until, for Izzy Dooley, their magic light suddenly blinked out forever.

4

Her feet were cold—so cold. It was so hard to see. But she could hear them.

"She thought she had us," Magaro was saying.

"She almost did," Zand answered, snorting something.

"No she didn't. It would have been better if we could have killed her like I wanted—"

Ringing. More ringing.

Nicole kicked, put her hands over her ears, then opened her eyes. Everything was blurry and dim.

Ring.

"Phone," she mumbled, throwing a hand over her eyes while she reached for the receiver with the other. " 'Lo."

"Mommy!" Shelley's voice, almost unbearably shrill and cheerful. "Were you still *asleep*?"

"Yeah. 'Fraid so. Something wrong?"

"No. Aunt Carmen thought you might like for me to call and say hi before I go to school."

"She was right." Nicole swallowed around the dry lump that was her tongue. "Have a good day, honey."

"Mommy, you sound funny."

"I do? Guess I'm just sleepy."

"No, you sound sick. What? Uh, wait a minute. Aunt Carmen wants to talk to you."

Nicole would have killed for a small cup of water by her bed. She felt like she'd eaten sand. In a moment Carmen came on the line. "Nicole?"

"Um-humm." She was aware of noise in the background. Something rhythmic.

"You sound *awful*. What's *wrong* with you?"

The sound was clearer. Music. "Can't 'splain right now."

Carmen lowered her voice. "Are you with a *man*?"

Nicole sat up in bed. "No! For heaven's sake, Carmen, I—" She broke off when she realized the music wasn't coming over the phone. It was in her own house.

"Nicole—"

"Shhh!" She listened. She recognized. She went cold all over.

"Nicole, you're scaring me! What—"

Nicole dropped the receiver and jumped out of bed. She weaved as her feet hit the floor and all the memories of the night before flooded over her. The attack. The police station. The hospital. The Seconal. The visual memories slid across her mind quickly, wiped away by the auditory memories conjured up by the familiar music coming from her living room.

"God, what's going on?" she mumbled, heart pounding.

"Nicole! *Nicole!*" she could hear Carmen shouting. "Answer me!"

She ignored Carmen's pleas and ran barefoot into the hall, then the living room. The stereo was on, the sound much lower than she usually set it, but still easily heard by anyone fully awake. Easily heard and dreadfully familiar.

"Rhapsody in Blue."

Nicole walked slowly to the stereo. She was used to listening to CD's, but what played was a cassette tape. The plastic container lay on a shelf beside the amp. She picked it up, knowing what she would see. Inside the front cover was a picture of Paul Dominic wearing a tuxedo and sitting at a Steinway grand piano. The title of the cassette read *Dominic, Gershwin, and Carnegie Hall*. "The new tape he played for me the last night we were together," Nicole whispered, dropping the cassette container onto the soft blue carpeting.

How long had the music been playing? It could have been hours, because the tape player would automatically flip sides and play a tape endlessly until it was removed.

She stood still, listening to the four-bar passage that bridges the long piano cadenza into the famous *Andantino moderato* melody. Then the music soared as the song moved into the development of the slow theme, the piano trading off with the orchestra until the rhapsody was brought to its spectacular conclusion.

Nicole closed her eyes, her breath coming in short, shallow bursts. There was a pause as the tape flipped sides. Then began "The Man I Love." She dropped to her knees, a deep, ragged moan escaping her. She wrapped her arms around her waist and rocked back and forth as tears rolled down her cheeks. "Paul," she cried, remembering this song playing in the background as they lay close together in the big, beautiful room on the third floor of the Dominic house, the room filled with roses and stereos, and Paul's grand piano.

"Paul, did you come into my house and put on this tape?" she asked aloud. "If you did, what does it mean? You're following me. Why? To love me or to torment me?"

She put her head down again, this time not closing her eyes. It was then she saw her bare feet and froze. The soles bore dark red streaks and smudges. She touched them gingerly, although she already knew she wasn't hurt. There was no pain. But instinctively she knew the stains were blood.

Not bothering to turn off the stereo, she stood and crept back into the hall, flipping on the light. Suddenly something seemed to coil and move in her stomach like a snake. She stared for what seemed an endless time at the huge circle of darkness on her pale blue carpet. A trail led from the circle to the back door.

Still barefoot, she walked through the stain and opened the back door, which was unlocked. First she looked at Jesse's empty doghouse. Then she looked at her futile attempts at a flower garden. Finally she looked at the figure hanging from a branch of the oak at the back of her yard.

Without hesitation, her face immobile, she drifted across the dry grass, the breeze blowing her flimsy nightgown around her legs. Her eyes were open, but she felt as if it were not sight leading her forward. The body was like a magnet, drawing her inexorably toward it. She didn't stop until her head bumped into a boot.

Suddenly she snapped back to acute consciousness. She gazed at the two booted feet, turning outward. Above them were jeans with ragged hems. Above the jeans, a white T-shirt and a leather jacket. And above the leather jacket was a black hood.

A black hood exactly like the ones found fifteen years ago on the bodies of Ritchie Zand and Luis Magaro.

TWELVE

"Paul, *no*," Nicole whispered desperately. "Please, God, don't let him have done this."

She stared at the figure. It wasn't just still. It was rigid. Rigor mortis. This was *death*. But whose? And when had he been hanged?

"I have to cut him down," she murmured, her stomach turning as she stared at the hood covering a head tilted on a broken neck. She turned and headed back to the house, wondering where she'd put the stepladder, which knife would be strong enough to cut the rope. She stepped on a rock with her bare foot. Pain shot up her leg, and with it mental clarity.

Cut him *down*? What did she think she was doing? Tampering with evidence, that's what she would have been doing. It was bad enough that she'd gone so close to the body. She could have already destroyed a small piece of evidence.

Normal emotion and reason flooding back through her like a charge of electricity, she ran into the house, slamming the back door behind her. Dashing into the bedroom, she spotted the phone receiver lying on the bed. She picked it up, listening to the rapid pulsing noise of a broken connection. Carmen had hung up.

Although Nicole's hands shook so violently she could hardly hold the receiver, she managed to punch the reset button, then 911. Eight days ago she'd done the same thing when her father shot himself in the head.

A hundred questions they asked. Three minutes into the call, Nicole snapped, "For God's sake, there's a dead body in my backyard. Do *I* have to solve the murder myself before I can get the cops here?'' Then she slammed down the phone on the still-chattering operator.

She looked at her flimsy nightgown. A robe? No, the police would be here soon, hopefully, and nightclothes made her feel too vulnerable. She reached for jeans, but they reminded her of last night and she tossed them on the floor. Finally she grabbed her gray sweatpants, then thought of her bloodstained feet. She couldn't face the police without a quick shower.

Nicole had scrubbed herself nearly raw last night after the attack, and the soap and hot water this morning was hardly soothing. She washed as quickly as possible, unable to ignore the dark water that ran beneath her feet. Last night that blood had given someone life. Now it was swirling uselessly down the drain with soapsuds. How fragile life could be, she realized with fright, how easily disposed of were its vital elements.

Uniformed police were the first to arrive, just as Nicole was tying the laces of her Reeboks. She ran to open the front door and watched the patrol car pull into the driveway. Then she looked down the block and saw another patrol car—the same one she'd seen parked there in the early hours of morning. Frowning, she looked at the clock. Eight-thirty. He should have been long gone. If she'd known he was still out there, she would have gone to him immediately.

She walked outside, her gaze, like those of the two officers who had just arrived, trained on the patrol car by the curb. One officer began striding toward the car. The other, a female, watched Nicole as she hurried across the lawn. ''What's he still doing here?'' Nicole asked. ''Why isn't he getting out of the car?''

''I don't know.'' The officer was young and very pretty and trying hard to look tough.

Nicole stood mesmerized as the young woman also began walking toward the other patrol car. By then the male officer was looking through the patrol car's open window. In a moment he withdrew his head as if he'd received an electric shock.

''He's dead!'' he shouted. ''Shot through the head!''

The female officer stopped cold. Nicole's breath left her in a long sigh and the scenery began spinning around her. A patrolman sent to protect her had been murdered. An unknown man had gotten into her house and been murdered, maybe just a few feet from her bedroom door, and then hanged in her backyard, all while she slept, dreaming of Magaro and Zand.

She collapsed into a lotus position and bent her head forward, willing the blood back to her brain. Forcing air into her lungs, she chanted, "I will not faint. I will not faint," like a mantra.

She was still sitting and chanting when someone put a hand on her shoulder. Nicole gasped and looked up to see Carmen, her face pale, her hair carelessly pulled back with a rubber band, her forehead creased. "You nearly scared me to death on the phone. What in God's name is going on here?"

"Is Shelley all right?" Nicole whispered.

"Of course. Bobby took her to school."

"Oh," Nicole managed. With death all around her, her main concern was her child's safety.

Carmen kneeled beside her, taking her chin in her large, lovely hands and forcing Nicole to meet her eyes. "What *is* it? Why are the police here? What's *happened*?"

"They're dead. Both of them."

"*Who's* dead?"

"The policeman in the car. The man in the backyard."

"The man in the back*yard*?"

"The one hanging from the tree." Nicole's voice quavered.

Carmen's face slackened. Then she gave Nicole a firm shaking. "Snap out of it. You're not making any sense. *Who* is dead in your yard?"

"I *told* you I don't *know*." The world was coming back into focus for Nicole and along with it her temper. Couldn't Carmen give her a moment to pull herself together? "Back off for a minute and let me get my thoughts straight."

People were coming out of their houses, and Nicole watched the uniformed officers begin to control the crime scene, backing people away, talking to them calmly. I'd be a terrible cop, Nicole thought. I could never keep my cool that way.

"Nicole?" Carmen persisted.

Nicole took a deep breath. "After you left last night, I was mugged."

"*What?*" Carmen trumpeted, drawing the attention of the neighbors and the police.

"Carmen, are you going to let me tell this or keep shouting at me?"

"I'm sorry."

"Anyway, the guy who mugged me got my keys and identification. Ray DeSoto, the detective I told you about at dinner last night, brought me home, then posted someone out here to watch the house. Someone got in anyway. When I got up, there was blood in the hall—so much blood—and I looked in the backyard and there was a man, dead, wearing a hood. A black hood. He's hanging from my tree. I called the police. When I came out to meet them, the patrol car from last night was still here. And they went to see why and . . ."

"And the officer is dead."

Nicole nodded. "Shot in the head."

Carmen sat down beside her on the grass, her mouth slightly open, her eyes dazed. "Nicole, are you *sure* about all this?" she said finally.

Nicole looked at her incredulously. "Do you think it was a dream?" Another patrol car pulled up, closely followed by a third unmarked car with a flashing light. "The black-haired man getting out of the car is Sergeant Ray DeSoto. Believe me now?"

Ray approached Nicole first. "Are you all right?" he asked, worry in his tone although his face was impassive. "Have you been hurt?"

"No, she's just frightened," Carmen answered for her.

Ray looked at Carmen. "And your name is?"

"Mrs. Carmen Vega. Nicole and I have been friends since childhood."

Ray nodded. "Would you two mind staying out here until we're ready to look at the other guy?"

"Why?" Carmen asked.

"So we won't disturb evidence," Nicole answered dully. "We're all right, Ray. Do what you need to."

Ray joined the officers at the patrol car containing the dead policeman. "I know this is a terrible time to say it, but he's great-looking," Carmen murmured. "It's obvious he likes you, too."

"You're right—this is an awful time, Carmen. But he *is* good-looking. However, he's just being nice to me."

"No he's not. I can tell."

"You can not. Besides, the last thing on my mind right now is romance. Can we talk about something else?"

"What? Dead bodies?"

Nicole closed her eyes. "I give in. Your subject is better."

Carmen jabbed her in the ribs and she looked up to see that Ray had returned. "Can you take me in the house now?"

"Yes, I think so." She and Carmen both rose.

"Mrs. Vega, I'd rather you stay out here," Ray said. "The fewer people we have contaminating evidence the better."

"I wouldn't mess up anything," Carmen protested, sounding disappointed.

Nicole looked at her. "Carmen, believe me, you don't *want* to see the house or the body. It's not like watching this kind of thing on television."

Carmen nodded. "Sure. I sounded like a ghoul."

Ray smiled at her. "That was just perfectly natural curiosity, Mrs. Vega." He took Nicole's arm. "Ready?"

"No, but I guess I have no choice."

As they walked back in the house, she noticed that Ray had taken out a notebook and he wore thin plastic gloves. He stopped in the middle of the living room, his expression baffled. "Did you put on music before or after you found the body?"

"I didn't put it on," Nicole said haltingly. "It was playing when I woke up."

Ray raised his eyebrows, then turned toward the stereo. "It's a cassette tape of Paul Dominic playing Gershwin at Carnegie Hall," she said.

Ray looked at her. "Your tape?"

"No. I have none of Paul's music."

Their gazes held for a moment. Then Ray wrote in his notebook, pressed the Stop button on the stereo with the end of his pen, and looked at the cassette case. "*Dominic, Gershwin, and Carnegie Hall.* His last concert. His last recording."

"How did you know that?"

"I've had reason to do research on Dominic lately." His eyes traveled beyond her to the large dark spot in the hallway. "Someone lost a lot of blood there."

"There's a trail leading into the backyard," Nicole explained. "I think he was killed or injured here, then pulled outside. I was out of it from the attack and the Seconal, but he still couldn't have made much noise. At least I don't think so. And I've told you I walked right through the blood, opened the back door, and ran barefoot to the body."

"By the way you keep referring to 'the body,' I'd say you've never seen this man before."

Nicole blinked at him. "I guess I never said anything to anyone except Carmen. Ray, I don't *know* who it is. He's wearing a black hood."

"A black hood?"

"Yes," Nicole said shakily. "Sound familiar?"

"Like the hoods over the heads of Magaro and Zand. Same material and everything?"

She lowered her eyes. "I never actually saw those hoods, just pictures. I never even understood their significance."

"The hanging and the hoods are what made some people think it was some kind of cult killing, like the Tate–LaBianca murders. Sharon Tate and Jay Sebring were hanged from a chandelier. Only back then, it was a bloody towel that covered Jay Sebring's face, not a hood."

"My, what a memory," Nicole said weakly, her stomach turning at the thought.

"I was fascinated by that case. It's one of the things that made me want to be a cop."

"But you would have been so young to have followed the case."

"Manson keeps coming up for parole and it's always carried by the news. It's hard to forget him or those murders." He glanced at the back door. "You went out that way."

"Yes. I woke up—actually, Shelley's phone call awakened me—and I heard the music and ran in here. I didn't even notice the blood on the carpet in the hall. Then I saw the cassette. *Then* I saw the blood. I followed the trail into the yard."

"Which is what we're going to do now."

"You want me to go with you?"

Ray's surly middle-aged black partner joined them. "Not necessary for you to go now. You'll just mess up the crime scene."

Ray shot the man an icy stare. "It *is* necessary for her to go, Waters. She might be able to identify him. And she won't mess up anything."

Nicole could almost hear Waters's teeth grinding in irritation. He was the same detective who was with Ray the morning her father had been found. She guessed him to be in his late forties or early fifties, slightly overweight and graying at the temples,

with a large face and eyes that seemed as if they could look right
into your soul. He'd be nice-looking if he'd smile, Nicole thought.
Smiles didn't seem to come easily to Waters, though.

They skirted the circular bloodstain, which Nicole guessed was
at least two feet across, and Ray opened the back door. "No
breaking and entering."

"Did you leave the door unlocked last night?" Waters asked.

"No. I'm certain I didn't," Nicole said with more assurance
than she felt. She'd been such a mess last night. She *always*
checked the doors before bed, but she didn't actually remember
doing it several hours ago.

"Don't touch anything," Waters ordered as they headed toward the body.

"Lighten up," Ray snapped. "I don't think you two have been
properly introduced. Nicole, this is Sergeant Cyrus Waters. Waters, *her* name is Mrs. Chandler and she knows not to touch anything."

"Well, excuse the hell outta me," Waters muttered.

Nicole smiled at him. "I'll be careful."

Looking slightly placated, Waters put his hands in his pockets
and turned down his scowl a notch.

Nicole's footsteps slowed as they neared the body. The beat-
up cowboy boots looked pathetic pointed outward. A fresh bird
dropping glistened on the ragged jeans. The fingers of the hanging
hands were dirty and stiff.

"Recognize him?" Waters asked.

"You haven't raised the hood," Nicole said.

Ray pulled her a step closer to the body. "We can't until we
get pictures. But is there *anything* you can see now that would
give us a clue—"

"The smell," Nicole interrupted. "Mildew."

"Mildew?" Waters repeated incredulously.

"She's got an incredible sense of smell," Ray said.

Waters rolled his eyes and looked at her as if she were an idiot.
"Maybe she should be in the canine corps. How are you at sniffing out cocaine, Mrs. Chandler?"

"Probably as good as I am at sniffing the garlic you had for
dinner on your breath," Nicole retorted, Waters's sarcasm spark-
ing her own.

Incredibly, Waters's mouth twitched as if he were actually going to smile. "Anything else?"

"There are also dog bites. This guy's right wrist has a dog's teeth marks. And look at his left jeans leg. It's torn near the knee. I think you'll find more bites under the tear." Nicole looked at Ray. "It's the man who mugged me on the River Walk last night."

THIRTEEN

1

After pictures had been taken, tape strung, extensive notes made, they finally lifted the hood. "Well, what do you know," Waters said. "Izzy Dooley."

"Izzy Dooley?" Nicole repeated dully.

"Yeah. I think Izzy is short for Isadore. The wacko thinks he's a vampire. He's been dragged in a couple of times for minor offenses but always manages to hit the streets before long." He frowned. "River Walk. That's not his usual area of business, though. Something strange about that."

"Why do you think he was there?" Nicole asked.

"No idea." Waters's frown deepened. "Would you believe the guy's only about twenty-four? Looks a good ten years older."

All Nicole could focus on was the stream of dried blood that ran down the right side of his face. It was so near his eye, it looked like a tear. Vampires are supposed to cry tears of blood, she thought.

"So he got in by using the keys he took earlier in the evening from Mrs. Chandler," Ray was saying.

"*After* he'd killed the officer in the car," Waters added. "Mrs. Chandler was attacked around ten. What time did the patrol car show up?"

"Not until nearly one in the morning," Nicole said.

"If Izzy got your ID when he attacked you, he knew where you lived. He had almost three hours to get out here before the patrol car arrived," Waters pointed out. "Why didn't he just come in the front door? Why did he smash the padlock on the fence?"

"Because our dog was out there," Nicole explained. "He must

have wanted to get Jesse out of the way so he wouldn't cause a commotion, so he let him out, then went into the house and waited. He could have gotten in while Sergeant DeSoto and I were at the hospital, which is why neither we nor the patrolman you put on surveillance saw anything when we got home.''

"I checked the house," Ray said.

"But not the backyard."

"You said you locked the back door," Waters reminded her.

"Yes, but if he had the keys, what difference did it make?" Ray argued. "He'd just let himself in again."

"Was the padlock on the fence broken when you got back from the hospital?" Waters asked Nicole.

"I discovered it fifteen minutes after I got home."

Waters's scowl was back. "I'm still troubled about this dog business. If Izzy's objective was to catch Mrs. Chandler alone in here and he had the keys, why didn't he just let himself in and hide? Why bother smashing the padlock to let the dog out?"

"The plan must have been to rob the place before Nicole got home and he didn't want the dog raising hell," Ray said, sounding irritated. "Seems simple to me."

Nicole's eyes met Ray's. "But none of this explains why Paul's music was on the stereo."

"Paul?" Waters asked immediately.

"Paul Dominic," Nicole forced out. "He was a concert pianist. I used to be involved with him. Fifteen years ago—"

Waters held up his hand. "I know the story, Mrs. Chandler. You probably don't remember, but I was on the case."

Nicole stared. "No, I didn't remember," she said faintly.

"Well, I'm not a pretty boy like DeSoto here. Women never remember me."

Nicole looked at him closely. "Actually, I think I *do* remember you." She swallowed. "Anyway, the cassette was playing on my stereo when I woke up this morning. It's not my cassette."

Waters gave her a penetrating look. "You're not thinking Dominic killed Izzy and the cop, are you?"

Nicole felt like something tiny trapped in a corner. "I . . . well, I know everyone thinks he's dead, but . . ."

"Cy, she thinks she's seen Dominic on several occasions," Ray said briskly. "At first I thought maybe she was imagining things."

"And now you don't?" Cy Waters asked.

"I'm pretty sure Paul Dominic is alive, that he's come back here, and that he's following Mrs. Chandler."

Nicole had thought this a hundred times, but having one police detective say it with conviction to another made it sound completely different.

Gradually she became aware of someone climbing a ladder. They were going to cut down the man who had hung, wearing his black hood, in her backyard half the night. Shivers ran over her and she clasped her arms across her chest.

Waters seemed aware of her drifting attention and startled her with a sudden question. "What makes you think Dominic's here?"

She swallowed. "There have been several incidents." He looked at her expectantly, and without thought she began telling him about the times she'd seen Paul. When she finished, she expected an argument, but Cy Waters merely looked at a gray cloud scudding across the sun.

"You know what all this means, don't you?" he asked Nicole. "If Paul Dominic murdered the men who attacked you fifteen years ago, then he probably murdered the man who attacked you on the River Walk last night." He gave her a bleak smile. "He sticks with Gershwin all the way, doesn't he?"

"What do you mean?" Ray asked.

"Another Gershwin song—'Someone to Watch Over Me.' If Dominic is alive, it looks like he's decided to watch over Nicole Sloan for the rest of her life."

2

It wasn't a cold day and Nicole wore a heavy sweatsuit, but she was still shaking when she left the house. She nearly fell into Carmen's arms. "Take it easy, kid," Carmen said.

"It was the man who mugged me last night," Nicole told her. "He must have used my keys to come in, and someone was waiting for him."

"Someone?"

"It looks like it was Paul."

Carmen held her away from her, her face turning stern. "Nicole, when are you going to stop harping on Paul Dominic? The police will think there's something wrong with you."

Ray and Waters appeared beside them. Ray said, "Mrs. Vega, it *is* possible that Paul Dominic is behind all this."

"What?" Carmen repeated faintly. "You *believe* her?"

"Carmen, you're making me sound like a lunatic," Nicole snapped, hurt.

"I'm sorry, but—"

"We think there is a *very* small chance that Dominic could be around," Ray interrupted. "If he is, there's also a chance that he killed Izzy Dooley, the mugger, as well as the officer in the patrol car."

Nicole glared at him. "A *very* small chance? I thought you believed me. Or do you think *I* killed those men?"

"Mrs. Chandler, I don't know who killed them," Ray said coolly.

Waters gave her a penetrating look. "Do you own a gun?"

Nicole was so startled it took her a moment to grate out a yes.

"Where is it?"

Nicole looked at Ray. Why didn't he say something in her defense instead of letting Waters take over? "The gun is in my bedside table," she managed. "The key to the drawer is under my mattress. But you can't possibly think *I* shot those men!"

"Why not?"

"Why *not*? Because a shot would have awakened the whole neighborhood."

"I'm aware of that," Waters answered. "A silencer must have been used."

Although Nicole trembled all over, she looked at Waters unflinchingly. "Sorry to disappoint you, but my gun is a revolver."

"I see you know about guns," Waters replied slowly. "Enough to know that it isn't impossible to use a silencer on a revolver?"

"*If* the barrel of the gun has been threaded. Mine hasn't."

"Nicole!" Carmen croaked. "Be quiet. You sound like a mobster!"

But Nicole couldn't stop. "Besides, you'll also see that the gun hasn't been fired in the last twenty-four hours."

"How do I know you only have one gun?"

"Because I'm telling you," Nicole returned coldly. "And what about my hands? Do a paraffin test—you won't find any nitrate residue.''

"Then why did you take a shower before we got here? The tub is still wet.''

"I took a shower because I had blood all over my feet. And Sergeant, that wouldn't get rid of all the traces of nitrate.''

"Mrs. Chandler, there's been an invention called the 'glove' that would protect your hands from residue. Besides, you're a little too savvy about handguns to make me comfortable.''

They glared at each other, nostrils flaring, until Ray said, "That's enough for now, Waters.''

"And furthermore,'' Nicole continued, ignoring him, "I suppose you think I *hanged* that man in the tree? Maybe you haven't noticed, but at five feet four and a hundred and ten pounds, I'm not exactly an Amazon woman.''

"The laws of physics—''

"The laws of *physics*!'' Nicole exploded.

Carmen grabbed Nicole's arm. "If you don't be quiet and get a lawyer, I'm going to tape your mouth shut!''

Nicole glared. "I'm only—''

"Shut *up*,'' Carmen hissed. "I mean it. Not another word.''

"This really isn't any of your business,'' Waters told Carmen tiredly.

Carmen whirled on him. "It is *too* my business! Nicole is my best friend and you're taking advantage of her shock to get her to say things she shouldn't.'' Her eyes narrowed. "It's not the first time you cops have done that to her.''

Waters gave her a sardonic look. "Just doing my job, ma'am. Besides, I didn't Mirandize her. You should know that means she's not under arrest.''

"How generous of you. I'll tell you what you can do—you can take your little Miranda spiel and stick it,'' Carmen stormed. "Nicole is coming with me for now.''

"She's not leaving the house yet,'' Waters snapped.

"I'm taking her to my car where I have a thermos of coffee, *if* that's all right, Your Majesty.''

"Fine,'' Waters said casually. "Just don't try driving off with her.''

Carmen rolled her eyes and muttered something in Spanish. Nicole didn't catch it, but she saw a twinkle in Ray's dark eyes.

3

Ray stayed on the street to question neighbors. Waters returned to the backyard. A young man from the medical examiner's office waved him toward the body, which had been turned on its abdomen.

"Both victims were shot in the left temple," he told Waters. "Both were contact wounds. I'd say a .38 caliber. The officer shows no other injuries in a preliminary examination. This guy is a different story." He pointed to Izzy's lower back. "That's a hell of a stab wound. It would have immediately paralyzed him from the waist down."

"No sign of a struggle?"

"No. He was probably taken by surprise in the house, stabbed, then dragged out. There's some bruising on the inside of his forearms. That means he wasn't dead when he was taken out of the house. He could have tried to hang on to the door frame and been jerked free. The arms would have hit the wood hard, causing the bruising."

"Any bruising or bleeding around the throat?" Waters asked.

"Some abrasions, but no blood. He was shot first, then hanged."

"I knew he wasn't hanged alive," Waters snapped. His feet hurt and he was hungry. His wife had him on a diet.

"There *was* some bruising around the mouth," the young man went on patiently. "I think something fairly rough had been stuffed in there to keep him quiet."

"Something rough? Like what?"

"Well, of course, I can't be sure. We'll know more after the autopsy, but I'd say something like terry cloth. Maybe a big washcloth."

"Interesting," Waters muttered. "I wonder if Mrs. Chandler is missing any washcloths."

4

Ray had questioned three people. Now he was talking to a middle-aged woman with hair dyed bright red who told him in detail about a violent argument Nicole had had with her husband Sunday night. "You should have heard her *language,*" she told Ray vigorously. "It was appalling."

"I see. How about Mr. Chandler? Was he shouting back at her?"

"Well, certainly," the woman sniffed. "No man would just stand there and take abuse like that. And I've seen plenty of *young* people at her house. She was entertaining a young, long-haired boy the very *night* of her father's funeral!"

"A funeral for which you refused to contribute one dollar for a wreath from her neighbors." Ray looked up to see a man in his late seventies—stick thin, white-haired, dressed in gray flannel pants and a navy cardigan—rushing toward him.

"Newton Wingate," he announced, sticking out a heavily veined hand toward Ray. Up close, Ray could tell the man was probably in his eighties, not his seventies, but his handshake was firm and his eyes a bright, alert blue behind his glasses.

"I've got some important information about those goings-on last night, Detective."

"Oh, what would *you* know?" the redhead said tartly.

Newton Wingate ignored her, addressing himself to Ray. "I have prostate trouble. Lord, boy, hope it never happens to you. Nothing but pure misery. The doctors wanted to take the thing out, but I said, 'No siree, I came into this world with all my parts and I'm taking them back with me.' "

The redhead rolled her eyes and stalked away as Wingate continued. "Anyway, I have to go to the bathroom constantly. Haven't had a full night's sleep for fifteen years. Last night wasn't any different. Well, I've developed a habit. Every night when I have to get up, I put on my glasses—all I need is to trip and break a hip—and I look out the bathroom window. The window's right above the toilet, you see. I could show you if you need proof."

"No, thanks, Mr. Wingate, I believe you."

"Good. Because I'd never lie to the police. Never have, never will. Anyway, around twelve forty-five I saw Mrs. Chandler walking up and down the street. I opened my window and I heard her calling 'Jesse.' That's their dog. Cute as can be, but full of the dickens. I knew the dog had gotten out, but I was in my pajamas and my dentures were soaking—lord, I'm a sight without teeth—so I didn't go out and help her look for him. I wish now I had. Half an hour later, I'm up *again*. I tell you, son, you don't know how miserable that damned prostate can make you. So I'm up, I look out, and I don't see Mrs. Chandler, but I see a police cruiser. I wondered about that. In fact, I lay in bed and worried about it for a while. I wondered if that louse of a husband had been bothering her again. Everything was quiet, though, and I know the guy's basically a coward who probably wouldn't come near the police, so I went back to sleep."

Ray had been furiously taking notes and he looked up. "Is that all you saw?"

Newton Wingate looked offended. "Is that *all*? Hell, I wouldn't have bothered you with that little bit of nothing. No, sir. Two thirty-five on the dot, I'm up again." Mr. Wingate glared at him defiantly. "And don't ask if I'm sure about the time because I *always* look at the clock before I go to the bathroom."

"I believe you. So it was about two-thirty and . . ."

"And I looked out the window, as usual, and I saw someone talking to that policeman."

Ray's attention quickened. "Was this person outside of the car?"

"Yes. The cop was still sitting inside."

"Man or woman?"

"He wasn't parked under a streetlight. I couldn't tell. Didn't get a look at the other face because the person's back was turned toward me. But I can tell you one thing for certain—the person was dressed in black and was a whole lot bigger than Mrs. Chandler."

"Big enough to be a man?"

"Sure. Or a tall woman."

"Then what happened?"

"Then I looked away." Mr. Wingate looked a bit abashed.

"Trying to get myself retucked in my pajamas, not that that's any major feat these days, and when I looked up, the person was gone."

"And the cop?"

"Sitting there, but motionless. Looking down, or so it appeared, but not moving a muscle. I didn't think too much of it at the time. Just went on back to bed." He sighed. "Now I know the poor fellow was dead."

FOURTEEN

1

Nicole huddled in Carmen's car, watching the activity outside. "Do you always have a thermos of coffee in your car?" she asked as Carmen handed her a cup. "Or were you expecting to bring it to me at a crime scene?"

"Bobby doesn't want me to take cream and sugar in my coffee anymore. The weight, you know. So since we take two cars and I usually leave first, I stop along the way, get my thermos filled with coffee just the way I like it, and hide it at the store."

"My goodness, you're devious!" Nicole smiled until she sipped the coffee. "This also tastes more like a banana split than a cup of coffee."

"*Half* that sugar is artificial."

Nicole took another sip of the hot if sickeningly rich coffee, and watched as Ray questioned her neighbors. She wondered what they were saying.

"The street is a mess," Nicole said. "Police cars. Patrolmen. Detectives. The ambulance. I'm glad Shelley's not here to see it."

"You're not going to bring her here this evening, are you?"

"No. We'll go to Mother's."

"That's an exciting prospect. A million questions. Lectures. And as I remember, your mother isn't crazy about Jesse."

Nicole's eyes filled with tears. "Jesse's gone, Carmen. When I got back last night, the padlock on the gate was broken."

"Oh, no," Carmen said sympathetically. "Well, he's run off before and he always comes back just fine."

"This isn't a case of the neighborhood kids letting him out, Carmen. Last night two men were murdered here, and a dog would have been in the way, making all kinds of noise." A tear ran down her cheek. "How do I tell Shelley that on top of everything else, Jesse is missing, maybe dead?"

"You *don't* say he might be dead. He's not."

"How do you know that?"

"Because if the police had found his body, they would have said something. It isn't lying around. Believe me, Nicole, whoever killed that cop and the bum was too busy to bury or hide Jesse's body. Besides, the dog moves like greased lightning. No one gets hold of him unless he wants them to."

"I didn't think of that," Nicole said hopefully, wiping at her wet face. "He *must* have gotten away."

"Sure he did."

Nicole looked up quickly and saw the false gleam in Carmen's eyes. She's only trying to cheer me up, she thought, and it almost worked. "I guess I'll just have to hope for the best," she said tonelessly. "But even if he comes back here tonight, the house will be empty."

"Then he'll keep coming until he finds you." Carmen stared ahead. "Nicole, Jesse being missing isn't your biggest problem right now."

Nicole didn't answer. Ray was talking to Newton Wingate. He'd been a widower for nearly twenty years, and Shelley and Jesse seemed to be his best friends. Nicole thought he was a sweetheart. Roger thought he was senile and a potential child molester.

"Nicole, are you listening to me?"

"Yes, Carmen, and I know Jesse isn't my biggest problem. I haven't lost my wits, as you implied to the police."

"Nicole, I'm sorry. It's just that I've had this idea in my mind ever since you brought up those masks. Or rather, ever since I talked to Bobby about who bought them."

Nicole looked away from Newton Wingate. "What did he say?"

"He said Roger has one. A wolf."

Nicole's facial muscles slackened. *"Roger!"*

"Well, not really Roger, Lisa. But she said she was buying it for Roger."

"Carmen, when *was* this?"

"Before Christmas, before her parents threw her out and she still had some money to toss around."

"Well, it *couldn't* have been Roger out in the backyard wearing the mask."

"Why not?"

"*Roger* wearing a wolf mask and scaring his daughter half to death? It's ridiculous, even for him."

"Maybe he hired someone to do it. Maybe they were supposed to look in *your* window and got the wrong one."

"Carmen, *why* would Roger do such a thing?"

"Because he wants Shelley." Nicole frowned. "Remember what he said to you at your father's funeral when you got in an argument about custody?" Carmen went on. "He said something like 'Don't forget your past emotional problems or the police investigation you went through. I've got a ton of ammunition on my side and I'm going to use it.' "

"I remember," Nicole said bitterly.

"So, I've wondered if he isn't trying to make you look unstable—thinking you see people wearing wolf masks in your backyard."

"Carmen, lots of people have prowlers. I don't think my having one would make me look unstable."

"But lots of people don't think they're being stalked by a guy who died fourteen years ago after murdering two men."

"*Think* they're being stalked?" Nicole returned hotly. "Thanks for having so much faith in me."

"I have all the faith in the world in you, Nicole, but you were *so* traumatized back then," Carmen explained urgently. "Your attack and Paul's arrest were bad enough, but I'll never forget when I called to tell you he was dead. You hung up. When I called back, your roommate said you'd fainted."

Nicole remembered that day. For almost a year she'd waited for Paul to call her, but he never had. Then Carmen told her he'd been killed in a fiery car wreck. The world had turned dark for her that day, and the light had never completely returned.

"Then you came back to a city you hate," Carmen went on. "Roger walked out on you and took up with a young woman half his age, your father committed suicide . . . My God, who *wouldn't* be off track after all that?"

"I am not off track," Nicole said through clenched teeth. "Ray believes me."

"Does he? He didn't sound like it to me. 'Mrs. Vega, there's a *small* chance that Paul Dominic is around.' That's what he said, and it doesn't sound to me like he's too convinced. I think you should stop talking about Paul.''

"Carmen, I *saw* Paul last night.'' She pulled the cross from beneath her sweatshirt and held it out to Carmen. "He gave me this.''

"What's that?'' Carmen asked.

"Something I've been wanting to ask you about. It's a silver and turquoise cross with wings engraved on the back made by your father-in-law. When I was nineteen, I told only you that I was seeing Paul, that I was having this necklace made for his birthday. Yet I saw Raoul when I dropped off Shelley yesterday and he asked if I'd married the handsome young man for whom he'd made the cross with the wings engraved on the back, the young man who was 'a genius,' who 'appreciated art.' He *knew* about Paul, Carmen. When did you tell him?''

All through her recital, Carmen's face had been growing redder. "I'm sorry, Nicole,'' she whispered. "I didn't tell Raoul. I told Bobby a long time ago.''

"You told *Bobby*?''

"Yes. You know how crazy I was about him. I wanted him to admire me. I was so impressed that you were seeing someone like Paul Dominic, and since Bobby was a musician, too, I thought he'd be impressed with you and with me for being your friend. I think it made him see me in a different light—you know, I wasn't just a girl with a good figure, I was best friends with someone who was dating one of the world's greatest pianists.''

"Oh, Carmen, that's pathetic. Why you *ever* thought you had to try so hard to win Bobby Vega's affection, I'll never know. I don't understand why you even believed he was worth it . . .'' Nicole's eyes narrowed. "Did you tell Bobby before or after Zand and Magaro raped me?'' Carmen bit her lip and said nothing, her throat muscles working. "Before,'' Nicole supplied. "And Bobby told Zand. *That's* how he and Magaro knew where to find me.''

Carmen closed her eyes and placed her hands together, as if she were praying. "Nicole, please forgive me. I was so young. I was so *desperate* to have Bobby. I had no idea he'd tell anyone else. If you knew all the circumstances . . .''

"But we'd been friends since childhood. This was a secret,'' Nicole said disbelievingly. "How *could* you?''

"I told you. I was stupid. And I only told Bobby. How could I possibly know what would come of telling him?"

Nicole glared at her. "Does he feel one iota of guilt for telling Magaro and Zand about my relationship with Paul and for what they did with that information?"

Carmen's large dark eyes were pleading. "I'm sure he does."

Nicole smiled without humor. "You're sure he does, but he's never said so. Just like he never said anything about Roger wanting to move out here to chase Lisa Mervin. He certainly knows when to blab and when to keep his mouth shut, doesn't he?"

Carmen drew back, offended. "You can't blame all your troubles on Bobby!"

"Can't I? It seems to me he's contributed quite a bit to them."

Carmen's head dropped. She twisted her watchband, and Nicole knew she was searching for something to say, but there was nothing. Not even Carmen could defend her adored Bobby this time. But she was also not responsible for his actions any more than Nicole was responsible for Roger's. Carmen had told Bobby about Paul when she shouldn't have, but she was only a teenager.

She looked at her friend. Her skin was pale, her eyes swimming with tears, her lower lip nearly bitten raw. Nicole knew she was writhing with guilt, and she hated to see Carmen in pain. Besides, the mistake Carmen had made fifteen years ago was such a tiny thing compared to all that had happened to Nicole later, things Carmen had always been there to cushion with unflagging love and support. At the moment Nicole was mad at the world, but she couldn't let anger and bitterness eat her up until it drove away everyone, including her best friend of so many years.

She reached out and touched Carmen's hand. "It's all in the past, now. Let's forget it."

"You mean it?" Carmen asked tremulously.

"Yes."

"Swear?" she asked the way she used to when they were children.

Nicole smiled. "Swear. But Carmen, I *did* see Paul, and he did put this necklace on me, *his* necklace."

Carmen closed her eyes. "Nicole, you were so shaken up after the mugging, you could have mistaken any man who looked remotely like Paul for him. And the necklace—Raoul could have made others."

"He promised me he wouldn't."

"He might have broken his promise. His Alzheimer's started long before he gave the store to Bobby. He probably forgot he even *made* a promise."

"I'm telling you, this necklace is exactly the same," Nicole burst out. "Why are you so stubborn on this point?"

"Because of how it makes you sound," Carmen retorted with equal force. She lapsed into an imitation of Nicole. " 'Paul Dominic is stalking me. I'm afraid he wants revenge. No, I was wrong. Paul and his heroic dog saved me on the River Walk and Paul put his necklace on me.' It sounds crazy, Nicole. Then you find a dead body in your backyard and you go and make everything worse by arguing with that policeman Waters, talking on and on about silencers and threading gun barrels and nitric acid residue."

"Nitrate residue."

"Oh, who cares? You scared *me*!" Nicole looked at Carmen, whose eyes brimmed with tears. "Nicole, *listen* to me. Don't you know what Roger could do with all this in a custody hearing?"

Nicole opened her mouth, but she had no quick answers. Carmen was right. She had no concrete proof of Paul Dominic's return besides the necklace, and there was no one but her to verify that it was Paul's. What she did have was two dead men she thought Waters would like to prove she killed. Roger *could* use all of this against her in court to get custody of Shelley, especially when he pointed out that fifteen years ago she'd almost had a nervous breakdown and had had to sit out a year of college until she was well enough to return. "What should I do?" she asked weakly.

"First, and most important, stop ranting and raving about Paul Dominic. And *stop* showing how much you know about guns, for God's sake."

"I don't know a lot about guns. What I threw at Waters was just trivia."

"Oh, sure. That's certainly how it sounded." Carmen looked at her earnestly. "It's perfectly obvious what happened. Don't forget that Roger showed up on the River Walk last night and got royally humiliated in front of you by one of your students. A couple of hours later, you got mugged by a guy who Roger probably paid to peek in your windows wearing a wolf mask Lisa bought. Roger saw you out with me. He could have called your

house and, when there was no answer, realized Shelley was staying somewhere else. So he got this guy to break in. He got carried
away and killed the cop DeSoto had posted out here. Then he
came in to do God knows what to you.''

"You've really thought this out, haven't you?" Nicole said
slowly.

"It doesn't take a lot of thinking."

"Well, it all makes perfect sense up to a point. Roger might
have paid Dooley to come in. Then what happened? Izzy Dooley,
in a fit of guilt, shot himself in the head and hanged himself in
my tree, being sure to don a black hood like Magaro and Zand?"

Carmen looked blank. "Okay, I don't *know* what happened
after he got in your house. But something did."

"That's an understatement."

Carmen raised her hands. "Maybe Roger came to his senses
and came to your rescue, killing this Dooley person before he
could kill you."

"And then *hanged* him and put on a tape of Paul playing at
Carnegie Hall?"

"All right, I don't know what happened. Let the cops figure it
out. That's their job. But *please* stop babbling about Paul Dominic. We're dealing with a real, live person here, Nicole, someone
who means you great harm."

"And you don't think Paul means me harm?"

Carmen looked as if she were going to scream. "Only if it's
from beyond the grave. He's *dead,* Nicole. Get that through your
head. Paul Dominic is *dead.*"

But he's not, Nicole thought stubbornly, shifting her gaze. Paul
is just as alive as you and I.

2

In spite of everything, Nicole was determined to teach her two
afternoon classes. "The police said they have nothing else to ask
me now, and I've already had a week off," she explained to
Carmen when she objected. "I went back yesterday. Now I can't
call in and ask for *another* day off. I can't risk this job, Carmen,

not with everything so unsettled between Roger and me, and his barely helping out monetarily!''

"Okay, settle down," Carmen soothed. "Get everything you and Shelley will need for the next couple of days and let's get the hell away from this house. We'll go to your mother's."

"Oh, great," Nicole moaned. "I hate having to face her before I go to school. I'll be too rattled to teach."

"Then my place."

"No," Nicole said quickly. "It's too far away. I'll ask Mr. Wingate if I can change at his house. Tonight I'll stay at Mom's."

"Who's Mr. Wingate?"

"The elderly man who's standing around. He's my only real friend on the street. I don't think he'll mind."

She was right. Newton Wingate seemed thrilled to be of service. He led Nicole and Carmen to his neat little house, tactfully kept the questions to a minimum, then insisted on fixing coffee and chicken-salad sandwiches before Nicole got dressed for school.

Later, as Nicole took her second shower of the day, she tried to think of what lessons she would present to her classes, but her mind had gone blank. A composition class and a creative writing class lay ahead of her. Writing assignments, she thought suddenly. When all else failed, an English teacher could always rely on a writing assignment, even if it wasn't planned.

When she stepped out of the shower and dried off, she spotted a set of scales. She stepped on to see that she'd lost five pounds in the last nine days. Looking in the mirror, she saw cheeks slightly sunken beneath the bones and dull eyes. How much longer could she go on at this rate? She would have to force herself to eat more, maybe even see a doctor and get a prescription for tranquilizers, because she couldn't get sick now. She'd meant what she said to Carmen about her job. Losing it would be a disaster.

For today she'd chosen a lightweight pearl-gray turtleneck sweater to hide the bruises around her neck, bruises left by a strange creature named Izzy Dooley who thought he was a vampire and ended up dead in her backyard. She slipped on the rest of her maroon suit, noticing that the waistband was loose, and brushed her hair, pushing it behind her ears, not bothering with styling.

"Why, you look like a new woman!" Mr. Wingate beamed when she returned to the living room.

"I look like a slightly improved woman. I'm afraid my students can't expect a very dynamic teacher."

"As I remember, I was always glad when occasionally the teacher wasn't gung ho," he said.

Nicole smiled. "I'm just glad I only have to get through two more days before the weekend."

But at the moment, those two days seemed like two weeks.

3

Nicole's in-class writing assignments elicited groans from her students. She tried to explain how they tied in with the work they'd been doing in class, but she had a feeling some of the students knew she was creating busy work.

She returned to her office with a stack of papers that would have to be graded over the weekend. A wonderful thought. At the moment, she couldn't imagine being able to concentrate on them.

Now her main worry was finding a place to stay tonight. "You can't put off calling Mom forever," she told herself aloud. She dialed her mother's number and was surprised when Phyllis answered breathlessly. "Nicole! What a coincidence. I was just about to call you!"

"Is something wrong?" Nicole asked cautiously, wondering if somehow her mother had found out about the murders.

"It certainly is! I've been feeling extremely drowsy most of the time. This morning I had the furnace checked and there's a carbon monoxide leak!"

"Good lord, Mom, you could have died in your sleep."

"I know. I've told Clifton several times the past few weeks we needed a carbon monoxide detector, but he just ignores me." She stopped abruptly, as if she just remembered her husband was no longer around to nag or blame.

"Can they fix the leak today?" Nicole asked quickly.

"Heavens, no! They have to replace the furnace. You should know that." Nicole smiled faintly. Her mother no doubt was absorbing everything the maintenance men were telling her, then spouting it back as if she'd known it all her life.

"Are you going to a hotel?"

"I'd planned to, but then Kay came along and very kindly offered to let me stay with her."

"And you're going to?"

"I hear that note of surprise in your voice. You thought I'd decline immediately because of how much I value my privacy. But I've decided it would be good for me to spend a couple of days with Kay." Her voice softened. "After all, we won't have her too much longer."

Nicole heard her mother's voice tightening. Why couldn't you have reached out to Kay before this? she thought. You both needed friendship. But both women were reserved. It took something drastic to force one to make the first move.

"I hope I don't react too badly to Kay's cats," her mother was saying. "I'm allergic to cats, you know."

"Mom, the allergist told you *years* ago you don't have animal allergies. You made that up because you didn't want me to have a pet, then ended up believing it."

"That allergist didn't know what he was talking about," her mother said firmly. "And speaking of mangy animals, how is that rough diamond of yours?"

"Jesse? Well, at the moment he's MIA."

"Missing? For how long?"

"Since last night."

"You *must* find him, Nicole," Phyllis said urgently.

Surprised by her mother's vehemence, Nicole said, "I thought you didn't like Jesse."

"Well, I suppose he does have a certain brand of charm. Your father certainly thought so. But it's Shelley I'm concerned about. She loves that little ragamuffin. I don't want her suffering another loss."

Nicole's voice thickened. "I don't, either, Mom."

"Are you about to cry over Jesse or is something else wrong?" her mother asked sharply. "I never did ask why you called."

"I was just checking in."

"That's a new one. And not very convincing. You made up better excuses when you were a teenager."

Nicole blinked fast, trying to clear her blurring vision. "I'm just feeling a little down. I thought Shelley and I might spend the night with you, but I guess that's out.''

There was a moment of silence. Why did everything have to be so awkward between her and her mother? Nicole thought. She wished she could just spill every trouble and fear thrumming through her being, then bury her head in her mother's lap and cry. But they'd never had that kind of relationship. Phyllis would either overreact and say she and Shelley needed to be in protective police custody, or she'd go rigid in a way that would make her father, the general, proud. Be a good soldier, Nicole, she'd heard Phyllis say a hundred times. Keep your troubles to yourself.

"You're perfectly welcome to drop by Kay's if you're lonely," her mother said in a businesslike voice. "I'm sure she'd enjoy it."

"No, we'll be fine."

"All right, whatever you want." There was another uncomfortable pause before Phyllis said, "I love you very much, Nicole. You've always been my angel."

Nicole was too shocked to answer. She could only remember her mother saying two or three times in her whole life that she loved her, and she'd never called her by any endearments. "I love you, too, Mom," she managed, "but I think you've breathed too much carbon monoxide." Immediately she could have kicked herself. Who was worse at expressing affection? Her or her mother? "Have fun at Kay's. I'll talk to you, soon."

Well, staying at her mother's was out. It probably hadn't been a good idea anyway. The woman had already withstood too much stress. Then a thought hit her. Her mother wouldn't have to know about the murders at all today if Nicole could control the situation.

Quickly she flipped through her Rolodex until she found Kay Holland's phone number. The woman answered on the second ring.

"Why, hello, Nikki!" she said in a pleased voice. "I was just making up the spare bedroom. Have you spoken with your mother?"

"Yes. She told me about the furnace and your kind invitation."

"Well, I can tell you, you could have knocked me over with a feather when she accepted. I'm just glad the gas didn't build up in the night. It could have killed her."

"I know. It's frightening. Kay, I have a favor to ask you."

"Anything, Nikki, you know that."

"There was some trouble at my house last night. It will be on the evening television news and in the evening newspaper."

"Oh, Nikki!" Kay cried. "What happened?"

"I'm in my office and I don't want to go into it right now."

"Are you and Shelley all right?"

"We're fine. But it's important to me that my mother not know tonight. Can you keep her shielded from the news?"

"I don't get the evening paper and as for the television news . . . well, I'll think of something. But I don't like this, Nikki. You sound awful and so many terrible things have happened."

"I know. But I promise you everything is okay. Just don't let Mom see any news. You'll both know tomorrow. And by the way, tonight Shelley and I will be staying in a motel."

"Nikki—"

"Bye, Kay, and thank you."

Nicole had just pulled out her phone book to look at motel listings when someone tapped on her door. Please, God, don't let that be Avis Simon-Smith, Nicole thought. "Come in," she called.

The door opened slowly and Nicole nearly jumped in her seat when Miguel Perez walked in. She had never really noticed his resemblance to Paul, unless subconsciously. Today his hair was pulled back in its usual ponytail, and his eyes were solemn. "Dr. Chandler, I need to talk to you about last night."

Nicole answered briskly, looking back at the phone book. "There's no need."

"I think there is." Miguel sat down across from her. "Look, Dr. Chandler, I know you're wondering why I was with Lisa."

"Whom you date is none of my business, although it didn't go over big with Roger."

"I date Lisa's friend Susan. The other guy at the table was Susan's brother. I didn't even know Lisa was going to meet us at the restaurant."

Miguel looked at her with misery in his eyes. He was making her uncomfortable.

"Miguel, I told you this is none of my business."

"But you're mad at me."

Nicole tapped her fingers on the table, realizing her coldness could be interpreted as jealousy.

"Miguel, I was shocked to see you with Lisa," she said slowly. "As you can guess, I don't have a high opinion of her. And I have to admit to feeling betrayed—I've been closer to you than any of my students, and you know about my husband's relationship with Lisa. When I saw you with her and it appeared you were on a date, or at least very interested in her . . . well, it was an unpleasant surprise."

"It wasn't a date."

"Fine."

"You still sound mad."

"Miguel, I told you—"

"I know. It doesn't matter to you." He got up, walked to the door, then turned around. "I just wish it did."

Nicole watched as the door closed quietly behind him. Now there was no doubt about his feelings for her. He cared. He cared deeply.

He was also on the River Walk last night. So many things she thought were secret about her relationship with Paul weren't secret at all. She'd learned that from Carmen. If Miguel were interested in her, would he have picked up every detail about her he could find? Would he have looked at old newspaper clippings and talked to people about her and Paul? Could it have been *his* eyes she looked into with her blurry gaze last night? Could he have slipped a cross like the one she'd had made for Paul around her neck? Could he have somehow latched onto the word *chérie*?

And more important, the day of her father's funeral he had been in possession of her house keys for several hours. Could he have had duplicates made?

"Miguel, could you have killed Izzy Dooley to protect me?" she whispered in horror. "Could you be trying to become my next Paul Dominic?"

FIFTEEN

1

Nicole nearly ran to her car, knowing she had to pick up Shelley instead of letting her board the bus for home. She drove faster than usual, hoping she wouldn't get a ticket. She'd meant to leave early, but she'd been delayed by Miguel.

She parked near the school and waited outside Shelley's classroom to make sure she didn't miss her. She couldn't resist peeking through the narrow window in the door to see Shelley gazing out the window. No matter how good a teacher you are, Nicole thought, you usually lose them the last five minutes. She had great respect for Shelley's teacher, and somehow seeing all those nine-year-old faces going blank made her feel better about her own students who tended to mentally drift near the end of the class.

When the bell rang, Nicole watched all the little bodies flood from the room, then reached out and touched Shelley on the shoulder. "Surprise!"

"Mom!" Shelley cried. "What're you doing here?"

"We're not going straight home."

Shelley immediately sensed trouble. "What's wrong?"

"I'll tell you in the car."

The worried look didn't leave Shelley's pretty face, but she didn't ask any more questions. They'd gotten in the car and driven about five minutes before she asked in a tiny, frightened voice, "Why can't we go home?"

Nicole hesitated. Should she make up an excuse? No. Shelley was almost ten. She couldn't hide the truth from her.

"Honey, last night someone broke into our house," Nicole began, deciding to leave out the part about the mugging on the

River Walk. "Apparently someone else was also hiding in there because . . . well, the intruder was murdered."

Shelley looked at her, her eyes huge and vivid blue. "Murdered!"

"Yes. A policeman Sergeant DeSoto had posted outside was also murdered."

"Wow!" Shelley exclaimed. "Didn't anybody try to murder you?"

"No. No one laid a hand on me."

"I'm so glad, Mommy! I mean, if you got murdered . . ."

Nicole looked over to see Shelley's eyes filling with tears and was glad she hadn't told her about the mugging. "I'm just fine, sweetheart."

"Okay." Shelley swallowed a couple of times and wiped at her eyes. In a moment she asked, "How did those people get murdered?"

"They were shot."

"Didn't you hear anything?" Nicole shook her head. "Oh, a silencer," Shelley said wisely.

"Yes."

"Gosh." Shelley stared straight ahead, then suddenly tensed. "Jesse! Did he get shot?"

"I don't think so."

"Don't you know?"

"Honey, he's missing."

"Missing!" Shelley cried, seemingly more upset about her dog than the deaths of two men. Nicole understood. The men were anonymous. The child loved her dog passionately. "Mommy, are you sure somebody didn't *kill* him?"

"I really don't think so. I believe he escaped. You know he can't be caught if he doesn't want to be."

"That's right!" Shelley said excitedly. "I bet he can run even faster than that big black dog."

Nicole went rigid. To her knowledge, Shelley had never seen the Doberman. "What big black dog?"

"The one outside our house the night Daddy brought me home late and you two had the fight in the driveway, and the same one I saw outside the schoolyard at recess today."

"Oh," Nicole said, trying to sound casual. "Was the dog alone?"

"No. It was with a man. He waved at me."

"Did he say anything to you?"

"No. He was too far away. He just watched me."

"Did the teacher see him?"

"No. Mommy, do you think Jesse will be home when we get there?"

"We can't go home tonight," Nicole said distractedly. "The police are still working there."

"Oh, sure. Crime scene."

Nicole looked at her. "Shelley, you sound twenty-five."

"Well, I'm not dumb. Do you want me to talk like I don't know anything?"

"No," Nicole said wearily.

"But what if Jesse comes home and we're not there?"

"Then he'll come back again. You know how persistent he is."

"What's persistent?"

"Good heavens, a word you don't know? I can't believe it. 'Persistent' means never giving up. He'll keep trying. Shelley, about the man at the school—"

"Are you sure he'll keep trying?"

Nicole looked at her daughter's beautiful, worried little face. "Sweetie, Jesse loves you as much as you love him. He won't give up on you after one day." Shelley looked slightly mollified. "Now tell me some more about the man at the school. What did he look like?"

"Ummm, tall. Dark hair. *Long* dark hair pulled back. Like Miguel's."

"Was it Miguel?"

"Maybe. He had on sunglasses, too. But Miguel never said he had a dog." Her forehead wrinkled. "I did hear him say something."

"If you weren't close enough to see his face clearly, how could you hear him say something?"

" 'Cause he said it loud. Not to me. To the dog. He started to leave and the dog stayed. He turned around and said, 'Come, Jordan.' I like that name, Mommy."

"I do, too," she said, thinking. The dog that had bitten Izzy Dooley wore an ID tag with an Olmos Park address. She was certain it was Paul's. Could Miguel also have a black dog named Jordan?

Unlikely but possible, she thought. But whether or not the man with the dog was Paul Dominic or Miguel Perez, what had he been doing outside the schoolyard looking at her daughter?

2

"I don't like this place very much," Shelley complained, looking around the motel room.

Nicole flipped open a suitcase and began removing clothing. "What's wrong with it?"

"It's not home," Shelley said dully. "Did you remember to feed the fish before you left?"

"Yes."

"What if Jesse comes home and he's hungry? There's no food."

"He'll go to Mr. Wingate's."

"Can we go home tomorrow?"

"Well, if we can't move back in, we can at least drop by and see if Jesse's back."

"I don't see why we can't move back in now," Shelley complained, stretching out facedown, head toward the foot of the bed. "Do they have cable here?"

"I'm sure they do." Nicole closed the suitcase. "All right, I think we're all set for tomorrow. Now I have a couple of calls to make."

Shelley let out an exaggerated sigh. "Can I watch TV?"

"Yes, you *may,* as long as you keep it low."

While Shelley listlessly flipped the remote control from channel to channel, Nicole called Vega's. Bobby answered, and without amenities Nicole asked to speak to Carmen. When she came on the phone, Nicole gave her the name of the motel and room number.

"Are you going to have police protection?" Carmen asked.

"I doubt it, although I'm going to let the police know where I am."

"Do you know anything else about the murders?"

"Nothing," Nicole told her. "I'm sure the whole thing will be on the evening news."

"No doubt. Nicole, I'm so worried about you."

"We'll be fine," Nicole said, just as she had to Kay. "It's sort of an adventure, being away from home for the night. Besides, hardly anyone knows where we are. If someone came looking for me tonight, he'd expect me to be at my mother's."

"But what about her?" Carmen asked. "All alone in that big house?"

"She's not home. Seems there's a carbon monoxide leak, and she's staying with Kay Holland. She doesn't know anything about all of this, and I don't want her to. And please, Carmen, don't you tell anyone, either."

"Nicole! Do you think you have to warn me about that? My lips are sealed. But if you need anything—"

"I'll call," Nicole said, knowing she wouldn't. There was nothing Carmen could do to help her. Besides, she didn't want to involve her any more than she already had.

Next she called police headquarters and asked for Raymond DeSoto. "Shelley and I are settled in at a motel," she told him. "Do you know any more about what happened this morning?"

"A little bit, but I don't think I should discuss it now. How about having dinner with me?"

"Dinner?" Nicole repeated blankly. "I'm with Shelley."

"I should have been more precise. Would you and Shelley like to have dinner with me?"

Nicole was so surprised, she found herself floundering. "Well, uh, just a minute." She put her hand over the mouthpiece. "Shel?" The child looked up from the television. "Would you like to have dinner with Sergeant DeSoto?"

Shelley's eyes widened. "He's asking me for a date?"

Nicole couldn't stifle a smile. "He's asking *both* of us."

"Oh." Shelley appeared to be thinking. "Sure."

"Shelley accepts," Nicole said into the phone. "So do I. But we have to be back early because it's a school night."

"I know a great little pizza place. It's rather secluded, and I really shouldn't been seen with you because of the investigation. Would that be all right?"

Nicole ignored her slight hurt over being regarded as a liability. "We love pizza."

"Good. Tell me where you're staying and I'll pick up you ladies around six."

3

Cy Waters stepped into his small home, kicked off his shoes, and sighed. He stood still in the entrance hall for a moment, sniffing appreciatively. Rich smells drifted from the kitchen. Unusually rich smells.

"Cy, that you?"

Aline had been calling this out every evening for the thirty-two years she'd been Mrs. Waters.

"No, it's Sidney Poitier," Cy returned.

"Make yourself at home, Sidney. Dinner will be ready soon."

Cy walked into the perfectly neat if comfortably worn L-shaped living room. Pictures of the three children who had kept this room in chaos for years hung on the walls. Cy glanced at them. Good kids. Attractive kids. Smart kids. And as much as he loved them, he was glad the last one had left to go to college in Dallas last fall. Being alone with Aline felt like they were newlyweds again, and Cy was enjoying it.

Aline, tall, full-figured, and stunningly attractive at fifty-one, walked into the room carrying Cy's glass of tonic with a slice of lime. "Hard day?"

"Brutal."

"You always say that." She sat down beside him on the couch.

"Something smells damned good in the kitchen."

"Beef Stroganoff."

Cy's eyebrows shot near his graying hairline. "What happened to that low-fat, low-calorie, low-flavor stuff you've been starving me on for the past three weeks?"

Aline took a sip of her own tonic. "I thought we needed a break."

Cy closed his eyes. "Praise the Lord."

"Cy, I spend a lot of time on those meals. I'm a nurse. I know what I'm doing. Besides, the doctor recommended that diet for you. He said in a few weeks you'd adjust to it."

"Sure. Bet he wouldn't go on it unless he had a gun to his head."

"Don't be such a grump." Aline touched one of her gold stud earrings absently for a moment, then said, "Speaking of being shot in the head, I heard you had a rather interesting case today."

"Yeah." Aline looked at him expectantly. "Where did you come by that information?"

"I have friends who are married to cops and friends who *are* cops."

"Okay. Today's business was pretty bad." Aline continued to stare at him. "You want to *hear* about it?"

"Might as well. Dinner won't be ready for twenty minutes."

"But you *never* want me to talk about work."

"That was when the children were home."

"No, just two weeks ago—" Cy broke off. He smelled the delicious meal bubbling in the kitchen. He looked into Aline's lovely doe eyes, and he understood. "You know who's involved in this case, don't you?"

She smiled sweetly. "You bet I do, honey. I was on duty in the emergency room when Nicole Sloan was brought in after those two animals almost killed her, remember?"

"Yes."

"Poor little thing was beaten to a pulp. They had to do plastic surgery to repair her face. It really got to me because she was only a couple of years older than our Carrie."

"I know."

"It isn't just that," Aline explained. "There was something about that case that bothered you. You tried to talk to me about it, but I wouldn't listen. The whole thing upset me too much. But I want to hear now."

Cy nodded. "It always bothers me when slime like Magaro and Zand go free. Zand bought that alibi that got him and Magaro off. Everyone knew it, but no one could prove it."

Aline shook her head. "That's not the part I'm talking about. I'm talking about the *murders* of Zand and Magaro."

"All the evidence pointed to Paul Dominic."

"But you had doubts."

"Until he ran. If he was innocent, he wouldn't have taken off like that."

Aline raised an eyebrow. "Cy, I know you. I know something

bothered you even *after* Dominic disappeared. And I know it's still bothering you now. I hear it in your voice. And it's connected to the murders this morning at Nicole's house.''

"Okay, you're right. But can't this wait until after dinner?''

Aline shook her head. ''No. No details, no Stroganoff.''

Cy groaned. ''So that's why I'm getting the good dinner tonight. Bribery.''

Aline grinned. ''That's right. So start talking, honey. I want to hear everything.''

SIXTEEN

1

Village Pizza Inn was small, cozy, and uncrowded at such an early hour on a Thursday. They sat at a table covered with red checked tablecloths. After a deep perusal of the menu, Shelley decided on an eight-inch veggie pizza. Then she pinned Ray with a stare. "Jesse was missing this morning. Is he home yet?"

"Not as of three o'clock, when I was last at the house," Ray said.

"Do you have any leads?"

Ray seemed nonplussed by Shelley's language. "She watches a lot of police shows," Nicole told him.

Shelley nodded. "*NYPD Blue* is my favorite. Are you conducting a search for Jesse?"

Nicole was glad Ray looked at the child without a trace of condescension. "No, Shelley, we aren't as of yet. Today we were working on other things. Besides, he hasn't been missing for twenty-four hours. It's also our belief that Jesse will come home in the next day or two."

"Do you know who killed the two men?"

Ray's dark eyes shot to Nicole. "I told her," she said. "She took it very well, like the brave, grown-up girl she is."

Shelley rolled her eyes. "Mommy, you're making me sound like a dork."

"Excuse me," Nicole said wryly. "I meant it as a compliment."

"I know." Shelley looked at Ray. "Well?"

"You're more demanding than my lieutenant." Ray smiled. "No, Shelley, we don't know yet."

"Any leads?"

"No, ma'am."

Shelley sighed. "After twenty-four hours, the trail gets cold."

Ray burst into laughter. "Shelley, you're a pistol."

"What do you mean?"

"He means you ask too many questions," Nicole said, getting irritated with the child's demanding tone. "Give him a break and be quiet."

"It's all right," Ray said. "Shelley, I meant you're very smart. Do you want to go into police work?"

"I'm not sure."

"She's torn between police work and acting," Nicole explained.

Ray nodded. "Just go to college like your mother did. That would help you in either field."

"But if I don't know which I want to do, how will I know what classes to take?"

"You could have a double major in criminology and drama," Ray said. "It would be unusual, but possible."

"I guess," Shelley said without enthusiasm. Not many nine-year-olds were planning their college majors. "Did you go to college, Sergeant DeSoto?"

"Yes. And why don't you call me Ray?"

Shelley looked at Nicole. "Is that all right?"

"Yes, if he says it is," Nicole said, glad that although the child spouted police terminology like an adult, she at least remembered her childhood manners.

"Where did you go to college, Ray?" Shelley asked sweetly.

He leaned back in the booth, seeming to be enjoying himself. "I went to college in New York City."

"That's far away," Shelley commented.

"I'd spent my whole life in Texas," Ray said. "I lost my mother when I was young and I was raised poor. I'd never even been on a vacation, so when I got some extra money and it was time to leave for college, I wanted to see a different part of the country."

"I bet you're a real good policeman."

Ray smiled. "I hope so."

After they ordered, Shelley asked for money to play the jukebox. Ray and Nicole each offered a dollar bill, and Shelley headed toward the machine.

"She's quite a kid," Ray said.

"That's an understatement. I'm sorry she's so persistent to-night. She's scared about the murders, and especially about Jesse. She's not usually so annoying."

"She didn't annoy me. She's just precocious."

"I know. She gets that from her father. Roger is brilliant, al-though his behavior has been less than exemplary lately."

Ray looked into her eyes. "I'm sure most of her intelligence comes from her mother."

Nicole smiled slightly. "Thank you, but believe me, I'm not brighter than Roger. He's been running circles around me for the past year."

"In what way?"

She didn't want to tell Ray about Roger talking her into a move to Texas so he could follow his girlfriend. It was too humiliating. "He just is, believe me." Ray's eyes probed hers, and she dropped her gaze, sipping her lemonade. "Can you tell me what you found out about the murders today?"

Ray looked over his shoulder, making sure Shelley was still out of earshot. "Don't worry. For Shelley, picking the correct songs is like choosing which wire to cut on a bomb. It'll take her forever."

Ray laughed. "Okay. For one thing, we did find your house keys in Izzy's pocket. That wasn't a surprise."

"But what about the other man? The one who killed Izzy?"

"There's no trace of a second person having broken in. Maybe he came in with Izzy, although that doesn't sound very likely. Maybe he followed Izzy in."

"That doesn't sound very likely, either, unless he was follow-ing Izzy."

"I know. We're still working on that. Anyway, both Izzy and the cop were killed with the same gun."

"An automatic?"

"Yes. Your revolver will be returned to you. We didn't find the murder weapon." A song by Hootie and the Blowfish began to play. "The cop had only one wound—the gunshot to the tem-ple. He died instantly. Izzy wasn't so lucky. All the blood in your hall probably came from the wound in his back."

"His back?"

"Yes." Ray pulled out a small piece of paper from his pocket

and began reading. "According to the autopsy, he was stabbed
with a four-inch blade. We didn't find the knife, either. Anyway,
it penetrated through an inner space in the lower dorsal spine,
transecting the spinal cord."

"Transecting the spine. That would have paralyzed him." Ray
nodded again. "But certainly he would have cried out. Why
didn't I hear anything?"

"There were terry-cloth shreds in his mouth. The killer must
have stuffed a washcloth in it before Izzy got over the shock of
the stabbing. Are you all right?"

"Yes," she managed, swallowing hard. "It's just so awful."

Ray's expression didn't change. "Keep in mind that Izzy might
have killed *you* if someone hadn't gotten him first. In fact, we
think that's what he intended to do. We found a small roll of
eighteen-gauge wire in his pocket. Ten years ago he tried to stran-
gle his father with wire. He probably intended to do the same to
you."

Nicole was astounded and repulsed. "Why wasn't he in
prison?"

"For the attack on his father? He was a juvenile and they
claimed temporary insanity due to drugs. He was out in the streets
in no time. We had another, similar murder a couple of years ago,
which I think Izzy committed, but we couldn't prove it."

"But why would he want to kill *me*? Just so he could rob the
place? There's nothing of any real value in my home."

Ray hesitated, his gaze shifting from hers to the window beside
them. "Nicole, we found three thousand dollars in Izzy's room.
We haven't had any robberies in the past few days where that
much cash was taken. Nor was Izzy at any of the pawnshops
lately. Besides, the money couldn't have been there long or he
would have spent it on drugs. We believe he was paid, probably
yesterday, to kill you."

"*What?*" Nicole blurted, ignoring the couple across the room
who turned to look at her. "But *who . . .*"

"Your husband is the most likely suspect."

Nicole stared at him for a moment, then shook her head violently. "No. Roger and I certainly aren't having an amicable divorce, but he would *not* do something like that. Besides, you don't
have any proof this Izzy person was paid to kill me."

"Believe it or not, Izzy had a girlfriend. Glorious young lady

by the name of Jewel Crown. Honest to God, that's her real name.
I think her mother knew she'd grow up to be either a hooker or
a stripper. We questioned her today. She told us about his being
paid for a hit. I quote,'' he said, his voice suddenly changing,
becoming high and nasal. '' 'On somebody's wife—she's a
teacher or somethin'. She's got a kid, but Iz wouldn't hurt no kid.
Just the wife.' '' Ray resumed his normal voice. "Now, as I said,
this young lady is a prostitute. She's also a coke addict. She's
not your ideal witness, but still . . .''

Nicole couldn't take it in. She felt cold, stunned, but stubborn.
"Ray, I'm telling you, Roger wouldn't *do* something like that.''

"Are you sure?''

Her mouth went dry as she thought of how he'd tricked her
into coming to San Antonio, of how erratic his behavior had become, of how determined he was to get full custody of Shelley.
"Three thousand dollars isn't a very high price to kill someone.''

"For Izzy, three thousand was probably a fortune. We're
checking your husband's bank account for any recent large with-
drawals,'' Ray said, just as their drinks were delivered.

Nicole took a gulp of her lemonade, wishing it were something
stronger, although after last night her stomach rebelled at the
thought. "I still can't believe it,'' she said finally.

"Who else might want you dead?''

"No one. Except maybe . . .''

"Paul Dominic?''

Nicole took another sip of her drink, then said slowly, "When
I first thought Paul was back, I believed he might want revenge
for my wrecking his life.''

"But now you think Dominic killed Izzy to protect you?''

"Maybe.''

"And the patrolman watching your house, Nicole? His name
was Jason Abbott, he was twenty-six years old, and he had two
little kids. Did Dominic kill him to protect you, too?''

Nicole drew back, the breath flooding out of her. "That's horrible. I'm so *sorry*.''

"It's not your fault.''

"I feel like it is, especially if Paul did it because of me . . .''

"You're not responsible for Dominic's actions.''

Nicole knew any good psychiatrist would say the same thing,
but as Shelley returned to the table, she thought of the young

patrolman Abbott's fatherless children. She'd never been convinced Paul killed Magaro and Zand, but if he had, it had been to avenge and to protect her—they had almost killed her, and if given the chance, they might have tried again. If Paul had killed Izzy Dooley, he had probably saved her life. But Abbott? Would Paul have killed an innocent man to maintain his own safety and anonymity?

"Mommy, you don't look so good," Shelley commented when she returned to the table.

"I'm fine, sweetie."

But as she forced down her food, everything tasted like cardboard that wanted to stick in her throat. Someone, maybe more than one person, wanted her dead. And she had a terrible feeling one of them would be successful.

2

Jewel Crown was on her way home after a long, disappointing evening. Not one john. But she supposed she understood it. She wasn't putting her heart in her work tonight. Izzy hadn't exactly been a girl's dream, but he'd cared for her. When she had a bad week, he'd always given her money to get by, to buy enough food and coke to keep her going. And he always said she was pretty. Not like the johns did because they wanted sex. Just because he meant it. Now he was gone.

Jewel hadn't liked talking to the police about his death. Hell, what hooker *did* like talking to the police? And the *way* Izzy had died. God, it made her sick to think about it. It also made her sick that the police took the three thousand dollars Izzy was paid, even though they gave her a little something for her story.

Jewel knew she shouldn't be afraid. She'd told the truth—Izzy *had* been paid to kill a woman, a teacher. He said she was a horrible person, a crazy woman who was hurting her kid, otherwise he wouldn't do it, and Jewel had understood. She didn't like it when kids got hurt by their parents the way she had. The only problem was that she wasn't supposed to know *who'd* paid Izzy, but she did. Iz had told her. Of course, she hadn't told the police who that person was. They couldn't have dragged the name out of her, no matter what they did. But maybe the person who hired Izzy didn't believe that. Maybe they thought she'd blab everything. Maybe they thought that just because she was a working girl, she was stupid. Or greedy, planning on blackmail. Jewel Crown was neither stupid nor greedy.

She turned her foot on a spike heel and cursed. Her feet hurt and her leather skirt and gold mesh top felt tighter than usual. She stopped and took off the shoes. There was nothing she could do about the skirt and top unless she wanted to walk home naked because she didn't wear underwear. The pavement felt cool under her bare feet. She'd elected not to wear the black fishnet stockings tonight. They were Izzy's favorite, but she was in mourning for him, so they remained in her dresser drawer.

Jewel turned down a dark street. She was tired, more tired than she could ever remember. She hadn't slept last night. Tonight she would sleep deeply and she knew Iz would understand. She was on her own now. A few more bad nights like this one and she'd be in trouble. She needed rest to get rid of the circles under her eyes and put some spring back in her step, give her the attitude that made her so popular with her clients.

Something whizzed past her face and buried itself in the sandstone building beside her. Jewel stopped, stunned, until a sharp pain pierced her left shoulder. Her right hand jerked up to the shoulder at the same moment she realized someone in the car opposite her was shooting at her. She dropped to her knees and crawled behind some garbage cans lined against the building. Another shot rang against the metal and she squealed, cowering lower, crawling forward. There were only three trash cans, and the last shot had pierced the one beside her. The next one could—

Voices. "Hey, what's goin' on out here?" one voice shouted. "Shots! Someone's firin' a gun!" yelled another.

The shots stopped. Tires screamed. Headlights disappeared as the car went tearing down the street.

Jewel, shivering and crying and bleeding, huddled behind the cans for twenty minutes before she finally crawled out and ran into the night, leaving her prized spike heels behind.

3

Ray watched until Shelley and Nicole were safely in their rooms. He knew he'd really shaken Nicole by telling her he thought someone had paid Izzy Dooley to kill her, but she had to be told. She had to be convinced that her life was in danger and that she shouldn't trust anyone, at least not Roger Chandler or Paul Dominic.

He had no doubt that Roger Chandler was having a nervous breakdown. His research confirmed what Nicole told him—Chandler was indeed brilliant. But a fuse seemed to have shorted out sometime last year. Ray didn't really believe Roger was so crazy about Lisa Mervin he'd do anything to get out of his marriage. After all, Nicole wasn't contesting the divorce, or to his knowledge, demanding anything except modest child support. Even the house was rented, not paid for by Chandler. But the man *was* determined to possess his daughter. Nicole would never acquiesce to that, and given his behavior, Ray couldn't imagine a judge giving him even joint custody. The only way Chandler could have his daughter to himself was if Nicole were dead.

And tonight he'd learned about a man named Miguel Perez. While Shelley ran ahead to jump in the car after their meal, Nicole told him about the man who'd stood outside Shelley's schoolground, who had waved to her, and whom she had described as looking like Miguel. She'd also told him about her meeting with Perez in her office, when he'd made clear his romantic feelings. Ray told her he didn't know why this man might want her dead, but he'd certainly check him out because if he weren't behind the mess with Izzy, he still might be causing trouble.

Then there was Paul Dominic. Although in front of other people Ray downplayed his belief that Dominic was around—he wanted to appear cool and objective—he knew in his gut Dominic was alive, here, and following Nicole. The question was *why*.

At ten o'clock, two hours after he'd left Nicole at the motel, it hit him—that sickening feeling that danger was near. Ever since he was a boy, he'd experienced waves of near nausea whenever peril lay close by, and he'd always been right.

He headed back for Nicole's motel and stopped the car in the parking lot, pulling into the shadows. He had a clear view of Nicole's second-floor room in his rearview mirror. The draperies were drawn, but he could see light around the edges. She was no doubt unable to sleep. Maybe she was watching television or grading papers. Although it was only ten-twenty, there was little movement around the motel. Someone pulled in, went into the office, then drove to the end of the lot and carried luggage into a first-floor room. A man came out of another room with an ice bucket, went into the alcove where Ray had already located the ice and soft-drink machines, then returned to his room.

Nothing looked out of the ordinary. But something was wrong.

Slouching down in his seat, Ray mentally prepared himself for an evening of surveillance. He could have requested a patrolman, but tonight he felt like handling things himself, even though he'd had a long, tiring day.

He'd thought he was wide awake. Then he saw his mother. She was smiling at him, her beautiful face alight, kneeling and holding out her arms. A little boy, he ran toward her, but the closer he got, the more her features blurred and coalesced until they were no longer beautiful and loving, but heavy and disdainful. His real mother was gone, and another had taken her place, her hand raised, waiting to slap his face or give him a painful pinch.

He jerked awake, sweating. He hadn't had the dream for years. He thought he'd left it behind with his youth. Disappointingly, he hadn't. Or maybe it had occurred only because he'd been thinking about his past this evening when he told Shelley about going to college in New York City. That had been his escape, his first step to freedom.

He looked at his wristwatch. Eleven-thirty. He'd been asleep over an hour. He was furious with himself as he sat up abruptly, looking at Nicole's room. Was that a shadow near the door? He squinted. The lighting was horrible here.

Ray frowned. Damn, he could swear there was something near her door, but it wasn't as tall as a man. A kid playing around? Someone crouching, trying to peek in. No. A *dog*. A big dog sat outside her door.

He grabbed his gun and bolted out of the car. "Dominic!" he shouted, turning in a quick circle, gun raised, and seeing nothing. "I know you're here, goddammit. You're not going to get away this time.'' He started toward the steps leading toward the second-floor balcony, gun raised, as he saw a few lights flicker on in various rooms. ''Dom—''

Something crashed down on the back of his head. Brilliant light flashed before his eyes as he dropped to his knees. He tried to lift the gun again, but consciousness slipped away. He never even felt his head scraping against the concrete parking lot.

4

Nicole turned restlessly in the unfamiliar bed. In her mind, she went over everything Ray had said. Izzy Dooley's girlfriend claimed he'd been paid to kill someone—a wife, a teacher. Would Roger really go so far to get rid of her?

Moonlight sliced through a crack in the draperies. She stared at it, her mind still racing. She'd told Ray about Miguel because she thought he may have been in her house last night. Izzy had her keys, but it was quite possible Miguel had duplicates. He might have killed Izzy Dooley. He might have killed the patrolman Abbott. But why would he have put on Paul's cassette to play over and over until she awakened? To mislead her? To make her believe Paul Dominic had killed the men? But how would Miguel know she thought Paul was back unless he too were following her and spotted Paul? It wasn't as if photos of Paul were hard to find.

But what did all this have to do with her father? Who had been sending the mysterious letters and the photograph of Paul to Clifton Sloan? And what in the name of God could have been in those letters to throw Clifton into the tailspin he'd suffered the last weeks of his life?

Shelley moaned a couple of times in her sleep, tiny, pathetic sounds that tore at Nicole's heart. Each time she got up and bent over her daughter sleeping in the other double bed. Her small, lovely face looked troubled, and Nicole feared she was dreaming of two murdered men or of her little lost dog.

Nicole tucked the covers up to Shelley's chin, as if that would protect her from harm, and crawled back into her own bed. She looked at the clock. Eleven-ten. In nine hours she had to be ready to teach a class. *Three* classes on Friday, and she couldn't get away with writing assignments. She had to get some sleep, which seemed impossible.

Twenty minutes later she was sleeping soundly. No tossing, no dreams. Later she was amazed that she'd been able to slip through REM sleep into the deep sleep of dreamlessness. Maybe that's why it took her so long to respond to the ringing phone. Shelley had already picked it up and was shaking her vigorously on the shoulder when she finally roused.

"Mommy, there's a man on the phone," she said.

"Who?" Nicole managed without opening her eyes.

"I don't know. I never heard the voice, but I don't like it. It's mean."

Good Lord, what now? Nicole thought before taking the receiver. "Yes?"

"Ah, little bird," a rough voice said in her ear. Nicole thought her heart would stop. After fifteen years she knew that voice as if she'd heard it yesterday. "Daddy's not around to protect you anymore, is he? And I haven't forgotten. I haven't forgotten anything you put me and Ritchie Zand through. And you'll pay, little bird. It won't be quick, it won't be painless, but it'll be final, both for you and your *puta* daughter."

The caller hung up. Nicole lay on the bed, frozen, shaking. "Mommy. Mommy, what *is* it?" Shelley demanded, her young voice rising. "*Who* was it?"

"Luis Magaro," Nicole said through chattering teeth. "A dead man."

SEVENTEEN

1

"A *dead* man!"

The raw terror in Shelley's voice pulled Nicole out of her own fear. "Of course it wasn't a dead man."

"You just *said* it was!" Shelley insisted.

"I was half asleep." Nicole realized she was still clutching the receiver in a death grip. She forced her fingers loose and replaced the receiver in the cradle. Then she sat up and pulled a shaking Shelley into her arms. "Don't be scared, honey. It was a crank call. I was barely awake. I didn't know what I was saying."

"But you looked so *scared*!"

"My dream scared me. Baby, it was *nothing*."

"I heard the mean voice. I want Ray," Shelley wailed.

In spite of her own shock and fear, Nicole noted that Shelley didn't ask for her father. Even she seemed to sense Roger was no longer someone to turn to in times of trouble. "Ray is probably asleep. I don't want to wake him up over a crank call. I'll tell him tomorrow."

"But what if that man has Jesse?"

"What would make you think he has Jesse?"

Shelley pulled away from her. "He didn't say anything about Jesse?"

"No. Absolutely not."

A scratching noise came from the area of the door. Both Shelley and Nicole jumped, clutching each other. "It's *him*!" Shelley shrieked. "It's the dead man come to get us!"

Nicole could have kicked herself for uttering "dead man" in front of the child. She'd scared her half to death. "Shel, there was no dead man on the phone. I told you. I was still almost asleep. I didn't know what I was saying.''

The scratching came again. Shelley let out another shriek. "It's the werewolf.''

"It is *not* a werewolf,'' Nicole said firmly. "There's no such thing.''

Again the scratching. The fear suddenly washed from Shelley's face. "It's Jesse! He's found us!''

"No—'' The child leaped from the bed, running toward the door. "Shelley, don't open that door!'' Nicole yelled, climbing from the bed.

"But it's Jesse!''

"No! Jesse couldn't make that much noise.'' Nicole's feet tangled in the covers dragging on the floor. She almost fell as she watched Shelley pull the chain free, then turn the door handle. "Shelley, no!'' she cried desperately.

But it was too late. Shelley yanked on the door. Oh, God, please help me, Nicole prayed as she freed herself from the sheet and floundered forward. She thought she would faint as Shelley swung the door wide, exposing the room to the dangerous night. "God, God, please,'' Nicole heard herself whimpering. "My little girl—''

But the desperate prayer was not necessary. Both she and Shelley stood rigid, stunned, as the big black Doberman pranced through the doorway, sat down, and held out a paw to Shelley. "It's the dog I've seen before!'' the child cried, taking the paw. "It's Jordan!''

Nicole couldn't speak. She simply looked at the dog, dumbfounded. Then she looked at the open door. Who would follow the dog inside? Paul Dominic?

But the doorway was empty. No one seemed to be following the dog, and the dog showed no sign of waiting for someone. It had simply arrived, looking as if it intended to stay.

Nicole ran for the door, shutting it, locking it, and replacing the chain. When she turned, Shelley was on her knees, hugging the dog around the neck. "You came to protect us from the dead man, didn't you, Jordan?'' she asked.

The dog licked her face, then looked up at Nicole with that strange expression of knowledge she'd noticed when she'd seen it earlier. Although her breath still came rapidly and her pulse still pounded in her abdomen, she managed a weak smile. Shelley was right. She knew it in her heart. Danger was near, and the dog had been sent to protect them.

But sent by Paul? How could he know she'd received a terrifying phone call?

2

The next morning, Nicole awakened to find the dog lying between her and Shelley's beds, her big dark eyes open and alert. Nicole crept from bed and kneeled beside the dog, stroking her head and neck.

"Paul sent you here, didn't he?" she whispered. "Is he nearby?" The dog looked soulfully into her eyes. "How did he know I was so frightened?"

"Who's Paul?" Shelley asked.

Both Nicole and Jordan looked at her. "I didn't know you were awake."

"Well, I am. Who's Paul?"

Nicole sighed, too tired to think up a lie or an evasion. "Paul Dominic. He's someone I knew a long time ago."

Shelley slipped from her bed, her little hand seeking the dog. "He was your boyfriend."

"How did you know?"

"The way you said his name. Also, that night you and Daddy had the fight in the driveway, Daddy said you thought he was *likable*, not *lovable* like Paul Dominic."

"You don't miss a thing, do you?"

"Well, you and Daddy *were* yelling."

"Yes, we were. That was disgraceful."

Shelley shrugged. "It's okay. I guess married people just do that. Uncle Bobby yelled like crazy at Aunt Carmen the night I stayed over."

Nicole raised an eyebrow. "You didn't tell me."

"I would have, but I forgot when you picked me up at school and told me about Jesse being gone and the murdered men. But Bobby was *so* mean, Mommy. He said he never shoulda married Aunt Carmen and he only did because of the kid. Jill said that was her baby brother that died. I didn't really understand, but it made Jill cry. Aunt Carmen, too. Then he left. Slammed the door and screeched his tires. Even *his* daddy was crying. Jill said he got scared when Bobby was so mad. I don't like Bobby for making everyone cry.''

''Bobby left?''

''Yeah. Aunt Carmen cried for a long time. Then I fell asleep. The next morning after I called you, Aunt Carmen left. I figured out later she came to our house because of the murders. Bobby took Jill and me to school, but he was a *huge* grouch. He wouldn't let us listen to the radio, and he didn't even say bye to Jill and me when he dropped us off at our schools.''

Nicole realized things were tense between Carmen and Bobby, but she didn't know they were having screaming arguments in the middle of the night.

Shelley crooned over the dog. ''Jordan, do you know where Jesse is?'' She leaned down and looked into the dog's eyes. ''Mom, she does!''

''Shelley, sweetheart, you don't know that. Jordan can't talk.''

''She can talk with her eyes, Mommy, really.'' Shelley sat back on her heels. ''Jordan, find Jesse.''

The dog immediately stood and walked to the door. ''See?'' Shelley squealed triumphantly. ''I *knew* it!'' She ran to the door and began unhooking the chain.

''Shelley, don't,'' Nicole said uselessly as Shelley flung open the door and daylight flooded the room.

The dog licked Shelley's hand, then bolted across the balcony and down the steps. ''Wait!'' Shelley called. ''We can't follow that fast!''

Nicole went to the door in time to see the dog disappear around the side of the building. Shelley looked at her tragically. ''Why did she run away?''

''She probably needed the bathroom and her breakfast.''

''And she wanted to see Paul.''

It sounded so strange to hear Shelley casually say the name of a man Nicole both loved and feared, a man of mystery, a man whose intentions she still didn't know.

''Yes, Paul was probably waiting for her,'' she said softly.

Shelley studied her. ''Mommy, did you love Paul Dominic?''

''Yes, Shelley, I did.''

"More than Daddy?"

Nicole hesitated. "In a different way."

"Oh. I think that means more than Daddy, but that's all right. Was Paul a teacher, too?"

"No, he was a concert pianist." When Shelley frowned, she amended her vocabulary. "Piano player. He played those big grand pianos and wore a tuxedo. He played in concert halls all over the world and made records. He was very famous."

"Wow," Shelley uttered appreciatively. "What happened to him?"

Nicole took a deep breath. "I don't know, Shelley. I honestly don't know."

3

Nicole barely made it to class on time. She immediately quelled questions about the murders, which her students had learned about from television and the newspaper. They seemed disappointed, even pouty about not getting any details, but Nicole didn't care. Her lecture, however, was disjointed, her manner nervous and stumbling. Half the students didn't seem to notice—they wouldn't have noticed if she began talking about Chaucer instead of Melville. But the other half were aware of her unease, particularly Miguel, who took few notes and stared at her intently throughout the class time, making her even more edgy. Was he totally innocent of all the mayhem going on around her, or was he right in the middle of it?

After class she rushed up to her office. She closed the door and called police headquarters, only to be told that Ray DeSoto had not reported to work that day. When she asked the desk sergeant why, he referred her to Ray's partner, Cy Waters.

Oh, no, Nicole thought. She was certain the man disliked and distrusted her. Her reluctance to talk to him grew when she heard his curt, "Waters, Mrs. Chandler. What is it?"

"I was trying to contact Sergeant DeSoto."

"Business or personal?"

"Business," she replied briskly.

"You can tell me."

"All right. My daughter and I stayed at a motel last night. Some time around one-thirty in the morning I received a crank call." Silence. She forged ahead. "The voice sounded like Luis Magaro. He called me . . ." Her voice broke. She took a deep breath. "He called me 'little bird,' just like he did the night he raped me. He called my daughter a *puta*. He said he hadn't forgotten anything I put him and Zand through. He said, oh God, I can't remember his exact words, but something about getting me and Shelley."

She could barely get her breath when she finished. For a moment Cy Waters said nothing. Finally he asked, "You say Luis Magaro *called* you?"

"*No*. Magaro is dead. Someone was doing a magnificent imitation of Magaro, someone who knew what Magaro said to me the night of the rape."

Some of the stiffness left Waters's voice. "Do you have any idea who did this?"

"None. I can't imagine who could capture that voice so accurately, much less know his words to me that night." She paused. "Will Sergeant DeSoto be in later?"

"Mrs. Chandler, last night Ray felt uneasy about you. He sat outside the motel for hours. Then he said he saw something suspicious. He was pretty vague on that point for some reason. Anyway, when he went to investigate, someone bashed him on the head."

"Good lord!" Nicole exclaimed. "Is he badly hurt?"

"Slight concussion. Drove himself to the hospital when he came to, which was a damn-fool thing to do. Did you hear any commotion in the parking lot?"

"No, I didn't." The police are going to think I need a hearing aid, she thought. I never seem to hear anything. Nothing except the scratching of Jordan on the door. But she wasn't going to mention that. If Jordan was there, Paul probably was, too. Had Paul attacked Ray?

"Is Ray all right?" she asked, forgetting formality and using his first name. "Is he in the hospital?"

"Should be, but he insisted on going home. You could probably reach him there."

"All right," Nicole said, suddenly realizing she had no idea where Ray lived. She hoped his phone number was in the telephone directory.

"Mrs. Chandler, give me the name of the motel and the room number." Pause. "Time of the call again?"

"Approximately one-thirty."

"Okay. I'm going to check this out. And by the way, we've finished with your house. You can return this afternoon."

"Great," Nicole said flatly.

"Thought doesn't thrill you? I don't blame you. If anything else happens, let me know."

"I will, Sergeant Waters," she said, thinking that if something else happened, she'd probably have a nervous breakdown.

4

Cy Waters leaned back in his chair. He knew from Ray that someone bearing a strong resemblance to Paul Dominic was following Nicole Chandler. He also knew Ray believed it *was* Dominic. He wasn't so sure. He'd thought for years Dominic was dead. But both Nicole Chandler and Ray were right—they had no definite evidence of his death. Even Aline agreed when he'd discussed the case with her last night.

Now Nicole said she'd received a call from someone imitating Luis Magaro. Cy was relieved there was no doubt in her voice on this point. She didn't believe it was Magaro, a man they *knew* to be dead—shot in the temple, hooded, and hanged exactly like Izzy Dooley.

"What the hell is going on here?" Cy muttered to himself, tapping his ballpoint pen against his teeth. Nicole's father's suicide, the reappearance of someone who both Ray and Nicole were convinced was Paul Dominic, Nicole's prowler wearing a wolf mask, the murders of the young patrolman and Izzy Dooley. Izzy's girlfriend claimed Izzy had been paid to kill someone's wife. If this were true, it appeared the "wife" was Nicole Chandler, and Roger Chandler was the most obvious suspect. But Cy believed everything that was happening now was tied to what happened fifteen years ago. That's what he'd told Aline last night.

"You weren't satisfied with that investigation," she'd reminded him, and he'd told her why.

"One, Dominic was brilliant," he'd explained. "Not just about music, Aline. Do you know he went to Juilliard when he was fifteen? Now, would a brilliant guy just dump a gun and his bloody shirt in a trash can in his mother's yard? He could have dropped the gun anywhere and burned the shirt. Instead, he might as well have left that stuff on his mother's front porch."

Aline frowned. "You're right. What's your second point?"

"Who was the anonymous informant? To my knowledge, no one knows. They had no idea about the credibility of this person. To me the whole thing had the feel of a setup, but Judge Hagan issued a search warrant anyway. I think the guy was getting senile."

"And your third point?"

"The gun. The serial number had been filed out, but they can usually bring that back with nitric-acid etching."

"And they didn't?"

"They said they tried, but the filing was too deep. If it had been drilled, I would have believed them. But filed? I was never convinced they tried hard enough to bring the number back. That serial number could have told us a lot."

"But what if Dominic just bought the gun from someone on the street?"

"That's possible. But as far as his defense went, at the very least, bringing back the serial number could have shown it wasn't registered to anyone in the Dominic family. At the best, it could have been traced to someone connected with Magaro and Zand. Hell, Aline, it was only because of the stuff found at Dominic's that everyone thought their murders were related to what happened to Nicole Sloan. But those guys were slime. You can bet she wasn't the only girl they'd raped, maybe even killed, not to mention all the other dirty stuff the guys in the band were into."

"All of them?"

"Oh, I don't think the others were as bad as Magaro and Zand, but they weren't choirboys. Anyway, maybe their murders had nothing to do with Nicole Sloan."

"But Dominic ran. Why would he do that if he were innocent?" Aline asked.

Cy leaned over and kissed the tip of her nose. "Because the

system doesn't always work. Sometimes innocent people get convicted. I'm sure Dominic knew that. Now can I have my dinner?''

"On one condition," Aline said firmly. "You watch out for that girl, Cy."

"I think Ray's doing his best to make that his job," Cy had said dryly. "Besides, she doesn't even like me."

"That's because you played your hard-nosed, crusty cop routine with her. But I'm not kidding. You look out for her."

"I will," Cy muttered now, a ringing phone bringing him out of the remembered conversation to the squad room. He leaned forward to pick up the phone. "Don't you worry, Aline, I will."

5

Nicole was exhausted after her first class. She felt as if she hadn't slept for a week, and the weekend seemed like a shimmering oasis she would never reach. She had an hour break between classes, and when she returned to her office, she put on a pot of coffee, mocha-flavored to wash out the taste of the abominable cup she'd had at breakfast. As the delicious smell of gourmet coffee began to fill the office, she downed two aspirin, sat down at her desk, and laid her head on her folded arms. She was almost asleep when the phone rang.

"Boy, I *do* need that coffee," she mumbled as she picked up the receiver and said in a thick voice, "Chandler."

"Good morning, Chandler," Carmen laughed. "You sound full of vim and vigor."

"I'm dead on my feet."

"You didn't sleep well at the motel?"

"No." Nicole stood and stretched the phone cord to the table where the coffeepot sat. She poured a full mug. "Someone who sounded like Luis Magaro called last night."

"Magaro?"

"Yes. He said he hadn't forgotten what I'd done to him and Zand. He threatened Shelley and me." She sat back down at the desk. "Carmen, are you still there?"

"Yes." Carmen paused. "Nicole, you do remember that Magaro is dead, don't you?" she asked carefully.

Nicole almost choked on her first sip of coffee. "Carmen, of *course* I know he's dead."

"But you think he called you."

"I didn't say *Magaro* called. I said someone who sounded like him called."

"Have you told the police?"

"Yes. Ray's partner. Ray's out today. It seems he decided to watch my room for a while last night. His partner, Sergeant Waters, said Ray saw something suspicious, got out of his car to check it out, and someone hit him on the head. He has a mild concussion."

"How awful! Did Ray see who did it?"

"I haven't spoken with him, but I got the impression from Waters he didn't know."

"Or Waters isn't telling."

"Maybe. At least Shelley and I get to go home tonight. I guess it's a mixed blessing. I can imagine what the place looks like after the police finished with it. Then there's all that blood in the hall . . ."

"Are you afraid to go back there alone?"

"No," she lied.

"If you change your mind, I'll spend the evening with you. You just call."

"I will," Nicole said, knowing she wouldn't. All Carmen needed was abuse from Bobby for spending more time with her.

After she hung up, she remembered the things Shelley said Bobby had yelled at Carmen—that he'd only married her because of "the kid." Bobby and Carmen had married just a month after Zand's and Magaro's deaths. Nicole had been unable to attend the modest wedding because she was recovering from the first of her plastic surgeries, but she understood the haste. Within two months, Carmen's pregnancy became visible. Four months later, Robert Vega, Jr., was born. In less than three months Bobby Junior died of crib death.

Although Nicole had always known Carmen was pregnant when she married, she never knew Bobby resented marrying her. They'd dated for two years. Carmen told her they'd always planned on marriage. But maybe marriage was only on Carmen's mind. After all, Nicole had heard the rumors of Bobby's indulgence in drugs and groupies while he was with The Zanti Misfits.

At the time of the Vegas' wedding, though, The Zanti Misfits were nonexistent. The band died with Ritchie Zand.

"You're not looking up to par today." Nicole glanced up and saw with a silent groan Avis Simon-Smith standing in her doorway regarding her with her large, dark, baggy eyes. "Being a bachelor girl again getting to you? Too many late nights?"

"Good morning, Avis," Nicole said evenly. "And I have lost a lot of sleep lately, but unfortunately it hasn't been because of romance."

"Oh, that's right," Avis said, snapping her fingers as if she'd just remembered. "You had a couple of murders at your place. I must say, Nicole, you do lead an exciting life."

"That depends on your definition of exciting. Would you like to come in and have a cup of coffee?" she asked reluctantly.

Avis raised her head and sniffed loudly. She wore huge, dangling earrings that suddenly reminded Nicole of floppy ears, and she had an abrupt mental picture of Avis as a bloodhound. Next she'll throw back her head and howl, she thought and promptly burst into badly concealed giggles.

Avis's head jerked toward her. "What's so funny?"

"Nothing," Nicole gasped, unable to get a grip on herself as the huge earrings swung an inch above Avis's shoulders. "Nothing, really."

"You're laughing at me, aren't you?" Avis demanded.

"No, honestly, I just thought of something—" At that moment Avis's large nostrils flared and she stepped forward. Nicole had never noticed how big and wide the woman's feet were, completely out of proportion with her body. Big paws for running through the woods after 'possums, Nicole thought, and lost the last of her control. She tried with all her will to stop the laughter, but it bubbled forth, loud, uncontainable, causing her to choke and tears to stream from her eyes.

"You are *such* a bitch!" Avis hissed, then vanished.

Oh, God, oh, no, Nicole thought, full of remorse although she was still laughing uproariously. Was she losing her mind? She didn't like Avis, but she knew the woman was troubled and suffered from a battered ego. The last thing she needed was to be laughed at, and Nicole would *never* have intentionally laughed in her face—no matter how outrageous her behavior—if she'd been herself. "But I'm not myself," she muttered, reaching for a tissue.

''I'm exhausted, I'm baffled, and I'm terrified, both for myself and Shelley.''

She wiped away the last of her tears and her laughter stopped as abruptly as it had begun. She would apologize to Avis. She would explain to her the strain she'd been under. Not in detail, of course, but enough so that Avis would understand. ''And maybe she'll forgive me,'' she said aloud.

But Avis didn't seem like the forgiving type. Nicole sighed and rubbed her temples, her head beginning to pound, when the phone rang. She picked it up and said hello. ''Is this Professor Nicole Chandler?'' a chirpy voice asked.

''Yes.''

''This is Mindy down at Dr. Linden's office.''

Nicole frowned. ''Who?''

''Mindy. Dr. Linden's receptionist.''

''I don't know a Dr. Linden.''

''You don't? Well, I don't understand that. Please don't tell me you don't know a Jesse Chandler.''

''Jesse?'' Nicole repeated blankly.

''About twenty-five pounds, most of which is unruly black hair, slightly crippled, a bark that could shatter your eardrums, under the impression he's a Rottweiler?''

''*You* have Jesse?''

''Yes, ma'am. He was brought in yesterday morning, and we were told to call your office and remind you to pick him up today. He had a checkup, a penicillin shot for a bad scratch on his side, and a bath, which he didn't like one bit. We're open until seven this evening, Professor Chandler.''

''You say he was brought in?'' Nicole asked, dumbfounded. ''Who brought him in?''

''Just a minute. I'll check the record.'' Mindy was beginning to sound exasperated with Nicole's ignorance of the situation. ''Here it is. Jesse Chandler. Brought in yesterday morning with a request for checkup, bath, medical attention, and boarding until today, when you were to be called.''

''Mindy, *who* brought Jesse in?'' Nicole persisted.

She heard Mindy's frustrated sigh. ''The dog was brought in by your friend Mr. George Gershwin.''

EIGHTEEN

1

Nicole had hoped to get home a bit early and do a little scrubbing on that blood in the hall before picking up Shelley, but the news about Jesse couldn't wait. She drove directly to the school and went to Shelley's classroom. When she looked through the narrow window in the classroom door and saw Shelley's head drooping, her eyes full of sadness and worry, she knew she couldn't wait another thirty-five minutes until class ended. She opened the door and told the teacher Shelley must come with her now. Apparently the teacher had read about the murders because her eyes became large and she said simply, "Of course. Shelley, go along with your mother immediately."

Shelley, too, looked frightened until they got outside the door. "Mommy, what is it?" she said, her voice quavering. "Did the dead man call again? Did someone else get murdered?"

"No one got murdered, and I've told you no dead man called. This is *good* news." She smiled broadly. "I know where Jesse is."

Shelley's mouth dropped. "Really and truly?" Nicole nodded. "He's all right?"

"He's *fine*. He just wants to come home. I'm sorry to pull you out of class, but—"

"Come on!" Shelley called joyfully, running down the hall. "We've got to get him!"

When they arrived at Dr. Linden's office, the waiting room was crowded. Shelley marched up to the desk and said, "We're here for Jesse Chandler."

Mindy, pert, pretty, and not over twenty-one, smiled at her. "Are you Jesse's mommy?"

"Yes, I am. Has he been asking for me?"

"Constantly," Mindy said with a straight face. "Do you have a leash?"

Shelley held up the leash they always kept in the car. Mindy took the leash and in a few moments returned with Jesse. He promptly pulled from her grip and ran to Shelley, yipping until Nicole thought her eardrums would burst.

A few moments later an older, graying man in a white lab coat walked out. "What's all the commotion?" he asked.

"Jesse is a little carried away with himself," Mindy told him.

The veterinarian smiled at Shelley. "Looks like he's glad to see you."

Shelley beamed. "Why don't you take him out to the car, honey?" Nicole said loudly over Jesse's barking. "I'll settle the bill."

Immediately after Shelley had dragged Jesse, still yapping shrilly, out the door, the doctor asked, "Mrs. Chandler, did Jesse escape or do you let him run loose?"

"I *never* let him run loose. My house was broken into the other night while I was out. Whoever did it let Jesse out."

"I see." She noticed the doctor frowning slightly. Then his eyes met hers, and she knew he'd finally connected the name Chandler with the murders. No wonder. The story, along with her picture, had been splashed all over the news. "Do you know how Jesse was found?"

Nicole shook her head. "I didn't even know he was here until Mindy called my office about an hour ago."

"It seems he'd gotten his collar caught on a fence he was trying to slide under. He was frantic and desperately thirsty when he was brought in, and he had a nasty scratch on his side, but otherwise he was unhurt. If he hadn't been found for a couple of days, though, he would have died of thirst or strangulation."

"Oh, thank goodness he *was* found."

"Mr. Gershwin seemed awfully worried about him," Mindy chimed in.

"Can you tell me what this man looked like?"

"Mr. Gershwin?" Mindy asked. Every time she said the name, Nicole wanted to scream. Obviously Mindy had no knowledge of classical music. She might as well have been saying Smith or Jones. "He was very handsome. Tall, dark-haired. Long hair pulled back in a ponytail. *Beautiful* hazel eyes.'' Mindy had a dreamy look on her face. She'd clearly been quite taken with ''Mr. George Gershwin.'' ''Don't you know him? He said he was a friend.''

''I'm not sure,'' Nicole said vaguely.

''Well, he seemed to know you. Even your department at the university, although I had to get your office number from a secretary. He was very emphatic about me calling you at a specific time. He said you would be out of class then.''

''Oh,'' Nicole said weakly, thinking how well he knew her schedule. ''Well, I'm certainly lucky that someone found Jesse. He means the world to my daughter. How much do I owe you?''

''Nothing,'' Dr. Linden said. ''Mr. *Gershwin* paid the bill ahead of time.'' Although Mindy didn't recognize the name, the veterinarian did. ''In fact, he has change coming since we didn't have to do any major repair work on Jesse. Of course there's that leg. It should have been set right after it was broken.''

''He was a stray,'' Nicole explained. ''When I found him, it had been broken for a few days and was already healing. The veterinarian back in Ohio said it was best left alone.''

''I disagree, although he seems to get around just fine.''

Mindy handed Nicole a fifty-dollar bill. ''This is Mr. Gershwin's change.'' She smiled brilliantly. ''And please tell him that if he has any pets, we'd be happy to have them as patients anytime, wouldn't we, Doctor?''

''I should say so.'' He winked at Nicole. ''Good-bye, Mrs. Chandler. I'm glad everything worked out so well for Jesse. And please say hello to Mr. Gershwin. I admire his music tremendously.''

''Does he play in a band?'' Mindy asked the veterinarian as Nicole walked from the office, smiling.

2

When they got home, Jesse jumped out of the car happily, dragging his young mistress behind him. Nicole was glad to see that all the yellow crime-scene tape had been taken down, although she noticed another patrol car was posted outside. Please let this young man have better luck than the last one, she thought.

Shelley asked, "Mommy, will Jesse have to stay in all night?"

"No. No damage was done to the gate and we can get a new padlock tomorrow. Let's let him out to check on all his buried treasures, although I'm pretty sure they're safe."

"Great!"

Before Nicole put her key in the front-door lock, she said, "Shelley, I'm afraid the inside of the house is pretty much of a mess."

"That's okay," Shelley said brightly. "I've seen it messy before."

"It's not just messy, honey. One of the men got hurt in here. There's blood on the carpet."

Shelley's smile faded. "A lot of blood?"

"I'm afraid so."

Shelley was quiet for a moment while Nicole watched her silently bracing herself. "Well, I guess it'll have to be okay," she said finally. "I'm not scared."

But when Nicole swung open the door, she saw an immaculate living room and a pristine carpet, although a new cream, peach, and blue scatter rug lay in the hall.

"I *know* the police didn't leave the place like this," she said in awe.

At that moment, a truck pulled up in front of the house. A young man emerged and walked toward her, glancing at a piece of paper. "Are you Mrs. Chandler?"

"Yes," she said tentatively over Jesse's barking.

"I'm here to install your new locks. Front, side, back doors, and a padlock for the gate."

"I didn't order new locks."

The young man looked at his work order again. "A Sergeant Raymond DeSoto did, ma'am. He said you might want to check things out." He handed her the work order. "His phone number's on there. I'll wait outside." He looked down at Jesse. "Hey there, little poochie."

Jesse let out a tremendous bark and sneezed all over the young man's shoes. "Sorry," Shelley said. "He doesn't like to be called 'poochie.' "

The young man laughed, ignoring his messy footwear. "No

sweat. I don't blame him. So what do you like? Duke? King? *Killer*?''

The young man was still joking with Shelley and Jesse as Nicole went inside and dialed what she assumed was Ray's home phone number. When he answered, she asked without preamble, ''Are you all right? Sergeant Waters told me you were hurt.''

''Well, hello, Mrs. Chandler, lovely to talk with you, too. I'm fine, thank you.''

''I'm sorry to be so abrupt,'' Nicole said. ''I've been worried. What happened?''

''I'll tell you all about it later. Is the guy with the locks there?''

''Yes. I assume you *did* order them?''

''Yes. Isn't that all right?''

''It's wonderful. I've been so busy today I forgot.''

''I didn't mean to be presumptuous, but I wanted the locks changed before you spent a night in that house.''

''Thank you, Ray,'' she said warmly. ''I don't suppose I also have you to thank for my spotless house, too.''

''Yes, indeed. I spent the whole day on my hands and knees, scrubbing and polishing.''

''Ray, you didn't!''

He laughed. ''No. I'm afraid I'm not up to that. I called a cleaning service. I hope they did a good job.''

''Ray, that was so thoughtful! And they did an excellent job. The place has never looked this good. I don't know how to thank you.''

Ray paused. ''When this is all over, you can go on a real date with me.''

Nicole suddenly felt sixteen and tongue-tied, but in a pleasant way. ''I think I could manage that,'' she said, wishing she'd come up with something more graceful. ''You're taking good care of us, Ray.''

''I must warn you, my motives aren't entirely altruistic.''

She smiled. ''Good. By the way, I have another piece of good news—Jesse has been found.''

''No kidding! Where was he?''

''At a veterinarian's. When he was found, his collar was caught on a fence.'' She took a deep breath. ''Ray, the man who brought him in called himself George Gershwin.''

''Oh, no,'' Ray moaned.

"Yes. The receptionist wasn't familiar with the name, but she described him. It was Paul. And there's something else. Jordan was at the motel room last night."

"Jordan?"

"The Doberman."

"Oh, right, I forgot the dog's name. I saw her outside your motel room. Rather, I saw a dog, just sitting there. I thought it was a person at first. That's what made me get out of my car."

"And that's when you were struck."

"Yes."

"I'm so sorry." She hesitated. "You might as well know the dog spent the night with Shelley and me."

"What!"

"Yes. I got a call—"

"Waters already told me about it."

"So, after the call there was a scratching at the door. Shelley thought it was Jesse. She had the door open before I could stop her. It was Jordan."

"And Dominic?"

"There was no sign of him. Just the dog. It was as if she'd been sent there to guard us."

"Dominic is the one who hit me on the head when I got out of the car."

Nicole hesitated. "Are you sure? Did you see him?"

"No. But who else would it have been?"

"Maybe the man who called me pretending to be Magaro."

"You don't think that was Dominic?"

Nicole sighed. "I don't *want* to believe it was Paul."

"After all that's happened? I know he was there last night, Nicole. His dog was, and I have a feeling those two are inseparable."

Nicole caught herself doodling outlines of dogs on a notepad and stopped herself. "I know it should make sense, but it just doesn't. Especially now."

"Especially now?"

"He found Jesse and took him to a veterinarian, Ray. He made sure the dog was treated and Shelley got him back. She's overjoyed."

"Are you *sure* the person who took Jesse to the vet was Dominic? Couldn't it have been that Perez guy?"

"I don't think so. Dr. Linden's receptionist said he had hazel eyes. Miguel's are brown."

"Hazel, brown, they're so close. Nicole, do you know how notoriously bad eyewitnesses are at describing what they've just seen?"

"Yes, but I believe Mindy was describing Paul," she maintained stubbornly. She paused. "Ray, I just can't believe a man who would go to so much trouble to save my little girl's dog would call me and pretend to be Luis Magaro, a man who's lived in my nightmares for years."

A short silence followed. "Nicole, did you ever describe Magaro to Dominic? I mean his voice, the words he used that night?"

"Yes."

"That's what I thought. Who else knows?"

She thought. "Roger. And Carmen. And if Carmen knows, so does Bobby."

"Roger is a possibility, but my money's on Dominic. And I'm not sure it was Dominic who took Jesse to the vet. You are. Let's say you're right. So what? Dominic is unbalanced. He's a *killer*."

"He didn't kill you."

"Do you think your husband killed Izzy Dooley?"

"Of course not. I don't believe he paid Izzy to kill me, either."

"Then who did? Miguel Perez?"

She began doodling again. "That's almost as hard to imagine."

"Maybe your neighbor, Newton Wingate."

She rolled her eyes. "This isn't funny."

"You're damned right it isn't funny. You're getting all soft because you think Paul Dominic found Jesse and took him to the vet. You're pointing out that if he attacked me in the parking lot last night, he didn't kill me. Wonderful. But think about this. If he killed Izzy Dooley, and he *is* the most likely suspect, he also killed that innocent young patrolman, Nicole—put a gun to his head and shot him in cold blood, just to protect his identity. *That* is what makes Dominic so damned dangerous. He's a murderer and he's totally unpredictable."

3

They had unpacked their clothes, the new locks were installed, including the new fence padlock, and Jesse had checked all his buried treasures when a car tore into the driveway, brakes screaming as it halted two inches from the garage door. Roger emerged from the Ford Explorer, but before he could reach the front door, Nicole ran outside to meet him.

"What the hell is this?" he said through clenched teeth. "Two men are murdered in my home and I have to hear it on the news?"

"This isn't your home anymore," Nicole said lamely.

"Oh, that makes a big difference. In God's name, why didn't you call me and tell me what happened? I must have called here a hundred times last night."

"You're right, Roger, that was an awful oversight. It just all happened so fast." Nicole was genuinely contrite that he'd been worried, but she knew last night would have been even worse if he'd known. "I apologize."

"Where were you?"

"A motel."

"Oh, *great*," Roger said scathingly, making a motel sound as bad as a brothel. "Is Shelley all right?"

"Of course. She wasn't even here when the murders happened."

"Oh, well, what was I even *worried* about?" He glared at her. "I want her."

He began striding toward the front door, but Nicole stepped in front of him. "You aren't taking her anywhere."

Roger put his hands on her shoulders and shoved her aside when the patrolman jumped out of the car and strode toward them. "Take your hands off her."

Roger whirled on him. "And who are you?"

"Who does it look like?" the young man replied harshly. "I'm a policeman."

Nicole could smell the liquor on Roger's breath and see people creeping out of their houses to watch. "Don't tell me what to do. I'm Roger Chandler. This is *my* house and *my* wife."

"Sir, I'm not going to tell you again."

Roger shoved Nicole out of his way before he took a step forward. Immediately the patrolman's hand clapped on Roger's shoulder. "Stop!"

"Aren't you supposed to say 'freeze'?"

The patrolman's lips pressed together. "This isn't a game. I said for you to stop and I meant it."

Roger spun, swung at the officer, who deftly darted out of his way, and continued the spin until his fist connected with Nicole's jaw. She staggered and heard Shelley scream from inside.

Roger looked horrified. "Nicole, I'm *sorry*—"

"That does it," the patrolman said harshly. In a moment Roger's hands were trapped behind his back in handcuffs.

"Ma'am, are you okay?" the officer asked.

Nicole's hand went to her jaw. It had been a glancing blow, surprising more than hurting her, but she backed away from Roger. Shelley ran from the house. "Daddy, how *could* you?" she cried. "You *hit* Mommy!"

"I didn't mean to," Roger said in a shaky voice. "I only came to get you."

Shelley grabbed Nicole's hand. "I'll never go anywhere with you again!"

"Shelley," Roger continued raggedly. "Don't be afraid."

"I *am*. I want to be with Mommy, not you."

"Dammit, Shelley, don't *look* at me that way!" Roger blasted.

Shelley's grip on Nicole's hand grew so tight it hurt, but Nicole said nothing. The child was terrified.

"Shut up," the patrolman said. "Roger Chandler, you are under arrest—"

Roger looked flabbergasted. "Arrest? For what?"

"For resisting a police officer, for one. For two, assault and battery on your wife."

"Assault and battery?" Roger echoed.

"Yeah. That's what it's called when you violently attack someone." He looked at Nicole. "You will press charges, won't you?"

"Assault and battery?" Roger croaked again. "That's absurd!"

The cop looked into his eyes. "There are about five witnesses in this neighborhood who don't think it's absurd, and one of them is a cop. Me."

"Are you really going to charge him with assault and battery on his wife?" Nicole asked.

The patrolman looked astounded. "You don't want me to?"

"Ni*cole*?" Roger pleaded.

She stared at him for a few moments, the bloodshot eyes, the hands opening and closing into fists. "Yes," she said firmly. "I want to press charges."

"Roger Chandler," the policeman began again, "you are under arrest . . ." The patrolman finished reading Roger his Miranda rights and left with the eminent professor in handcuffs. Nicole sagged into the house and flopped down on the couch. Shelley cuddled against her.

"Mommy, does it hurt?" Shelley asked, looking at her jaw.

"Not much."

Shelley was quiet for a few moments, then she ventured, "What's wrong with Daddy? Does he act this way because of Lisa?"

Nicole shook her head. "No, baby, I don't think so. I did at first, but not anymore, and it's not fair to blame her. I think he's sick."

"You mean he's crazy?"

"*No,*" Nicole said emphatically. "I think he just got a little mixed-up from so many pressures over the years. His parents pushed him so hard to succeed. Then he worked extra hard in school and got his Ph.D. with honors. Finally he married me and we had you. He took *such* good care of us, Shelley, only I'm afraid I was a little too much for him."

Shelley's face puckered. "What do you mean?"

"I had problems because of things that happened to me when I was a teenager."

"What kind of problems?"

"Things I'll tell you about when you're older."

"I'd understand."

"I'm sure you would," Nicole said gravely, "but I'm just too tired to go into all of that now. Anyway, my point is that I don't want you to blame Daddy for what's going on. He's not himself."

"Who is he? Freddie Krueger?"

Nicole laughed in spite of the situation. "You're not supposed to watch the *Nightmare on Elm Street* movies."

"I've seen 'em all."

"I have no doubt," Nicole said hopelessly. "But Daddy isn't anything like Freddie Krueger."

"Will Daddy go to prison?"

"No. He'll probably be out on bond tonight."

"That's when you pay money to go free, right?"

"Yes," she said vacantly, thinking of Paul. His bond was a million dollars. It had been so easy for his mother, Alicia, to come up with a hundred thousand dollars. He hadn't been considered a flight risk because he was so attached to his ailing mother. But as soon as he was freed on bail, he was gone.

"Will Daddy have a trial?"

"Maybe we can work out something else. I can drop the charges and we can have counseling or something . . ."

"Are you sure?"

"I'm not a lawyer. I'm not sure of anything. But I'll try to keep Daddy out of jail."

I'll try to keep Daddy out of jail. The words rang in Nicole's head when later she looked in the bathroom mirror at her bruising jaw. She remembered Ray telling her the police suspected Roger of paying Izzy Dooley to break into her house, maybe even to kill her. The thought gave her chills and definitely dampened both her guilt and her sympathy. Perhaps jail, maybe even a long prison sentence, is exactly what Roger Chandler not only needed, but deserved, because after all, she had no idea what the man was capable of anymore.

4

Nicole, Shelley, and Jesse cuddled on the ugly couch together, watching television. The carpet was still slightly damp from a professional cleaning, but for the first time Nicole found the smell pleasant. It was certainly better than the smell of fear and death that had filled her nostrils when she left here yesterday.

"I'm glad it's Friday night and we don't have school tomorrow," Shelley said.

"Me, too," Nicole agreed. "I think I'd scream if I had to teach tomorrow."

"Mommy, do you think Daddy's in jail now?"

"No. I think he's probably already out."

"What if he comes back here and tries to take me away?"

Nicole hugged her. "The policeman is still outside. He won't let Daddy in." He won't let Roger *near,* Nicole thought. Not with a restraining order. Lisa had come for his car earlier.

"Could we have some popcorn?" Shelley asked.

"Sure, kiddo."

She had just placed a bag of popcorn in the microwave when the phone rang. Nicole picked it up to hear her mother blurting, "Nicole Marie Sloan, murders happened in your *house* and you didn't tell me!"

"I didn't want to upset you, Mom. There was nothing you could do."

"I could have been there for moral support. But this *person,* this Iggy Dooley, what was he doing in your house?"

"Izzy Dooley," Nicole said, setting the microwave for two minutes. "I didn't invite him here, Mom, he was robbing the place." At the very least, she thought.

"Well, who killed him?"

"I don't know."

"So there were *two* people in your house, one robbing it, one killing the robber, and you didn't hear anything?"

She wasn't about to tell her mother about the drinking, the mugging, the Seconal. Phyllis would be even more appalled. "I know it sounds incredible."

"And a young police officer was also killed?"

"Yes. That was very sad."

"It's awful. It's also awful that you didn't tell me."

"Mom, I—"

"Didn't want to worry me. Kay's been saying the same thing. You were in on this together."

"Mom, don't you get mad at Kay. She didn't know what happened—only that I didn't want you to read the newspaper yesterday evening."

"I'm not going to get mad at her, especially knowing how persuasive *you* can be. She's as much of a pushover when it comes to you as your father was."

The first kernel popped and Nicole jumped. "Mom, I'm sorry you feel betrayed, but I really was trying to protect you. Besides,

Shelley wasn't even here—she was spending the night with Jill—and I wasn't hurt.''

"But you must have been shocked out of your mind. And I didn't even have a safe place for you to come because of that ridiculous carbon monoxide leak," Phyllis snapped, as if she held the leak personally responsible for everything that had happened.

"Is the new furnace in?"

"Yes. I'm going home tomorrow. Then you and Shelley will move in with me."

"We're settled back in our own house, Mom."

Phyllis's voice became shrill. "You are *not* staying in a place where murderers lurk!"

"Murderers don't usually *lurk* here, Mom. Besides, the house has been completely cleaned and we have a patrolman outside."

"That didn't help much the last time. That unfortunate young man."

"I know. I feel terrible about it. I ordered flowers for his funeral, although I don't know how his wife will feel about that—he did die because of me."

"He died doing his duty, Nicole," Phyllis said firmly. "You have nothing to feel guilty about. And flowers are always appreciated."

"Mom, I do have a piece of *good* news. Jesse was found."

"Oh, thank goodness!" her mother exclaimed. "I was so worried about what losing him might do to Shelley. Who found him?"

"I'm not sure," Nicole said vaguely. "He was taken to a veterinarian's, and they called me."

"How did they know where to call?"

"His ID tag." Nicole hated lying to her mother, but she certainly couldn't tell her the truth. "He had a bad scratch on his side, but otherwise he's fine."

"I'm glad. And I'm sure Shelley is ecstatic."

"She is."

Her mother paused. "Well, if I can't talk you into moving in with me, will you at least come to the house tomorrow afternoon, just so I can assure myself you and Shelley are really all right?"

"Sure, Mom," Nicole said, then remembered the bruise on her jaw. Tomorrow would call for heavier makeup than usual and staying out of bright light. "Will you be home around noon?"

"Yes. I'll fix a light lunch." She paused. "And you may even bring that little ragamuffin dog, if you like."

Her mother must really be worrying about them to issue an invitation for Jesse, too, Nicole thought. "I'm sure Shelley would love to bring him."

The corn was now popping wildly and Shelley appeared in the kitchen. "Aunt Carmen's here."

Nicole nodded. "Mom—"

"I heard. You have company. Have a nice evening and I'll see you tomorrow."

Carmen had come armed with some late-edition fashion magazines "which I'm sure you haven't had time to read," and their senior high school yearbook "for laughs."

Nicole took up the popcorn, melted a whole stick of butter in the microwave (so much for calories and cholesterol, she thought), and drizzled it over the bowl. Then she fixed soft drinks and carried everything back to the living room.

Carmen really looked at her for the first time. "What happened to your face?"

Nicole was about to say she'd bumped it on the door when Shelley volunteered, "Daddy was here, shouting and stuff about the murders. He wanted to take me away, and when Mommy wouldn't let him, he tried to hit the policeman and then he *did* hit Mommy. The policeman put him in handcuffs, read him his rights, and took him to jail."

Carmen's lips parted and she looked at Nicole. "Really?"

"I'm afraid so."

"I can't believe it!" Carmen exclaimed. "Well, yes, I guess I can. He's out of control."

Nicole sat down on the couch. "Oh, it wasn't such a big deal," she said for Shelley's benefit. "He didn't mean to do it, and my jaw doesn't hurt at all." Carmen looked as if she didn't want to let go of the subject, but Nicole's voice was firm. "Why didn't you bring Jill?"

"Jill is spending the night with a friend. I thought you might find it creepy being back here, so I decided to spend the evening with you."

Nicole smiled. "It's a pleasant surprise. Just the three of us girls, hangin' out."

"Us girls and Jesse," Shelley said, burrowing between Nicole and Carmen on the couch, reaching forward for the popcorn bowl and offering it to Carmen. She stared at it for a moment then dived in, obviously not worrying about the diet tonight. When the bowl was empty, they turned to the yearbook. Shelley looked at her mother's senior picture—stiff, unnatural, her young face crowned with layered, puffy hair—and laughed. "Your hair doesn't stick out like that anymore, Mommy."

"No. Styles change, thank goodness. You don't know how much time I spent trying to get my naturally straight hair to curl and pouf. I hate to think of how much hair spray I used. Your Aunt Carmen was blessed. Her hair curled all by itself."

They looked at Carmen's photograph. Her hair was indeed full, her face thinner. "Aunt Carmen, you look sad in that picture," Shelley said.

"Yeah, I guess I do," Carmen said softly.

Nicole remembered the day those photos were taken. Carmen and Bobby had had a fight in the morning. Carmen was upset out of all proportion, it had seemed to Nicole. She didn't know then that Carmen thought, probably correctly, that Bobby would immediately turn to another girl.

"Let's look at some more," Shelley said. "Are there any other people in here I know?"

"I don't think so," Carmen told her. "But there are others of your mother and me." Carmen flipped pages. "Here's your mother—the head cheerleader all the boys wanted to date."

"Oh, sure," Nicole laughed. "I sat home lots of Saturday nights. I was afraid I wasn't even going to be asked to the prom."

"That's because your parents scared off everyone," Carmen said. "Boys nearly had to be cleared by the FBI before they could date you."

"Blame that on Mom. The general taught her interrogation techniques that would frighten off the bravest soul."

"Were you a cheerleader, Aunt Carmen?" Shelley asked.

"No, I was in the band. I wore a heavy uniform and hid behind a saxophone."

"Were you a good player?"

"No, I was awful."

"Then how come you did it?"

"I guess I just wanted attention." Carmen turned more pages. "Oh, look, Nicole. Here we are in that Thespian Club play."

Nicole peered closely. "We are? What play?"

"Don't you remember? The principal's son was a drama major in college. He wrote that horrid play about the Salem witch trials, and the principal nearly forced the Thespian Club to put it on. It was long, boring, factually inaccurate." Carmen laughed. "There we are—Witch Number One and Witch Number Two. We had to wear hoods, Shelley, which the real victims of the witch trials never wore."

"Hoods?" Shelley echoed as Nicole felt herself going hollow.

"Yeah. Hoods to symbolize death—we all had to come back and give a speech after we'd been hanged, and the hoods were sort of gruesome reminders to the audience that we were dead. You made such a big deal about it all, Nicole. About the hanging, and especially about the silly hood. You hated it. You were nearly obsessed with it. You threatened to burn yours after the play."

"I'd forgotten," Nicole said weakly. "In the play we were hanged as witches and wore hoods."

Carmen suddenly frowned. Shelley touched Nicole's arm. "Mommy, why do you look so weird? And how come you're so cold?"

Nicole couldn't answer. She simply stared at Carmen and saw one word mirrored in her eyes: "hood." Hoods exactly like the ones Magaro and Zand wore fifteen years ago. Hoods like the one Izzy Dooley wore yesterday morning as he hung from the tree in her yard.

NINETEEN

1

Phyllis half rose from the couch. "Nicole, he's raising his leg again," she said nervously.

"Shelley, take Jesse outside," Nicole said for the fifth time since they'd arrived an hour ago. As Shelley called for Jesse to follow her into the large fenced-in back lawn, Nicole looked at her mother apologetically. "Sorry, Mom. I guess we shouldn't have brought him."

"No, that's all right," Phyllis said insincerely, "but I thought he was house-trained."

"He is. He's only putting a drop here and there to mark his territory."

"Oh, how charming."

Nicole smiled. "Mom, you're making a tremendous effort today, but we'll go soon. I know you don't like animals."

Phyllis shook her head. "I don't want you to leave. I've been so worried about you. And I *don't* dislike animals. Kay finally told me about her illness last night, and I've promised to take her cats when she's no longer able to care for them."

Nicole looked at her mother in shock. "Her cats! *Both* of them?"

"Well, don't look at me in such amazement, Nicole. I do have a *few* warm bones in my body."

"I think they're all warm, although you try not to show it. What about your animal allergy?"

"Apparently the allergist made a mistake. Kay's cats didn't bother me in the least. It might be nice to have them here."

"Pets are a big responsibility."

"I'm not a child, Nicole, I know they are. But what am I supposed to do with my life now?"

"You still have Shelley and me."

"Shelley is getting older. She'll be dating soon and wanting to run around with her own friends. When you get out of this mess with Roger, you'll start dating again, too. The last thing either of you will want to do is spend every Saturday or Sunday entertaining me."

"But what about your friends?"

Phyllis hesitated. "My only real friend was your father. He's gone. I could have been great friends with Kay, but I waited too long to find that out."

"But what about all the ladies in your reading club?"

"Oh, like Mildred Loomis? Good heavens, every visit from her would clean out the kitchen. And she's a dreadful gossip. The others? They're involved with their own families. So what do you suggest? I've explained why I don't want to keep the store. I don't believe anyone is going to hire a sixty-year-old woman who has never had a professional job, who can't even type much less work one of those wretched computers. I really don't see myself sitting here day after day watching soap operas and crocheting doilies."

Nicole smiled. "Some days that would sound like heaven to me."

"That's only because your life is so full and you don't *have* to do it. No, I don't want to drain other people, but whatever I occupy my time with, I want it to be warm and alive, someone, or something, who can love me in return."

Nicole had never felt she loved her mother more than at that moment. She knew how proud of her Clifton Sloan would have been, as well. Nicole's father had adored animals. Maybe that was figuring into Phyllis's offer to take Kay's cats, too.

A thought suddenly struck Nicole. "Mom, before Shelley comes back in, I need to ask something." Phyllis raised a penciled eyebrow. "Do you remember a play Carmen and I were in during high school?"

"The senior play?"

"No. Something the Thespian Club produced. It was a dreadful thing about the Salem witch trials—"

"Oh, *yes*!" Phyllis burst out. "The worst play I've ever seen.

And the gruesome costumes! A lot of pretty girls wearing those awful hoods.''

Nicole grew tenser. "It's about the hoods I'm concerned. Do you know what happened to mine?"

"Your hood from that play? Why on earth would you want it?''

"I just want to know if *you* know where it is."

Phyllis raised her hands. "Well, I made it—"

"You *made* my hood?" Nicole asked in surprise.

"They don't sell glamorous hoods like that in local department stores," Phyllis said dryly. "Yes. I had to make it. On the first try I got the eye holes too low. The second one was all right."

"So there were *two* hoods?" Nicole asked slowly. "What did I do with them *after* the play? Throw them away?"

Phyllis was looking at her strangely. "Why are you so interested in those hoods?''

She's forgotten about the hoods on Magaro and Zand, and she knows nothing about the hood on Dooley, Nicole thought. "Carmen was over last night. She brought our senior yearbook. There was a picture of us wearing the hoods. I'd completely forgotten about it, but I got curious. It's not important."

"I don't think he could squeeze out one more little drop of water," Shelley exclaimed, bounding back into the perfect living room with Jesse, who let out a noisy sneeze.

Shelley looked at her grandmother. "Sorry. Sometimes he sneezes when he doesn't like someone. Sometimes he sneezes when he's happy. It's kind of a problem."

"Jesse has many problems," Phyllis said forbearingly, "but he's still a good boy who loves his mistress."

Shelley beamed. Nicole sat astounded by her mother's good will. Jesse looked as if he were going to sneeze again in pure joy.

The phone beside the couch rang and Phyllis picked it up. She listened for a moment, then said in a tense voice, "Yes, she's here. What's the problem?" Another pause. "Well, I don't see why not. I *am* her mother."

Nicole rushed to the phone and took the receiver from her mother's hand. "This is Nicole Chandler."

"Mrs. *Roger* Chandler?"

"Yes. To whom am I speaking?"

"Mrs. Chandler, this is the Texas Medical Center. Your hus-

band has just been brought in. He was in a bad car wreck and
has serious injuries.''

2

Nicole hung up. ''Roger's been in a car accident. I have to go to
the hospital.''

''*You* have to go?'' Phyllis said indignantly. ''Why?''

''Because he's still my husband.''

''Daddy's hurt?'' Shelley asked, her voice distressed and guilty
at the same time. She thinks I'll be angry with her for caring,
Nicole thought.

''Yes, Shelley, he's hurt. I know you still love Daddy and
you're upset, but I'd like for you to stay here with Grandma while
I go to the hospital.''

''Why can't I go?''

''Because I might have to sit around for hours in an emergency
room, and that's no place for a child.'' Nicole went to her,
kneeled, and put her hands on Shelley's shoulders. ''I'll call you
the minute I know something. Okay?''

Nicole glanced up at Phyllis, who looked as if she'd like to
keep Nicole from going, too, but she only said, ''Yes, Shelley,
stay with me. Emergency rooms are full of germs. You don't want
to get sick, do you? How will you take care of Jesse?''

''I don't want Mommy to get sick, either.''

''I won't,'' Nicole said. ''I'm older and tougher than you.''

''But you got hurt last night,'' Shelley argued, reaching out to
touch her mother's jaw.

Phyllis's gaze snapped to the spot. ''Nicole, I thought I saw a
shadow on your face, although you've tried to keep that side
turned away from me. What happened?''

''I banged my jaw on a cabinet door,'' Nicole said quickly,
winking at Shelley.

But Phyllis wasn't fooled. ''You're so creative, Nicole, I
wouldn't think you'd use the oldest excuse in the book for that
kind of bruise. And you're rushing off to *see* him?''

Nicole stood. ''Mom, he's Shelley's father.'' She kissed Phyllis
lightly on the cheek. ''I'll call soon.''

Nicole drove quickly to the hospital, surprised by how much concern she still felt for Roger's welfare. He'd never been the love of her life, and for the last two months, he'd embarrassed her, deserted her, threatened her, and even hit her. But she still cared. She didn't want her marriage resurrected, but she wanted Roger's health and well-being restored.

As soon as she entered the emergency waiting room, her eyes fell on Lisa Mervin. She sat huddled in a corner chair, her legs tucked beneath her, her long hair pulled over one shoulder so she could comb her fingers through it nervously.

"Lisa?" The girl looked up with mascara-smudged eyes. She was deathly pale and she held her right arm as if it hurt. "Lisa, were you in the car with him?"

Lisa shook her head mutely. "I fell down," she said like a child. "He got mad and went tearing out to the car. I was running after him and I fell."

"Was he drinking?" Nicole asked, sitting down beside her.

"No. But he was so *mad*." She looked away. "You had him arrested last night."

"He tried to take Shelley and he hit me. But he would have been arrested even if I hadn't pressed charges. He also assaulted a police officer."

Lisa tensed. "He hit you *and* a cop?"

"He hit me and he *tried* to hit a cop. Why? What did he tell you?"

"That you had him arrested for coming near the house just to check on Shelley."

"Good old Roger and his lies," Nicole sighed. "Have you had word on his condition?"

"Not yet. I'm not next of kin, anyway. They wanted next of kin."

"How did you know to reach me at my mother's?"

"I didn't. When you weren't home, I called Vega's. Carmen said you might be at your mother's house and gave me the number."

"Oh." Nicole sat down beside her, feeling awkward. The two women in Roger's life, one the wife, one the mistress, and both were worried. What did you say in a situation like this? Nicole couldn't bring herself to try to comfort Lisa, so she fell back on questions. "Where did the wreck happen?"

"At the end of the street. Roger just pulled out of the apartment-house parking lot, went shooting down the street, and didn't stop at the intersection. I saw the whole thing because I was chasing after him since he was so mad and all. Two cars hit him."

Nicole looked at her in amazement. "He didn't stop at the intersection? He'd be pulling onto a busy street. Are you *sure* he wasn't drunk?"

"Absolutely. He just paced around all morning drinking coffee, raving about you and . . . well, how he was going to take Shelley away from you for good because you were a crazy woman and everyone knew it, what with you carrying on about Paul Dominic, who is dead, and those murders at your house . . ."

Nicole raised an eyebrow and Lisa's face reddened. So Roger was accusing her of being crazy and saying that's why he had a right to take Shelley away from her. Hadn't Carmen claimed that was his game plan? To prove her unstable so he could have full custody of Shelley? And the whole thing had started with the prowler in the wolf mask.

"Lisa, I'm going to ask you something and I need to know the truth." The girl looked at her warily. "I want to know about the wolf mask you bought at Vega's. Did you really buy it for Roger?"

Lisa blinked blank green eyes. "Wolf mask?"

"Yes. The heavy Indian wolf mask. Bobby said you bought it for Roger."

Lisa continued to look maddeningly blank. "I don't know what you're talking about." Her voice held the ring of truth.

"I believe Roger might have worn a wolf mask you bought to scare me."

Lisa looked at her as if she were indeed the crazy woman Roger claimed. "Why would he?"

"I don't know. You tell me."

Lisa seemed to draw away from her slightly. "Look, Nicole, I'm not saying someone didn't do that, but if they did, they weren't wearing a mask *I* bought." She frowned. "*Bobby* told you I bought a mask?"

"Yes. Well, actually, he told Carmen and she told me."

"Oh. So you really heard this from Carmen."

"Yes."

Lisa shrugged. "That explains it."

"What are you implying?"

"That I wouldn't believe anything Carmen has to say."

Nicole stiffened. "Carmen is my best friend. Besides, you don't even know her."

"Who says I don't know her?"

"She does."

Lisa huffed. "Carmen has known me since I was a little kid."

Nicole stared at her for a moment before she said, "I don't believe you."

"I don't care what you believe, but when I was a kid, Mrs. Vega baby-sat for a lot of people. I was in the Vega house every weekday. Carmen was always there, drooling around over Bobby."

"Lisa, you couldn't have been more than five when Bobby and Carmen were dating."

"So what? I wasn't deaf and blind. Besides, they lived with the Vegas after they got married. Mrs. Vega didn't like her. She told my mother that Bobby didn't want to marry her, even when she got pregnant. She said although it was the right thing to do and she encouraged him, she didn't think he would have gone through with it if that band Bobby was in hadn't fallen apart."

"Maybe you misunderstood. You were so young."

"It was hard to stay young at my house. My parents didn't believe in protecting children. But I didn't have to be told. Even when I was little I could tell Carmen acted funny around Bobby. She was obsessive. I think she got pregnant on purpose. I don't know what she would have done if Bobby had *still* refused to marry her, pregnant or not."

Nicole sat in silence, torn between further questions and hot denial. She and Carmen had been almost like sisters since they were six. Carmen was the only person she'd told when she was involved with Paul. She was the first person Nicole had called when she'd accepted Roger's proposal, the matron of honor at her wedding, the person with whom she'd been in constant contact during her pregnancy with Shelley, the first who knew Roger was leaving her. Why would she lie about knowing Lisa Mervin or claiming that Bobby said Lisa had bought the wolf mask?

She'd decided to pick up a magazine and ignore Lisa when a doctor appeared. "Are you Nicole Chandler?" he asked Nicole.

"Yes. How is Roger?"

"Not good," he said seriously. "He's being taken to surgery now with a ruptured spleen. He also has a couple of broken ribs on the left side, and a broken left arm, along with multiple contusions and lacerations, the worst laceration being on his scalp. He's lost a lot of blood."

"Is he conscious?" Lisa asked.

The doctor glanced at her. "Not now, but he was for about five minutes."

"Did he ask for me?"

"What is your name?"

"Lisa Mervin. I'm his fiancée."

The older doctor gave her a brief look that all but said he doubted the formality of this relationship. "He never mentioned a Lisa *or* a fiancée." His cool gray gaze fell on Nicole. "He just said over and over that his wife cut his brake line because she wanted to kill him."

TWENTY

1

Nicole sat in the surgery waiting room for an hour, not talking to Lisa, her mind racing. If Roger was not drunk, then the only explanation for his barreling into a busy intersection was that he'd lost his brakes. Brakes rarely failed on their own. Besides, this potentially fatal car crash had happened within twenty-four hours after Roger struck her. It seemed more likely her unknown protector had once again punished someone who tried to hurt her. Roger's car was an easy target because it sat in the open at the apartment complex.

Finally she went to a pay phone and called her mother. She got the answering machine, which Phyllis rarely used. "Nicole," the tinny message ran, "I have taken Shelley out for ice cream. We'll be home around four." After the beep, Nicole left her own message saying Roger was in surgery and she would call again as soon as she knew something.

Hanging up, she was glad her mother had taken Shelley out of the house. The child had been through a lot lately, and hearing of her father's accident had probably upset her more than she'd let on in front of Nicole. Phyllis was trying to divert her in any way possible.

After another endless hour and two cups of bitter coffee, a female surgeon came out to tell them Roger had come through the surgery well and was in the recovery room.

"Will he live?" Lisa asked.

"Unless some unexpected complication arises."

"When can I see him?"

The doctor looked closely at Lisa. "Are *you* his wife?"

"No, I am." Nicole spoke up. "But we're going through a divorce. He'd rather see her."

"Are you sure?" the doctor asked.

"Yes. I'll be leaving now. Let her see him when he's able." Her eyes met Lisa's. "Call me if . . ." If what? she thought. If you need a shoulder to cry on? "Please keep me posted on his condition." Lisa gave her a truculent look that hinted she never intended to talk to Nicole again. "Lisa, Roger is Shelley's father," Nicole reminded her. "She has a right to know how he's doing."

"Oh, all right," Lisa said grudgingly. "I'll call sometime tomorrow."

"Call tonight."

Lisa nodded curtly and Nicole hurried out. How strange it felt to know that she, Roger's wife of twelve years, the mother of his child, couldn't even look in on him because he thought she'd tried to kill him.

And I didn't, she thought grimly as she crossed the parking lot to her car. But someone did.

2

Instead of driving back to her mother's, Nicole went to the big white house in Olmos Park. The place looked as empty and neglected as usual, a monument of faded grandeur, now deserted. But it wasn't deserted. People lived inside. Just how many people, she wasn't sure. But she intended to find out.

She knew in her heart Paul Dominic was back, but she had no one else's confirmation. If he were in San Antonio, though, he would come to see his mother even if he weren't actually living in her house. He had adored her. And they had been so close, Alicia would know if he had killed anyone. She had to see Paul's mother.

She parked in front of the house and strode up the front walk. She thought she saw draperies beside the door move slightly, but she tried to keep her eyes straight ahead. Leaves and dirt littered the wide front porch. At one time it was spotless and plants grew in the giant urns on either side of the double front doors. "I keep a key under the left urn," Paul had told her once. "It's silly—a holdover from my teenage years when Mother watched me like a hawk. You think *you* have overprotective parents! My mother outprotected *both* of yours. If I wanted to have any fun, I had to sneak out and make sure the key was someplace Rosa would never find it. She thought I didn't know, but she searched my room regularly for signs of infractions she could report to my mother. She's never liked me."

Nicole used the lion's head knocker. She could almost feel Rosa on the other side of the door, counting off the proper number of seconds before she finally opened it. Her flat black eyes swept disdainfully over Nicole before she finally asked, "Yes?"

"I'm sure you remember me," Nicole said firmly. "I'm Nicole Sloan. Chandler now. I'd like to see Mrs. Dominic."

The woman stared at her for a moment, almost as if she hadn't understood what Nicole said. At last she answered, "Señora Dominic isn't well enough to see visitors."

"This is very important, Rosa."

Gray threads wove through the heavy black hair, but the style hadn't changed. It was parted in the middle and drawn back in a braid and she wore a long black dress. She looked stolid, humorless, and intractable. There was even a hint of cruel satisfaction in her expression. "I told you. Señora Dominic doesn't see visitors. Especially *you*."

Ignoring the insult, Nicole persisted. "Would you just ask her if she'll see me?"

"No. She won't want to see you."

"Do you have the right to answer for her?"

"Good-bye, Señora Chandler. Don't come again."

Rosa slammed the door.

Nicole stared at the dirty wooden door in front of her, the door whose elaborate carving used to gleam with varnish, and shook her head. "Don't count on scaring *me* off, you old harridan," she muttered. "I *will* see Alicia Dominic before this week is out, even if I have to break into the house to do it."

3

Nicole's next stop was Vega's on the River Walk. She walked into the shop and was greeted by Bobby, standing behind the counter. "Well, hello, Nicole!"

She looked at him coolly. He appeared puffy, tired, and perpetually petulant. And *he* was constantly criticizing *Carmen's* appearance, she thought angrily. "Hello, Bobby."

"How's your loving husband? I heard he was in a car wreck."

She walked to the counter. "He's alive and recovering with Lisa Mervin by his side."

"Ah, young, delectable Lisa." Bobby came close to smirking, and Nicole was certain if there hadn't been a couple of customers browsing in the store, she would have slapped him.

"Lisa told me today you've known her since she was a child," she said.

"My family wasn't well-off, like yours. My mother kept her and a few other children during the days to make ends meet."

"I also know that you knew she was involved with Roger last year and that she's the reason he dragged Shelley and me back to San Antonio. You could have told me before the move, Bobby, and saved me a lot of trouble."

He shrugged. "I stay out of other people's marriages."

"How discreet of you." Nicole's anger grew with his smugness. "You weren't always so discreet, were you?"

Bobby's smirk faded. "Nicole, if you're looking for Carmen, she's home with our daughter where she should be, not chasing around after you, holding your hand through your unending troubles."

"You didn't answer my question, Bobby. You weren't always discreet, especially back in the days of The Zanti Misfits, were you?"

She was aware that a female customer stood with a vase in hand, openly listening to them, but she didn't care. The rage she'd felt toward Bobby ever since she learned he knew about Roger's affair with Lisa long before Roger tore up their lives was bubbling to the surface and she couldn't stop it.

Bobby's face tensed. "I loved that band. It was my future. Ritchie Zand's death was a tragedy."

"Oh, yes, it's always *so* sad when such a fine young man is cut down in his prime."

"Don't be such a smartass about someone you didn't even know."

Nicole leaned across the counter, her face inches from Bobby's. "Oh, *I* knew him, Bobby. You want me to describe how well I knew him?"

Bobby's cheeks were growing red. "Shut up. Do you know how many women would have given anything to sleep with him?"

"I didn't *sleep* with him. He *raped* me. And if someone hadn't come along, he would have helped Magaro kill me."

"*If* he did what you said, it was because he was messed up on something Magaro gave him."

"*If* he did what I said?" She glared at him. "You *know* he did it. He *bragged* about it."

Bobby was almost shaking with anger. Both customers stared at them openly. "You came out of it all right. You didn't need to have him murdered!"

The woman nearly dropped the vase. "I didn't have anyone murdered," Nicole hissed.

"Sure. The lily-white Nicole Sloan would never do such a thing." Bobby's puffy eyes narrowed. "But looking at what's happened lately, I'm beginning to think maybe you *didn't* have him murdered. Maybe you did it yourself."

"And set up Paul to cover my crime?"

"Who knows what you're capable of? Who knows what *any* woman is capable of? I know Carmen would do anything to get what *she* wants."

Nicole slowly shook her head. "I never knew what she saw in you to begin with. Now I wonder how she can bear to be near you."

"Oh, she can bear to be near me, all right. She just doesn't get the chance very often."

"Bobby, you are such a *jerk*!"

"And you are—" The woman had carefully placed the expensive vase back on the shelf and was cringing through the doorway. The man watched her, looking as if he too planned a hasty escape.

"Get out of my store, Nicole," Bobby said with quiet venom. "You're scaring away my customers."

"So I see." Nicole drew back, smiling, her even voice denying her pounding heart. "I'll go if you answer one question for me." He stared at her, his round cheeks now crimson. "Did Lisa Mervin buy one of those Indian masks from you? A *wolf* mask?"

Bobby laughed without humor. "If Lisa had that kind of money, she'd spend it on clothes for herself. She'd never *waste* it on art."

"Not even if she were giving it as a gift to a man who *could* appreciate art?"

"Listen, Lisa's idea of a gift for a man is Old Spice cologne. That's as imaginative as she gets. Check old Roger's medicine chest—you're sure to find a bottle. Believe me, Roger's interest in her isn't her mind. She was a great lay when she was fifteen, and I'm sure she's even better now."

Nicole's face slackened. "You and Lisa . . ."

Bobby smiled. "Don't think you'll get any thrill from telling Carmen. She already knows. Now get out of my store before I call the police."

4

Nicole thought about going by Carmen's, then dropped the idea. She'd already been thrown out of two places today. She didn't have the energy to go for three. Besides, she knew her mother and Shelley would be home, with Shelley anxious to hear news of her father's condition.

The front door opened before she'd even reached the porch. Shelley ran to greet her. "Mommy, is Daddy all right?"

"Yes, honey," Nicole said, bending to hug her. "He's going to be fine. You don't have to worry about him."

"Does he want to see me?"

"Not tonight. They had to do surgery. When I left, he wasn't even conscious yet. Lisa is with him."

Shelley made a face. "Oh, *her*."

"Yes, *her*," Nicole said, not attempting to add something nice, or at least temperate, about the young woman. She was still seething over Bobby's revelation that he'd been cheating on Carmen with her five years ago. The thought that she might one day be Shelley's stepmother made her almost physically ill.

"Did you have ice cream?"

"Butter rum and walnut. Two bowls."

"Two!"

"For my nerves."

Nicole laughed. "I guess that's a harmless tranquilizer."

Phyllis appeared in the doorway. "You look very tired, Nicole. Come in and have some coffee."

Nicole stepped into the cool perfection of her mother's home. She'd never thought of the place as a haven until today. Phyllis insisted she sit on the couch while she brought in a silver coffee service. As she poured, she said, "Now, tell us about Roger."

"He had a ruptured spleen, some broken ribs, a broken arm, and some cuts. The doctor said he'd lost a lot of blood, but he came through the surgery just fine."

"What caused the wreck?" Phyllis asked, handing her a cup. "Driving when he shouldn't have been?"

Nicole knew her oblique phrase meant her mother thought he was drunk. "His brakes failed."

"His *brakes* failed?" Phyllis looked at her closely. "Shelley, would you run out to Grandma's car? I think I dropped my lipstick on the floor and it will melt in the heat." Shelley looked suspicious but complied without an argument. As soon as she cleared the door, Phyllis said, "There's more. What is it?"

"Roger is claiming that I cut his brake line in retaliation for his hitting me last night."

Phyllis folded her arms across her chest and let out a disgusted sigh. "Is there any further trouble that man can cause? What is wrong with him?"

"I don't know, Mom. Maybe he's having a breakdown." Nicole wouldn't tell her mother the police believed he was trying to have her killed.

"I think you and Shelley should move in with me. At least for a little while."

There was no way Nicole was going to bring the havoc that followed her to her mother's home. The woman was sixty and still recovering from her husband's shocking suicide. "Thanks, Mom, but Shelley and I belong in our own home. Besides, Roger is safely in the hospital for the next few days. He won't be paying me any visits, and I don't think the police will take his accusations seriously."

"I'm not worried that the police will believe Roger. The very idea of your cutting his brake line is too absurd for anyone to believe. But those murders at your own home—" Phyllis broke off, shuddering. "How can you stay there?"

"We have police protection, Mom."

"That didn't do any good the other night."

"Mother, I don't want to quarrel about this."

Phyllis gazed at her seriously. "I know why you don't want to come here. You're worried about me. I also know better than to argue with you. It's useless. You've always been so stubborn. But what about Shelley? If you won't come here to live until this mess is straightened out, won't you let her? I truly believe she would be safer here."

Nicole drew a deep breath, thinking. No matter who committed the murders, they were connected to *her,* not Shelley. She was the lure for danger, but by keeping Shelley with her, she was placing her child in the path of danger as well.

Shelley bounded back in the house. "No lipstick."

Nicole made an instant decision and turned to her. "Shel, Grandma is awfully lonely without Grandpa. What would you think about keeping her company for a few days?"

Shelley's face clouded. "You mean leave you all alone?"

"Just for a few days."

"But what about Jesse?"

"Jesse can stay here, of course," Phyllis said, with a look of resignation. Nicole knew her mother would prefer to have him return home with Nicole, but she realized Shelley would probably refuse to stay without him.

Shelley looked undecided. Although she had adored her grandfather, she had always been intimidated by Phyllis. She didn't feel close to her grandmother. At least she hadn't until now. Since Clifton's death, Phyllis seemed to be unbending, perhaps because she had always depended on him to fulfill all her needs for affection and companionship. Now she was forced to turn to others. The result was that today Shelley seemed more comfortable with her grandmother than she ever had before.

"Well, Shelley?" Nicole asked.

"Sure, I'll stay," Shelley said magnanimously. "Don't worry, Grandma. I'll think of all kinds of fun things for us to do."

"Thank you, my dear," Phyllis said in her formal way, although Nicole saw the genuine warmth and gratitude in her eyes.

5

The evening seemed especially long without Shelley. Nicole hadn't realized that even if she were working and the girl was in her room, she was still so aware of her warm, loving presence. Tonight she felt all alone in the world with only the patrol car sitting in front of her house and the television rattling on from program to program that couldn't hold her attention.

She thought about calling her mother to see how Shelley was faring, but she was afraid the child might take the call as a sign of Nicole's loneliness and want to come home. She considered calling Carmen, then rejected the idea. She had a lot of questions for Carmen, such as why she'd denied knowing Lisa and why she claimed Bobby said Lisa bought a wolf mask, but those questions would have to be approached carefully, in person, not blurted out over the phone.

At ten she checked all the doors and windows, glanced out at the patrol car, and allowed herself a wistful look into Shelley's empty room, wondering how she and Phyllis and Jesse had managed during the evening. Two months ago she could not have imagined a more unlikely threesome spending the night together, and she smiled. So much had changed in just two months. She supposed change was what kept life interesting, but right now she would give a great deal for one boring week.

She was just ready to undress and go to bed early when someone tapped on the door. Nicole stiffened, then went to look out the peephole at the same time a man was yelling, "Nicole, it's Ray DeSoto."

Nicole opened the door and Ray stepped in. He wore jeans and a pale blue shirt beneath a windbreaker. "Come in," she said, genuinely happy to see him. "I'm alone tonight. Shelley is staying with her grandmother."

"Really?" Ray said, shrugging out of his windbreaker and smiling at her warmly. "Whose idea was that?"

"Mother's, but it seems wise considering all the trouble that's following me."

"Definitely."

She looked at his handsome, solemn features. "I know you've heard about Roger's wreck and that's what you're here to talk about. Would you like something to drink?"

"A glass of wine, if you have it."

Ten minutes later Ray sat on the couch and Nicole in the chair, each holding a glass of chardonnay. "I hate to get into this, but I assume you've heard Roger's charge that I cut his brake lines," she said.

Ray nodded. "The back lines are steel. The front ones, where about eighty percent of the braking power is, are rubber. A sizable cut had been made in the front so most of the fluid drained out. There was a pool of it where his car had been parked. He'd backed into his parking space and according to his girlfriend, he pulled straight out of the space, then shot out of the lot without even slowing down. If he'd attempted to stop, he would have realized he didn't have much brake power before he picked up speed and reached that intersection."

Nicole's hands had grown cold. "So I'm the likely suspect for doing the damage. After all, if all I would have had to do was cut a rubber line . . ."

"Slow down, Nicole. Brake lines aren't like a rubber garden hose. They're braided and very strong so they can handle high pressure. It would take quite a bit of strength to cut one."

"Are you saying the police think I wouldn't have been strong enough?"

"I'm saying *I* don't think you're strong enough to make a cut like that, even if I believed you would even consider doing such a thing. I *know* you didn't do it, Nicole."

"Could it have happened by accident?"

"No. The cut is too clean."

Nicole took a sip of her wine. "I guess this eliminates Roger as a suspect in the murders of Dooley and Officer Abbott."

"No it doesn't."

"But if the person who killed them tried to kill Roger—"

"*If* it were the same person. The police won't necessarily make that assumption."

Nicole sighed. "I guess that puts me back in the hot seat where Roger is concerned."

Ray leaned forward, looking at her earnestly. "Nicole, *I* believe the person who killed the cop and Dooley is the same person who sabotaged Roger's brakes. And I believe that person is Paul Dominic. The only problem is that I have *no* proof to show anyone else that he's back in town or even alive, for that matter. And without proof, there's not much I can do except try to protect you from him and from the police myself."

TWENTY-ONE

1

The next morning Nicole awakened with a dull headache and a slight sense of disorientation. Confused, she lay still for a few moments before the events of the last days swept over her: her father's suicide; the murders; Roger's near-fatal accident. And along with the memories came the image of Paul. Paul and his dog. Ray believed he was back. She believed he was back. But no one else did.

I have to know, she thought. Maybe I can't be certain whether or not he actually hurt anyone, but I have to be certain about whether or not he's *really* here, or if I've just imagined his presence and managed to convince Ray of it, too.

She sat up in bed, thinking. She must talk to Alicia Dominic. If Paul were here, she alone would know for certain. But Rosa wouldn't let Nicole in the house. She couldn't storm the bastion, knock the woman out of the way, and force herself inside. Maybe Alicia wasn't even in the house. Maybe she was in a nursing home.

No, she's in there, Nicole mused, sweeping back her tangled hair. Otherwise Rosa wouldn't have been so determined to keep her out. If Alicia weren't there, if Rosa were merely maintaining an empty house while its mistress spent her last years in a home, she wouldn't be such a bulldog. But the only way Nicole could get into the house was by stealth.

She looked at the clock. Six-thirty. So early considering how hard it had been for her to fall asleep. Early Sunday morning. Sunday. "Mass!" she said aloud. She remembered Paul laughing, "*That woman* spends so much time at mass, she must have a really guilty conscience. Mass every day. Twice on Sundays."

Nicole bolted out of bed, took a quick shower, pulled on jeans, a blouse, and a jacket, and left the house without even bothering with makeup. She didn't know whether or not the patrolman had been given orders to follow her, but it didn't matter. She could certainly go visiting if she chose.

She drove to Olmos Park and parked down the street from the Dominic house. She sat restlessly in the car for nearly an hour before she saw Rosa, dressed in black, go to the garage. Five minutes later she pulled out in a dark sedan that looked at least ten years old. Nicole slid down in her seat, hoping that Rosa wouldn't recognize her car from yesterday. Apparently she didn't because her car went to the end of the street, turned the corner, and disappeared.

Nicole waited another five minutes just to be safe, then emerged from her car and hurried to the house. She had no hope of Paul or Alicia opening the door if she knocked. She would have to enter by herself, but she'd already planned this on her way to the Dominic home.

Long ago Paul told her that when he was young he kept a key hidden under the urn to the left of the door. Could the key possibly still be there? She kneeled and pushed the concrete urn with all her strength. It tilted slightly and she almost cried out in triumph when she saw a key underneath. She snatched it up and dropped the urn with a thud.

The key was cold in her hand. Cold and shining. Either a new copy was made or the original had been cleaned recently. "Now who would do that?" she mumbled with a small smile. Certainly not Rosa or Alicia.

Nicole glanced around. She didn't see the patrolman. Maybe he hadn't been following her. Or maybe he was merely waiting to see if she were going into the house and lead the police to Paul. She had to take the chance.

Using a key and entering by the front door would not cause the suspicion opening an unlocked window and crawling through would if any neighbors were watching, she reasoned. She straightened her shoulders and tried not to look furtive as she slipped the key in the lock, swung open the door, and walked in.

The large entrance hall was dim, the curtains over the sidelight windows drawn, no lights turned on. Certainly unsafe if anyone, particularly a weak Alicia Dominic, tried to descend the spiral staircase. But then maybe Alicia was beyond such action.

Nicole remembered meeting her three times. She'd been ill with pneumonia during Nicole's relationship with Paul, but he'd taken Nicole into her bedroom to visit her. She'd always rested propped up in a king-sized bed draped with a gold satin spread. She wore delicate, lovely bed jackets and, although she was thin and pale, Nicole thought Alicia was the most beautiful woman she'd ever seen, with her thick, gleaming black hair spread over her shoulders, her sculpted nose, sensual mouth, and large, dreamy violet eyes. Paul looked incredibly like her except for the eyes. ''I inherited those from my father,'' he'd told her. ''My mother said that until the day he died, Dad's eyes were full of spirit and intensity. I don't remember them that way, but then he seemed like a very old man to me and he was extremely distant. I think he was disappointed I wasn't going to turn into a business tycoon like he was.''

How could anyone have been disappointed in Paul? she'd wondered. Alicia certainly wasn't. Her adoration of her son made her almost glow in his presence. I probably glowed, too, Nicole thought, beginning to climb the stairs, certain that if Alicia were in the house, she was upstairs in her bedroom. Roger never made me glow, but Paul did.

When she reached the top of the stairs, she hesitated. The ''ballroom,'' which Paul had turned into his music room, was on the third floor. Family bedrooms and guest rooms were on the second. But the hall stretched to her right and her left, lined with doors. Which was the correct one? She closed her eyes, trying to recall in detail the evenings Paul had taken her in to see his mother. Then she opened them, looked hard down the dim hall to her left, and began walking. In a moment she saw the double doors leading to the master suite.

Nicole stepped into the large, gloomy room. She smelled medicine, rubbing alcohol, and menthol rub. A television sat against a wall, loudly playing a religious show. At the other end was a king-sized bed. Nicole saw no one on it.

''Mrs. Dominic?'' she asked softly. Nothing. Then a bit louder. ''Mrs. Dominic?''

She became aware of bedding rustling. ''Who is that?'' a thin voice rang out. ''It's not Rosa.''

Nicole crept closer to the bed. As her eyes became more accustomed to the dimness, she saw a frail figure slightly raising a bedspread, its head lying beside pillows propped against the head-board.

"Oh, you've slipped off your pillows," Nicole said, hurrying to the woman. "Did you hurt your neck?"

"My neck's fine and I slipped off the pillows on purpose," the reedy voice answered. "I hate religious television shows. Rosa always makes me watch them on Sunday mornings."

Nicole looked down into the face of Alicia Dominic. Only the aristocratic bone structure remained. The rich black hair was mostly gray, the flawless skin dry and webbed with fine wrinkles. Even her beautiful eyes looked cloudy. She frowned, squinting furiously, then said, "Nicole!"

Nicole was so shocked she was speechless for a moment. Finally she said, "Mrs. Dominic . . . I . . . can I do anything for you?"

"You can prop up my head and turn off that damned television. And how about a little light in this room? We're not growing mushrooms in here!"

"Certainly." Nicole gently lifted the woman's small head to the pillows, shut off the television, and opened the draperies a bit. She didn't want to flood the room with light when the woman's eyes were so weak.

She went back to the bed. "Mrs. Dominic—"

"I can't believe Rosa let you in."

"She didn't. I came before but she wouldn't allow me to see you. So I . . . well, I broke in."

The woman's face twisted and Nicole couldn't tell if she were smiling or grimacing. "It wouldn't be the first time you sneaked into this house."

Nicole's gaze dropped. "Mrs. Dominic, as I started to say earlier, I'm not sure how you feel about me—"

"My Paul loved you."

"Yes, at one time."

"No. Still."

Nicole's heart quickened. "Still?"

"Forever. I loved like that once."

"You did? Your husband?"

"He was much older than I," Alicia said, her gaze wandering. "We married when I was eighteen. Arthur was forty-nine. He was my father's business partner. My father wanted the marriage. I loved my father so much."

"I see."

"Arthur tried to make me happy. He loved me." She beamed, showing slightly yellowed teeth. "And he gave me Paul." She reached out and grabbed Nicole's hand. "Wasn't Paul magnificent?"

"Oh, yes," Nicole breathed.

"He was my world. My beautiful boy. So good. So loving. So talented. Have you ever heard Paul play the piano?"

She was drifting, Nicole thought, although her eyes were still open. "Yes, Mrs. Dominic, I've heard him play."

"A genius, my boy. A gift from heaven. I admired Arthur," Alicia rambled on. "A good man, a good husband. And with Paul, I was happy. And then I met *him*."

"Him?" Nicole asked, baffled.

"Arthur was gone so much. I met Javier. He was *so* handsome. Younger than I. At first I tried to make him go away."

Alicia lay quietly for a few moments, her mind skimming back over the years. "Did you fall in love with Javier?" Nicole prompted.

Alicia fingered a rosary held in her frail hands, her eyes filling with tears. "Yes. And I made such a mistake."

An affair, obviously, Nicole thought. Paul had once told Nicole his mother was deeply religious. She must have suffered over the affair for years. Maybe guilt was responsible for the chronic bad health, the premature aging.

"God made me pay," Alicia began again, tears running down her face. "I tried to make amends, but it didn't work because I was still lying, still hiding. He hates me, you know."

"I thought God didn't hate anyone," Nicole said.

"Not God. *He* doesn't hate me. But He does punish, you know. I've been punished. He doesn't let you get away with things."

Nicole stroked her hand. "Mrs. Dominic, I'm sorry about Paul being charged with murder and then . . . going away."

"That wasn't the beginning. I've been punished ever since Javier. I tried to do the right thing. No, no, that's not honest. I tried to eat my cake and have it, too. So I was doubly punished. The other one . . ." She shook her head. "Could I have done something for him to change things?"

"Mrs. Dominic, I don't know what you're talking about," Nicole said gently. "Who's 'the other one'? Javier?"

"I can't talk about him. No, no, I can't talk about him except with my priest." She looked at Nicole who saw clarity come back into the woman's fogged eyes. "Rosa won't like it if she finds you here. She never did like you. *I* did." She reached up and delicately touched Nicole's face. "So perfect for my Paul."

Nicole swallowed hard, trying to control her sorrow, her guilt. "Mrs. Dominic, I came here to talk about Paul. Is he alive?"

The woman's gaze shifted and she chanted, "My son died in a car wreck a long time ago."

"I know a lot of people believe that, but it seems to me I've seen him. He's always with a dog."

Alicia smiled slightly. "The dog? The big black . . ." Her eyes widened and the parrot tone returned. "My son died in a car wreck a long time ago."

"Please, Mrs. Dominic," Nicole begged. "I need some answers. Your son comes to see you, doesn't he?"

"Why, just last night—" The woman caught herself again. Her head turned and the eyes looked directly into Nicole's. "Did the police send you?"

"No. They don't even believe Paul's alive. I only came for myself. Anything you tell me is just between us. Believe me, Mrs. Dominic, you can trust me, even though you might hate me."

Alicia's face twisted into that unrecognizable expression. "I don't hate you. I don't understand what happened—it's not clear anymore. My memory, you know . . . But I remember that you're good. I see goodness in your eyes. I always have."

Nicole smiled weakly. "Thank you, Mrs. Dominic. You don't know what that means to me. All these years I've thought you must blame me for what happened to Paul. I'm sorry. I never meant to hurt him. I would have died before I intentionally hurt him. The situation spiraled out of my control. But I must know the truth about Paul now."

"My son died in a car wreck—"

"Please stop saying that! I haven't believed for quite a while that Paul is dead. I know he has a big black Doberman named Jordan. He's been to see you, you can't deny it. I just need to know how *he* feels about me. Does *he* hate me?"

Alicia looked away. "If I'd just owned up to what I'd done, maybe everything would have been different. We must own up to our sins, you know. And upbringing is so important. I failed him, and I was punished."

"You failed Paul?"

"Everyone," Alicia said irritably. "The other one. He was involved—I know it. I've always known it."

"Mrs. Dominic, I don't know what you're talking about. Please explain."

She looked at Nicole. "You have a little girl with the name of a poet."

"Yes. Shelley." She paused. "How did you know that?"

Alicia's eyes circled the room lazily. "For a long time I didn't know about Paul." Her eyes filled with tears. "They told me he was dead."

"But now you know that's not true, don't you?" Nicole asked eagerly.

"My son died—"

"Mrs. Dominic, *please*!"

The woman looked cowed. "It's what I'm supposed to say."

"I understand," Nicole said gently, angry with herself for speaking harshly to Alicia.

"What are *you* doing in here?"

Nicole and Mrs. Dominic both jumped as Rosa tromped in, heavy browed, unsmiling, her eyes brimming with hostility.

Nicole stood up. "I told you yesterday I needed to see Mrs. Dominic."

"And I told you she doesn't receive visitors." Her eyes narrowed. "You broke in here! You always were a sneaky little tramp who thought she could do what she pleased. Well, not this time. I'm calling the police and having you arrested for breaking and entering!"

"*No.*" Rosa turned back and looked at Mrs. Dominic who was struggling to sit up in bed. "You will not call the police."

"This woman, this *slut* who ruined your son's life, has broken into *your* house—"

"Yes, *my* house," Mrs. Dominic said forcefully, sounding much the way she had fifteen years ago even though Nicole could see the effort it was taking. "A judge hasn't declared me incompetent and you are not my guardian. *I* give the orders here, and I'm telling you no police will be called."

Rosa glowered at her, then at Nicole, who put her hand on Alicia's arm. "I'm leaving now, Mrs. Dominic. Thank you for speaking with me."

She started toward the door, the heavy, bull-like Rosa breathing loudly behind her when Alicia called, "Nicole?" She turned. "Remember, some loves are forever."

2

As Nicole drove home, she thought about her talk with Mrs. Dominic. The woman had been visited probably as recently as last night by her son. Her love for Paul was clearly unqualified. But who was "the other one" to whom she disdainfully referred? The mysterious Javier, the man she'd loved and maybe spurned?

Nicole shook her head. The visit had answered two important questions. Paul was definitely in San Antonio and still cared for her. But it had also raised more questions than it had answered.

When Nicole reached home, she was dismayed to see Carmen's car in her driveway and Carmen sitting on her front porch. Normally she was always glad to see her friend, but today she had a lot of disturbing questions to ask Carmen and she already felt drained by her visit to Alicia Dominic.

She took a deep breath and forced a smile. "Good morning, Carmen."

"I've had warmer greetings." Carmen studied Nicole's face. "And you're not looking up to par."

"No makeup and a rough couple of weeks." She withdrew her keys from her purse. "Why are you here so early?"

"Your mother tried to reach you several times earlier. When she couldn't, she called me."

"Is something wrong?"

"No. She said Shelley wanted to say hello to you, but when they couldn't reach you, your mother got alarmed. After the last gory disaster here, she didn't want to come by with Shelley, so she asked me to come."

"I'm sorry, Carmen. What a millstone I've become to everyone."

"No you're not. And it was no trouble for me to come this morning. Bobby took Jill to church. By the way, your mother told me about Roger's wreck."

"Which he claims I caused." Carmen looked blank and Nicole

knew her mother hadn't given her the details. She opened the door and motioned for Carmen to enter. "He thinks I cut his brake line."

"That's crazy!" Carmen exploded. "He was probably drunk."

"No he wasn't. Ray came by last night and said the front line *was* cut."

Carmen's face sagged. "You're kidding."

"Hardly."

"Well, the police can't believe you had anything to do with cutting it."

"Ray doesn't. I don't know what everyone else thinks. I'm beginning not to care. Have a seat. I'll put on some coffee, then call the hospital. Lisa said she'd call last night with word on Roger's condition, but she didn't."

"Big surprise," Carmen muttered, sitting down on the couch. "She's so reliable and considerate."

While the coffee brewed, Nicole called the hospital and was told Roger was in stable condition although he remained extremely agitated. Next she called her mother and gave the excuse of going for a drive for her absence early in the morning. "My, you've been going for a lot of drives lately," Phyllis said dryly, and Nicole immediately remembered she'd used that excuse before. Quickly changing the subject, she described Roger's condition, spoke to Shelley, reassuring her that her father would be fine, and promised to call back later.

When she hung up the phone, the coffee was ready. She placed cups along with cream and sugar on a tray. At the last minute, she added a few cookies on a saucer. She hadn't eaten any breakfast and her stomach was growling.

"So, how is the charming Roger?" Carmen asked as Nicole carried a tray into the living room.

"Stable."

"I assume you mean physically, not mentally. I suppose Lisa's sticking to him like glue."

"Probably." She braced herself and decided if she didn't bring up the subject of Lisa abruptly, she might lose her nerve and not get around to it at all. "Carmen, speaking of Lisa, we sat in the hospital waiting room yesterday while Roger was in surgery. We talked."

"That must have been interesting."

"It was. She told me you've known her since she was little."

Carmen had been stirring sugar in her coffee. The spoon abruptly stopped spinning. *"What?"*

"She said Bobby's mother baby-sat for her. That's how the Vegas and the Mervins became friends. According to her, she was around all the time when you were dating Bobby and after you were married and living with the Vegas. Carmen, you said you didn't know her."

"I *don't*. I mean, maybe Bobby's mother did baby-sit for her, but she would have been a child. Besides, she baby-sat for several children. I never paid much attention to them. First I was a teenager all wrapped up in Bobby. After we were married, I was pregnant, then the baby died. I honestly don't remember her or any of the other kids. They were just a mass of little anonymous faces to me."

Nicole reached for a cookie, thinking about what Carmen had said. Hadn't she told Lisa the same thing—that she was only a child when Carmen was around her? No doubt Lisa's appearance had changed radically during adolescence. And when they were teenagers and Carmen was seeing Bobby, she'd never mentioned by name any of the kids for whom Mrs. Vega baby-sat.

Carmen was staring at her. "What's the matter? Don't you believe me?"

"Yes, I believe you, Carmen."

"You sound strange. What else is wrong?"

Nicole took a bite of cookie although her hunger was gone, her stomach churning with tension. Should she even mention the other thing? She didn't want to offend Carmen, but she had to have an answer to Lisa's accusations. She took a deep breath. "Lisa also said she never bought a wolf mask. You told me she did."

Carmen's eyes widened. "But she did! Bobby said so."

"He told me she didn't."

"But he told *me* she did. You misunderstood him."

Nicole sighed. "No, I didn't. Someone is lying."

Carmen set down her mug with a crash. "Nicole Sloan, how dare you! First you accuse me of lying about knowing Lisa, then you accuse either me or Bobby of lying about her buying the wolf mask—"

"I said *someone* is lying."

"Well, you certainly didn't sound like you thought it was Lisa, even after all she's done to you and the kind of person you know she is!'' Carmen's dark eyes blazed. ''What the hell is *wrong* with you? You're doubting me, your best friend of nearly thirty years. You're romantically obsessing about Paul Dominic, a known murderer. You've never even cried over your own father, the man who doted on you and you professed to adore.''

''Carmen—''

''Save it!'' Carmen rose. ''I think you're losing it, Nicole. You don't trust me? Well, I don't trust you anymore, either.''

''Carmen!''

''I mean it!'' Carmen shouted, stalking toward the front door. ''Maybe *you* killed the cop and Dooley. Maybe you even killed Magaro and Zand.''

''Carmen, I know I've hurt your feelings, but how can you say such cruel things?'' Nicole cried.

''Easy. You're acting so weird, just like you did back then, after your attack. Maybe that's because you killed Magaro and Zand on one of your midnight walks.''

''My midnight walks?''

''Your sleepwalking. Or are you going to claim you don't know anything about it? That would be convenient.'' Carmen snatched her purse off an end table. ''Oh, hell, what does it matter now?''

Nicole grabbed her arm. ''It *does* matter! Tell me what you're talking about, Carmen, *please.*''

''Why bother? You think I'm a liar. You wouldn't believe me.'' She jerked her arm from Nicole's grasp, opened the door, and stormed out onto the front porch. ''Don't call me until you're ready to apologize. Better yet, don't ever call me again!''

As Nicole watched Carmen's car shoot out of the driveway and head down the street, her eyes filled with tears. How many more people were going to walk out of her life? How many more could she stand to lose?

3

Nicole lay on the couch, listening to music, when someone knocked on the door. She jumped up, hoping it was Carmen returning to patch up their earlier falling-out. Instead, Lisa Mervin stood on her porch. Nicole was so surprised, she said nothing.

"I knew you'd be overjoyed to see me," Lisa quipped tartly. "Roger wants me to bring Shelley to visit him."

"He does, does he?" Nicole returned, finding her voice. "She's not here."

Lisa shrugged. "I told him you wouldn't let her come."

"Lisa, she really *isn't* here. But even if she were, *I* would take her to see her father. I wouldn't turn her over to you."

"Look, I don't care one way or the other," Lisa snapped. "I'm just doing what Roger asked."

She turned to go. "Lisa, wait. If you'll come in, I'd like to talk to you."

Lisa looked back. "You want to talk to *me*? About what? Cutting Roger's brake line?"

"I didn't cut his brake line," Nicole said tiredly. "I don't know why, but I have a feeling you believe me." Lisa merely stared at her, but she knew she was right. Nicole held the door open wider. "Please come in."

Lisa took a deep breath, her large breasts straining against her skintight sweater, and walked inside. "Nice house," she muttered.

"Thank you. Have a seat. The couch and chair are Roger's."

Lisa looked at the brown monstrosities, and for the first time a ghost of a smile crossed her face. "Wow. Talk about ugly. I can't imagine him buying furniture like that."

"I think it must have been during an LSD flashback," Nicole said dryly.

Lisa laughed out loud. "Miguel said you were funny."

"You're friends with Miguel?"

"He dates my friend Susan." She looked edgy. "Why are you asking about Miguel?"

"No particular reason," Nicole lied. Lisa's nervousness spoke volumes. She was attracted to Miguel at the least.

"What did you want to talk to me about?"

"Carmen. She was here earlier. She swears she didn't know you—that when her mother-in-law baby-sat for you, she never even knew your name. She also swears Bobby told her you bought the wolf mask from him."

"Have you asked Bobby about the mask?"

"Yes."

"And he says I *didn't* buy it, doesn't he?"

"Well, yes," Nicole said reluctantly.

Lisa tucked her long hair behind her ears, looking bored. "Nicole, I *told* you I didn't buy that mask. I also told you Carmen's a liar. I think she's nuts. It wouldn't surprise me if *she* was looking in your windows wearing that mask."

"Lisa, that's ridiculous! Why would she do that?"

"I don't know. To make *you* look crazy."

"That's exactly what she said about Roger."

"Well, he sure didn't cut his own brake line. And what about those murders a long time ago? You know, those guys who raped you."

Nicole looked at her in shock. "Magaro and Zand?"

"Yeah. Bobby's mother said if the band hadn't broken up, Bobby probably wouldn't have married Carmen, even though she was pregnant. Without Ritchie Zand, there wasn't a band anymore. Zand's death was pretty convenient timing for Carmen, wouldn't you say?"

Nicole drew back, horrified. "Lisa, my God, you think *Carmen* killed Magaro and Zand?"

Lisa stood. "It's just a theory, one I'm sure you won't give a second thought because it came from me. But she's jealous as hell of you. She always has been."

"I don't believe that," Nicole said staunchly.

"Believe what you want. Roger says you never see what's right in front of you. So what do I tell him about Shelley?"

"What about her?" Nicole asked blankly.

Lisa sighed in exasperation. "Will you take her to *visit* him? That's what I came here for, remember?"

"Yes, I remember. Tell him I'll bring her tomorrow."

"Okay, but he'll be mad."

Lisa didn't say good-bye and neither did Nicole. She sat motionless on the couch after Lisa left, replaying Lisa's words: *Zand's death was pretty good timing for Carmen, wouldn't you say?*

TWENTY-TWO

1

Nicole was furiously vacuuming the living room. She let out a little shriek when the front door opened and she saw a man's face before she realized it was Ray.

Switching off the vacuum, she yelled, "Have you ever heard of knocking? You nearly scared the life out of me!"

Ray held up both hands. "*Sorry!* I knocked about five times."

"No, I'm sorry," Nicole said, regaining her composure.

"The door was unlocked. It's not such a hot idea to leave yourself so vulnerable when you're being stalked."

Nicole ran her hand across her forehead. "It was damned foolish. My only excuse was that my last visitor upset me badly."

"It couldn't have been Roger."

"No, it was his sweet young thing, Lisa Mervin. Sit down and I'll get you something to drink."

Ray came over and put his hands on her shoulders. "No, *you* sit down and I'll get *you* something to drink. I know where the refrigerator is."

Nicole smiled into his dark eyes. "Thanks. Iced tea. The glasses are—"

"I know where they are."

Nicole sank down on the couch and put her feet up on the coffee table, an act unheard of in her mother's house. She glanced over at the fish, swimming in their beautiful, perpetual tranquility. Shelley had every one of them named, but at the moment Nicole could only think of half of them.

"Here you go," Ray said, carrying two tall glasses. He sat down on the couch about a foot away from her. "Why was Lisa here? Begging you to take Roger off her hands?"

Nicole managed a wry smile. "Even *she* knows that would be an impossible sale. Roger wanted to see Shelley and expected me to turn her over to Lisa for the afternoon. I told her that even if Shelley were here, I wouldn't do that."

"It must have been a short visit."

"Not as short as you might expect. I told you she said Carmen knew her and that she'd never bought a wolf mask. Well, before Lisa's visit, Carmen was here. I asked her about those things."

"Oh, no," Ray said. "No wonder you look so depressed today. I can guess Carmen's reaction."

"She was outraged. Then she went off on this tirade about how weird I've been acting, not even crying over my father's death. Finally she said she wouldn't be surprised if *I'd* killed Officer Abbott and Izzy Dooley, even Magaro and Zand."

Ray looked stunned. "She said all that?"

"Yes. Very loudly, very angrily."

"Phew!" Ray shook his head. "I can understand her being offended by your questions, but talk about an overreaction!"

"That's what I thought. Considering what Lisa said this afternoon, I believe it was a suspicious overreaction."

"What do you mean?"

"Carmen was pregnant when she and Bobby married. Lisa said that if the band Bobby was in, The Zanti Misfits, hadn't broken up, he wouldn't have married Carmen, pregnancy or not. If Ritchie Zand hadn't been killed, the band wouldn't have collapsed. She said Zand's death was awfully convenient for Carmen."

Ray turned his glass in his hands, watching the ice cubes move. "So she's implying that Carmen killed Zand and Magaro?"

"Yes."

"Bullshit."

"You think it's out of the question?"

"Don't *you*?" Ray looked at her intently. "Nicole, I'm surprised. She's your best friend."

"I know I sound terrible, but considering her reaction—not to mention the things she said to me . . . well, I guess I'm just hurt."

Ray reached over and took her hand. "I know. But what would Carmen have to do with the deaths of Abbott and Dooley? Dominic is the man, Nicole. Fifteen years ago *and* now."

Nicole still didn't believe that. She hedged. "I suppose she upset me the most by implying she suspected me. She talked about my bouts of sleepwalking.''

Ray's eyebrows rose. ''Do you sleepwalk?''

''Not that I know of. But she said I did after my rape. She said I could have killed Zand and Magaro while I was sleepwalking. And about a week ago, I started having these strange dreams in which I hear Magaro and Zand talking *after* they were cleared of my attack. I'm always in Basin Park, near where they raped me.''

Ray looked at her steadily. ''Nicole, your hand is trembling. For God's sake, do you really think you killed those guys fifteen years ago and hung them in trees? Do you think you killed Dooley and Abbott? Or cut Roger's brake line?''

''No, but the dreams . . .''

''Do you see anyone in the dreams except Magaro and Zand?''

''No. I don't even clearly see them. I just hear their voices.''

''And you're in Basin Park, where they raped you. Doesn't it make sense that you'd dream about that place?''

''After all these years?''

''After all that's happened. Your husband left you. Your father committed suicide. You're being stalked by Dominic, who *did* kill Magaro and Zand. That's why the dreams started. Stress and reminders of the past.''

''I don't know, Ray,'' Nicole said doubtfully.

''Listen, I really came here today to tell you some news that I know will ease your mind.''

''Good. It could use some easing.''

''It seems some teenagers were out near Roger's parking lot the night he was in jail, the night his brake line was cut. Two of them claim they saw someone hanging around a Ford Explorer. Roger is the only tenant with an Explorer.''

''Did they get a good look at this person?''

''No. Not at the face, anyway. There's some dispute over the height—one witness says the guy was about five foot ten, the other at least six feet. But they both agree on long dark hair and some kind of bulky jacket.''

Nicole swallowed. ''Long dark hair?''

''Yeah. The description matches that of the person seen talking to Abbott in a patrol car before he was shot. It's Dominic, of course.''

"Maybe. Don't forget that Miguel Perez also has long dark hair."

"Nicole, I haven't found out one wrong note about Perez. Not even a parking ticket."

"Okay. Did these teenagers say they saw this person actually *do* anything to Roger's car?"

"He was on his hands and knees beside the car. The police are taking that seriously."

"But there's still no proof that this guy did anything to the brake line, is there? I mean, no fingerprints or anything."

"No."

"So I'm still not off the hook, either with the police or myself," Nicole said dismally.

Ray was still holding her hand and he squeezed it. "Nicole, you are a beautiful, gentle, loving woman. You are *not* a murderer."

"Do you really believe that?" she asked tonelessly.

"I *know* it." Ray leaned closer to her. "I *know* you would never hurt anyone."

They looked into each other's eyes. Ray's face was so close to hers she could feel his warm breath on her face. She felt like leaning toward him, letting him hold and kiss and comfort her the way she knew he wanted to do. But something held her back, some deep irrational reserve kept her from letting Ray get any closer.

"I'm starving," she said abruptly. "Would you like a tuna-salad sandwich or something more sophisticated?"

She couldn't miss Ray's fleeting look of disappointment. "A tuna sandwich is fine."

2

That evening Nicole looked out the window a dozen times, wondering if she would spot Jordan, but there was no sign of the big dog. She thought about calling her mother to see how Shelley was faring but was afraid Phyllis might start another campaign to get her to move home. And she certainly couldn't call Carmen.

She considered calling Ray, but rejected the idea. He'd seemed vaguely unhappy during their lunch, and she knew it was because she had nearly pushed him away earlier when they sat on the couch. That action still puzzled her. She was attracted to Ray, and he'd certainly been kind and gentle to her, a champion throughout this whole mess. But she wasn't ready for a new man in her life. Also, she felt guilty that she hadn't told him about her visit to Alicia Dominic. She promised the woman the conversation was just between them, and she meant to keep that promise. Besides, Alicia hadn't told her anything pertinent that she and Ray didn't already know—that Paul was in town. The revelation about her affair had nothing to do with the case.

Around ten o'clock, Nicole again glanced through the yearbook Carmen had left behind. She turned to the picture of them in the Thespian play, wearing the hoods. If their names hadn't been under the photo, she wouldn't have known which of the three hooded witches she was. Then she looked closer and recognized a pair of shoes she'd owned in high school. And Carmen was so much taller than she and the other girl playing the witch. She was only a shade shorter than the boy portraying one of the judges.

So much taller. And now heavier than she had been as a teenager. Nicole's mind spun back to Ray's description of the person who had been seen hanging around Roger's car the night his brake line was cut. Long, dark hair, wearing a bulky jacket, and between five foot nine and six feet. Carmen was five foot nine and would have been even taller wearing shoes with any kind of heel. Ray had also told her Newton Wingate saw a tall, dark-haired person talking with the young patrolman Abbott the night of the murders. And what about the prowler wearing a wolf mask? Carmen claimed Bobby said he'd sold one to Lisa. Both Lisa and Bobby denied this. But as Lisa had pointed out, Carmen had access to the masks all the time. She'd also said Carmen had always been jealous of her and maybe wanted to make her appear crazy.

But why would Carmen want her to look crazy? Nicole leaned forward on the couch, putting her head in her hands and thinking hard. Could it be because Nicole was back in San Antonio claiming that Paul Dominic was, also? Even Ray believed he was here. But Carmen, usually so open-minded, steadfastly rejected any such notion. Was she afraid if given a chance Paul could prove his innocence? What would Carmen have to lose if it turned out he could?

Nicole abruptly lifted her head from her hands. Everything, if the case were opened again and, as Lisa insinuated, Carmen herself had killed Magaro and Zand.

But as things stand now, what if the case *were* opened again soon? Nicole thought. Who might the police look at first? Carmen? Of course not. They would focus on the unstable woman whose enemies had been experiencing violent accidents or deaths.

Her stomach turned over at the thought. Carmen? Carmen, who had been her friend for *so* long? Could she have planned such a complicated, diabolical scenario? No, it was impossible. Carmen might have been obsessed with Bobby Vega, even desperate to marry him because of her pregnancy, but she didn't have it in her to kill Magaro and Zand, much less Abbott and Izzy Dooley.

I'm tired, she thought, so tired I'm even entertaining Lisa Mervin's theories. If that's not a sign of a brain on overload, I don't know what is.

Exhausted, Nicole fixed some warm milk, checked all the doors and windows, then went to bed. She propped pillows behind her, intending to read, but within ten minutes her head had slid sideways.

It was night. A warm breeze blew her pale, silky robe around her legs. She walked through the brush, which pulled her robe aside whenever it snagged on a twig.

Voices floated toward her. "She thought she had us," Magaro was saying.

"She almost did."

"No she didn't. It would have been better if we could have killed her like I wanted, but she still couldn't hurt us. I got too many friends, man. I *told* you I'd come up with an alibi." Her right hand squeezed around something metal. It fit perfectly within her palm. It gave her a feeling of power.

Now she was closer to the voices. "I should be on drums."

"Vega's on drums."

"Get rid of him or he might meet an unfortunate fate, worse than the girl's. At least she lived, although I'd still like to get this knife in her throat for all the trouble she caused."

And then there was a crunching in the grass. Someone was approaching the two men, someone tall, someone she couldn't quite see. Her fingers tightened on the object in her hand . . .

Nicole jerked up in bed, drawing in her breath so sharply it hurt. She trembled all over and she felt perspiration dampening her hair, trickling down her temples.

A dream, she told herself. Ray had said after all that had happened to her the past few weeks, it was no surprise she was dreaming of Basin Park, of Zand and Magaro . . .

But this wasn't about the rape, she reminded herself. It wasn't even about that night.

"Maybe you killed Magaro and Zand on one of your midnight walks," Carmen had said to her just that morning. Oh, God, Nicole thought. In the dream there had been something in her hand. Could it have been a gun?

She glanced at the clock beside her bed. Eleven-fifteen. Very late to be calling her mother, but she had to know.

Phyllis's voice was crisp and alert when she answered. "Nicole! Do you know what time it is?" Before Nicole had time to say anything, Phyllis exclaimed, "Oh, my God, what's happened now?"

"Nothing, Mom," Nicole said. "I hope I didn't wake up Shelley, but I just had to ask you a question."

"The phone in your old room, where Shelley is staying, has a different number."

"I'd forgotten," Nicole breathed. "Did I wake you?"

"No. I was reading. Now what is this all about?"

"Sleepwalking. Mother, after my attack, did I sleepwalk?"

There was a slight pause. "What would make you think that?"

"Because Carmen told me I did."

"Oh." Another short pause followed. "Yes, Nicole, you did."

"For how long?"

Phyllis took a deep breath. "Well, your attack happened in February. I believe the sleepwalking stopped in May."

"Did I just walk around inside the house or did I go outside?"

"Inside, mostly, but there were a couple of times when it seemed you'd been outside. Your feet and legs were dirty and scratched. But you never remembered a thing."

"I see," Nicole said slowly. "Did I ever have access to a gun?"

"A gun! Of course not. Your father deplored guns."

"He used one on himself."

"He was ill," Phyllis said in a pained voice. "Besides, he used a gun he'd bought recently. He never kept one at the store or the house for protection."

Nicole wished she felt better, but she didn't. "Mom, do you remember the night Magaro and Zand were murdered?"

"Nicole!" Phyllis's voice was developing an edge. "These questions are very alarming. What are you driving at?"

"I want to know, Mom. Was I back in the hospital for plastic surgery? And don't say you don't remember. If you say that, I'll check the hospital records."

Phyllis sighed. "Don't threaten me, Nicole. You don't have to look up hospital records. You hadn't had the plastic surgery yet. You were home."

"You're sure?"

"Yes, because I tried to keep the newspaper from you, but you saw a report about the murders on the morning newscast. You became very upset and I had to call the doctor. He gave you a tranquilizer. Then the police were here. It was awful."

"I remember being home, now. Did I sleepwalk that night? The night of the murders?"

Phyllis's voice tightened. "Nicole, I really don't see why this is so important to you. Why does it make any difference after all this time?"

"It does, Mom. Believe me, it does. Just tell me."

"All right. You did not sleepwalk that night."

"You're certain?"

"Absolutely," Phyllis said.

But Nicole heard the doubt in her voice.

TWENTY-THREE

1

"For today I asked you to read Melville's 'Bartleby the Scrivener,'" Nicole began, facing her Major American Writers class. "What was your impression of Bartleby?"

"I think he was nuts," one student near the front volunteered.

"No, he *ate* nuts," another countered, throwing the class into gales of laughter.

Nicole, who usually didn't mind a bit of levity in classes, was uncharacteristically annoyed. "Those were very perceptive comments," she said tartly. "Can anyone offer a more sensitive analysis of the character?"

Sensing her mood, the class fell silent. She waited. She looked at Miguel, whom she could usually count on for an intelligent comment, but he stared steadily down at his open book, clearly determined not to respond to her.

"All right," Nicole said with forced patience. "Let's start with something easier. What is a scrivener?" Silence spun out. Finally a mousy girl in the back row volunteered a halting answer.

Nicole was never able to get the class off the ground, and as she trudged back to her office, she blamed herself. When students sensed the teacher's lack of enthusiasm, they responded in kind. And I *like* that story, she thought. But with all the other stuff going through my mind, it's hard to work up any fire for sad young Bartleby.

When she returned to her office, she called her mother. "Feeling better today?" Phyllis asked.

"Yes. I'm sorry I disturbed you last night. I must have sounded like a lunatic."

"No daughter of mine could ever sound like a lunatic."

I wish everyone thought that, Nicole thought. "Mom, Roger wants to see Shelley. He sent Lisa to pick her up yesterday afternoon."

"Well, that's nerve!"

"I thought so, too. But he does have a right to see her. I told Lisa I'd bring Shelley to the hospital this evening."

"You will do no such thing," Phyllis said firmly. "I don't want you around that man. I don't want Shelley around him, either, but as you said, he has his rights. *I'll* take her."

"Oh, Mom, I hate to ask you to do that."

"That's the way I want it. For once indulge me, Nicole. After all, you know Roger won't get violent or obnoxious around me. He's always been intimidated by me."

"I didn't think you knew that!"

"Of course I know it. I deliberately cultivated it in him. I always sensed he might someday turn into a man who needed to be kept in line."

Nicole laughed. "You read him better than I did."

After a slight pause, Phyllis said, "Nicole, you've always wanted to see nothing but good in people. Sometimes I think you wouldn't know evil if it looked you right in the face."

Nicole was silent. Had she been unable to see it in Paul? In Carmen? Or maybe, if her fears about what she'd done during her bouts of sleepwalking were true, had she been unable to see it every time she looked in the mirror?

2

After her classes, none of which went much better than the first, Nicole hurried to the university library. Using one of the computers, she looked up articles on somnambulism. Finally finding one that looked promising, she began printing it out.

"Finding everything you need?" a librarian asked.

Nicole stiffened irrationally, feeling that if the woman saw the subject matter of the article spinning out from the printer, she would know Nicole's purpose for wanting it. "I'm doing fine, thank you," she said in a strained voice.

"If you need any help, let me know."

"I teach here. I know how to use the library." The woman looked slightly affronted. "Thank you for your help, but I think I've found exactly what I was looking for."

"Well, good for you," the woman muttered as she turned away.

Nicole was ashamed of snapping at the woman, but her nerves felt raw. After the printer finally stopped, she hastily gathered the pages of the article, stuffed them in her briefcase, and left the library.

She had almost reached her car when she saw Avis Simon-Smith heading toward her own old brown Mercedes. "Avis!" she called.

The woman stopped and turned toward her. Students filled the parking lot. Some of them glanced up at Nicole as she reached Avis. "I'm glad I caught you," Nicole said, slightly breathless from her dash in high heels. Avis looked at her expressionlessly, her baggy pants flapping in the breeze around her skinny legs, her short, overpermed hair looking dry as a tumbleweed. "I wanted to apologize for my behavior the other morning."

"You mean when you laughed at me right to my face?" Avis asked coldly.

"I wasn't laughing at you, Avis."

"Really? You could have fooled me."

"No, honestly, Avis. I'm telling you the truth." Or part of it, Nicole thought. "I've been under such a strain lately—my father's suicide, the murders. I'm sure I don't have to explain to you what that kind of tension can do to a person."

One of Avis's scanty eyebrows rose. "What makes you think you wouldn't have to explain acting crazy to me? *I* don't act crazy."

This isn't going well, Nicole thought. She was tired, her briefcase suddenly seemed to weigh a ton, and the two big books she'd tucked under her right arm were causing a cramp. "Avis, I wasn't implying you act crazy. I was only saying that you must be able to *imagine* what the recent events in my life have done to me. I'm very nervous. When I'm nervous, I'm prone to laugh over nothing at all."

"You *do* seem to be having a run of bad luck, but that doesn't give you any right to take it out on me." Avis's voice rose. "But you *like* taking it out on me. You think I'm comical."

Nicole blinked at her in surprise. "Avis—"

"Shut up! Let me finish. You think I'm comical because I'm over fifty, plain, and generally considered a washout."

"Avis, I *don't* consider you a washout—"

"Yes, you *do*. But let me tell you something." Avis stepped closer to her, the hollows under her eyes looking cavernous in the bright sun. "I've written a book—you haven't. I've taught for years—you haven't. I've spoken to hundreds of people at literary conventions—you haven't. But I'll tell you what I've never done that you have—I've never lost a man to a Kewpie doll whose IQ is less than her breast measurement."

Anger flooded through Nicole. "That's probably because you've never had a man to lose!"

Avis's eyes narrowed, her gaze brimming with pure hatred. Suddenly she reached out, placed both hands on Nicole's shoulders, and shoved. Nicole staggered backward. She could have caught her balance if her high heel hadn't landed on a pebble. Instead, in a flash she lay sprawled in the parking lot, her briefcase and books scattered around her.

As Avis stalked to her car, students surrounded Nicole. "Are you all right, Dr. Chandler?" they asked. "Are you hurt? Everyone knows she's wacko, but how could she *do* something like this?"

For the most part unhurt but embarrassed, Nicole pulled down her skirt, which had ridden up to expose her hips, and rubbed at her elbows, which had borne the brunt of the fall. "I'm fine, really," she assured the students, her cheeks scarlet. "Gosh, what a scene. So much for winning friends. Could someone help me up?"

But while other students gathered around Nicole, murmuring comfort, offering help, Miguel Perez stood rock-still thirty feet away, his venomous gaze following Avis Simon-Smith's Mercedes out of the parking lot.

TWENTY-FOUR

1

Two hours after Nicole returned home, she felt slightly more relaxed but very tired, so tired she might never be able to summon up any energy again. If only it were summer break, she thought. If only none of this were really happening.

When the phone rang, she lay on the big, ugly couch wearing a silk robe, her body feeling so tender and weak from fatigue she couldn't even bear the weight of clothes. She groaned and went to answer it.

"So how are you today?" Ray asked.

"I have sore elbows and a bruised ego." Nicole explained her earlier encounter with Avis. "At least we provided some entertainment on campus this afternoon."

"The woman sounds like she needs some psychiatric help. She also sounds like she should be charged with assault and battery. You have plenty of witnesses."

"You want me to charge two people in one week?" Nicole laughed. "I don't think I'm up to it, although I *am* beginning to feel like a punching bag. It's like I'm wearing a big sign saying HIT ME."

"I'm sorry that happened," Ray said sympathetically. "I don't expect you're up to a quiet dinner tonight."

"Thanks, but not really. I still have to prepare for school tomorrow, and then I thought I'd go to bed early."

"Sounds like a good plan. But may I reserve a space on your calendar soon for a nice dinner at the Tower of the Americas?"

"Oh, Ray, I haven't been there for years! I'd love it, but I thought you weren't allowed to date suspects and that's such a public place."

"This will all be settled within a couple of weeks."

"From your lips to God's ears."

"I have a direct pipeline. Do we have a date, then?"

"Yes. Definitely."

"Great," Ray said enthusiastically. "I'll keep you informed about the case this week. Be sure to keep all your doors and windows locked, call me anytime if you need me, and try to quit worrying and get some sleep tonight."

"Yes, sir. Talk to you soon, Ray."

What a nice man, Nicole thought. Nothing like that partner of his, Waters. And he's good-looking, too. I'm very lucky he's working this case. I was very lucky to meet him.

She smiled, going to the refrigerator and pouring a glass of orange juice. She hadn't eaten dinner, and the thought of food was unappealing now although she hadn't eaten since breakfast and knew she needed to gain weight. The cold, tart juice tasted delicious, though, and she poured a tall glass, carrying it back to the living room with her.

Nicole sat on the couch and placed her briefcase beside her. Tomorrow she would teach the stirring Composition I, which was never a problem. She did, however, need to refresh herself on how to create believable characters for Creative Writing. She opened her briefcase, looking first for the page of partial notes she'd already made for the class, then at the folded pages of the article on somnambulism. Her hand went to the article.

Twenty minutes later she'd learned that sleepwalking is one of the parasomnias that include night terrors, nocturnal enuresis, and nightmares. She also learned that it typically happens during stages three and four of sleep when there is no rapid eye movement, and that it is more common in children than in adults. Episodes can last between thirty seconds and thirty minutes, although sometimes they are longer.

But it wasn't until she reached the end of the article that her heart began to pound when she read that sleepwalkers rarely remember their episodes, which are often caused by stressful or traumatic events. She leaned forward and read the last sentence of the article aloud, her hands trembling: "Somnambulists often inflict violent or even fatal injuries on other people during their episodes."

She looked straight ahead. "They're capable of inflicting violent or even fatal injuries to others," she repeated emptily. Injuries like gunshots to the head?

2

Nicole wasn't aware of exactly how long she had sat holding the article in her hands when the phone rang. It was her mother reporting that she'd taken Shelley to see Roger. "He looks awful, but the nurses say he's doing fine. He seemed totally deflated when I walked in instead of you," Phyllis said with satisfaction. "I think he had quite a tirade prepared. One look at me, though, and the wind went right out of his pompous sails."

Nicole laughed. "Mom, you're incredible."

"You're just realizing that?" It was the nearest thing to a joke Nicole had ever heard her mother make and she was too surprised to respond. "Your daughter wants to speak to you."

"Wonderful," Nicole said. "And Mom, thanks for keeping her and taking her to see Roger."

"You have nothing to thank me for."

A moment later her daughter's buoyant voice sounded in her ear. "Hi, Mommy! We went to see Daddy."

"Grandma told me. How is he?"

"Pretty messed up. He's got bandages all over and he complained like crazy. The nurses said he was the worst patient they've ever had." Shelley giggled. "I think they'll all be happy when he goes home."

"Then he's Lisa's problem."

"She wasn't there, Mommy. I was glad, but it was one of the things Daddy was so cranky about."

"Maybe she just needed some time to herself." Or maybe she had a date, Nicole thought. The cat was flat on his back and it was time for the mouse to play. But with whom?

"Nobody else has come to see him. There was only one vase of flowers. I told you his friends didn't like him anymore."

"Well, at least he got to see you, honey. I'm sure that meant more to him than a dozen vases of flowers."

After the call, Nicole's mind immediately returned to the article and she decided she needed a drink. Five minutes later she sat on the couch again, the article lying on the floor at her feet and a glass of vodka and tonic in her hand.

Oh, God, was Carmen right? she wondered. Could she have killed Magaro and Zand? She'd certainly suffered a traumatic event—the brutal rape and beating that probably triggered the sleepwalking episodes. Basin Park was only half a mile from where she'd lived. The article said the episodes were characteristically short, but it wouldn't have taken much time for her to get to Basin Park and back, even on foot. And the hoods. Her mother had said she made two and didn't know what happened to them. "Maybe I do, Mom," Nicole said, taking a gulp of her drink. "Maybe they ended up on the heads of Magaro and Zand."

I couldn't have killed them, she thought. I just couldn't have. Still, she couldn't get the sound of their voices out of her head as they sat beneath the overpass.

Nicole slapped her hands over her ears. "Maybe I didn't kill them," she moaned. "But I was there the night they were murdered. I know it. I was *there*."

3

Avis poured another glass of burgundy, started out of the kitchen with only the glass, and paused. "Oh, to hell with it," she muttered and went back for the bottle. Carrying both the half-empty bottle and the glass, she walked down the long hall of the house to what her parents had always called the "drawing room." It was cavernous, decorated with valuable, if dusty, antiques, and very chilly on cool Texas winter nights. As a child she'd never been allowed in the room. Now that her parents were dead and the house was hers, it gave her great pleasure to eat and drink in it, knowing her mother and father would be horrified by such uncouth behavior.

Her father had been a famous lawyer, the kind who took on the glamour cases, always traveling around the country with his beautiful young wife. They were a dazzling couple who had been immensely proud of their handsome, equally dazzling son, John, and immensely disappointed in their plain, bookish, gawky daughter. Avis had spent her childhood trying unsuccessfully to win their love, which was focused on John. When Avis was seventeen, her brother was killed in Vietnam performing a stupid, reckless act that her parents, if not the army, labeled "heroic." After John was gone, Avis believed her parents would turn some of their love her way, particularly if she distinguished herself in some way. But graduating from Harvard with a Ph.D. in English had not done the trick. Neither had the publication of her critically praised book on Samuel Johnson, of whom they had never heard. And after her father died abruptly of a heart attack and Avis had given up her position at Brown University in Rhode Island to come home to a mother who perpetually complained of loneliness, there had been no difference. It seemed to hurt her beautiful mother even to look at Avis's face, which aged before its time, making her look middle-aged by the time she was thirty-three.

Avis gazed up at the portrait of her mother above the mantel. It had been painted when she was twenty-two, one year after her marriage. She had blond hair, startlingly blue eyes, high cheekbones, a porcelain complexion, and Avis thought she looked remarkably like Nicole Chandler. Nicole should have been her daughter, Avis thought bitterly. She would have been proud of Nicole.

Avis's jaw tightened. She raised her glass to the portrait. "Here's to you, Mother," she ground out. "And here's to your daughter in spirit, the one who looks and acts so much like you." Avis giggled. "She didn't look so beautiful sprawled in that parking lot today."

She gulped the wine, almost choking, then burst into laughter at the thought of Nicole lying on the concrete, her skirt up around her hips. Then she thought of how the students had rushed to help Nicole, how concerned they'd looked, how someone had called *her* a wacko, and her laughter died. They didn't care that Avis had once been considered a brilliant young scholar, that she'd written articles and a book, that she had just finished what she considered a pivotal book on Alexander Pope, even if those idiots at the university presses to which she'd submitted it said the manuscript was rambling, the criticism unsound. "As if they'd know unsound criticism if they heard it!" she said to the room at large. "They just can't accept anything as sophisticated as what I've done. They don't understand it."

Thinking about the much-rejected manuscript made her feel

worse. She emptied her glass, then filled it again to the brim. She addressed the portrait. "Yes, Mother, I know the glass shouldn't be full, but who cares? There's no one here to see my breach of good form. There's never anybody here. *Never.*"

Her eyes welled with tears. How long had it been since she'd had company? Nancy Silver and her husband used to come, but they hadn't visited her for over a year. Her few other friends had vanished long before. And men? Several years ago there had been a man, a handsome, sensitive man who'd gone to foreign films with her, talked of literature with her, had even eaten dinner with her and her mother in the big dining room that hadn't been used since her father's death.

Then, one hot summer evening when they'd sat in this room, Avis, summoning all her courage, took his hand and raised it to her lips. She kissed it and looked deeply, meaningfully into his dark eyes. He'd blushed, averted his eyes, and haltingly told her that while he cared deeply for her, he was afraid she didn't realize he was gay.

Her mother had laughed when, the next day over dinner, Avis had burst into tears and told her. "You mean you didn't *know* he was gay?" she'd asked incredulously.

"How could I have?" Avis had asked in bewilderment.

Her mother shook her head. "Avis, did you really believe a heterosexual man *that* good-looking would want to spend so much time with *you?*"

Avis had leaped up from the table, turning over her chair as she went. Two days later her mother was found at the bottom of the steep staircase, her neck broken. The death was ruled an accident, although Avis knew the police had their suspicions.

She quickly turned her mind away from the image of her mother's glassy eyes staring up at her. Even in death Avis thought she saw disappointment, even repulsion in them. After that the house had been all hers and she'd made changes. She closed off both her parents' and John's bedrooms, and virtually abandoned the upstairs. She'd fired the housekeeper, then thrown away the key to the wine cellar, indulging herself in all the fine vintages her mother had reserved for company. After all, what did it matter? There was very little company anymore, and there was no one to whom she could leave the house and its treasures, including the wine cellar. At one time Avis had planned on leaving it to Nancy Silver, but three months ago she had changed her will, bequeathing it to charity.

She took another sip of wine, then slipped a CD into the portable player she kept in the room. Just before Handel's *Water Music* began, she thought she heard the tinkling of glass coming from the back of the house. She cocked her head, but the music obliterated all further sound. Probably nothing, she thought. She hadn't washed dishes for three days. Maybe one of the glasses stacked in the sink had fallen over and broken.

Avis drained her glass and refilled it, emptying the bottle. "Oh, well, the hour is young and many more bottles await." She set the glass down on a dusty Sheraton drum table and reached out her hand to a handsome, invisible suitor. "Yes, sir, I would most surely enjoy a dance." She began an elaborate gavotte, preening and dimpling at her imaginary lover, picturing herself in a gown of lavender satin, her thick blond hair piled high, her ample breasts nearly spilling from the top of her low-cut gown, her beauty the desire of all the men, the envy of all the women.

She tripped, almost fell, and giggled loudly. The room seemed to be moving. "Please forgive me, sir. I fear I'm dizzy from dancing," she told her dance partner.

The music softened during one of the string movements and she heard it. A thump. Then another and another. Near the stairs. *On* the stairs. The stairs where her mother had died.

The simpering smile faded from Avis's thin lips. She stood still for a moment. Finally she moved from the drawing room to the hall. She never turned on many lights at night, mostly because bulbs had burned out and she never bothered to replace them. This was true of the crystal chandelier in the hall, which had ceased to glisten and glow two years ago. She slept downstairs, so the only light on the stairs was that filtering from the drawing room. She crept forward, alternately frowning and squinting as she tried to focus on the mound at the bottom of the stairs. She stepped closer and closer. Was it a body? Was it . . .

"Mother!" she screamed. "Mother, I didn't mean to do it! I was just so angry. You were laughing at me. You said I was comical! And I pushed you—"

Avis was screeching, her face blanched, her eyes huge and burning in their cavernous sockets. Her hand clapped over her mouth, and she backed slowly away from the mound, horrified.

You're drunk, she thought with a brutal clarity she rarely allowed herself. You're hallucinating. Mother has been dead for four years. Dead and buried. She *couldn't* be lying, once again, in a broken heap at the foot of the stairs.

She kept backing up, nearly gibbering with fear and guilt and shock, when she bumped into someone. Instead of turning to see who it was, she froze, terrified that if she turned, she would see the face of her mother.

Flutes, oboes, bassoons, and strings sounded in the other room. "Scared?" a voice asked in her ear.

Avis opened her mouth, but nothing came out. If I could just talk, she thought. If I could just say *one* word, this hallucination would end. One word . . .

An arm circled her waist and jerked her backward against a body that felt abnormally warm. "Did you think that was Mama at the foot of the stairs? Did you relive that moment when you *pushed* her, just like you pushed Nicole Chandler today? You got all mixed up, didn't you, Avis? You thought Nicole was your mother."

"No, no I didn't," Avis whispered frantically. "I didn't mean to push her."

"Who? Your mother? Or Nicole?"

"Nicole."

The gun jammed against her head, feeling as if it were going to push a hole in her temple. "Liar."

"Okay. Just for a moment. They look so much alike. I didn't mean to hurt her. I *wouldn't* hurt her. I wouldn't hurt anyone."

"Liar!"

Avis was beginning to hyperventilate. "All right. I don't like her. But she laughs at me."

"Who? Nicole or your mother?"

"I don't know. Both."

"No wonder. You're pathetic."

"Yes, yes, you're absolutely right," Avis panted. The hall was beginning to circle around her. Too much wine and too little air in her lungs. "I'm sorry. I won't hurt her again."

"You're damned right, you won't. You won't hurt Nicole or anyone else ever again," the voice grated. The arm moved up, encircling her throat, completely constricting her breathing. Everything went black, even though Avis knew she was still alive.

She tried to move her hands, to claw at the arm around her throat, but she was paralyzed with fear. She knew what was coming and she wished she would faint, but she'd never fainted in her life. "You'll never hurt anyone again."

Even if the gun hadn't been silenced, the shot couldn't have been heard over the soaring, triumphant trumpet ending of Avis's favorite musical composition.

TWENTY-FIVE

1

Nicole left her office, turned a corner of the hall, and near ran into Nancy Silver who looked at her with beleaguer eyes. "What's wrong?" Nicole asked.

"Avis didn't show up to teach today. She didn't call. No o can reach her. I even went by her house. Her car is there, but s didn't answer the door, so I came back to school." Nan frowned. "Nicole, I heard about what Avis did to you in t parking lot yesterday. I wondered if she called you or came your house last night to apologize."

Nicole started to say she doubted if Avis were the least sorry for what she'd done, then realized Nancy's genuine wor didn't deserve a sarcastic answer. "No, Nancy, I haven't seen talked to her since yesterday afternoon. But she was in quite mood."

"I know it's none of my business," Nancy said hesitant "but I've wondered—"

"What we argued about? The other day Avis was in my offi and I started laughing. I've been under a lot of pressure and y know how strange she acts sometimes. She did something th struck me as hilarious. It was inexcusable of me to laugh like did and she was terribly offended. In the parking lot yesterday was trying to explain my mental state and apologize, but she w having none of it. She made some scathing remark about n husband leaving me, and I took the bait and shot back an insu and she pushed me."

"Oh, God, Nicole, I'm sorry."

"It's not *your* fault. Besides, I wasn't hurt and maybe I d served it."

"Don't be silly. I've been friends with Avis a long time. I've seen her change dramatically over the years. My husband and I don't even visit her at home anymore because, frankly, she started giving him the creeps. He thinks maybe she killed her mother—"

"Killed her mother!" Nicole burst out.

Nancy's dark eyes clouded. "I suppose you've never heard the story. Anyway, I always thought it was an accident. Nevertheless, after her mother's death, she went from eccentric to downright strange, and no one knows better than I how she can goad you into saying things you'd never usually say. Just because you reacted to her insults doesn't mean she had the right to knock you down. I think she's going to lose her job."

Nicole was genuinely upset. "Not over that silly incident! She didn't even knock me down. She just pushed me and I lost my balance. Good heavens, if I thought she were going to be fired because of *me*—"

"Not only because of you. The incident yesterday was just the final straw after four years of inappropriate behavior and terrible comments to students and teachers. They've bent over backward for her here, given her every chance." Nancy bit her lip. "I'm afraid she realizes that maybe she *will* lose her position here and she's done something to herself. After all, this job is all she has left."

"Come to my office, Nancy," Nicole said briskly. "I have a friend on the police force. I'll call him and see what he can do about locating Avis as soon as possible."

2

"Ray, this is a job for uniforms, not for us," Cy said as they sped north.

"Normally I'd agree, but I think this woman's disappearance has something to do with the Chandler case."

"What it has to do with is the fact that Nicole called and asked you to check it out, so you jumped like a puppy on a leash."

"It has to do with the fact that this woman is a teacher in the same department as Nicole and yesterday she threw a fit in the parking lot and knocked Nicole down." He looked over at Cy.

''And we both know what's been happening to people who do harm to Nicole Chandler.''

''She offs them, or attempts to.''

Ray stiffened. ''That's an assumption.''

Cy laughed. ''Get off your high horse, Ray. I know how you feel about her. That's why you need me around. I've got a more objective view of things.''

''It sounds to me as if your mind is already made up.''

''I've got some thoughts about all of this,'' Cy said vaguely. ''In the meantime, we're off on a wild-goose chase, two homicide detectives looking for a woman just because she didn't show up for work this morning. The lieutenant would be thrilled.''

''The lieutenant doesn't have to know if we don't find anything.''

Cy fell into a deep silence. Probably thinking about what he was going to have for dinner, Ray mused disdainfully. All the guy seemed to care about these days was food.

Ten minutes later they pulled up in front of a rambling Victorian house. Like the Dominic home, it had obviously once been beautiful, although not so grand, but suffered from neglect. ''This Simon-Smith woman isn't into home repair,'' Cy commented. ''This place needed a coat of paint about three years ago. Car in the driveway.''

''Nicole told me the woman drives a brown Mercedes. That's it.''

They climbed the verandah steps and knocked on a heavy door wreathed with beveled glass. After four tries, they gave up. ''Let's check around back,'' Ray said.

''Oh, good lord, Ray. What's the big deal?''

Ray sighed. ''Five minutes. That's all it'll take to knock on the back door.''

''Okay,'' Cy said. ''But I still hate wasting my time just to impress your girlfriend.''

''She's *not* my girlfriend.''

''Whatever you say.''

They walked across the grass and around the side of the house, where there was no door but a multitude of dirty windows and faded green shutters.

No fence surrounded the large backyard. A once-beautiful gazebo stood in the center of the yard, but its shabby condition indicated it was never used. A shame to let a place like this go, Cy thought. Aline would love this house, and she'd manage to make it look like a showplace without spending a lot of money. They could sit in that gazebo in the evenings, drinking mint juleps and discussing their day . . .

While Cy stood contemplating the gazebo, Ray started to knock on the back door. Then he stopped. ''Cy, a pane of glass in the door is broken. Come here and look. It's right beside the door-knob. Looks like a little blood on the glass, too.''

But Cy didn't answer. His gaze had drifted from the gazebo to the back of the lawn, where a hooded figure with long, skinny legs dangled from a branch of a huge, beautiful live oak.

3

It was seven o'clock. Nicole had promised to call Nancy as soon as she learned anything about Avis, but she'd called Ray three hours ago and still heard nothing. She paced around the living room, dusting furniture she'd just dusted two days ago, talking briefly on the phone to Shelley, who was growing increasingly restless at her grandmother's, and trying vainly to concentrate on lesson plans for the next day. When someone knocked on the door, she ran to it, flinging it open.

''Ray!'' she cried. ''I've been waiting to hear from you.''

He looked tired as he stepped through the doorway, his smile strained. ''I'm sorry I didn't call earlier.''

Nicole searched his face. ''Something's wrong. Avis is dead. She killed herself, didn't she?''

Ray drew a deep breath. ''She's dead,'' he said softly, ''but she didn't kill herself.''

''An accident?'' Nicole ventured with a sinking heart, knowing she was only hoping it had been an accident.

Ray put his hands on her shoulders. ''Nicole, she was shot in the head, then hanged wearing a hood.''

Slowly the world went dark for Nicole. Then she was being placed on her bed. In a moment Ray was back with a cold cloth for her forehead. ''Nicole, you fainted.''

Nicole nodded. ''Avis was murdered like the others.''

"Yes. She was in her backyard."

"Oh, God, Ray. I don't suppose a tall, dark-haired person was spotted at the scene."

"We haven't found any witnesses so far." He looked down. "You'll be formally questioned tomorrow."

"And arrested?"

Ray clearly didn't want to answer the question. "There's no physical evidence against you."

"But there *is* motive. And I don't have an alibi."

"We only found the body three hours ago. Evidence pointing to someone else might turn up. And don't worry about an alibi."

"What do you mean?" Nicole asked, her voice high-pitched. "I was here at the house all evening, no visitors, no witnesses."

"You let me worry about that."

"What are you talking about? Inventing an alibi for me?"

"If I have to."

"Ray, I can't let you do that. Your career—"

He turned toward her, his eyes burning. "Nicole, I'm not worried about my career right now. I'm worried about you. I'm not going to lie to you. You're in deep trouble. This murder looks really bad for you on top of everything else. But I *know* you didn't do it. Dominic did."

Nicole swept the cloth off her forehead. "How can you be so sure it was Paul?"

Ray looked at her in disbelief. "Nicole, someone hurts you, or attempts to hurt you, and they wind up with a bullet in the head, hanging from a tree and wearing a hood. It happened fifteen years ago and it's happening now. Paul Dominic was arrested for the murders of Zand and Magaro. He ran, disappeared, but now he's back. How much more proof do you need?"

"I suppose I shouldn't need any," Nicole said weakly. "Ray, I know you're convinced Paul committed these murders. What does your partner, Waters, think?"

"Waters only sees what he wants to see."

"And he wants to see me as a murderer, doesn't he?"

"Yes, he suspects you," Ray said reluctantly. "But that's what Dominic wants. That's why he's lying so low, why he's only shown himself to you. No one but you." He looked at her soberly. "But I know he's back and he's killing like the madman he is."

4

"Can't sleep?"

"How'd you know?" Cy asked.

"You're not snoring loud enough to rattle the windows." Aline propped herself up on her elbow. "You're thinking about Nicole Sloan."

"Nicole Chandler, Aline. She got married. Now her husband claims she slit a hole in his brake line and nearly killed him."

"That little bitty thing? I don't believe it. Brake lines are tough."

"She could have managed it. And he *was* at her house the night before. Hit her in the jaw. Then there's that Simon-Smith woman. She pushed Nicole in the parking lot yesterday. Knocked her down. Today Ray and I found her dead and hanging in a tree, just like Magaro and Zand and Dooley."

Aline shivered. "That's grotesque. Surely you don't think Nicole could actually *hang* people in a tree."

"Now *that* doesn't seem too likely. Still . . ."

They lay in silence for a moment. "Cy, have you looked into those murders that happened fifteen years ago?"

"Yeah, but so far I haven't learned anything new. I'm not through, though."

"The other night you sounded like you didn't think that pianist could have killed them."

"Paul Dominic. And I didn't say he couldn't have killed them. I just wasn't convinced."

"You said you thought he'd be smarter about disposing of the evidence."

"That, among other things, bothered me." He sighed. "There was something about him. Maybe it was those fine manners, or the respect he showed me. Or maybe it was the look in his eyes that got to me. I've heard people protest their innocence until they're blue in the face. I've seen them cry, and swear on their children's lives, and ask God to strike them dead if they aren't telling the truth, but their eyes give them away. But this guy's eyes looked, well, bewildered, hurt, like he honest to God didn't know what the hell was going on.''

''How did he defend himself?''

''He didn't. He didn't confess, but he didn't say one word in his defense, either. His lawyer did all the talking for him.''

''That was smart if he was guilty.''

''Yeah, but it's unusual. Unless you're dealing with an habitual offender, or somebody in organized crime—you know, the type that's always in trouble and always hiding behind a lawyer—the accused usually make an occasional outburst about their innocence, whether they are or not. Dominic didn't say a damned word. Just sat there looking flabbergasted.''

Aline stroked Cy's arm. ''You're not going to give up on this, are you? After all, you said you thought what happened fifteen years ago is connected to what's going on now, and there's a whole mess of trouble around that girl. Those murders at her house, her husband, now this college professor . . .''

''Things look bad for her, Aline. Coincidences happen, but not *constantly*. Yet everyone who does her wrong ends up dead or seriously hurt.''

''But Cy—''

''Look, Aline, I *am* working on this. I've already retrieved the gun that killed Magaro and Zand from Evidence. I'm having Ballistics make another stab at recovering that serial number.''

''Do you really think the serial number is so important?''

''I think it could be.''

''Is that *all* you're doing?''

''For now.''

''Doesn't sound like much to me.''

''It's about all I *can* do. A trail gets mighty cold after fifteen years.''

''If you say so. Oh, by the way, I forgot to tell you. Someone named Jewel called here for you.''

Cy sat up in bed. ''Jewel! Jewel Crown?''

''Jewel Crown? What kind of name is that?''

''Aline . . .''

''Okay. She didn't give her last name. She just said she wanted to talk to you. I told her to call headquarters. She said she couldn't do that, then she started to cry.''

''Did she say where I could reach her?''

"No, or I would have told you earlier. I thought maybe it was a crank, her refusing to give a last name or to say where she could be reached or to call you at headquarters. Is she important?"

"She could be."

"Oh, Cy, I'm sorry I forgot to tell you. You know I wouldn't deliberately keep a message from you—"

Cy leaned over and gave her a quick kiss. "Don't worry about it, darlin'. If she didn't say where I could reach her, there's nothing I could do anyway."

"Well, why wouldn't she call you at work if it was so important?"

"I don't know. She's a hooker, Aline. Hookers aren't fond of police stations."

"Does this Jewel have anything to do with Nicole Chandler?"

"Yeah, indirectly. At least I thought it was indirectly. She was Izzy Dooley's girlfriend."

"His girlfriend! A guy like that could have a girlfriend?"

"They say there's someone for everyone." Cy sighed again. "Look, Aline, I'll make you a deal. I won't make up my mind about Nicole Chandler's guilt or innocence, and I won't give up checking into the murders fifteen years ago, on one condition."

"Oh? And what's that?"

"Well, that tofu-and-soybean dinner you served earlier was healthy but left me feeling completely empty. I want a sandwich. A *real* sandwich with meat and cheese and pickles and mayonnaise and about a thousand calories."

Aline laughed and kissed his cheek. "You got it, honey. We'll consider it brain food."

5

Nicole lay in bed, knowing sleep would elude her again tonight. Worried, she knew if she didn't get some rest, she would collapse from exhaustion.

Ray had left three hours ago, but it seemed like twelve. With every passing minute, her fear of being arrested grew.

Another person had been murdered. Poor Avis. Nicole hadn't

liked her, but she certainly didn't want her dead. And to think Avis might have been murdered because of her was unbearable. She shuddered. Ray was convinced Paul had done it, not just because Avis had pushed her in the parking lot, but because Paul was a "madman." Paul Dominic, a madman. She shook her head.

Nicole rose, went to the stereo, picked up the tape *Dominic, Gershwin, and Carnegie Hall*, and put it in the slot. A few moments later the first seductive strains of *Rhapsody in Blue* filled the room. How long had it been since she'd listened to the song all the way through? Every time it came on the radio, she turned it off. If she was at a party and someone put it on, she left the room. To her it had come to represent death—the death of love as well as the rape and the subsequent deaths of Magaro and Zand, for which she'd been considered indirectly responsible.

She sat down on the couch just as the piano began. Paul playing the piano. Paul at Carnegie Hall. She closed her eyes and it was fifteen years ago. Paul and she lying on cushions in the big music room. Vanilla-scented candles flickering. Her hand in his. The song ending and Paul leaning over, his penetrating hazel eyes gazing into hers. "Do you believe in destiny, Nicole? . . . I believe I was destined to come back to Texas and meet you again." She opened her eyes. "Will I see you tomorrow?" he'd asked at the door. "I have to go to the Mission San Juan to finish my research." "Then I'll meet you there," he'd promised. He said the day they'd spent at the mission earlier was one of the happiest days of his life.

She smiled, remembering how they'd wandered around the grounds, talking about everything, taking pictures of each other, holding hands. "I love you very much, *chérie,*" he'd told her before she left his house that last night. And he'd saved her on the River Walk when she was attacked by Izzy Dooley. He'd slipped the cross around her neck and gazed once again at her with his intense hazel eyes. "Some loves are forever," his mother had said.

The song soared into the famous *Andantino moderato* melody. "Yes," Nicole said softly. "Forever. I loved you then, Paul, and God help me, I love you now. You love me, too, but I don't believe that love means you'd kill for me."

The song concluded and she got up, walking restlessly again around the living room. Paul Dominic murdering five people, one an innocent young policeman sent by Ray to protect her? It was ridiculous.

As she paced around the living room, her gaze fell on the mail lying on a small table by the front door. She had brought it in but promptly forgot it. Now she picked it up, sorting through it quickly. "Bill from the electric company, bill from the phone company, bill from the water company. Wonderful," she said aloud, tossing aside the bills along with an alumni newsletter. Then she lifted a postcard. On the front was a Spanish mission. "The Mission San Juan," she murmured. Turning it over, she saw there was no stamp—only the printed words "Meet me here at midnight." Beneath them was a sloping *P*.

"Paul!" she gasped. "Paul wants to see me."

She stood still for a few seconds, undecided. Then she rushed to the bedroom.

6

Nicole peeked out the window over her kitchen sink. There was a patrol car. "Damn," she muttered.

She glanced at her watch. Eleven-twenty. Quickly she went to the phone, called for a taxi to pick her up on the street behind hers. Then she checked her wallet to make certain she had plenty of money, went to the basement, retrieved the aluminum stepladder, and carried it to the backyard. Placing it beside the back fence, she climbed up and grabbed hold of an overhanging branch, the same one Izzy Dooley had used. She flung her legs over the six-foot fence, hung by the branch with one hand, and leaned down, straining to grab the top of the ladder. She managed to drag it over the fence, cringing at the grating sound it made, and dropped it onto the neighboring backyard so she could use it when she returned. Then she dangled for a moment, took a deep breath, and plummeted. She landed just two inches clear of the ladder and flat-footed, not turning an ankle as she'd feared, and sprinted across the lawn of the vacant house.

For the next few minutes Nicole stood on the sidewalk, terrified a neighbor had seen her climbing over the fence, mistaken her for a prowler, and called the police. How could she explain her actions, especially to Ray? In her mind she invented one lame excuse after another until the taxi appeared. Sighing with relief, she hopped in and said, "The Mission San Juan."

The driver turned in his seat. "The *mission*! At *this* hour?"

"Is it your company's policy to question the passenger's destinations?"

"Well, no, but—"

"Then please get me to the mission as soon as possible."

During the day they could never have made it across town in time. So late at night, though, they arrived only a couple of minutes after midnight. The driver pulled the taxi into the gravel parking lot.

"I want you to wait for me," Nicole said.

The middle-aged driver turned and looked at her querulously. "*Wait?* That'll cost you double time."

"Fine."

Nicole started to get out, but the driver said, "No, *you* wait." She turned back to him. "Pay me your fare to this point."

"How do I know you won't just take off and leave me?"

"How do I know you won't do the same and stiff me for the fare?"

"Oh, all right," Nicole snapped. "But don't you *dare* drive away as soon as I'm out of the taxi."

"I won't. But I don't like sittin' out here. This place is spooky at night."

"Lock the doors and I'm sure you'll be fine."

"Easy for you to say."

Yes it was, Nicole thought a minute later as she walked away from the cab. Look at what had happened to the patrolman, Abbott. It was one thing for her to risk her own life, but the life of someone else? But I'm here to meet Paul, she reminded herself. If in my heart I believed Paul had killed Abbott, I wouldn't have come.

The Mission San Juan was more isolated than some of the other missions along the river, forming the San Antonio Missions National Historic Park. She knew the park officials left at five and the church, which was still active, closed at seven except for special events. She walked through an opening in the stone walls surrounding the grounds, which she hadn't seen for fifteen years, not since she and Paul had spent the day here together. One of the happiest days of her life, also.

Beyond the wall, the grounds looked huge. Unlike at the Alamo downtown, there was no outside lighting and she depended only on a bright moon that cast its glow on the faded white walls of the church and threw shadows on the trees and the large, rough wooden cross standing like a sentinel inside the mission square. It was hard to believe the place had once bustled with activity, within the compound the Indian artisans producing goods from the workshops and outside the farmers cultivating crops that sustained the whole community. But that had been over two hundred years ago. Now the compound was empty and silent, although she thought she could feel the ghosts of those long-dead people all around her in the deep quiet of the night. The cab driver was right. The place *was* spooky. She was glad she'd brought her gun.

Nicole's footsteps slowed. What am I doing? she asked herself silently. I've been afraid for days that Paul wants revenge, yet I get a postcard and a cryptic message and here I am. What if something happens to me? Shelly certainly can't be raised by Roger. Not by Mom, either. She hasn't gotten over Dad's death. Maybe Roger and Carmen are right about me. Maybe I *am* crazy.

But she couldn't stop. She walked toward the ruins of the unfinished church the missionaries had begun in the 1760's but had had to abandon because of lack of funds and manpower. She had pulled a windbreaker over her blouse and she now wished she'd worn something heavier. Chills ran up and down her arms.

Nicole stopped, then turned toward the parking lot. She was far away from the cab now. She couldn't even see it clearly. If someone attacked her, the cab driver couldn't reach her in time to help her. He didn't seem like the chivalrous type, anyway. If she screamed, he'd probably be flying out of the parking lot in seconds.

Shadows moved across the moon, shifting the light. She could have sworn the large cross moved. The spreading juniper behind it rustled as the wind changed. She'd only been here during the day. She never knew how night transformed the grounds, and she was alone . . .

Nicole let out a tiny cry when something touched her. She looked down to see a large black Doberman forcing its muzzle into her hand.

"Jordan!" she cried, inexpressibly happy to see the dog. "You certainly are the quiet one. Are you here with Paul? Of course you are. You never leave his side, do you?"

"Only when I ask her to."

The voice floated out from behind the walls of the unfinished church. "Paul?"

"Yes, Nicole. Come here."

Nicole suddenly felt rooted to the spot, unable to move. Jordan looked up at her, back at the place where the voice had come, then gently clamped her jaws around Nicole's wrist, pulling her forward. She passed through an opening in a low stone wall. Before her stood a statue of Jesus holding a baby. Beside the statue stood a man.

"Paul," she said softly.

"I wasn't sure you'd come." He walked toward her. "I'm so glad you did."

She hadn't remembered how tall he was—over six feet—or how broad his shoulders were, or how he moved with a dancer's grace. The years had not changed his body. But his face? She stared at it in the moonlight. Yes, the face was harder, the forehead more lined, the cheekbones more prominent. The eyes were just as intense, although she caught a trace of wariness in them that had not existed fifteen years ago.

"Nicole?" he asked tensely when she didn't answer. "You did come alone, didn't you?"

Overcoming the shock of speaking to him after so long, she managed a weak, "Yes."

"No one else saw the postcard?"

"No. And I went over my back fence and got a taxi on a different street so the policeman in the patrol car wouldn't see me."

Paul smiled. The same even white teeth, the same dimples, although they were deeper. "My dear Nicole. After all these years you still have to sneak around to see me. I'm sorry."

They stood about five feet apart, Jordan sitting between them and turning her sleek head as each spoke. "Paul, everyone believed you were dead. Where have you been all these years?"

"Everywhere, making a living any way I could."

"But your things were found near that terrible car wreck. The police thought the man inside was you."

"The guy gave me a ride. Then he pulled a gun and took my money. I thought he was going to kill me. He probably would have if he hadn't been so drunk. I managed to get away, without my knapsack, and later in the day he wrecked. The car was stolen and the police assumed I'd been driving."

"I see." Nicole took a deep breath. "Why did you jump bail?"

"I didn't think I stood a chance of being found innocent."

Nicole's throat felt tight. She took a step closer to Paul, looking up into his eyes. "But you were innocent?"

His eyes searched hers. "You're really not sure, are you?"

"I . . . I'm sorry, Paul. I never believed it for a moment until you ran—"

"You *really* aren't sure."

"Paul, as I said, you *ran*." Nicole heard the agony of guilt in her voice. "And there was so much evidence against you . . . I'm sorry if my doubts make you angry, but—"

"Make me angry? Make me *angry*?" Nicole stood slightly open mouthed as Paul burst into laughter. "Your doubts don't make me angry. They lift the weight of the world off my shoulders. All these years I thought . . . well, never mind what I thought."

"What? *Tell* me what you thought." Paul shook his head, but suddenly realization dawned on Nicole. "You thought *I* murdered Zand and Magaro! That's why you never defended yourself. You thought you were taking the blame for me!" Paul smiled ruefully. "But what about the gun? You believed I planted it at your house and you still protected me?"

"I thought *if* you planted the gun, you couldn't have been in your right mind. You were so young, so traumatized. You might have thought I deserved punishment for not walking you to the car that night. Or you might have thought no one would find the gun."

"My God, because of me you've been on the run for fifteen years!" Nicole flung herself at Paul. His arms immediately closed around her. "Oh, Paul, I'm *so* sorry!"

"I'm not, at least not completely," he said, hugging her. "I was so spoiled. Soft. Pampered. The last few years I finally grew up."

"But your mother . . ."

"Yes, what all this did to her was terrible. But I've always been in touch with her. She's *always* known I was all right except for a couple of weeks after the wreck. I didn't even know about it. Nicole, *she* encouraged me to go.''

''Certainly not because she thought you were guilty.''

''No. Because she was convinced I'd be found guilty, and she knew prison would kill me.''

Nicole looked up at him. ''Did she know you thought you were protecting me?''

''Yes. And she said it was silly—that you would never have killed those men and set me up. But she also recognized that there was no evidence against you, only motive. The evidence was all against me. She saw the reality of my situation, but she never blamed you.''

''She's a remarkable woman. I saw her on Sunday.''

''She told me. She said you were as beautiful and resourceful as ever.''

Nicole smiled. He touched her face gently and leaned down to kiss her, but she turned her head. ''I'm sorry,'' Paul said humbly.

''Oh, Paul, I'm so happy to see you. It isn't that. It's . . .''

''It's what?''

''Well, what about all these recent murders?''

''You think I'm behind them?''

''You called me the night Roger and I had a fight in the driveway. You said if he talked to me that way again, you'd kill him.''

Paul looked at her in shock. ''Nicole, I made no such call.''

''But it was your voice. You even called me *chérie*.''

Paul looked at her earnestly. ''Nicole, I swear on my mother's life that I never made that call. I have *never* called you. I was afraid your phone was tapped.''

''But it sounded so much like you . . .'' She trailed off, twisting the cross at her neck.

''You're wearing it.''

''I have since the night you gave it to me on the River Walk. And don't try to tell me *that* wasn't you.''

''Certainly it was me. You saw Jordan. You looked right into my eyes.''

''Yes, I did. You protected me from that awful person, even though you were right out there in the open where you could so easily have been caught.'' Her gaze dropped. ''Paul, there's another reason I didn't let you kiss me.'' He was quiet. ''I'm afraid I *did* kill Zand and Magaro.''

She could feel him stiffen against her. ''But you said you had doubts about *my* innocence.''

''I didn't clearly say what I meant. I've been having these dreams lately.'' Paul frowned. ''In the dreams I see Zand and Magaro where they were murdered. They're talking about me *after* the attack, *after* they'd been cleared of my rape.''

Paul seemed to relax. ''I don't understand why you're upset. They're just dreams.''

''But they don't *feel* like dreams. They feel like a memory. And I've recently learned that I was sleepwalking during that time and that sleepwalkers are capable of violent acts and—''

Paul placed his fingers gently over her lips. ''And then you put the gun in my trash along with one of my shirts stained with Zand's blood?''

''Maybe.''

''I don't believe it. Do you realize the time and planning those murders required? In a sleepwalking state you believe you remembered to bring a gun and hoods and my shirt—which by the way I never knew how you could have gotten—then killed Magaro and Zand, hung them in trees, and finally came on over to Olmos Park to plant evidence? No, Nicole, whoever murdered those two wasn't committing a random act of violence while sleepwalking.''

''But you thought I might have done it deliberately?''

''You were so traumatized. I thought maybe it was an act of temporary insanity.''

''Temporary insanity? Thanks.''

''Wouldn't that have crossed your mind if our positions were reversed? After all, you weren't just raped. You were beaten so badly you required plastic surgery. And it was a miracle you weren't killed. All because you were sneaking around to see me, a man who didn't even walk you to your car that night.''

''I wasn't temporarily insane. I don't *feel* like I killed them. I don't believe I did. *You* didn't kill them. Then who?''

''I don't know. Those two must have had a lot of enemies.''

''Enemies who would set you up?''

''Why not? I was a likely suspect with all my talk of how I was going to get even with them.'' He laughed dryly. ''My plan to get even with them was to get their contract with the music company broken. I had friends at Revel Music who were already looking for loopholes in the contract. They weren't anxious to be connected with a band whose lead singer had just been arrested for nearly killing a girl.''

They walked to the low wall and sat down, right arms wrapped around each other, left hands clasped. Paul's hands had always been strong, but the skin was soft. Now the skin was rough and callused. They were silent for a moment before Nicole asked, ''Do you still play?''

''Whenever I'm near a piano and no one else is around. It would take a long time for me to get back to my former level. Maybe I never could.''

''I'm *sure* you could,'' Nicole said fervently. ''Paul, why did you come back now?''

''I was here when your father killed himself. I knew you'd be shattered, so I stayed to watch over you for a while.''

''You risked remaining here because you were worried about me, even though you also believed I might have murdered Zand and Magaro?''

''If you had killed them, I wouldn't have blamed you.''

''Even if I'd set you up, allowed you to take the blame?'' Nicole asked incredulously.

''Nicole, I told you I knew that if you hadn't been at my house that night, those two wouldn't have gotten you. And you were so battered, physically and mentally. You were also young. I could understand you blaming me. I felt what happened to you was my fault. So I had to come back now and help you if I could. But I haven't helped. I've just made everything worse.''

''No, you haven't.'' Nicole was beginning to shiver with cold and nerves. Paul pulled her closer to him. She looked up at the strong profile, the dark hair pulled back in the sleek ponytail exposing the strong neck. Her protector, she thought. Even with his doubts about her, he'd still risked his freedom, maybe his life, to help her. ''But Paul, all these recent murders are connected to me. The police suspect me.''

''They're supposed to.'' He looked at her. ''Now *you* are being set up.''

''*Why?* Who could hate me so much?''

''Your husband?''

"Carmen thought it was Roger wanting me to look crazy so he could get full custody of Shelley."

"Killing people is an extreme way of making you look crazy."

"The girlfriend of the man who was killed and hanged in my yard said he'd been paid three thousand dollars to murder someone's wife, a teacher."

"Your cop friend told you that."

Nicole felt a stab of guilt at the thought of Ray. What would he think of her sneaking off to see Paul, clinging to him and immediately accepting everything he said as truth? He would be appalled. He might even stop believing in her innocence. "Yes, he told me," she said softly. "His name is Ray DeSoto. He's been wonderful to me, Paul."

"He knows I'm in San Antonio and the very thought of my being near you makes him draw his gun."

"You hit him in the motel parking lot that night, didn't you?"

"Yes. He almost caught me. I've been following you everywhere, doing my best to look out for you and your daughter. I didn't feel you were safe in that motel room. Somehow he knew I was there."

"Someone called the room, pretending to be Magaro."

"*Magaro!*" He shook his head. "Not only I, but a dead person is supposedly calling you. But I knew something was going to happen that night. I just couldn't stay after hitting DeSoto. I was afraid that after he regained consciousness, he'd call in backup. I had to leave the protecting to Jordan."

"She did a fine job." Nicole reached out and petted Jordan's head. She licked Nicole's hand. "Thank you for saving Jesse, Paul."

"You should thank Jordan. I saw you going up and down the street, looking for Jesse. Then a patrol car came. I thought you were safe, so Jordan and I went looking for Jesse. She found him around four in the morning."

"Around the time Abbott and Dooley were being killed at my house."

"If I hadn't been looking for Jesse, I would have seen who killed them."

"Whoever *did* kill Dooley saved my life. But the others—the patrolman Abbott and Avis Simon-Smith—I wasn't in danger from them."

Paul looked at her blankly. "Who's Avis Simon-Smith?"

"She was a woman I worked with. She was very unstable and she hated me. We had a fight yesterday. She knocked me down in the parking lot. Late this afternoon she was found dead, hanging from a tree in her backyard with a bullet in her head and wearing a hood."

"Good lord," Paul breathed. "I saw what Dooley did to you on the River Walk. I've even seen what goes on between you and your husband. But I didn't know anything about this Smith woman."

"Ray found her."

"Tell me about Ray."

"I don't know much. He's a couple of years younger than I am. He wouldn't have been around when you were arrested."

"It seems so long ago," Paul said.

"It was."

"Long enough for you to find someone else to love and marry and have a child with."

There was no rebuke in his words, only sadness and a note of loss. "It was a kind of love, Paul. Not like mine for you. Roger was strong and smart and if he was a little dull and stodgy—"

"At least he wasn't the killer you thought I was."

Nicole looked at him regretfully. "Paul, I never really believed you killed anyone. But you never called me after you ran away. Why?"

"I was afraid you would tell the police."

"I wouldn't have, not back then. Later I thought you'd died." She closed her eyes. "God, Paul, I was devastated. If only you'd let me know you were alive."

"Again, I was afraid. The police believed I was dead. They stopped looking for me. But if I called you and you told them . . ."

"They would have resumed their search. I understand."

"And I understand why you married. You deserved a normal life. And a beautiful daughter. She looks like you."

"She's a great kid." She frowned. "Did you watch her at the playground one day?"

"Yes. I wasn't trying to frighten her."

"You didn't."

"I didn't mean to frighten you at your father's funeral. I didn't think you would see me. When you did, I froze.''

''Why did you come?''

''Partly out of respect for your father. He was nice to me when I was very young, even if he came to dislike me later. And because I wanted to see you.''

''I thought maybe you'd come back for revenge.''

Paul's jaw dropped. ''Revenge! Good God, it never occurred to me you'd think that. I must have scared the daylights out of you.''

Nicole smiled. ''Yes, Paul, you did.''

''But you're not scared now?''

''Would I have come here if I were?''

''I suppose not. Still, it took a lot of nerve to meet me out here. But then, you were always brave.''

''I don't feel too brave these days, Paul. Carmen pointed out to me none too gently that I haven't even cried over my father's death. I guess I'm in shock—his death was so horrible. Then all this started. I can't mourn my father when I'm scared to death I'm going to be arrested for these murders. What will happen to Shelley?''

''You won't be arrested if I can help it,'' Paul said fervently. Then he paused. ''Nicole, are you sure your father committed suicide?''

Nicole's stomach tightened. It was a question that had run through her mind for days, although she hadn't let herself dwell on it. She combed fingers through her long, wind-tossed hair. ''The police are, but I'm not, although both Mother and his assistant, Kay, say he was upset those last weeks. He was also receiving mail that disturbed him. No one knows what the letters said or where they came from, but the last one had a picture of you in it.''

Paul looked genuinely surprised. ''A picture of *me*!''

''Yes. Kay found it partly burned in Dad's wastebasket in his office.''

''Burned? Why would he burn my picture?'' Nicole was silent. ''Oh. He was still angry over my relationship with you. But why would someone send a picture after all this time?''

''I have no idea. It wasn't as if Dad had anything to do with your arrest. It's true he didn't like you, but he never said you killed Magaro and Zand. He believed it was some kind of cult

killing and you'd been set up because by then everyone knew
about our relationship. You were a convenient scapegoat. He
didn't think their deaths had anything to do with me. But Dad's
death was the beginning of this nightmare.''

''No,'' Paul said slowly. ''The nightmare began fifteen years
ago. Everything goes back to your attack and the deaths of Zand
and Magaro, even your father's suicide, if it *was* suicide. The
mysterious mail and the picture of me sent to him convince me
of that.'' He hesitated. ''Good lord, you don't think he believed
I was sending the mail and that I was coming after him!''

''He was afraid you were going to kill him, so he killed himself
first? That doesn't make sense.''

''No, I guess not.''

''Besides, he thought you were dead. We *all* did.'' Nicole
reached up and touched his face. ''Paul, I'm so sorry. You had
such a fabulous life until I came into it.''

Paul looked at her tenderly. ''I have quite a few regrets about
my life, but meeting you isn't one of them. I feel the same way
about you as I did the last time we were here. Do you remember
that day?''

''It was sunny and beautiful. We talked endlessly. We took
pictures of each other. I knew that day that I loved you. Yes,
Paul, I remember. I'll remember it forever.''

Slowly Paul's face lowered over hers. The kiss was gentle and
tentative at first, then increasing in passion. Nicole's mind spun
back fifteen years, and suddenly she felt as if she hadn't been
kissed since Paul said good night to her at his door before she
left his house that last night. A wave of love that she'd been trying
to suppress for so long washed over her and she returned his kiss
with equal passion, her slender body seeming to melt into his,
their souls seeming to meet the way they had the very first time
they kissed. ''Some loves are forever,'' Alicia had said. She was
right. Her love for Paul had never died.

She wasn't sure how long they kissed before Jordan abruptly
stood up and growled. Paul broke away from Nicole, who felt
weak and disoriented. ''What is it, girl?'' he asked the dog.

She stood rigidly, gazing out onto the vast, unlighted grounds.
''Paul?'' Nicole's voice quavered.

He continued to hold her. ''Jordan.'' The dog glanced at him,
then focused again on the grounds. ''Someone is out there.''

"Oh, God," Nicole said. "What should we do?"

"We stay calm."

"Go inside," Nicole ordered, her wits coming back to her. "The first room is still intact. Go in there. I'll see who it is."

"I'm not leaving you alone."

"Hey, lady!" a voice shouted. "I'm not waitin' no more. If you're out here, come on. I'm leavin'."

The pent-up air fled from Nicole's lungs. "It's the taxi driver. I told him to wait."

"Then go," Paul said. "I can't have you stranded out here."

"But when will I see you again?"

"Soon." He kissed her, a quick, hard kiss on the lips. "I love you, *chérie*. As always. Now *go*."

In an instant he and Jordan had disappeared like ghosts inside the unfinished church. Nicole sat for a moment, overwhelmed by the meeting, the kiss, their abrupt disappearance.

"Lady, this is your last chance!" the man yelled. "I'm goin' back to the cab now."

Nicole jumped up and ran into the open, spotting the man almost immediately. He was only about fifty feet away. "Wait!" she called to his retreating back. "I'm coming."

He turned to look at her, his heavy face annoyed. "Well, at last. You're gonna have a helluva fare, you know."

"That's all right," she said breathlessly, catching up to him. "It was worth it."

TWENTY-SIX

1

After Nicole had returned home that night, she couldn't sleep. Well, that was nothing new, she thought as she lay on the bed. And tonight it really didn't matter. She felt energized, even lighthearted. She still didn't know who was committing the murders, she was still under suspicion by the police, but she knew that Paul was innocent and that he still loved her.

"He still loves me," she said aloud, touching the cross hanging from the chain around her neck. She wished she had someone to tell. At one time she could have told Carmen, but not now. Not even before she'd slammed out of the house on Sunday. Carmen was too determined to believe that Paul had killed Zand and Magaro. But Lisa said maybe Carmen had actually been the killer. It was true Zand's death had given her Bobby. The question was, would she have killed to have him?

When the alarm went off the next morning, Nicole was still awake and staring at the ceiling, trying to find answers. But she couldn't. All she knew was that she believed with all her heart in Paul's innocence.

When she left for school, she felt better than she had for weeks. When a sad-eyed Nancy stopped her before she got to her office, she had to camouflage the improvement in her spirits.

"Nicole, I'm so horrified by what happened to Avis!" Nancy said. "When I was at her house earlier in the day, she was dead in her backyard. If only I'd gone on around."

"It wouldn't have made any difference," Nicole said gently, aware that Nancy did not know all the details of Avis's death. As with Dooley's death, the police were withholding that information.

"Yes, I guess you're right. It wasn't suicide, though. Your friend with the police—did he tell you if they have any suspects?"

Yes, I'm the prime suspect, Nicole thought. "He didn't say."

Nancy sighed. "I can't help feeling this has something to do with Avis's behavior lately. She's been saying the most awful things to just about everyone, and I'm sure there have been other incidents like the one with you in the parking lot yesterday. I begged her to get help—"

"Nancy, you were a good friend to her. You did all you could. Don't torture yourself."

"That's what my husband says. And the Avis who was my friend hasn't existed for a long time. I was so hoping this sabbatical would help. Three months. Three more months and she would have been in England doing research." Nancy sighed again. "Oh, well, I'm handling the funeral arrangements. I doubt if you want to attend, but there will be so few people, so few flowers . . ."

Nicole put her hand on Nancy's arm. "I'm not sure I'll be able to attend." I might be in jail, she thought with a shiver. "But I'll certainly send flowers. Just tell me where to send them when the arrangements are made."

After her first class, Nicole returned to her office to find Ray and Cy Waters waiting for her. She'd been telling herself all morning to expect this—after all, Ray had told her she would probably be formally questioned today. Still, seeing Ray in an official capacity jolted her, especially after her meeting with Paul last night.

"Do you want me to go to headquarters?" she asked.

"No, Mrs. Chandler," Waters said. "We can talk here for now."

"All right." Nicole closed her door. "Would you like some coffee?"

"This isn't a social call," Waters snapped.

Nicole's gaze fluttered to Ray, but he was taking out a pen and notebook, his face impassive. "I'm sorry. I wasn't trying to make light of this," she said.

Waters nodded. "Good. Now, we've heard you and Ms. Simon-Smith weren't the best of friends."

Nicole sat down behind her desk. "No, we weren't. She was

rather odd. She *was* close to Nancy Silver, who also teaches in this department. Nancy could tell you more about Avis's personality than I.''

''But you had a fight in the parking lot day before yesterday.''

''Yes. I'd said something last week that made her mad. I was trying to apologize, but she wouldn't listen. She insulted me, and I insulted her back, and she shoved me. Not hard—I wouldn't have fallen if I hadn't been in high heels.''

''But you *did* fall and you were furious.''

''No, Sergeant Waters, I wasn't furious. I was surprised and embarrassed.''

''If someone pushed me down like that, *I'd* be furious.''

''Well, I wasn't.''

''But you didn't like her.''

''No, I didn't.''

''Is it true that the next day you called Sergeant DeSoto and asked him to check on this woman because she hadn't shown up for work and no one could reach her?''

''Yes.''

''Hmmm.'' Waters looked up at a framed print of a Degas painting that hung over a bookshelf, then back at Nicole. ''Mrs. Chandler, why were you so concerned about a woman you admit you disliked?''

''Because I know she has . . . had mental problems. When Nancy said she might have killed herself because she thought the incident in the parking lot was going to cost her her job, and I had provoked that incident by saying something cruel when I should have simply ignored her taunting . . .'' Nicole raised her hands. ''I felt responsible. I wanted to make sure she was all right.''

''That's very noble.''

Nicole was silent. She glanced at Ray again. He had not said a word.

''Mrs. Chandler, where were you between ten and twelve night before last?''

''At home,'' she said promptly.

''Did you have any visitors?''

''No.''

''Do you have any way of proving you were there during those hours?''

Ray was still gazing at his notebook. "There was a patrolman out front," Nicole said. "He can verify that I didn't leave."

"You could have sneaked out the back."

Nicole could feel herself coloring as she thought of last night's secret flight. "The backyard is fenced in. I'm afraid I'm not up to jumping a six-foot fence."

"Your prowler managed to get over it."

Nicole's mouth went dry. "Yes, he did. But I didn't climb a rope and go over the fence that night."

Waters wrote in his notebook. Ray wrote in his. He said he was going to give me an alibi, Nicole thought. I told him not to lie for me. But now I'm scared. Now I wish he'd say *something*. "Sergeant Waters, I believe I've said all I want to without my lawyer being present."

"What are you afraid of?" Waters asked.

"I'm not afraid. I'm just not stupid." She glanced at her watch. "Besides, it's time for my next class, so unless you plan to arrest me . . ."

"Not now," Waters said lazily. "Ray, the lady's got a class. Guess we'd better be on our way."

Ray nodded. They stood. "We'll be talking with you again, ma'am," Waters added.

"Very well," she said in a steady voice that belied her pounding heart. "But the next time my lawyer will be present."

After they left, Nicole put her head on her desk. Oh, God, she thought. Now I know how Paul felt fifteen years ago—scared, baffled, all evidence building against him, and no one to come to his defense.

2

Nicole was just leaving her office when the phone rang. She almost didn't answer but at the last minute decided it might be something important.

"Nicole," Ray said. "I was afraid I'd miss you."

Nicole could hear traffic noises in the background. "Where are you?"

"I'm using my cell phone. Cy's in a restaurant picking up coffee for us."

"Isn't that what drive-through windows are for?"

"Cy likes the coffee here. You sound angry." Nicole was silent. "You're wondering why I didn't say anything in your office today. Look, Nicole, I have to appear somewhat objective. Cy's already making assumptions about our relationship. What I wanted to tell you is you don't have to worry about an alibi. The patrolman outside your house saw you moving around inside, even saw your face at a window at the approximate time of the Smith woman's death."

Nicole breathed in relief. "Why didn't Waters tell me?"

"He wanted to scare you. But Nicole, I had every intention of telling him I'd had a long phone conversation with you from about ten-thirty to eleven-thirty if it had come to that."

"I'm glad it didn't. I wouldn't want to be the cause of problems with your career. But I wish I'd known this morning. Waters *did* scare me."

"Sorry. I didn't find out about what the patrolman said until a couple of hours before we questioned you. I never had a minute alone to give you a call."

"All right, Ray. I'm glad you let me know. Maybe I can stop shaking now."

"Just relax, Nicole. I know this has been awful, but justice *will* be served."

The phone went dead. Probably Ray had seen Waters coming back to the car. "Justice will be served," Ray had said. She wished that made her feel better, but it didn't because she knew Ray believed justice would only be served if Paul Dominic were captured and prosecuted.

3

"Thank goodness today is over," Nicole muttered, closing her briefcase, picking up a couple of books and her purse, and leaving the office. She knew she'd been more on target with her teaching than she had for days, but she was still exhausted.

She took the elevator down. In the large main hall, students milled around, forming into groups, laughing, picking up pamphlets someone was handing out. The place was always a scene of activity, a place to hang out between classes or just get together to socialize. Nicole passed through the crowd, nodding at familiar faces. Then her steps slowed as she saw Miguel and Lisa. Clearly they were arguing, Lisa's color high, Miguel gesticulating, his voice loud. As Nicole neared them, she heard Miguel say, "I don't know why I even bother with you!"

Miguel stalked off without ever seeing Nicole. She walked up to Lisa. "You're in love with him, aren't you?" Lisa's cheeks grew even redder. "That was a shot in the dark, but I'm right."

"Miguel doesn't have anything to offer me. I'm with Roger."

"And what does *he* have to offer you? I know he's nice-looking and well educated, but he's also twenty years older than you and a college professor. After he pays child support, he's not going to be able to give you the good life."

"Not now."

"What do you mean, not *now*? What do you think is going to change?"

"His mother can't live forever."

"You're counting on an inheritance. Well, don't. She's furious with Roger for deserting Shelley and me."

Lisa's eyes simmered. "I *know* that. She hangs up when he calls. But she'll get over it."

"I wouldn't count on it. She's never exactly doted on Roger, and now she's angry with him and disappointed in him. I doubt if she gives him a penny."

"She *would* have. She would have forgiven him. Everything would have been great."

Her eyes filled with tears while Nicole's eyes narrowed. "I've taken one shot in the dark. Let me try another. Roger no longer wants to marry you."

Lisa's face set obstinately. "Yes he does."

"I don't think so. I think he realizes he made a big mistake getting involved with you. That's what you mean by 'would have.' Things *would have* been great if he hadn't decided to throw in the towel."

"That's not true! He doesn't *love* you anymore, Nicole."

"I know. But in leaving his family, he tore up his life. His mother won't have anything to do with him and will probably write him out of her will, not that she had a fortune to leave, anyway. He's separated from Shelley, whom he *does* love. She's so bitter she doesn't even want to be around him. His friends don't accept you or him when he's with you.'' Nicole tilted her head. "That's why he's drinking so much. He's miserable.''

"You just want him back!''

"No. If he came to me tomorrow, I wouldn't take him back. The damage is done. He's already lost everyone who meant anything to him.''

Lisa glared. "He'll feel different when *everyone* realizes what a nut you are,'' she shouted. "When everyone knows all the awful things you've done lately, they'll understand why he left you. They won't blame him *or* me. His mother will forgive him, and he'll get Shelley like he wants. Then he'll be happy again. *We'll* be happy.''

"You'd like that, wouldn't you?'' Nicole said slowly. "You'd like for everyone to think I'm crazy. How far would you go, Lisa? Far enough to make me look like a murderer?''

Lisa's eyes flashed at her. Then she turned and ran from the building.

4

Nicole's mind churned as she drove home. So Roger didn't want Lisa anymore. She supposed she should feel like gloating, but she didn't. She realized now that her marriage had been over long before Roger left in January. Lisa had simply speeded up the inevitable.

Besides, it was clear both Roger and Lisa had each lost what they wanted most. Roger wanted Shelley and the respect of his mother and his peers. His colleagues might be more receptive to him after he got rid of Lisa, but the damage his relationships with his mother and Shelley had sustained could probably never be completely repaired. And Lisa had apparently lost Miguel, which meant he'd been lying when he said there was nothing between them. How many other things had he lied about? Carmen had said Lisa's parents sent her to college in Ohio to get her away from "some weird guy" in San Antonio. Could that have been Miguel?

Nicole stiffened. Had Miguel been watching her the last two weeks? Could all along Miguel have been both her protector and her tormentor?

If that were true, then *he* would have made the call she'd received from someone imitating Magaro. But how could Miguel have possibly known what Magaro said to her the night of the rape?

Simple, she thought as she stopped at a light. The information highway. Magaro told Bobby, Bobby told Lisa, and Lisa told Miguel. Maybe Miguel was going along with Lisa's plan back then. Or maybe he was just trying to scare me so I'd turn to some man for protection, hopefully him. Or perhaps the information stopped with Bobby. Maybe it was *Bobby* on the phone that night. He'd certainly love to frighten me.

When she pulled into her driveway, she noted that the patrol car was still in front of the house. Well, at least she was providing fodder for the local gossips, she thought. Probably the only person who found it exciting instead of frightening was Newton Wingate, whom she frequently saw talking to the patrolmen. "Just brushing up on my police procedure," he'd called to her one day, smiling merrily. "I'm thinking of writing a murder mystery."

"Am I your inspiration?" she'd asked, amused.

Newton looked at her waggishly. "My dear, you'd inspire any man."

But Newton was nowhere to be seen today. Maybe hard at work on his typewriter, she thought. Inside the house, Nicole sorted through the mail, noting there were no bills and no postcards, kicked off her shoes, and poured a glass of iced tea. I am *so* tired, she thought. So terribly tired. She set her glass on the coffee table and stretched out on the couch. In five minutes she was sleeping soundly.

It was night. She walked through the brush and voices floated toward her. "She thought she had us," Magaro was saying.

"She almost did," Zand answered, snorting something.

"No she didn't. It would have been better if we could have killed her like I wanted, but she still couldn't hurt us. I got too many friends, man. I *told* you I'd come up with an alibi." Her right hand squeezed around something metal. It fit perfectly within her palm. It gave her a feeling of power. "I said I'd keep you out of prison, didn't I?"

"Yeah, you did."

"And you promised me something in return. I'll tell you what I want. No more of this roadie stuff. I got talent, man. I shouldn't be haulin' around equipment. I should be on the drums."

"Vega's on drums. He's been with the band from the beginning."

"So? You get rid of him. No big deal."

"That wouldn't be easy, man. I wouldn't know how to do it."

There was a long, ominous silence. "You never know how to do anything, do you?" Magaro hissed in disgust. She saw the flash of an all-too-familiar knife. "You get rid of Vega, or he might meet an unfortunate fate, worse than the girl's. At least she lived, although I'd still like to get this knife in her throat for all the trouble she caused."

And then there was a crunching in the grass. Someone approached the two men, someone tall, someone she couldn't quite see. Her fingers tightened on the object in her hand.

"All right, Magaro, take it easy," Zand was saying. "If you want Vega out, he's out. Put that damned knife away."

The shadowy figure was off to her right, moving toward Magaro and Zand. She frowned, her sharp eyes piercing the clear night. Then, in the light of the moon, she caught a glimpse of the face . . .

The figure turned. Clifton Sloan looked directly into her eyes. "Nikki!" He rushed to her. Magaro and Zand were laughing uproariously at something. They hadn't seen or heard them. They also didn't see a third figure hovering near Nicole and Clifton. Clifton peered at her. "You're sleepwalking again." He dropped a gun into the grass. "Oh, God, you're barefoot." He lifted her, knocking the flashlight out of her hand. "We're going home, sweetheart. We're going home and you're going to forget all about this."

As he swung her around, heading for the road, she caught one last glimpse of the other figure standing absolutely still, watching them. The face. She could barely see the face . . .

Nicole bolted up from the couch, her heart hammering. "Oh, dear God!" she cried. "I *was* there that night. And so was my father. With a *gun*. My father had come there to kill Zand and Magaro!"

TWENTY-SEVEN

1

At dusk Nicole was still pacing around the living room, stunned by the buried knowledge her dream had revealed. Her gentle, gun-hating father had intended to kill Magaro and Zand. What was his plan? To leave his hotel in Dallas and drive to San Antonio, kill Zand and Magaro, then drive back to Dallas and be there for his morning meeting? It could be easily done. Dallas was less than two hundred miles from San Antonio. And the police had verified that he was seen in the hotel at ten o'clock in the evening, and again the next morning at eight. His plan would have worked, but he hadn't counted on seeing his daughter in Basin Park. That had stopped him from committing murder.

Or had it? Had he taken her home, put her to bed, and gone back to finish the job? Would Zand and Magaro have still been there? Would he have been able to find the gun again? Would he have set up Paul to look like the murderer?

She sat down, twisting her hands in her lap. What should she do with this knowledge? Call Ray? Would it diffuse his certainty that Paul was a killer? Maybe. It would also cast a terrible light on her father.

But there was a third person out there that night. She'd seen the silhouette. Could she identify that person? No. Could she prove that person had murdered Magaro and Zand after she and her father left? No. If Ray even believed her story about the third person, he would probably think it was Paul.

She was certain it wasn't. So who was it? Carmen, as Lisa believed? Nicole concentrated on the memory. The person had been taller than she, and certainly heavier, but beyond that she could remember nothing. Could it have been Bobby, wanting only to kill Magaro because he was forcing Zand to kick him out of The Zanti Misfits? But why would he have killed Zand? Could *that* murder have been an accident? Or could it have simply been an unknown, crazy person who'd seen her father drop the gun and seized an opportunity?

Abruptly Nicole realized she had a splitting headache. She went into the kitchen, downing two more aspirin as she glanced out the window. It was dark now. She'd been pacing and thinking for over an hour, and she still didn't have any answers.

She went back and lay on the couch, waiting for the aspirin to take effect, glad Shelley wasn't here to see her in this condition. Would her life ever return to normal? Would this mystery ever be solved? Or would she end up in prison?

She was still lying in the dark when the phone rang. Oh, no, she thought. How can I possibly sound normal if it's Shelley or Ray?

Nicole rolled off the couch and stumbled into the kitchen, banging her knee on the coffee table along the way. "Hello?"

A moment of silence spun out. Finally Paul said in a raspy, pain-ridden voice, "Nicole, come to the Mission San Juan. I need you."

Then the line went dead.

2

Nicole stood holding the phone for a few seconds. What could have happened? Had she led someone to Paul less than twenty-four hours ago?

Without hesitation, she bolted for the bedroom, and nearly tore off her suit. Within minutes she was in jeans and a sweater. She pulled a jacket over her clothes, stuffed her gun in the pocket, then picked up the bedroom phone and called the taxi company, once again directing them to pick her up on the street behind hers as soon as possible.

As she ran through the darkened living room, she remembered Ray saying the night Avis had been murdered, the patrolman outside had seen her moving around inside. The men sent to watch her were clearly alerted to survey for normal light patterns, and here it was pitch-dark, not one light glowing in the living room.

Quickly she went around, turning on lamps and even the television. She pulled back the sheer curtains, looking outside, just in case he was looking back and could see her face. Then she drew one set of draperies. All looked normal for eight-thirty on a week night.

Next she went to the basement and retrieved her ladder. She went out the back door and propped the ladder against the fence. Two minutes later the ladder lay in the backyard of the empty house, and she had made another successful drop to the ground. She arrived at the sidewalk just as the taxi pulled up.

"The Mission San Juan," she said, climbing into the backseat.

The driver turned around. "Not *again*!"

Nicole looked at him. "Good lord, what are the chances of getting the same taxi driver two nights in a row?"

"Slim. Look, lady, I told you I don't like it out there."

"Didn't I pay you double last night? Didn't you make more than you would have in a normal night?"

"Yeah," he said grudgingly.

"Did any harm come to you?"

"Well, no."

"Then what's the problem? I'll pay double the fare again tonight. You could use the extra money, couldn't you?"

"Okay." He shook his head. "But if you're havin' an affair, lady, I'd suggest you find a better place like everyone else. This is weird."

"Please just drive. I'm in a hurry."

"You're *always* in a hurry. I'd sure like to know what this guy's got goin' for him. No woman would do this for me."

You're not Paul Dominic, she thought. I'd do anything for Paul if he needed me.

But what could be wrong? Nicole asked herself as they crossed the city, this trip slower than the last one because it was earlier in the evening. If someone *had* caught up with Paul, why would they be holding him at the mission? It certainly couldn't be the police or Paul would be in custody. What about Miguel? Carmen? Maybe even Lisa or Bobby?

But perhaps Paul wasn't being held at all. Maybe he'd been badly hurt and taken refuge at the mission instead of going to a hospital, which would be too dangerous. If that were the case, though, why hadn't he gone to his mother's? Fear of Rosa? And what could she do for him?

After what seemed an interminable ride, they finally arrived at the mission. "Don't tell me," the driver said. "You want me to wait."

"Yes. Do I have to pay up to this point?" Nicole asked.

"No. You were good for the fare last night. I guess I trust you."

Thank heavens, Nicole thought, remembering she only had ten dollars in her purse and no checkbook. He'd have to wait until she returned home to get paid.

She jumped out of the cab, passed through an opening in the stone walls, and crossed the grounds. The tall wooden cross looked more stark and rough than it had last night. She stopped. Something was different. It was the light. The cross wasn't bathed in only the softening sheen of moonlight. She looked toward the church to see light flickering through the open doorway. There must be a special event tonight because the church was open. In that case, she had to be extra careful.

Nicole ran to the ruins of the unfinished church where she had met Paul last night. Moonlight played over the statue of Jesus holding the baby in one arm. Someone had placed a bouquet of flowers in the statue's free hand. Slowly she went into the first room on the left, which she knew had been intended as the baptistery. No Paul.

She searched all the rooms of the ruins, then went outside. "Jordan?" she called softly, hoping the dog would come to her again and lead her to Paul. But the dog didn't appear.

Next Nicole went to the *hospedería*, or guest lodgings, but to no avail. She emerged again onto the open grounds. Where could he be? The historical museum was closed. Only the church remained open.

Music floated from the open door. Gregorian chants, beautiful and haunting. And loud. Then it hit her. If there were a special event going on, where were the cars in the parking lot? There were no cars, no sign of activity. Paul was in the church. It was the only place left. But he certainly wouldn't turn on lights and play loud music.

He wasn't alone, she thought with a chill. Someone had him.

Nicole approached the door slowly, afraid to go in, afraid not to. Finally, getting a firm grip on the gun in her pocket, she stepped inside.

She'd always thought the inside of the church was beautiful, although outside it was the most austere of the missions. The walls were snowy white, the ceiling high and lined with rough beams. A simple circular chandelier decorated with only six candles hung high above. But the altar was magnificent, with its crimson hangings, golden pillars, vividly colored religious statues, and more candles. Fresh baskets of poinsettias sat beneath a delicate, lacy white altar cloth.

To her right on a table, votive candles burned. *All* of them, nearly fifty. The music soared, filling the old church with the reverent, perfectly pitched *a cappella* voices.

"Paul?" Nicole called over the music. "Paul, are you here?"

At first there was nothing but the sound of the chants. Then she heard it. Groans. Someone kicking the wooden floor near the front of the church.

Slowly she moved forward, still holding the gun in her pocket. How strange that felt. To be in a church, holding a gun.

Another groan sounded at the front of the church. Nicole bolted forward, then stopped. A man rose up from behind the altar. He held a battered, gagged Paul. He was also holding a gun to Paul's temple.

"Ray?" Nicole's voice was high with disbelief. "Ray, what are you doing?"

"I knew you'd come if *he* asked you. You still love him, don't you? After all this time." Nicole went hollow inside. "*He* wouldn't make the call," Ray said. "*He* wouldn't lure you out here. Not even when I got . . . *persuasive*. So I had to imitate his voice again."

"*Again?*"

Ray lapsed into a perfect imitation of Paul's voice. "Nicole, come to the Mission San Juan. I need you."

Suddenly Nicole remembered Paul saying he would never call her because he was afraid her phone was tapped. She also remembered Ray imitating Izzy Dooley's girlfriend's voice. Obviously he had a faculty for mimicry. How many times had he used it?

"Ray?" Nicole asked, feeling as if the words were coming from someone else. "Did you call me pretending to be Magaro?"

"Yes. After Dominic hit me, I made the call on my cell phone when I regained consciousness. Scared you, didn't I?"

Nicole was shivering, but her voice was steady. "You're the person behind all of these murders, aren't you?"

He looked at her nonchalantly. "Certainly, Nicole."

Horror engulfed her. How many times had he sat in her living room, offering comfort, delivering bad news with soft words and kind eyes? She'd believed in him. She'd considered a relationship with him when this ordeal was over. This ordeal he'd created. But she knew it would be a mistake to let him see her revulsion. Somehow she knew he would expect surprise, even be pleased by it, but he wouldn't tolerate revulsion.

She swallowed. "So you're responsible for the murders lately, but not fifteen years ago. You didn't kill Zand and Magaro."

"Oh, yes, them, too."

"Them, too?" she echoed in shock. "Why?"

"Because they hurt you."

"Because they *hurt* me? Ray, you didn't even *know* me."

"Yes, I did. Sort of." He smiled sweetly. "You don't recognize me, do you?" Nicole slowly shook her head. "You don't remember Rosa's son, Juan?"

Nicole's mind spun back over the years. The shy teenager, always darting out of the way, never meeting her eyes. And Rosa's last name was DeSoto. She hadn't thought of that for years. Besides, there were so many DeSotos in the area. "You're Rosa's son?" she repeated dumbly. "But your name . . ."

"Raymond Juan DeSoto." He smiled. "Don't feel so bad. Paul here didn't recognize me, either, did you, Paul?"

He tore the gag from Paul's mouth. Dried blood streaked down from a corner. One eye was circled with purple, and his right cheek bore a long cut. "No," he croaked.

"How about that?" Ray said, smiling. "Didn't even recognize his own brother."

Paul's head jerked toward him and Ray pushed the gun harder against his temple. "Be *still*," Ray hissed.

"What are you talking about?" Nicole asked. "Paul doesn't have a brother."

"Not one that he knows about. Not a *full* brother. I'm the product of an affair the saintly Alicia Dominic had when Paul was about twelve."

My God, Nicole thought. She had considered that the affair with Javier resulted in a child, but she'd thought that child might possibly be Miguel Perez because he looked so much like Paul. There was no resemblance between Paul and Ray besides dark hair.

"Alicia doesn't think I know," Ray went on, "but I've *always* known. She was too religious to have an abortion, so she found a woman who was an illegal immigrant and promised that if she'd pretend the child were hers, she'd pull strings to get the woman's citizenship papers along with giving her a permanent home in a mansion. She and Rosa left San Antonio, Alicia supposedly for Europe. Actually, they were both in California. Shortly after Alicia had me, giving *her* name as Rosa DeSoto in the hospital, she came home. Three months later Rosa showed up with a baby and was hired as the housekeeper."

"The other one," Alicia had said. Ray was "the other one," the son of Javier.

"I don't believe you," Paul grated out.

"Well, it's true." Ray jerked him and Paul cried out. Obviously his left arm was broken. His face paled, and Nicole saw the gleam of sweat on it. "Not that I was ever treated like your brother. Oh, I lived in the same house, but I was kept away from you as much as possible. Your mother was always afraid some resemblance between us might show up. That's why you've never recognized me. You left home at fifteen—I was only three—and when you were back on visits, I was ordered to stay out of your way. That was part of it, anyway. The other part was that your mother, *my* mother, could barely stand to look at me. I was a reminder of her great sin. Rosa told me that one night when she'd had too much to drink. She drinks in secret, you know."

Nicole thought of Alicia's words: "God made me pay . . . I tried to make amends, but it didn't work because I was still lying, still hiding."

"Oh, materially she did all the right things," Ray continued sarcastically. "Saw that I was well dressed, sent me to a good college. But Rosa! The woman is a sadist. She hated me. She tortured me in a hundred little ways. One day I gathered all my courage and told Alicia. I even showed her the bruises on my arms from Rosa's vicious pinching. You know what your wonderful mother did, Paul? She averted her eyes and said, 'You probably got those playing. Don't be so imaginative, Juan.' She knew, but she didn't care. All her attention was focused on her golden boy, the legitimate one, the talented one. I abhorred you, Paul. I always have.''

Nicole closed her eyes, still unable to believe what she was hearing, yet knowing it was true. ''You were in Basin Park the night my father went there to kill Zand and Magaro.''

Ray gave her a coy look. ''Oh, you remembered! Or did you really know about your father all along?''

''I just remembered this afternoon.''

''How convenient that you'd remember today of all days. Yes, I was there. I simply picked up your father's gun and killed them.''

''And the hanging and the hoods?''

''He'd brought the rope and the hoods, too. Didn't you see that in your dream? I think he wanted to make it look like a ritual killing. I just followed the plan, only *I* knew people would think it was the kind of macabre thing Paul might do.''

''The shirt,'' Paul rasped.

''I had access to your clothes, so I wrapped the murder weapon in your shirt. I knew you didn't have an alibi. You were lying around in your music room, listening to yourself on that damned tape and pining over Nicole. Alicia was in the hospital. She couldn't provide an alibi. Dear Rosa was closeted in her room, as usual, reading those smutty romances and drinking.''

''So you left the house and no one knew,'' Nicole said.

''I left the house *every* night. It was the only time I had to do what *I* wanted, my only freedom. I knew where Dominic's secret key was under the urn. I hung out with Zand and Magaro. They liked me because occasionally I'd bring them a bottle of wine I'd sneaked out of the house. When they were high, they told me what they'd done to you, Nicole. Magaro kept giggling about calling you 'little bird.' He thought that was hilarious. I pretended to think it was funny, too. That's why they didn't panic when I came up to them that night. They thought I was just some seventeen-year-old fan. They called me Ray, but they had no idea who I really was or where I lived. They just enjoyed having me around, seeming to worship them.'' Ray laughed harshly. ''All along I thought they were a couple of pigs.''

Nicole still held the gun in her pocket. She took a small step closer to the altar. "Ray, you said you killed them because of me."

"Yes. The beautiful Nicole who never looked twice at me because she was too dazzled by Paul. But I looked at you. I wanted you more than anything I've ever wanted in my life except Dominic's destruction."

"You didn't know me. You only wanted me because I was Paul's."

"That was part of it. The rest was just *you*. I loved the way you looked, the way you moved, the way you talked. Everything."

"So you punished those who hurt me and tried to destroy Paul at the same time. But what about now?" Nicole's vision darkened for a moment as an awful thought struck her. "Ray, did you murder my father?" she asked shakily.

He blinked at her. "Nicole, I *told* you it was suicide."

"You told me a lot of things."

"Yes, but *that* was true. Suicide isn't as easy to fake as it is on television. And I had that damned Waters along with me. He would have picked up on the fact that it wasn't really suicide, even if I *had* murdered your father and tried to cover it up."

"But you sent Dad the letters and the photo of Paul?"

"Yes. When I heard you were back in San Antonio, I knew fate had brought you back to me. But there were so many people around you. I was trying to figure out what to do about your husband when he did it for me." Ray laughed. "Stupid fool. But there was still your father. You were crazy about him. So I decided to slowly make him fall apart by reminding him of what he'd done."

"He didn't kill Zand and Magaro!" Nicole shouted.

"No. But he was there that night. He saw someone else. He looked right into my face, Nicole. He didn't know who I was, but he knew I wasn't Dominic. But did he come forward after Paul's arrest? Did he admit the gun was his? Did he say he'd seen someone else out there? Did he do *anything* to deflect suspicion from Dominic? No."

Nicole felt sick. Ray was clearly unbalanced, but he was right about her father. Clifton Sloan wasn't a murderer, but he hadn't done anything to save Paul.

"I couldn't murder him because *no one* would believe you

would kill him," Ray said. "I hoped he'd just crack up and admit
what he'd done. That would certainly have damaged your love
for him. Instead he killed himself. That turned out to be fortunate,
though. It got rid of him and brought me into your life."

"Yes, how fortunate," Nicole said weakly. "But if he really
did commit suicide, why didn't he leave a suicide note?"

"He did. It was a full confession of what happened fifteen
years ago. I didn't want suspicion shifted from Dominic. Fortu-
nately, the note had slipped under the desk. I found it and tucked
it in my pocket when Waters wasn't looking. It's easy to fool
Waters about little things."

A note. Her mother had been crushed because Clifton hadn't
even left a note to explain why he'd done such a terrible thing.
His confession would have been shocking, but at least it would
have been an explanation, because Nicole was certain her mother
didn't know what had happened that night fifteen years ago. But
Ray had hidden it. Hatred for him rose up in her like gall. But
she wouldn't show it. She couldn't. Right now she had to concentrate on trying to save herself and Paul.

Nicole took a deep breath and another small step forward.
"You said no one would believe I killed my father. But your goal
was to make everyone believe *I* killed those other people?"

"Yes."

"*Why?*"

"So you'd turn to me because I'd be the only one who believed
you. Then I would become your protector and you'd fall in love
with me."

"But you didn't count on Paul returning."

Ray hesitated, a fretful look passing over his face. "No. Oh, I
knew he wasn't dead. Rosa told me she'd caught glimpses of him
at the house over the years. She still hates me, but she's also
afraid of me." He smiled with satisfaction. "You see, she's always suspected *I* was the one who killed Zand and Magaro. She
knew Paul didn't have the guts to do it. But she wouldn't say
anything because I knew her immigration papers were faked. She
made a big mistake telling me that. But Dominic coming back
turned out my way, too. No one else believed you when you
claimed he was in San Antonio. Everyone thought you'd flipped
after Roger left you and your father committed suicide. But *I*
believed you. You appreciated me for that."

"Yes, I did."

"And it tarnished Dominic's image in your eyes. You were suddenly afraid he *did* murder Magaro and Zand and had come back to murder you in revenge for what happened to him."

"Yes. But only for a while."

Ray's smile faded. "So I saw for myself last night. You know, it always bothered me that you kept such a physical distance between us. You never even kissed me, but I told myself you had too much propriety to throw yourself in another man's arms when your husband had left less than two months ago.

"Then I saw you with Dominic here at the mission, and I knew I was wrong. You didn't have any trouble throwing yourself in *his* arms, not even after all this time, after all your suspicions of him. I'll bet you never even gave *me* a thought."

"That's not true, Ray."

"After all I did for you. Hell, I even offered to invent an alibi for you for the Smith woman's death. But it didn't make any difference. You didn't care about me. No one has *ever* cared about me."

"That's not true. I *did* care. If it weren't for Paul—"

"If it weren't for Paul, what? You would have been in *my* bed before long? You would have married *me* after your divorce?"

"I don't know, Ray. I couldn't see that far into the future."

"I can." The flickering candles cast shadows on Ray's face, making him look gaunt and hollow-eyed. "It wouldn't have happened. You would have used me to help you. Then you would have forgotten I existed."

"That's not *true*." Nicole took another small step forward, as if she were genuinely agonized by Ray's words. "I would never have forgotten what you did for me, and our relationship could have become romantic." It sickened her, but she had to add the following sentence. "It still can."

Ray sneered at her. "Do you think I want you *now,* after what I saw last night?"

"What did you see, Ray? Me hugging someone I hadn't seen for years, someone I once loved, someone I realized hadn't done anything to hurt me? Is that such a terrible thing? Besides, how did you know I was meeting Paul here?"

"When you had your little fainting spell after I told you about the Smith woman, I saw the postcard with the mail and read it. I watched that night to see what you'd do. I know you so well, I even figured you'd go over the back fence. But as for your simply hugging someone you once loved, you must think I'm a fool. You didn't just *hug* him. You kissed him. Passionately. It was like something out of some damned corny movie. It nauseated me. And I stopped caring about you, Nicole. Right then and there, I stopped caring.''

His coldness in the office earlier that day when Waters was questioning her so relentlessly. He'd been furious. Then later he'd decided that in order not to make her suspicious of him, he'd better smooth things over, so he'd called and lied to her about the officer seeing her moving around in the living room. She knew now it was a lie because she remembered that between ten and twelve, when Avis was killed, she'd been in bed.

''So, Ray, what's the plan?'' Nicole asked. ''What are you going to do with us?''

''You'll both be found here, dead. Dominic, of course, managed to lure you here.''

''How could he do that if I'm supposed to be afraid of him?''

''We have Carmen to attest to the fact that you'd stopped fearing him. Or, since she's now convinced you're off your rocker, she might claim you came out here to kill Dominic. In any case, there will be a record that a call was placed to your house from here. Obviously it was from Dominic. We also have the cab driver who will testify that he brought you out here.''

Nicole was close enough now to see that Paul's eyes were red-rimmed. He looked shockingly pale and exhausted. Obviously Ray had grabbed him last night, after she'd left. He'd been a prisoner all day. And he'd been beaten. Badly.

Her hand clenched around the gun in her pocket. ''Ray, you never finished telling me what your plan for us is.''

''Dominic will kill you, and I'll kill Dominic. I'll probably get a commendation for it.''

''Paul will kill me with *your* gun? That won't work.''

Ray looked disgusted. ''*No,* Nicole. The gun I'm holding to Paul's head, the gun that will kill you, isn't mine. It came from the Dominic house. And by the way, you might as well take your hand out of your pocket. I know you have your gun in there, but it isn't loaded.''

Color drained from her face. ''You unloaded it?''

"Yes, today. I pick locks, remember? I was in your house."

Anger soared in her. "You thought of everything, didn't you? You even planted the money in Dooley's apartment."

"I didn't *plant* it. A couple of years ago I destroyed evidence and saved Dooley from a murder charge. He owed me, but I paid him anyway. I told him I wanted you killed, and I told him what lie to tell Jewel about how he got the money. I had him follow you. He let me know you were on the River Walk. I ordered him to rough you up and get your purse, that's all. Later he was to go to your house and murder you. Meanwhile, I smashed that padlock and let Jesse out. When I took you home, I searched the house to make sure all was safe, remember? Only while I was in the basement, I unlocked a window and pulled a chest underneath it."

"But why did you put a patrolman outside? That only made things more dangerous."

"That was unfortunate. Erwin, the officer who questioned you after your attack on the River Walk, likes to make women uncomfortable to their faces, but underneath he has this disgusting soft streak. He dispatched Abbott. He spotted a man walking toward your house. He was starting to get out of the cruiser, so I walked up to him like I had nothing to hide, and I killed him. I had no choice. Then I came into the house via the window and waited for Dooley. It was always my plan to kill him before he got to you. Simple."

"But you didn't count on Newton Wingate seeing you."

"He saw *someone* talking to Abbot. Someone with long dark hair. So did those kids who spotted somebody messing around with Roger's car. Long dark hair. Like Dominic's."

"A wig."

"Sure." He sighed. "The only thing that went wrong was Jewel. That idiot Dooley told her who *really* gave him the money. She stuck to the story, but I could tell she knew the truth by the way she looked at me when Waters and I questioned her. I tried to kill her, but I wasn't successful."

Nicole released her grip on the gun. If it were unloaded, what good was it except as an object to strike him with? Ray, on the other hand, had at least two *loaded* guns. All she could think of to do at the moment was to keep talking.

"But why didn't you kill Roger like you did the others?"

''Roger had an annoying habit of never being alone. He's always with his girlfriend. I had to find another method. It didn't quite work, but it didn't matter. Things still looked bad for you, and you came running to me. Just what I wanted.'' He sighed. ''So much planning. So much energy. I thought it was worth it. I thought *you* were worth it.'' He gave her a piercing stare. ''But you aren't.''

''What if I hadn't met Paul last night? What if your feelings for me hadn't changed? I would surely have been arrested, maybe even found guilty of the murders.''

''No. I knew I could lure out Paul when the time was right. Then I would kill him. And there was evidence to link him to the crimes. He'd been in his mother's house, remember? I'd told Rosa to be on the lookout for *any* signs of Dominic. She did a pretty good job. Fear will sharpen the senses, you know. By now she's scared stiff of me. She knew if she didn't come up with something, she might not live long. She got strands of Dominic's hair from Alicia's bedspread. They would match the strands found on Dooley's shirt, where I'd placed them. Dominic had also cut himself shaving in his mother's bathroom. He didn't do a very good job of cleaning up. Rosa found the blood. She had sense enough to save traces for me, which I added some water to and put on the broken window in the Simon-Smith woman's door. You didn't know about this evidence, of course, but you were always fairly much in the clear. *I* couldn't have provided an alibi for you by claiming to have a long phone conversation with you between ten-thirty and eleven-thirty the night I killed the Smith woman.''

''I know. Phone records.''

Ray smirked at her. ''Very good. Catching on at last.''

''But what about the prowler in the wolf mask?''

''Dooley.''

''Where did he get the mask?''

''Rosa bought it for herself. I took it. Then I called Bobby and told him if anyone asked, he was to say Lisa bought it.''

''Then Carmen *wasn't* lying,'' Nicole said with a wave of guilt.

''No. She told you what Bobby told her. She always told you the truth, but I wanted you to doubt her. I didn't want you to believe in anybody except me, so I told Bobby to lie about the mask.''

Nicole frowned. "I don't understand. Why would Bobby lie for you?"

"Bobby's afraid of me because way back when I knew Magaro and Zand, I learned about his taste for underage girls. After I became a cop, I kept up with him. You never know when you'll need dirt on someone," he said matter-of-factly. "I've got so much evidence against him, I could ruin his life. He wouldn't dare disobey me." He tilted his head. "Of course, the same was true of Avis Simon-Smith. Four years ago she killed her mother. At that time I was a detective investigator assigned to the case. Foul play couldn't be proved, but I knew she did it, and she knew *I* knew. The crazy bat was terrified of me."

"You ordered her to push me in the parking lot?"

"Not specifically. I just told her to publicly humiliate you."

"That's why you became a cop, isn't it? It gave you power over people. Power you never had as a child."

"Forget the amateur psychology, Nicole. You can't have power unless God lets you have it. God is on my side."

"God, or the devil?" a man's voice rang out.

Ray's gaze shot behind Nicole. She turned. Cy Waters stood in the door of the church, his gun drawn.

"Waters!" Ray shouted. Nicole looked back at him. His face transformed. The weird smirk was gone. He looked tough, businesslike, in control. "I've got Dominic. He was going to kill Nicole."

"Won't work, Ray," Waters said. "I've been standing outside the door for ten minutes. I wanted to hear this."

Ray jerked Paul, causing him to flinch in pain, jamming the gun into his temple. "What are you doing here?"

"I followed you. I got a call from Jewel Crown earlier this evening. She had some interesting things to say about your paying Izzy to kill Nicole, then shooting at her on the street the other night."

Ray laughed emptily. "And you took her seriously? She's a hooker and a coke addict."

"It wasn't just Jewel. I've never trusted you, DeSoto."

"Never trusted me?" Ray sneered. "Oh, that explains it. Well, tell me something, Cy. If you didn't trust me, why didn't you say so to someone?"

"Because you're a super cop. Never made a mistake. Made

sergeant at thirty-one. Commendations up to your neck. What was I supposed to do—complain about you just because you gave me the creeps but I didn't know why?''

Ray gave him a lopsided grin. ''What about your attitude toward Nicole? You seemed convinced she was guilty. You dragged her over the coals. What was that all about?''

''Partly because that's my way—I always play bad cop. But partly because when I first suspected what you were up to, I couldn't believe it. I decided to act normal and just watch to see if you made any mistakes. And you did. You've screwed up a couple of times lately, Ray.''

Ray stiffened as if affronted by an insult. ''Like when?''

''Like taking the gun used in the Zand–Magaro murders out of Evidence the day after I said I was going to have Ballistics go over it again.''

''What's the big deal about that? I put it back.''

''*After* you were satisfied that the serial number couldn't be recovered. They told me in Ballistics you'd brought the gun over and asked. But you got too cocky. You didn't let them try. *I* did. This time they were able to bring it up. The gun was registered to General Ernest Hazelton, Nicole's grandfather.''

Ray pulled a face. ''I guess that means Nicole killed Zand and Magaro.''

''My father tried,'' Nicole said desperately to Cy. ''But he couldn't go through with it. He dropped the gun. Ray picked it up. He was in Basin Park that night. He knew Magaro and Zand. Sergeant Waters, he's Paul's half-brother.''

''So I heard,'' Cy said slowly. ''So, Ray, Alicia Dominic is your mother, but you were raised by Rosa DeSoto.''

''So what?''

''So you were in the vicinity of the Zand–Magaro murders. So you knew Paul Dominic, but you never said anything in all these weeks. So you had a very good motive for trying to pin a murder on him.''

''That's not *proof*.''

Cy went on equably. ''I'll tell you another thing that bothered me. You've always been a stickler for rank. Yet you insisted we go check on that Simon-Smith woman. That's not our job, Ray. But you had to go to her house. You even dragged me around back so we'd be sure to find her body and Dominic's blood on the broken window.''

''That's ridiculous!''

Cy stepped into the room. ''None of this explanation is necessary. I just don't want you to believe I'm as dumb as you've always thought I was. But even if I were, I *heard* what you said to Nicole. You told her everything, including the fact that you killed Zand and Magaro.''

''Well, now, that's just your word against mine, isn't it?'' Ray asked.

So fast that Nicole hardly saw it, Ray swept the gun from Paul's temple and fired. The bullet whizzed past Nicole's face. Abruptly Cy cried out in pain.

Nicole couldn't duck. She couldn't take her eyes off Ray as he leveled the gun at her. This is it, she thought, frozen. There's nothing I can do. I have no weapon. Dodging behind a pew won't help. He'll just keep firing until he hits me. Good-bye, my darling Shelley. Good-bye, Paul.

Suddenly Paul lunged to the left, throwing Ray off balance. His gun went off, hitting the iron chandelier and sending it dancing wildly. Ray screamed in rage. He whirled, pointing the gun at Paul's head.

''No!'' Nicole screamed a second before another explosion sounded in the church, ripping through the sound of the beautiful chants.

Nicole's hands covered her head. Who'd fired a gun? she thought frantically. Cy or Ray?

Her heart thudding with fear, she slowly lifted her head. Ray stood behind the altar. Paul stood beside him.

For a moment, neither Paul nor Ray moved. Then she watched in amazement as Ray's features softened. His eyes looked beyond her, looked at nothing, really. Finally he smiled. ''Mother!'' he said softly.

Then he pitched forward on his face, toppling off the altar into the flowers, his blood splattering the delicate white altar cloth.

EPILOGUE

Nicole, Paul, and Shelley crossed the cemetery grounds. Jordan trotted alongside Paul. Shelley held Jesse on a leash.

Paul wore a cast on his arm and a bandage on his cheek. Jordan bore a bare spot and stitches on her head from a laceration above a concussion. Ray had left her for dead on the mission grounds when he'd taken Paul home and kept him tied in his basement without food or water. When Jordan revived, she'd hidden on the mission grounds, waiting for her master to return.

Paul, Nicole, and Shelley all carried flowers. They stopped at Clifton Sloan's grave.

The wind blew Nicole's hair around her face. She looked beyond the grave to the knoll where the large Pinchot juniper grew. "It seems like months ago that Dad's funeral service was being held and I looked up to see you and Jordan standing on that knoll. You looked right into my eyes."

"And you went all white," Shelley said.

"I hadn't seen him for fifteen years, honey. I thought he was dead."

"But you're sure glad he's not." Shelley looked at Paul and beamed. "Me, too. Mommy told me she used to love you. I think she still does."

Paul smiled at her. "I hope so."

"I'm still a little sad about Ray, though." Shelley frowned. "I thought he was our friend."

"He fooled a lot of people," Nicole said. "He wasn't what he seemed to be."

"Yeah, I know." Shelley laid a single red rose on her grandfather's grave. "Do you think Grandpa knows we're here?"

"I don't know," Nicole said.

"I think he does. I think he knows it's a pretty day and we're all here, even Jesse." Then with a child's quick change of attention, she asked, "Can I take Jesse and Jordan to look at some of the other flowers?"

"Yes," Nicole said.

Paul nodded to Jordan, who trotted along with Shelley and an exuberant, sneezing Jesse.

When they were a few feet from the grave, Paul put a hand on Nicole's shoulder. "How do you feel?"

Nicole shrugged. "Sad. Strange. Paul, I didn't know my father at *all*."

"Yes you did," he said gently. "You know he loved you. That's all that's really important."

"I'm surprised you can say that. What about what he did to you?"

Paul's gaze dropped. "When Ray first told us the truth, I was furious with your father. Enraged. But then I thought about it. What would his coming forward have accomplished? Who would have believed his vague story about a third figure he couldn't identify in the park? All the police would have concentrated on was him. He had the motive, the opportunity, and the means. The gun was part of your grandfather's estate left to your mother. She told us it was kept in a locked chest in the attic. She never looked at the guns, never even knew it was missing from the collection."

"But she suspected I'd been sleepwalking the night Zand and Magaro were murdered."

"Suspecting isn't knowing. She didn't want to upset you. And she *didn't* know your father had come back from Dallas that night."

"But he had. And he could have cleared *you*."

"I think he was taking the chance that I would be found innocent."

"That was quite a chance."

Paul smiled. "Nicole, your father was human. He made a mistake. Just like my mother. But they paid for their mistakes. Your father probably never had a moment's peace of mind for fifteen years. The guilt must have been awful. That's why he left the church. Finally, when Ray's tormenting started, he just couldn't stand it anymore. And Nicole, with the exception of your father's death, everything *did* work out for us in the end. The real killer is dead. I've been cleared. We're together again. You have a beautiful daughter. Your husband has left Lisa. Even Carmen has forgiven you.''

"I guess you're right," Nicole said listlessly. "But *none* of this had to happen if Dad had just told the truth."

Paul's voice was gentle. "Nicole, please remember all the things you loved about your father. That's what I've tried to do with Mother. Don't let one bad mistake negate all the good things he did in his life. And you know, I'm convinced that if I hadn't run, if I'd gone to trial and he'd seen that it was going badly for me, he would have come forward."

"Do you really think so?"

"Yes, I do."

"I can't believe how forbearing you are."

"I told you I learned a lot during my years on the road. One of them was tolerance for people's weaknesses. After all, look what I did. Instead of facing my troubles, I ran. I put the people who loved me through a lot of pain because of that decision. I hope they can forgive *me*. I've tried to forgive my mother for how she treated Ray, pushing him aside, leaving him in that devil Rosa's care, ignoring the abuse. It made him what he was. And I think you should forgive your father. He was a good man, Nicole. He just panicked. So did I."

Nicole sighed. "You're right. Dad *did* make a mistake—a huge one." She looked up at him and smiled sadly. "But I still love him."

"Of course you do."

She kneeled and put her bouquet of pink chrysanthemums on the grave. Then Paul kneeled also, placing a bunch of hyacinths beside her bouquet. "White hyacinths," he said. "A long time ago my mother told me they mean, 'I'll pray for you.' "

They both stood. Nicole looked up at Paul, her eyes brimming with tears. "I think I can finally cry for him, now."

Paul wrapped his good arm around her, pulling her close. He kissed the top of her head. "Let the tears come, Nicole. You can always cry to me because I'll never leave you again."

Read on for an excerpt from
Carlene Thompson's next book

YOU CAN RUN...

Coming soon from St. Martin's Paperbacks

The child slid out of her window into the smothering folds
of a hot summer night. Her mouth slightly open, she turned
in a circle, gazing upward at the dome of sky, thinking stars
looked like silver glitter sprinkled on Mommy's black velvet
dress. She'd never seen so many stars twinkling around a fat
moon white as fresh snow. Maybe the moon *was* made of
snow, she mused. Maybe up so high, it was too cold for snow
to melt.

She pulled her thoughts away from the beautiful night sky
and directed them to her task. The girl grasped a glass jar sitting on the windowsill. She checked to make sure the lid bore
several tiny holes for air. Then she listened for a moment. The
sounds of a song floated from the house. She knew the name
of the song was "In My Room," sung by some boys who lived
at the beach. Mommy always listened to that song when she
was sad, and tonight she'd played it again and again.

Mommy wasn't just sad, though. For the last few days,
while the little girl had been getting well from an operation
on her tummy, Mommy hadn't laughed like usual. After
Mommy had brought her home from the hospital this morning, she'd kept walking through their little house, sometimes
crying. When the child asked what was wrong, Mommy always said, "Nothing at all! Everything is fine, Willow."

But Mommy didn't look like she believed everything
was fine. That's why Willow had decided to make a surprise
even if Mommy might get a little mad because Willow was

supposed to be in bed. She had to hurry, though, before Mommy looked into her room like she'd done so many times today. If she saw the bed was empty—

Willow decided she just wouldn't think about that now. She had work to do and if she moved real fast and tried real hard, she could be back before Mommy even noticed.

Willow dashed across the yard as fast as her five-year-old legs would carry her. She loved the backyard where she had a swing set and a little rubber swimming pool. She vaguely remembered once living in a big building—a place up high with lots of windows. There was no yard and no swing set, but sometimes Mommy took her to a huge place called Central Park. Central Park had grass, but Willow liked her grass much better.

She liked her grass so much she couldn't resist smelling it. She winced with pain before she remembered she was supposed to bend at her knees, not from her tummy. Too late now, though, and her tummy didn't hurt very much. Besides, she'd spotted a dandelion. She sniffed it, too, loving its tangy smell. Willow thought dandelions were beautiful, all bright yellow and fluffy. This summer she'd often picked bouquets of dandelions for Mommy who always put them in a glass of water.

Willow pushed aside her long red-gold hair and tucked the dandelion behind her ear. Then she headed farther back, toward the woods at the edge of the backyard. The moon and stars were so bright, she hadn't needed to bring along her little plastic flashlight. She held her precious glass jar with both hands. If she dropped it and broke it, she'd ruin the surprise. She knew she had to be very careful.

Willow stepped just inside the line of trees. Then she removed the lid from her jar and stood still, hardly breathing, waiting. And waiting. And—

There! A tiny yellow flash higher than her head, but not too high! She reached up, gently closed her hand around an insect, dropped it in her jar, and put the lid on top. She held up the jar and looked. Blink, blink, blink! Her friend would have called this a lightning bug. Willow thought that was silly. These bugs didn't shoot out scary spikes of blinding light. Some people called them fireflies, but they didn't set things on fire, either. No, these bugs were nice and they flashed soft, glowing colors that didn't hurt anyone. Mommy called them sparkle bugs and so did Willow. This sparkle bug she named Dandelion.

Willow took one more step into the woods and stopped. Mommy didn't like her to go into the woods at all, which made them even more enticing to Willow. The woods were darker than the backyard, though, and Willow had to admit they looked a little bit scary at night. Besides, she didn't need to go into them. If Dandelion had been floating around right here, other sparkle bugs would be, too.

Willow again went completely still, trying to take little, silent breaths. Little breaths weren't easy, though. The night was so hot she felt as if a blanket covered her head. A breeze blew, but it was hot, too. Sweat had popped out on her forehead and she didn't feel as good as she had when she climbed out the window. She thought briefly that maybe she should have waited one more night after her operation before she'd come out looking for sparkle bugs. Mommy needed cheering up *now*, though.

At that moment, a tiny light blinked right in front of her face. Willow giggled, gently grasped the bug and put him in the jar with Dandelion. The bug blinked again, his light the color of the cantaloupe slice Mommy had given her with lunch. Willow named him Cantaloupe. Cantaloupe and Dandelion blinked at the same time. They'd made friends!

Willow wanted to get at least one more sparkle bug. She'd planned to get five because she was five, but she was just too hot and all at once, very tired. Just one more bug would be perfect. She'd have three bugs, and they would make Mommy as happy as five sparkle bugs.

"Willow!"

The little girl almost dropped her glass jar when she heard her mother yell from the back door of the house. Willow whirled around and hurried out of the woods. She saw Mommy coming down the three steps from the back porch, heading directly for her. Now I'm gonna get in trouble, Willow thought dismally. She'd get in trouble, she didn't feel good, and she only had two sparkle bugs. Her wonderful plan was shattered.

"Willow Conley, what are you doing out here?" Mommy's usually soft, sweet voice sounded high and sharp. "You know you're supposed to be in bed. Do you want to end up in the hospital again? Because that's what will happen if—"

Willow stood frozen in the face of Mommy's anger when a tremendous blast shook the earth. Her mother pitched off the bottom step into Willow's little rubber swimming pool just as a funnel of fire shot through the roof of their house. Vicious yellow flames darted like snakes' tongues through shattered windows and burst through the open back door.

Stunned, the little girl stood rigid, paralyzed by shock and fright. Burning pieces of wood soared through the night, some landing only inches from her. She did not retreat into the woods away from them, though.

Willow simply clutched the jar of sparkle bugs, her terrified eyes fastened on Mommy lying motionless in the swimming pool as the hungry fire swept over her.